Praise for *The T*

"Ellen Feldman has done it again. This time she conjures up New York City in the postwar years, as loyalty oaths and blacklists begin to take their toll, and as the irresistible Fanny Fabricant grapples with familial expectations and societal conventions. The result is an indelible novel suffused with heart and history, fresh, fast-paced, and exhilarating."

—Stacy Schiff, *New York Times* bestselling author

"An inspiring and thoughtful exploration of female ambition, creative spirit, and what it means for a woman to defy expectations in order to build the life she deserves . . . A compelling and insightful novel."

—Lynda Cohen Loigman, bestselling author of *The Matchmaker's Gift* and *The Two-Family House*

"Emotionally compelling and gorgeously written, full of Feldman's trademark wit and wry observation, *The Trouble with You* is as addictive as the world of the 1950s soap operas in which the novel is set, and as serious and satisfying as the finest fiction being written today."

—Liza Gyllenhaal, author of *A Place for Us* and *Local Knowledge*

"A big-hearted novel that takes the reader through history . . . It's the NYC of automats and radio serials, the America where women are expected to stay home and raise kids. But Fanny finds independence, a career, and even love. . . . I cheered for her every step of the way."

—Ann Hood, *New York Times* bestselling author of *Fly Girl* and *The Knitting Circle*

"A heartbreaking joy to read, an entertaining ride through the exuberance of New York City following the Second World War. In the end, this wonderful book is an ode to the power, resilience, and ambition of women everywhere in any era."

—Jessica Anya Blau, author of *Mary Jane*

"A captivating read, set against the backdrop of the Red Scare. Beguiling characters abound, in all senses of the word. At a time when book banning and threats of censorship are increasing, Feldman's story reminds us of the human cost of the loss of freedom to believe, to read, and to write. A bonus: that a library, my very own, gets a star turn as Fanny's and Charlie's writers' haven, made this novel even more of a treat!"

—Carolyn Waters, head librarian, The New York Society Library

"Feldman is at the top of her game in *The Trouble with You*. She displays a perfect grasp of the postwar era, its politics, her characters, and the human heart. It is a masterful performance—and a great read."

—Kevin Baker, author of *Dreamland*

"I love this book in so many ways. . . . The descriptions of Charlie and Fanny working together amount to, for me, expert instruction in the craft of storytelling."

—Frederick E. Allen, former editor at *New York*, *American Heritage*, and *Forbes*

Also by Ellen Feldman

The Living and the Lost

Paris Never Leaves You

Terrible Virtue

The Unwitting

Next to Love

Scottsboro

The Boy Who Loved Anne Frank

Lucy

The Trouble with You

A Novel

Ellen Feldman

ST. MARTIN'S
GRIFFIN
NEW YORK

This is a work of fiction. All of the characters, organizations, and events portrayed in this novel are either products of the author's imagination or are used fictitiously.

First published in the United States by St. Martin's Griffin, an imprint of St. Martin's Publishing Group

www.stmartins.com

Design by Meryl Sussman Levavi

Library of Congress Cataloging-in-Publication Data

Names: Feldman, Ellen, 1941– author.
Title: The trouble with you : a novel / Ellen Feldman.
Description: First edition. | New York : St. Martin's Griffin, 2024.
Identifiers: LCCN 2023036048 | ISBN 9781250879462 (trade paperback) | ISBN 9781250879479 (hardcover) | ISBN 9781250879486 (ebook)
Subjects: LCGFT: Novels.
Classification: LCC PS3572.I38 T76 2024 | DDC 813/.54—dc23/eng/20230828
LC record available at https://lccn.loc.gov/2023036048

First Edition: 2024

10 9 8 7 6 5 4 3 2 1

For the docs in my life

Michael Schwartz

and

Stephen Reibel

Your education will prepare you to be splendid wives and mothers, and your reward might be to marry Harvard men.

—Wilbur Kitchener Jordan, president of Radcliffe College, in his welcoming addresses to incoming students, 1950s

There is much you can do about our crisis in the humble role of housewife.

—Adlai Stevenson's address to the graduating class of Smith College, 1955

In dealing with a male, the art of saving face is essential. Traditionally he is the head of the family, the dominant partner, the man in the situation. Even on those occasions when you both know he is wrong, more often than not you will be wise to go along with his decision.

—*The Seventeen Book of Young Living*, 1957

For the male, sex involves an objective act of his doing but for the female it does not. Her role is passive. It is not as easy as rolling off a log. It is as easy as being the log.

—*Modern Woman: The Lost Sex* by Ferdinand Lundberg and Marynia F. Farnham, MD, 1947 bestseller

The Trouble with You

Prologue

December 25, 1947

She was going to be a flower girl. She was six years old, well, five and a half, and had a red velvet dress with a red satin sash because it was a Christmas wedding, and she was going to walk down the aisle with a basket of rose petals and drop them on a long silk carpet. Her cousin Belle was going to be a flower girl too, but she wasn't even five and would probably do something dumb like forget to drop the petals or cry. The wedding hadn't started yet. They were still home, and she was coming down the stairs in the red dress that her mother called wine-colored. Her father was standing at the bottom, watching. He was dressed up too, in a black suit with shiny lapels, and a wide thing around his waist that she'd never seen him wear before, and a snowy white shirtfront with what looked like tiny colored ladybugs he said were studs running down the front. His hair was smooth, his mustache trim, and his cheeks pink the way they were after he shaved. Sometimes he let her sit on the closed toilet seat and watch him shave. She loved the way he whipped up white foam in a wooden bowl and spread it over his face, then cut paths through it with his razor. And she loved the smell. Sometimes, since he'd come home from the war, she went into the bathroom when he wasn't there, picked up the wooden bowl with his shaving cream, and put her nose to it because it smelled so good. It smelled like Daddy.

When she reached the next-to-the-last step where she usually jumped to the bottom but didn't now because of the velvet dress and her slippery new Mary Janes, he put both hands over his heart, staggered backward like when someone gets shot in the funnies, and shouted, "I am struck. I am struck by beauty."

She told him not to be silly, though she liked it when he was silly that way, and went and stood by him and took his hand. He had big hands with long fingers, and her own disappeared in them. A moment later, he called up the stairs.

"If you don't get a move on, Fanny, we'll be celebrating their first anniversary instead of their wedding."

Her mother came around the landing at the top of the stairs. During the war, when her father was away, they'd lived in an apartment where there were no stairs, only a hall from the kitchen and living room down to the bedroom where she slept in a crib beside her mother at first, then in a big-girl bed in what her mother called an alcove at the end of the hall. Now there were more rooms, and steps from downstairs to upstairs, and she had a bedroom of her own. At first, she was scared, but not anymore.

"'Rivers know this,'" her mother said. "'There is no hurry. We shall get there some day.'"

"Winnie-the-Pooh!" Chloe shouted.

"I'm glad my girls are up on their literary references," her father said, "but I'd rather get there tonight."

Her mother started down the stairs. Her dress was velvet too, but black not red, and it didn't have a sash. It didn't have anything at all, unless you counted the long white gloves that went all the way up her arms, the strings of pearls around her neck, and the pearl earrings that you could see because her coppery hair—that was what everyone called it—that usually hung down and curled around her cheeks was piled on top of her head. It made her neck look almost like the giraffe in the book about Noah's ark. Chloe didn't like that one as much as *Winnie-the-Pooh*. She and her father watched her mother as she came down the stairs in her high strappy shoes. When she was almost at the bottom, her father spoke. He didn't shout. He didn't grab his chest and pretend to be shot. He was almost whispering.

"It's not fair, Fanny. You're going to put the bride in the shade."

His tone made Chloe look up at him. Sometimes she thought of them as separate—ask Mommy; wait till Daddy gets home; at least wait till Daddy gets home now that he was home from the war—but most of the time they were one person, MommyandDaddy. But that was to her. Until that moment, she'd never thought of them the way they were to each other. Now, standing in the front hall, all of them dressed to kill, as her father called it, she sensed something went on between them that had nothing to do with her.

Her mother buttoned her into her coat, her father helped her mother on with hers, then got into his own, and they went out the side door through the screened porch that was empty now because the furniture was in the basement for the winter. In the driveway, a plume of smoke was coming out of the back of the Buick her father called his other baby because he'd had to wait so long to get it after the war.

"I started the engine," he said. "Couldn't take a chance on my girls getting cold and Chloe having to walk down the aisle with goose bumps."

He put his hands under her arms and lifted her into the middle of the front seat, helped her mother in, came around the car to the other side, and got behind the wheel. He started to back down the driveway. When her mother did that, she opened the door and leaned out to see the edge of the pavement. Her father didn't even turn around. He just kept his eyes on the mirror that showed him what was happening out the rear window.

Her legs were straight out in front of her because the seat was so deep, and as they passed under a streetlamp, the light sparked off her Mary Janes like stars.

"Poor Mimi," her mother said. That was what people always called her. When Chloe was little, she thought that was her name. Poor Mimi. Then her mother explained that her name was Mimi but everyone put "poor" in front of it because they felt sorry for her. Chloe asked why they felt sorry for her, and her mother said because Mimi's husband, Norman, didn't come home from the war.

"But Daddy did," Chloe said.

"Thank heavens."

"Thank heavens," Chloe repeated, though she wasn't sure what she was saying. She was little then.

"It's Barbara's wedding," her father said now. "Barbara's night."

"Which is one of the reasons I feel sorry for poor Mimi. It can't be easy being a widow at her age and watching your younger sister walk down the aisle. It seems like only yesterday we were going to Mimi's wedding."

"How old is Belle?"

"She's almost five, not even," Chloe said.

"So the wedding wasn't exactly yesterday." Her father's voice had changed.

Her mother looked over at him, but didn't say anything.

❦

Fanny cursed herself. She shouldn't have mentioned Mimi. It wasn't as if Max was likely to forget her, or more to the point, forget Norman. The two of them had shipped out at the same time.

She turned to look out the window on the passenger side. Here and there, open curtains revealed Christmas trees blinking anticlimactically and families sprawled in exhaustion. At the end of the block, a semicircle of four small faces and two larger ones glowed cadaverous gray in the darkness.

"The Fentons got a television set for Christmas," she said.

"I didn't know you and Mrs. Fenton were so tight you compared notes on these things."

"We don't, but when we passed just now, you could see into their living room. The whole family was lined up watching."

"I read the other day that there are something like ten million sets in the country. In a decade, half of all American families will be sitting around those things. Or so the article said."

He turned the car onto Lower State Street. A handful of stores already had sale signs in the windows. It was just the letdown of Christmas night, even if you didn't celebrate it, Fanny told herself. Her mood had nothing to do with poor Mimi.

Years later, when Fanny thought about the night of Barbara's wedding, two images would come back to her. Actually, one wasn't a recollected image but an actual picture. The professional photographer had captured her and Max on the dance floor. His hand is on the small of her back, his mouth is at her ear, and their cheeks are pressed together. When she looked at the picture, she tried to remember what it had felt like, but she couldn't summon the sensation, only the memory. The other image would be of her neighbors looking gray and inert as corpses in the sepulchral light of their living room.

❦

They came out of the Pierre Hotel into a world hushed by a dusting of snow. The wind hadn't yet picked up, and the white flakes fell silently from a cloud-pale sky. The quiet reminded Fanny of that moment in Penn Station more than four years earlier when Max and the other men had pounded down the steps to the waiting train, leaving the women and children stunned and mute. But that quiet had been barbed with fear. This hush made her want to lift her face to the sky in celebration of the sheer beauty of the night. She turned up the collar of her coat, slipped her arm through Max's though he was carrying a sleeping Chloe, and they started toward Sixty-Third Street, where he'd found a parking spot.

When they reached the car, she opened the back door, he leaned in, put Chloe on the back seat, and arranged a blanket over her. The snow was starting to fall a little faster. Later, the US Weather Bureau's chief meteorologist would say he'd never seen so much snow come down so quickly, but that would be later. No one had seen the storm coming. Even the weather experts on the twenty-ninth floor of the Whitehall Building at 17 Battery Place still hadn't an inkling that before it was over, 26.4 inches of snow would fall in Central Park, more in some parts of New Jersey; stalled and abandoned cars would clog the streets and highways; hotels would overflow with the stranded; more than five hundred flights would be canceled at La Guardia Field, New York's major airport; and seventy-seven people would be dead. The count included only those who lost their lives due to the storm. Other fatalities were not part of the tally. Afterward, fingers would be pointed at the Weather Bureau and other government agencies for the disastrous lack of preparedness, but in fact no one except Mother Nature could be blamed. Most storms in the Northeast travel from west to east with the prevailing winds, enabling weather stations along the way to pass on information. But this storm was moving from east to west. There were no weather installations in the Atlantic.

It wasn't a blizzard, yet. There wasn't even enough snow to necessitate chains on tires. Max had had a drink or two at the reception and a glass of champagne during the toasts to the happy couple, but he'd stopped drinking after that and had had two cups of coffee with the wedding cake.

He eased the car out into the traffic, and turned on the heater. By the time they emerged from the Holland Tunnel, the snow was coming down more heavily. He turned the windshield wipers back on, then reached out and rubbed the inside of the front window with his gloved hand.

"Can you clear your side?"

She hesitated for a moment, debating whether to use her glove, her hand, or her handkerchief, then unbuttoned the lower part of her long evening glove, slipped out of it, and cleared the windshield with her bare hand. A horn shrieked. Max's foot started instinctively toward the brake. He checked the impulse. This was skidding weather.

He was leaning forward now, trying to see through the snow and the glare from the oncoming cars that had turned on their brights.

"Idiots," he muttered at the offending drivers.

The wipers dragged back and forth through the accumulating snow, making dull thumping sounds as they went. Fanny kept looking from the road to Max and back again. Now and then she peered into the back seat. Chloe was curled on her side with her fist in front of her mouth. She turned back to Max. The interior of the car was dark, but she was dimly aware of his knee going up and down as he tried to play the gas pedal to keep from using the brakes.

A flash of light seared the windshield.

"Watch out!" she shouted.

Again, his foot started for the brake. Again, he caught himself, eased off the gas, and guided the car through the swerve.

"Don't do that!" he said when he had the car under control.

"I'm sorry."

He didn't answer.

It went on that way for some time. She tried not even to gasp.

He turned the car off the highway onto a local access road. The snow accumulation was deeper here, but there were no other cars or oncoming lights. They made it to Maple Avenue, then turned onto Oak. They were almost home.

He was creeping along the road now, still hunched forward, trying to make out the entrance to their driveway. The snow was an undifferentiated blanket. Only the dark shadows of the house and the trees were visible.

"I think it might be here," she said.

He didn't answer, but turned the wheels slowly to ease the

car into what might or might not be the driveway. It skidded to the left and came to a stop.

He maneuvered the car back onto what ought to be the driveway in view of where the house was. The garage loomed ahead. He inched the car into it.

She pushed open the door on her side of the car, climbed out, and stood looking across the yard. The path to the back steps wasn't even an outline.

"I'll carry Chloe in, then come back for you."

She didn't argue with him, but she had no intention of waiting like a prima donna while he tramped back and forth through the snow.

He lifted Chloe from the back seat and started out of the garage with her in his arms. Years later when they talked about that night, Chloe would wish she could recall the trip from the garage to the house. Did she wake? Did she reach sleepy arms around her father's neck? Did she nuzzle against his snow-dampened cheek? She would give a lot for that memory.

Fanny hiked up her long dress and stepped out of the garage into the snow. She'd ruin her shoes, but she didn't care. The three of them were home in one piece.

He was coming out the back door when she reached it.

"Why didn't you wait?" he asked as he came down the steps and took her arm.

"I can manage. And I didn't want you to have to come out again."

"You could have fallen."

As if on cue, her heel slipped on the ice, but he caught her before she went down. When they reached the small back porch, he held open the door for her and followed her into the kitchen.

"But I didn't," she said as she bent to take off her ruined shoes.

They made their way to the front hall closet, hung up their coats, and started up the stairs. Exhausted but vividly and gratefully, oh, so gratefully alive, he reached out and palmed her behind as they climbed.

Chapter One

1941

She'd married him a little recklessly. War did that to people. Across the country, girls were slipping into hastily made wedding dresses or newly bought suits and walking down an aisle or into a flower-bedecked living room where men in recently acquired uniforms stood waiting nervously.

They'd known each other only a month; they'd fallen in love in three days. She'd expected her aunt Rose to try to talk her out of it. What she hadn't counted on was that Rose, practical no-nonsense Rose, had a reckless streak of her own. She was also a romantic, though no one in the family would have believed it. Rose knew what her family, and the world for that matter, saw when it looked at her. Rose, the old maid. Rose, who couldn't possibly know the ecstasy and pain of love, the urgency and heat of sex, the terror and heartbreak of a back-alley abortion. Rose, whose very name was a joke, like the names of so many of the girls with whom she'd grown up and worked in the factories. Rose. Iris. Flora. Pearl. Ruby. Golda. They gave them names that connoted beauty or opulence, then sent them to work sewing hats or gloves or dresses so their brothers, Fanny's father among them, could graduate from college and even professional schools. Rose had worked to put both of her brothers through school and been so successful at it that she'd gone from a sweatshop to her own little business. That merely validated their view of her. Everyone knew what business took out of a woman. Sometimes Rose wanted to throttle the world for the arrogance of youth, the stupidity of the married, the sheer lack of imagination of everyone who saw only this short, now stout, bossy woman with wiry red hair that made her look, she said, as if she'd stuck her finger in an electric socket, and an astonishing complexion that would have been rare on a fifteen-year-old girl and was unheard of in a menopausal woman. Rose was the only one Fanny had ever heard use the word. Even the books called it "change of life."

Rose wasn't opposed to Max. The rest of the family was—or in the case of Fanny's deceased mother, would have been—unabashedly enthusiastic. He met the late Celia Baum's criteria for men in general and future husbands in particular. He was tall, good-looking, and would be what was known as a good provider. Fanny's father was less particular about appearance and didn't think height mattered unless you were going to be a professional basketball player, a breed any daughter of his would marry over his dead body, but Max was Jewish and would be a professional man, a distinction Milton Baum, an accountant, appreciated. He could turn his daughter over to Max with a clear conscience and a palpable sense of relief. The extended family shared the feeling. Fanny hadn't been exactly rebellious, but no one had ever described her as docile. That was Rose's fault, but what could be done? The other aunts, by both blood and marriage, had children and concerns of their own. They did their best. Aunt Sarah, married to Fanny's father's brother, couldn't have been more generous with gifts of twin sweater sets and charm bracelets and invitations to join her, Mimi, and Barbara on their mother-daughter outings, but her own two were a handful. Fanny's aunts on her late mother's side were almost as generous, but they lived in New Jersey, closer to Philadelphia than New York, and you couldn't raise a teenage girl long distance. So, much as the family worried about Rose's influence, Fanny fell under it by default.

The irony was that if it hadn't been for Rose, Fanny never would have met Max. If it hadn't been for Rose, Fanny never would have been at Barnard in the first place. She wouldn't have been at any college. Fanny's late mother hadn't been an advocate of higher education for women. She hadn't been against it; she just hadn't seen the point. Fanny's father, however, was vehemently opposed. Too much education was likely to give a girl ideas.

"Exactly," Rose said.

Milton didn't get the quip, though unlike his sister, he did have a college degree, thanks to the years Rose had spent hunched over a sewing machine.

Rose didn't persuade him. She threatened him.

"If you don't send her to college, I will."

Milton shrugged. He was careful with money and liked a good bargain.

"And tell the entire family that Milton, the man I put through college, is too cheap to give his only child what I gave him."

The only thing Milton valued more than a bargain was respect. Somewhere along the way, he'd come down with the idea that he was a paragon of many virtues.

So Fanny went off to Barnard. The choice of schools had something to do with Rose too. Fanny had flirted with the idea of Smith. The campus looked idyllic in the catalog. But Rose did alterations for a woman whose daughter was at Smith. The girl, who was Jewish, had been assigned as roommates the only other Jewish girl in her dorm and the one Negro girl in the class. Rose, the old leftie, loved the idea of a Negro roommate, but felt Fanny might be more comfortable at a school with less prejudice and more of what were called, though never by Rose, "her own kind." The irony was that Fanny ended up rooming, by choice rather than assignment, with Susannah Bennett, who'd strayed from the Episcopal Church. Fanny wasn't thumbing her nose at her family, who, with the exception of Rose, were nothing if not tribal. She and Susannah had simply hit it off when they'd both had their short stories read aloud in freshman English and each had admired and envied the other's.

Then, during her senior year, she met Max, who was speeding through medical school at Columbia. The government, eager to get physicians into action as soon as possible, had reduced training to seventy-two weeks. By the end of the war, the course would shrink to a mere sixty weeks, but by then Max would be in France.

At the end of their first month together, on the afternoon that broadcasts of philharmonic concerts and football games were interrupted to announce that the Japanese had bombed Pearl Harbor, an American military base in a place so obscure most people couldn't find it on a map, they decided to marry. If medical training could be rushed, certainly marriage didn't have to dawdle. Everything was speeding up, like the pages being torn from a calendar in a movie sequence to show the passage of time.

Her recklessness was rewarded. Unlike many people in love, they were well suited. There were, of course, minor disagreements over matters like his inability to empty an ashtray, her overreaction to the dog-earing of a page in a book, and why you could maim a magazine that way but not a hard-bound or even paperback volume. Nonetheless, their worldviews meshed. They agreed about politics. They liked many of the same movies, paintings, music, and books, even if he didn't treat his as well. They were besotted with each other. He made her feel not only desired but desirable, though not with empty compliments. He was too canny for that. He knew the way to her heart was through her mind. When she'd confided the story of the freshman mixer she'd spent in the ladies' room because no one had asked her to dance, he didn't tell her the boys at the mixer must have been blind. He merely pointed out that she hadn't stood much chance of being asked to dance in the ladies' room. God, she loved him.

They were also of the same mind about the most important issue of the day. All around them, men who were going off to war and women who were being left behind were wrestling with the decision. Some were determined to have a child. If the man didn't come home, he would leave something of himself and the girl would have something of him to hang on to. Others were more cautious. Husbands thought it would be unfair to the offspring and the girl. Wives could not imagine raising a child alone. Max and Fanny had no trouble making up their minds. He said his genes were crying out to go on, the noisy little buggers. She wanted his child. And though neither of them would dare to say it—they didn't want to tempt fate—both were functioning on the assumption that he would come home. The red crosses painted on the tops of hospital tents weren't an insurance policy, but at least he wouldn't be storming beaches or parachuting out of planes.

Although Rose hadn't opposed the marriage, she thought

they should wait to have a child, but said nothing. Her familial reputation for bossiness wasn't any more accurate than the view of her as an inexperienced spinster.

A year after they married, eight months before Max shipped out, Chloe was born.

❦

The crowd milling in the heartless winter sunshine pouring through the steel-and-glass roof of the Pennsylvania Station churned with tension. Men lit one cigarette from another, stamping out the last with an army boot or oxford; made jokes; and repeated last-minute instructions. The bankbook is in the top left-hand drawer of my desk. Remember what I told you about the fuse box. Be a good boy/girl and listen to Mommy. The women held their faces, shadowed by their best hats, because this would be the image he would take with him, rigid with determination not to cry. Children stood docile and frightened or chased siblings around their preoccupied parents. The handful of WACs, WAVEs, and nurses waited in twos and threes. Strangely enough, no one came down to see them off. When Fanny thought about it later—she was too distraught to at the time—she couldn't imagine why. Perhaps their families didn't approve of their leaving home to go gallivanting around the world, even if they were doing it for patriotic reasons. All she knew for sure was that *Life* magazine had commented on the fact in a pictorial essay.

Max made no jokes. He was unhappy and apprehensive, but not awkward. He repeated no instructions. Fanny had a good memory and knew her way around a checkbook if not a leaky faucet. But he did light one cigarette from another.

Fanny wasn't wearing her best hat. Somehow worrying

about clothing at a time like this struck her as frivolous. Besides, she was fairly sure this image of her standing on the concourse of Penn Station was not the one he would carry with him. The night before, after they'd made love, she'd started to pull the sheet and blanket that had slid to the floor back over them. She wasn't modest, merely chilly now that the sweat was beginning to dry. He'd stopped her, got out of bed, turned the three-way bulb in the lamp on the night table that was on dim two notches up to bright, and stood looking down at her.

"What is it?" she asked.

"I'm taking a mental snapshot. It's the one I'm going to carry with me."

She'd reached up and pulled him down, and they'd made love again.

An unembodied voice floated out over the station concourse, calling out a list of southern cities, and said the train would be boarding on track 4. Couples embraced, some of them crushing children between them, as if there were no tomorrow, and for many of them there wouldn't be. Holding Chloe in one arm, Max put his other around Fanny and drew her close.

Men stooped to pick up duffels and rucksacks and suitcases. Max let go of Fanny, handed Chloe over, and bent to pick up a Gladstone in one hand and a valise in the other. The voice repeated the names of the cities and the number of the track. Suddenly a couple of hundred men were stampeding down the steps to the train platform. Reluctant as they were to leave, anything was better than that agonizing drawn-out goodbye.

Fanny watched Max disappear into the crowd. She tracked his shoulders, then the back of his head, then only an anonymous hat lost in a sea of officer and garrison caps.

The sudden quiet was eerie. It fell over the station concourse like a thick blanket. Even the children who had been so noisy a moment ago went silent. They knew something was up. Years later, coming out of a wedding, Fanny would liken the hush of the falling snow to this unnatural stillness. But then she'd have no premonition. Standing alone among the crowd in the vast soaring space of the Pennsylvania Station, she felt fear crowding in. Suddenly the thought of the red crosses painted on the tops of hospital tents offered scant comfort.

A feeling of hollowness, as if her insides had been scooped out, overcame her. She was insubstantial. Light as a helium balloon, she could easily float up to the steel-and-glass ceiling and bump there aimless and sore until she disintegrated. Only Chloe's small arms hanging on anchored her. But children were known to loosen their grip. Helium balloons were always floating off into space.

She held her daughter tightly and started across the concourse toward home, wherever that was now.

Chapter Two

SOMETIMES FANNY THOUGHT IT WOULD HAVE BEEN better if they'd had less time before Max shipped out. No, she didn't mean that. She was grateful for every moment. It was only that they'd had weeks and months to move from falling in love to loving. She would have missed him in any case, but in the infancy of their marriage she would have missed him as a girl misses her daydream. Now she missed him as a part of herself. Reading a book, she'd look up to tell him something and realize he wasn't there. Washing dishes or making the bed, she'd sense his presence behind her and turn her head only to find empty space. It was like the stories she'd read about men who had lost an arm or a leg in the war. The appendage was gone, but they still felt sensation in it, and pain.

At least she had the part of him that was Chloe. Chloe hadn't loosened her grip, and Fanny hadn't floated off. She fed her daughter and bathed her, diapered and dressed her, walked her to the park and pushed her on the swings. She held her breath as Chloe let go of a chair and staggered toward the sofa, unsteady as a drunk on her short fat legs. When she reached her destination and flung herself onto the cushions, Fanny applauded. When the small hand did loosen its grip and she climbed a step on her own, Fanny cheered. She exulted in the achievements, but silently willed her daughter not to rush. Save something for Daddy.

Her former college roommate, Susannah, a rangy big-boned girl who always looked, she said, as if she ought to be carrying a hockey stick, had no child to keep her anchored. "I feel so frivolous," she confided to Fanny as they sat drinking coffee in Fanny's small kitchen or walked behind Chloe's carriage to the park. "Jeff is risking his life on some hellish island in the Pacific while I spend my days working my way through Revlon's spectrum of lip and nail colors and reading. I'm racking up a book a day."

"I'm impressed," Fanny said.

A few weeks later, Susannah turned up at Fanny's apartment with a wheelie toy for Chloe and an announcement that she'd gotten a job at a women's magazine.

"Most of the editors, who were all men of course, are doing something in the war, so they're hiring girls to fill in. I had to promise to give it up when the real editor comes back. As the editor in chief who hired me pointed out, the real editor is a man with a wife and children to support; I'm a girl with time on my hands. But I won't want the job when Jeffrey comes home. In the meantime, I know I'm not exactly furthering the war effort. Not the way I would be if I were working at the Brooklyn Navy Yard or Sperry Gyroscope in one of those nifty Sperry Girls coveralls designed by Vera Maxwell. But I'm uncoordinated, and I'll be helping the girls who are doing that, in a way. The magazine publishes all kinds of useful stuff like recipes for getting dinner on the table in twenty minutes when you come home from eight hours on an assembly line or how to sew blackout curtains. It may not be much, but it's something."

On her knees bending over the tub where Chloe was splashing happily that night, Fanny told herself she was doing something more important than working at a magazine. She was raising the future. But she couldn't help feeling . . . not envious exactly, merely a little overshadowed.

She tried to do her part. She saved tinfoil; pitched in at the small victory garden on the block; and *used it up, wore it out, made it do, or did without,* as the slogan went. She also took a first aid course. Rose had signed up both of them. They learned to make splints, apply bandages, deal with shock, and treat burns from mild first-degree cases to life-threatening fourth degree. The training, invaluable in wartime, would come in handy in peace, they agreed, as they tried out their newly acquired skills on each other. Rose was more adept, but then she always had been.

Years earlier Rose had started doing private alterations after factory hours for women on the Upper West Side, where the brothers she'd put through school were living. Women began to tell other women about this girl from the Lower East Side who was a wiz with a needle and thread. She raised hems and lowered them, which was harder, let dresses out so no one could guess at those extra ten pounds, and transformed an old coat into the latest fashion. Her reputation spread. Clients came from all over the city. Some of them began bringing her photographs from *Vogue* and *Harper's Bazaar* to copy. A few of the more enterprising, or perhaps only less scrupulous, brought the garment itself, which they returned to the store after Rose made a sketch. Rose didn't mind the work. She was proud of her skills and, as a former union organizer, believed in the dignity of labor. What she did mind were the women who swore they needed whatever it was overnight. She found them even more irritating than those who complained about how much she charged, though she knew that some of them confided to their friends that they'd gotten a Mainbocher suit that cost several hundred dollars at Saks or Bergdorf's for twenty-five.

As her clientele grew, she left the Lower East Side and found a place in a handsome redbrick apartment building with terracotta-framed windows on West End Avenue. Her home, studio, fitting room, and office, it was only a few blocks from Fanny's tiny walk-up on West Seventy-Sixth Street. That made it convenient for her to stay with Chloe on evenings when she sent Fanny off to the movies with Susannah or her other two nieces, Mimi and Barbara. Sometimes, she paid Charity, a tall thin woman who came down from Harlem three times a week, to do housework, or a high school girl in the building to stay with Chloe while she and Fanny went to the theater. Rose had always taken Fanny to the theater. She'd introduced her to *Waiting for Lefty* and *Awake and Sing!* as well as less contentious plays like *The Barretts of Wimpole Street* and *Romeo and Juliet*. Once she'd taken her to hear Norman Thomas speak, though she'd made her promise not to tell her parents. In the end Rose had voted for Roosevelt, because in this country a vote for socialist Norman Thomas, she said, was a wasted ballot, but she'd told Fanny it was important to hear all sides.

A few months after Max shipped out, Rose came up with a volunteer job for Fanny. One of her clients was a writer for several daytime radio serials. Rose was careful never to call them soap operas or soaps in hearing range of the client. As a contribution to military morale, the network that carried the serials gave servicemen free tickets to broadcasts. Broadway shows, nightclubs, and Radio City Music Hall were bigger draws, but being in the studio for broadcasts of *Ma Perkins, Our Gal Sun-*

day, and the other shows their mothers and wives were tuning in to every day was something to write home about. The network, Rose's client explained, needed volunteers to check the credentials of the men on leave and hand out the tickets. Three afternoons a week, while Charity kept an eye on Chloe as she cleaned or took her to Central or Riverside Park, Fanny put on a Rose-altered suit from her undergraduate days in winter or one of the similarly made-over linen dresses and her straw pinwheel hat in summer, and rode the subway down to Rockefeller Center, where broccoli, cabbages, tomatoes, and other edibles flourished in a victory garden, to sit behind a desk in the lobby of the network's building, smiling at enlisted men and officers, brushing off invitations to dinner or dancing or a movie, and handing out passes for various programs. She knew she wasn't furthering the war effort the way the girls who volunteered for civilian defense teams or the Red Cross were, but she was making some of those lonely men a little happier. They would have been a lot happier if they'd been able to talk her into bed, but she had a way of twisting the gold band on the third finger of her left hand while fending them off that convinced them she wasn't being coy. Her efforts boosted her own morale as well. Sometimes she managed to go for ten or fifteen or even thirty minutes at a time without worrying about Max.

Occasionally she took Chloe to see her father, who lived on Riverside Drive with his new wife, though the visits didn't always turn out well. Her father's second wife did not enjoy having proof of his first—two proofs—underfoot. She was also a fastidious housekeeper who despaired of sticky hands on furniture or crumbs anywhere. The visits to Max's parents in Brooklyn were more successful. Both of them doted on Chloe.

Since Susannah had begun working at the magazine, Fanny

spent more time with her cousin Mimi. As babies, she and Mimi had been walked in their carriages together; as girls, they'd played together; and in school Miriam Baum's desk had always been behind Florence Baum's. Their families and the New York City educational system had thrown them together, but their temperaments had divided them. Mimi not only played by the rules; she took it upon herself to make sure others did as well. Fanny preferred to flout them. But now the conditions of their lives overcame the differences in their natures. All that mattered were the two children—Mimi's daughter Belle was a year younger than Chloe—and the two men whose whereabouts they were unsure of and whose current lives they could only imagine, and tried not to. When one got a letter or a trove of letters, both celebrated. Sometimes they read snatches aloud. The result was that they grew closer not only to each other but to each other's husbands. Before Norman had shipped out, Fanny had barely known him. Now she regarded him as a part of her life and worried about him accordingly. Mimi felt the same about Max. The perceptions might not be accurate, but they were comforting.

There was, however, one crucial difference between their lives. Fanny was still in the small apartment she and Max had moved into after they'd married. When Norman shipped out, Mimi returned to her parents' place on Central Park West. Fanny had tried to talk her out of the move. It would be like returning to childhood, she warned.

"That's why I'm doing it," Mimi said. "I have enough to worry about without having to take care of the practical stuff. Norm tried to teach me how to balance the checkbook and stuff like that. He finally gave up and turned everything over to his father. Now I don't have to bother about it, and Norm doesn't have to worry that I'm messing things up." She smiled, and the dimples on either side of her rosebud mouth emphasized her pleasure at the arrangement.

❦

Mimi and her sister, Barbara, were standing in the foyer of the family apartment as Fanny buttoned Chloe into her coat. It was the fall of 1944, and everyone was saying the war couldn't go on for much longer. Even the trove of letters Mimi had gotten from Norman that morning predicted the end was in sight. Fanny was telling them about a newspaper column she'd read a few days earlier that had predicted the men would be home by Christmas, when the doorbell rang. Mimi, who was standing closest to it, lifted the metal disk on the peephole and looked out. She dropped the disk and leaned her back against the door.

"Who is it?" Barbara asked.

Mimi didn't answer.

Barbara tried to move to the peephole, but Mimi pushed her away.

"Don't open it."

"Who is it?" Barbara insisted.

"No one," Mimi said. "A mistake."

"What do you mean a mistake?" Barbara asked.

"Go away." Mimi was shouting at her sister now. "It's a mistake. Whoever is out there has the wrong apartment."

Barbara was trying to get around her sister to reach the door, Mimi was holding Barbara off with both hands, and Fanny would have laughed at the replay of their childhood, but she was beginning to realize who was on the other side of the door. She didn't want to open it either, but someone had to.

She put her hand on the knob.

"Don't!" Mimi screamed.

She twisted it.

"Please don't." Mimi was sobbing, and by now Barbara must have figured out who was there too, because she wasn't wrestling with her sister but holding her, or trying to. Mimi's legs had given out, and she was sinking to the floor. "Please don't," she moaned again.

Fanny opened the door. A boy in a Western Union uniform was standing in the hall. The telegram in his hand glowed like a hot yellow sun. Fanny knew it would scald anyone who touched it. She reached out and took it from the boy. The name in the telegram that would begin THE SECRETARY OF WAR DESIRES ME TO EXPRESS HIS DEEP REGRET would not be Captain Max Fabricant, but Lieutenant Norman Kraus. The burn to her would be only a singe. For Mimi it would be fourth degree. Permanent damage to the body and possibly the organs. You didn't need a course in first aid to know that.

❦

They stood in the lobby of Rose's building waiting for the elevator, Fanny impatient because they were late, Chloe counting off the numbers as the hand on the metal dial above the elevator door inched down.

"One!" she shouted when the hand stopped moving and the door opened.

A woman stepped out. Fanny took Chloe's hand and started into the elevator cab. As she did, a boy in a Western Union uniform appeared beside them. He hesitated, waiting for her and Chloe to precede him. Fanny stepped back. Chloe tugged her forward. The boy went on waiting. "Going up," the elevator operator said. The boy nodded for her to enter. Chloe tugged at her hand again.

"You go ahead," Fanny said to the boy. "I forgot something."

She wasn't superstitious. She just didn't like the idea of riding beside that poor boy on his heartbreaking mission. It was a brutal job, impossible for an adult, unthinkable for a growing boy. Pity, not fear, held her back, she told herself.

❦

Mimi's life had snapped in a moment. She was no longer the girl she'd thought she was. The world saw her differently too. Fanny tried not to, but she couldn't help herself. The concerns that had once bound them now divided them. The harder Fanny tried not to mention Max, the more his name slipped out. His letters were secrets rather than celebrations. But something in her face or manner must have given her away, because more than once Mimi asked Fanny if she'd received a letter on a day when she had. Sometimes Fanny lied and said she hadn't; others she admitted she had. The answer made no difference. The look on Mimi's face remained the same. The only alteration was now her cheeks were plump, almost puffy. Instead of growing thin and gaunt as newly minted widows were expected to, she could not stop eating. She was desperate to fill the void.

❦

Then it was over. In Times Square crowds cheered, men and women embraced, and people mugged for the camera. All across the country, strangers kissed and husbands and wives who didn't yet know they'd become strangers fell into bed. A joke went around. "What's the first thing you're going to do when you get home?" the reporter asks the soldier. "Throw my wife down on the bed and make love to her." Only everyone but the most sheltered mothers knew he hadn't said "make love." "What's the second thing?" the reporter asks. "Take off these damn boots."

Wives and mothers stopped waiting for the mailman and fearing the appearance of the Western Union messenger. Men staggered off ships and planes, blinking at the country they'd been fighting for. Neon signs still goaded them to drink Ballantine beer and chew Wrigley's gum and smoke Chesterfield cigarettes. Traffic lights changed from red to green, and drivers gunned their engines and raced into the future. Had reports of gas rationing and tire shortages been myths circulated at the front? Men in business suits hurried to make a killing or at least a living. Women strode to the dentist and the hairdresser and lunch. Boys lounged against buildings or on steps ogling girls in thin summer dresses. No blasted tanks, bombed-out buildings, or twisted bodies littered the landscape. The men who'd laughed at the government pamphlets warning them of problems in picking up their old lives—"Coming Home," "Since You Went Away," "Readjustment Tips"—began to wonder if they'd been too cavalier.

Max hadn't been cavalier. He knew the experiences and images of the war would stay with him all his life. The boy whose blown-away face no amount of plastic surgery would ever let express joy or sorrow or love again, though Max had assured him that the specialty had come so far during the war that it would. The young man who refused to speak, though his vocal cords were intact, but his two arms and one leg had been amputated. The men on the ship returning home whose hard stares, trigger tempers, and sudden starts at unexpected sounds and movements gave away wounds no X-ray would ever reveal. But if the scars of war were seared into Max's memory, the miracle of his own survival was a guilty wonder.

He showed up in the middle of the night. She wasn't expecting him for another day or two. The troop ship he'd returned on had docked in Miami, but back in France he'd refused to risk waiting for one headed to New York. He'd called from Florida to say he was working on getting a flight out. The sound of his voice stunned her. She had framed photographs of him all over the apartment and scrapbooks brimming with their brief past. She had a drawer full of letters. But for a year and a half she hadn't heard his voice.

"Are you all right?" the voice that was suddenly in her ears again asked.

"Are you?" she answered.

She told him to hurry, hurry, hurry.

That had been at one in the afternoon. She heard the door to the apartment open at three the following morning. She was out of bed in seconds.

Neither of them knew how long they stood in the darkness holding each other.

"Are you all right?" he asked again.

"Are you?" she repeated.

They went on holding each other.

"I'm filthy and sweaty," he murmured against her mouth.

"And here," she added without letting go of him.

Finally, he said he really did need a shower, because he couldn't remember when he'd last had one, and she asked if he wanted something to eat or drink, and he said he didn't.

A little later he came out of the bathroom. She was sitting on the side of the bed waiting for him. She'd combed her hair, but hadn't put on lipstick. They lay down facing each other. She could tell when he drew her to him that he'd shaved. But the funny thing was that despite the joke about the sequence of sex and the removal of boots, they did not make love immediately. They lay holding each other. They didn't move. They didn't speak. They just clung. Finally, as the world beyond the window began to go from black to gray and they were sure this wasn't a dream, he was home and they were safe, they made love.

Afterward, as they lay in the tangled sheets and she could tell from his breathing that he'd fallen asleep, an image flashed through her mind. Poor Mimi stared out from her round no-longer-dimpled face with sore, accusing eyes.

Chapter Three

THEY WERE GOING TO BUY A HOUSE. THEY COULDN'T afford one, at least they couldn't have in normal times under normal circumstances, but they were going to buy one all the same. Uncle Sam was going to help them. The men who'd served deserved to get college educations, start businesses, and own their own homes. The government decreed it. The GI Bill made it possible.

For the first year and a half after he'd returned, they'd sublet an apartment from another doctor who was leaving Bellevue, where Max had a surgical residency. He'd had plenty of experience in various field and evacuation hospitals, but he wanted formal training. He was determined to make up for whatever he'd missed, and he needed it to qualify in the specialty.

The one-bedroom apartment was too small for a couple with a child, but it was only a block from the hospital. The location made it convenient for Max's work and difficult for sleeping, reading, listening to music, calming a crying child, and most other endeavors. Sirens shrieked by at all hours. Nonetheless, in view of the housing shortage, they'd been lucky to find it. But now it was time to move on. The city was no place to raise a child. Children, they were hoping.

Most of their contemporaries wanted a new house in one of the new suburbs that were sprouting across the country like mushrooms after the rain. Of the girls Fanny had known in school and waited with during the war, only Mimi and Susannah were staying in the city. The suburbs were no place for a widow. Susannah's husband, Jeffrey, was in law school. But the others were fleeing to leafier pastures, or so the brochures promised they'd be in the future. The trees had been cut down to facilitate speedy building and new ones had not yet been planted. Fanny and Max understood the attraction. They went to look at several models in several developments, but something about those unfinished houses and unplanted yards struck them as unwelcoming.

"It's like a moonscape," Fanny said.

"The grass will grow," Max pointed out. But he understood what she meant. He usually did. She'd thought they'd grown close before he'd shipped out. She still remembered those months alone when she'd sense his presence and turn her head only to find emptiness. But there was an even deeper bond now. In those days, she wouldn't have been able to remain silent in the face of his silence. What are you thinking? she would have asked. Are you worried about something? Now she knew not to intrude. Even intimacy had dark unknowable corners. It demanded them.

Another aspect of living in one of those houses troubled her. There were various models. Colonials, split levels, saltboxes. Floor plans differed. Some had larger kitchens, others an extra closet. The houses had minor deviations, but no idiosyncrasies. Part of her thought it would be reassuring to look out her kitchen window as she made dinner or put dishes in the dishwasher that came with the house, as did the other modern appliances, and see a reflection of her life. Part of her was frightened at the idea of being a type. A line from F. Scott Fitzgerald's *The Rich Boy*, which she'd read in her modern lit course, kept coming back. "Begin with an individual, and before you know it you find that you have created a type: begin with a type, and you find that you have created—nothing." She feared becoming nothing.

Max found a real estate agent. They spent weekends tramping through houses that were too big for them, too small for them, too expensive, in need of too much work. Then, when they'd decided they'd give it one more Sunday, and if nothing turned up, they'd sign a contract for an unfinished house on a barren street in a new development, they found it.

The house was in a residential section of a town not far from the city. In less than half an hour, Max could drive through the Holland Tunnel and be at the hospital. There was even an older doctor in the town who wanted a younger man to cover for him evenings and weekends and might want to sell his practice before long. Their lives were falling into place.

❦

They closed on a hot breezeless Friday at the end of July. Fans whirred in the open windows of the bank that was backing the GI mortgage, while the two lawyers slid papers back and forth across the table, and Fanny and Max and the man who was selling the house signed on the proper lines. Their lawyer had asked Max if he was sure he wanted Fanny's name on the deed, and Max had said he was sure. The process took less than half an hour.

They came out of the hot office into the long rays of the late-afternoon sun. Max was carrying a sign saying THE FABRICANTS in big block letters, which the real estate agent had given them for the front yard and Fanny had no intention of putting anywhere other than the back of a closet. Max slipped out of his seersucker jacket and hung it on the hook in the back seat of the old prewar Chevrolet. She took off her white cotton gloves and put them in her handbag. They climbed into the boiling car and rolled down the windows. She didn't have to ask where they were headed.

He pulled up in front of the house and came around the car to open her door, and they made their way up the flagstone path shaded by two old oaks. The grass needed cutting. Later Fanny would see the unkempt yard as a sign. Why had they needed the extra worries? But that would be later. When they reached the front door, Max took the key from his pocket.

"Should I carry you over the threshold?"

"Only if you want to spend tomorrow in bed with a bad back."

"I resent that. I came back from the war an excellent physical specimen."

"You can say that again." Standing behind him, she reached around his body to embrace him as he opened the front door.

They went through the rooms, sometimes holding hands, sometimes standing with their arms around each other's waists, occasionally going single file down a hall or up the stairs.

"We could make that into a breakfast nook," she said of an alcove in the kitchen.

"We could, except that if we start renovating, we won't be able to afford breakfast to eat in the so-called nook."

"I see a breakfront there." She pointed to one wall of the dining room.

"That's funny. I see a bare wall until we pay down the mortgage a little."

"The sofa will go there," she said in the living room, "and two chairs facing each other in front of the fireplace." She envisioned them sitting of an evening, reading, his long legs stretched out so that, still keeping her nose in the book, she could slip off her shoe and tease him with her toes.

They climbed the stairs to the second floor.

"This will be your study."

"Until we need another bedroom."

They reached the master bedroom, and he let go of her waist and crossed to one of the two windows overlooking the backyard. She followed him. Several streets over, an egg-yolk sun dripped toward the roofs of other houses, none of them replicas of this one. In the near distance, a child's voice shouted home-free-home. From the other direction came the crack of a bat hitting a ball.

"Tell the truth," she said. "You hired an army of kids to put on this show."

He had his arm around her again. "The kids came cheap. The setting sun cost a bundle." He went on looking at her, and she recognized the expression.

"There's no bed."

"Bed? What happened to the girl who thought a chair in a locked med school lab was pure luxury?"

"Her lustful heart still beats, but I don't see a chair either, and the floor doesn't look as if it's been swept anytime recently."

"Fortunately, I happen to have a blanket in the car."

"What are you doing with a blanket in the car in the middle of July?" she asked when he returned with it.

"I like to be prepared."

He spread the blanket on the floor. She reached behind her to unzip her dress. As she tugged at the zipper, it caught.

"Damn," she said.

He came around the blanket, unzipped the dress, and reached inside it. The last thing she thought before she stopped thinking was that a child conceived their first afternoon in the new house would be a miraculous down payment on the future.

❦

Two months after they moved into the house, Mimi's younger sister, Barbara, got engaged, and Fanny gave her a shower. She didn't particularly want to. She didn't approve of showers. That was Rose's influence again. It was one thing in the old country, Rose insisted, when everyone was poor and a couple starting out needed all the eiderdowns, cooking utensils, and other household items they could get, but now it was merely a stickup for more presents. Fanny agreed with her, but went ahead with it. No one could expect poor widowed Mimi to take on the task.

There was one fortunate dividend, at least for Chloe. Barbara asked her to be a flower girl in the wedding.

Chapter Four

SHE CLOSED THE DOOR TO THE BEDROOM BEHIND THEM and walked to the windows to pull down the shades. The snow was an impenetrable curtain of white shutting out the world. They'd gotten home just in time. She pictured the other wedding guests who'd stayed even later tripling and quadrupling in the few hotel rooms left, if they were lucky, sleeping on a row of spindly wedding chairs, if they weren't.

He sat on the side of the bed, pulled open his tie, and slipped out of his jacket. "That was one hell of a ride," he said as he reached around to unhook his cummerbund. "There were a couple of moments when I was sure we were going to end up in a snowdrift and freeze to death before anyone found us."

"Thanks for not telling me at the time."

He fiddled with the hooks for a moment, then stood and crossed the room to the dresser where she was taking off her pearls. "Whoever invented these things ought to be taken out and shot."

"But you look so dashing in it," she said to his reflection in the mirror.

He grinned, then turned his back so she could undo the hooks.

He sighed. "Now I know how you feel when you take off your girdle."

"Are you kidding? That thing's child's play compared to a Lily of France straitjacket."

He sat on the side of the bed again, removed the ladybug studs from his shirt, shrugged out of it, stood, and started for the closet, carrying the shirt, cummerbund, and jacket. She knew that tired as he was, he'd hang up the suit and put the shirt in the laundry basket.

She slipped off her earrings and inserted them in the velvet row in the top compartment of the jewelry box, then closed it and stood holding on to the dresser for a moment. She was so tired that she flirted with the idea of not taking off her makeup, but it was only a flirtation.

She heard a thud from the closet. He must have bumped into the shoe rack again. She loved him dearly, but he was a bull in a china shop in that closet. He insisted he hadn't been until she'd had him put up the second rack.

"What is it about women and shoes?" he'd asked.

"What is it about men and ties?" she'd answered.

Sometimes she varied the reply. "It has to do with my legs," she'd say.

"What does it have to do with your legs?"

"The way you can't keep your eyes off them."

"Guilty as charged."

She twisted around to reach the zipper on the side of the dress. Side zippers were supposed to be easier than those at the back, but they rarely were. Nonetheless, she was too tired to struggle. She started for the closet.

"Honey, can you—" She stopped. What were the clothes—his suit, several of her dresses and skirts and blouses—doing on the floor? Later she'd realize he must have pulled them down when he'd grabbed the pole to keep from falling. But he had fallen. He was lying on his side, his body twisted, his face as white as the pleated shirt she'd danced against all evening, his eyes terrifyingly blank.

She didn't remember calling the ambulance, but she must have, because it came, though it took forever to get through the snow. All she remembered was sitting beside him, holding his hand in both of hers, begging him not to leave her.

Chapter Five

SHE KNEW AS SOON AS SHE CAME DOWN THE STAIRS AND stepped into the living room that she never should have let them hold the service here. Not that anyone had asked her permission. They plied her with pills and tiptoed around her, while she moved through them like a sleepwalker. Now the sight of the plain pine box shocked her awake. It radiated menace, like a wild animal that has stumbled into the house and, unable to escape, was poised to strike. But the funeral home would have been worse. She couldn't leave him with strangers.

Someone—her father? Max's? The insincerely sympathetic man from the funeral home? She couldn't bear to lift her eyes to discover who it was—led her through the maze of rented chairs that crowded the room. The extended family was large. Max had a lot of friends. And people were eager to show their indignation. A man in the prime of youth. A man, as his father kept saying, who'd returned from the war safely only to be done in by the peace. This was not the way the world was supposed to work.

She felt their eyes boring into her as she took the seat left open for her. Her knees were almost touching the pine box.

She reached for Chloe's hand. Her daughter grasped hers in return. He couldn't be in there. It was impossible. She fought the urge to fling open the coffin. You see, she'd scream to the ghoulish mob who didn't belong in their living room, it's a mistake. It's a bad joke. Max is upstairs, waiting for you all to clear out so he can come down and we can be alone.

Another hand at her elbow guided her out of the house down the shoveled path to the long black car waiting at the curb. Later, she had no idea how much later, other hands helped her out of the car at the cemetery and steered her along the path that had been cleared between the banks of snow.

The blizzard had camouflaged the hard truth of the field of death. Only the occasional white-blanketed rise of an overly tall headstone gave away what lay beneath the snow and dirt. They reached a raw gaping hole in the ground. Later, years later, she'd wonder how they'd managed to dig a grave in the frozen earth. Now she merely averted her eyes.

The rabbi's words were foreign to her, though he spoke in English. She and Max weren't believers. It was all a meaningless performance going on behind a scrim. A mistake, like the pine box in the living room. She'd wake up from it soon.

The rabbi finished speaking, picked up a shovel, slid it into the pile of soil that had somehow been defrosted, and turned the blade into the open grave. The sound of the earth hitting the coffin shocked her awake again.

The rabbi held the shovel out to her. She stood staring at it. He leaned toward her, urging her to take it. She went on staring at it. He murmured something. She looked from the shovel to the grave and back again. She closed her eyes. The moment seemed to go on for some time. Behind her, someone coughed.

She opened her eyes. The rabbi extended the shovel another few inches toward her. She took one more look at it, then turned, walked down the gravel path, and out through the gates of the cemetery. She would not bury Max.

❦

Years later, Chloe would remember three things about her father's funeral.

She would recall sitting beside her mother in the living room trying to keep her Mary Janes, the same shoes she'd worn to be a flower girl three nights earlier, from touching the big wooden box that they said her father was lying inside. She didn't believe that. Not for a minute.

She'd remember Belle asking to see her flag.

"What flag?" Chloe answered.

"When my daddy died, I got a flag."

Chloe didn't particularly want a flag. It certainly didn't seem much of a trade for a daddy. But it didn't seem fair that Belle had gotten one and she hadn't.

And she'd remember the slap. That came a few days after they took the wooden box out of the living room, but the funeral still shrouded the house. It would for a long time, maybe forever.

Her mother was sitting at the kitchen table. There was a cup and saucer in front of her, but she wasn't drinking from it. She was just sitting there, with her eyes wide and staring, like one of Chloe's dolls. When you laid the doll down, her eyes blinked shut, but her mother's didn't close even when she lay down. Chloe knew because the night before she'd gone into MommyandDaddy's room that was only Mommy's now and asked if she could get in bed with her mother. Her mother didn't say anything. She just lifted the covers and moved over to make room for Chloe. And until Chloe fell asleep, every time she looked at her mother, her eyes were still wide and staring.

Now her mother was at the kitchen table staring, Aunt Mimi was telling her mother she had to eat something, Belle was pulling on Chloe to go out and play in the snow, and Aunt Rose was leaning against the counter watching. Chloe wished they'd all go away, all except Mommy. And that her eyes would stop staring.

"Come on." Belle tugged on her arm again, and before Chloe knew it, her hand flew up and pushed Belle, Belle fell back onto the floor and started to cry, and another hand flew out and smacked Chloe's cheek. Then people were shouting, and Aunt Mimi was picking up Belle and carrying her out of the kitchen, and Mommy was hugging Chloe tight, so tight she could barely breathe, and saying I didn't mean it, I didn't mean it, forgive me, I didn't mean it.

Aunt Rose pried her and Mommy apart, took her into the dining room, sat, and pulled her onto her lap. "Mommy's not herself," she said quietly, as if it was a secret between them. "She didn't mean to slap you. She never would have if she were herself."

Later, when the slap faded and she stopped hating her mommy, because now that Daddy was gone Mommy was all she had, she realized what Aunt Rose said was true. Mommy wasn't herself. A new mommy had taken her place. She even had a new name. Poor Fanny. The words hummed through the house on the day of the funeral and for the days after it when people came to visit bringing baskets of fruit, platters of cake and cookies, and dishes of food that other people ate, because her mommy turned away from them. Poor Fanny.

❦

For the next several weeks, Fanny avoided the living room. If she had to cross it, she hugged the walls, like a cat slinking around the perimeter in stealth. The only consolation was that she wouldn't have to avoid it for long. The house was already on the market.

The family had expected her to go to pieces at the realization that she'd have to sell it. She didn't. A strong woman, some said. Still numb, others observed. No one suspected the truth. She was glad. She hated the house.

The house was the enticement that had duped them. It was the booby-trapped stuffed animal the enemy leaves behind in retreat to seduce a homesick soldier to pick it up and blow himself sky-high. Before the house, they'd been happy. Before the house, he hadn't had to worry about clogged gutters or aging furnaces or a tree that hung dangerously over the porch roof. Why had they needed trees in the first place when the city was full of parks? Then there was that damn shoe rack she'd insisted on. All it had done was clutter the closet. He hadn't been able to turn around without bumping into something. It was one more inconvenience, no, injustice, she'd visited upon him. Before the house, he hadn't had to wear himself out driving back and forth to the city. He could saunter the block to the hospital. He could even come home for lunch, which admittedly he'd never done, but he could have, or she could take Chloe and sandwiches to meet him for a picnic, which she had now and then. The sirens had been a comfort rather than a hardship. The noise had signaled help was on the way. If an ambulance had been able to race to him on city streets that were already being plowed rather than slog through miles of snowed-in roads, the hospital might have been able to save him.

❦

She was at the stove scrambling an egg for Chloe. She didn't bother cooking for herself. Chloe sat at the table watching her, though when Fanny glanced over, she could tell from her daughter's expression that she was thinking of something else.

"If Daddy—" she began, then stopped abruptly and put her hand over her mouth.

Fanny slid the egg onto a plate, turned off the burner, carried the plate to the table, and sat across from Chloe. She tried not to look at the empty place at the end of the table.

"You can talk about Daddy. You're supposed to talk about him. That's the way we keep him alive."

It was a nice statement, perfectly crafted for a child, but Fanny hated the lie. Nothing could keep Max alive. They could talk about him till they were blue in the face, and he'd still be dead. Even Chloe knew that.

❦

Fanny had listed the house with the same real estate agent from whom they'd bought it. She didn't know any others, and Max had trusted him. It sold for several thousand dollars more than they'd paid for it. Between that and Max's insurance, she could live for a while, but, as everyone in the family was quick to point out, only a while. She had a cushion, not a sinecure. The family telephone wires vibrated with possible solutions to the problem.

Her father invited her to move in with him and his wife.

"How does Adele feel about that?" Fanny asked.

"She likes the idea."

"Your nose is growing longer, Pop."

"Okay, but I put my foot down. You're my daughter."

She was touched. She might not want to live with her father and his wife, but she did like the idea that he still cared enough about her to suggest it. She told him that and thanked him, but added that it wouldn't work.

A few days later, Mimi telephoned. "I have a wonderful idea," she began, and Fanny knew what was coming. Still holding the dish towel, she sat in the chair beside the telephone shelf in the corner of the kitchen. "You and Chloe can move in with Belle and me. I spoke to Norman's parents about it."

Norman's parents were paying the rent on the apartment on Riverside Drive. Mimi had married well, as the saying went. Her late husband had been heir to a wholesale paper company. In one of those improbable but not unusual chains of events, Norman's father—who'd come to America at the age of twelve and begun selling paper goods from a pushcart—had managed to parlay it into several wholesale dealerships, and ended up buying forests in this country and Canada. He would take care of his only son's widow. He'd already established a trust fund for his grandchild.

Fanny, the family shook its collective head and agreed, was not so fortunate. Max's parents were schoolteachers. Good people, the salt of the earth, but Fanny couldn't expect any help from them. Fanny's father was retired from his job as an accountant, and he was, the family had always known if not said, tightfisted. There would be no trust funds for Chloe.

"The girls will be the sisters they're not likely to have now," Mimi went on, "and it will be like old times for us."

Fanny closed her eyes for a moment before she spoke. She

didn't know which was worse, the idea of erasing her entire adult life or the prospect of two widows racing toward old age together. Widows. The mere sound of the word made her flinch. The pinched first syllable that gave way to the open-mouthed howl of outrage.

She thanked Mimi, as she had her father, and told her the invitation was generous, but she didn't think it would work. "I can't live on charity."

"It won't be charity," Mimi assured her. "You'll contribute to the household expenses."

Exactly, Fanny thought. I'll contribute, but it will always be your apartment where Chloe and I live on sufferance.

"Just think about it," Mimi insisted.

Fanny promised to, though she knew she wouldn't.

Some of the family thought Rose should take her in. That wouldn't be charity, but familial responsibility. Heaven knew Rose was an expert at that.

Rose and Fanny killed the idea in its cradle.

"She has objections to everything, but how will she live after the money runs out?" various members of the family asked Rose, because the question seemed too cruel to pose to Fanny.

"She'll get a job," Rose said.

With those four words, the mantle of "poor" was lifted from Mimi's shoulders—she was widowed, but at least she didn't have to work—placed squarely on Fanny's, and reinforced. Poor, poor Fanny.

❦

She stood in the middle of the bedroom. The movers had already carted out the furniture. The space was as empty as it had been the day of the closing when they'd made love on the floor.

With nothing to absorb the sound, their cries had echoed off the walls and through the house.

She crossed to the window. The only sound now was the squeak of her shoes on the bare floor. The June sun beat down on the greening yard. She would have preferred rain. This clement summer day was a reproach. She'd already gone through the house closing the windows. No children's voices sailed into the room. No cracks of balls against bats shattered the quiet. Life had lost its soundtrack.

❦

Chloe waited until her mother was downstairs going through the empty rooms, checking to make sure they hadn't forgotten anything. She crossed the hall, went through her parents' bedroom, and stepped into their bathroom. The black-and-green tiles were smudged. The toilet seat where she used to sit to watch Daddy shave had an old washcloth on it. She opened the medicine cabinet. It was still there. She'd been afraid it wouldn't be. She stood staring at it. She knew she wasn't supposed to take things that didn't belong to her, but she had to have this. Anyway, Mommy probably wouldn't know. She just wanted to get out of the house. She didn't say that but Chloe could tell. So it would be her secret. Like the mints that used to be in the candy dish on the coffee table in the living room. In the old days, *before,* her mother had never noticed how many were gone.

She took the wooden bowl from the shelf. She had to be quick. She didn't want to be caught. But she couldn't resist a sniff. She lifted the top, held the bowl to her nose, and inhaled. Daddy was back.

She put the lid on the bowl and, holding it behind her

in case Mommy came upstairs again, went back to her own room. A bag with some books, a doll, and a few toys stood in the middle of the room. Her mother had told her not to pack them in the cartons so she'd have some of her things while they stayed with Aunt Rose until the new apartment was ready. She slipped the wooden bowl into the bottom of the bag. She didn't know if her mother would stop her from taking the bowl of shaving cream with her. She never knew what her mommy was going to do these days. Like that slap. Her mother had never hit her before. But she had to have that bowl that smelled of Daddy.

Chapter Six

They moved back to the city. The decision was practical. According to Rose, there were more jobs in the city. It was also sentimental. Fanny had been happy with Max in the city.

Rose found the apartment for them. She knew everything that went on in the neighborhood and heard through the grapevine that an army vet, his pregnant wife, and their child were moving to the suburbs, leaving behind a flat on the third floor of a four-floor eclectic Renaissance revival building, or so the landlord designated it, only two blocks from Rose's own place and three from the school Chloe would start in the fall. The ceilings were high, the living room was big enough to use a corner of it as a dining area, and a bay of three tall windows protruded out over West End Avenue. Rose was already sewing a cover for a cushion to put on the long, curved seat that ran beneath the windows over a line of built-in walnut cabinets. The two bedrooms in the back were narrow, too narrow to fit the double bed from the house. That was all right. Sleeping alone in the constricted twin bed was no worse than nights in the big double bed when she kept reaching for Max and finding only cold sheets.

During the day she went through the motions. She got Chloe

off to school in the morning and picked her up in the afternoon. She cooked meals, washed and ironed laundry, cleaned the apartment. She must have done all that relatively competently, because there were no complaints from the school about Chloe's absenteeism, slovenliness, or malnutrition; no lectures from Rose. She moved through the neighborhood, made distracted conversation with neighbors when she ran into them, with Rose and Mimi and Susannah when they forced her to do something. She even read books. *Gentleman's Agreement* with its treatment of antisemitism almost held her attention, but when she finished *B.F.'s Daughter* by Marquand, whose books she'd always enjoyed, and couldn't remember most of it, she went back to old friends like *Middlemarch*, *Madame Bovary*, and *Anna Karenina*. She knew those stories well enough not to miss much if her mind wandered to her own misery.

Everything came to her from a distance. Even she came to herself from a distance. She'd see herself standing at the kitchen counter slicing an onion, walking up Broadway to buy groceries, sitting on a park bench with Mimi while the girls played nearby, and watch with disbelief. Who is that woman who seems to be functioning?

Occasionally when she passed other women and men in the neighborhood whose hand-me-down clothes, haunted eyes, and bizarre navigations to avoid a policeman or even a doorman, anyone in uniform, marked them as refugees from the war and the attempt to wipe out an entire people, she chastised herself. She'd lost a husband. These people had lost husbands and wives and children and whole families. These people had suffered concentration camps and death marches and horrors she could only imagine. But grief is not a competition. The greater loss of others is no balm for your own.

The one task she couldn't carry off, however, was looking for a job. And no one rushed her. Even Rose agreed she needed time to learn to live in a world she'd had no preparation to inhabit, to make up new rules as she went along.

During the second summer after Max's death, however, Rose decided time was running out. "Have you even tried looking for a job?" she asked.

"What's the point?" Fanny said, and cited one of the few newspaper articles she'd read and managed to retain. The fact that it happened to suit her needs was purely coincidental.

The wave of unemployment everyone had feared when twelve million men took off their uniforms, put on civvies, and returned to their old jobs or went looking for new ones hadn't materialized. Nonetheless, employment was for men, especially men who had families to support. Women need not apply.

"The point," Rose said, "is that you have to find work."

"You tell me how. Even the girls who had jobs during the war were forced to give them up. My old roommate Susannah had to promise when the magazine hired her during the war that she'd go quietly once the real editor came home. He did, and she was so furious she picked up her typewriter and threw it at him."

Rose laughed. "I always liked that girl. But as for how, you might start with the 'Help Wanted—Female' pages in the papers. That's what most people who are serious about finding a job do."

The next morning Fanny bought a copy of the *Times,* carried it home to the apartment, sat at the dining table, opened it to "Help Wanted—Female," and began to make her way through the ads. BILLING CLERK. BOOKKEEPER. COMPTOMETER

OPERATOR. She didn't even know what a comptometer was. COOK EXPD. EXPORT ASSIT-PERFECT SPANISH—ENGLISH REQUIRED. She began to sweat. MODEL SIZE 12–14. MODEL 5' 5" TO 5' 7"—ATTRACTIVE. STENOGRAPHER. STENOGRAPHER. STENOGRAPHER. SALESWOMAN. SALESWOMAN. SALESWOMAN.

She couldn't imagine herself in any of those jobs. She tried to think of women she knew who worked. Rose, of course, but she had a skill. A few of her professors had been women, but they had advanced degrees and, as far as she knew, didn't have children. She thought of other women whom she'd read about. Eleanor Roosevelt. Clare Boothe Luce. Martha Gellhorn. She admired them all, but couldn't imagine being in their shoes. She didn't have their ability, or their passion, or their courage. All she had was a cum laude degree in English literature, which hadn't equipped her to do anything but raise intelligent, well-behaved children, further a husband's career, and volunteer for good causes. She looked down at the want ads again and pictured herself applying for the jobs. They'd laugh her out of the office. They'd tell her to stop wasting their time. She threw the paper in the trash.

Another six weeks passed. "Have you been looking at all?" Rose asked one night when they were in Fanny's small kitchen cleaning up after dinner.

Fanny put another dish in the draining rack. "I went through the want ads, as ordered, but I'm not qualified for anything."

"Come on, Fanny, you have a degree from one of the seven sisters."

"Where I was told repeatedly that everything I learned there would make me a sterling wife and mother. I'd be able to discuss art and lit-tri-ture at dinner parties with my husband's colleagues and polish my children to a glossy shine."

She turned off the water and faced her aunt. "You don't understand. I wasn't brought up to work. I was brought up *not* to work."

Rose picked up the dish and began drying it. "Not by me you weren't."

Fanny was silent for a moment. Then it burst out. "I'm scared, Rose. I'm really scared."

"Of what?"

Fanny had to think about that for a moment. "Everything."

Rose leaned against the counter. "You know what Mrs. Roosevelt says."

"I can't believe it. I tell you I'm terrified and you quote the former first lady."

"Can you think of someone better?"

"Okay, what does Mrs. Roosevelt say?"

"Do one thing every day that scares you. Or something to that effect."

"I'd be happy if I could do one thing one day."

"You don't have a choice."

"Now I wish I had taken some courses at Teachers College."

"No tears over the milk you spilled in your carefree youth. Just get on with it."

The next morning Fanny bought the paper again, took it back to the apartment again, and opened it to the "Help Wanted—Female" pages again. They looked as daunting as they had the last time she'd read them, but as Rose said, she had no choice. She began circling ads.

No one laughed her out of an office. No one told her to stop wasting the company's time. But no one offered her a job either. Summer cooled into autumn. The city began gearing up. As she paged through the paper to the want ads, she saw announcements for the reopening of supper clubs, new Broadway shows, and CBS television's star-studded fall lineup. On her way to interviews, she passed window displays for Scottish cashmeres in Peck & Peck, campus tweeds in Paul Stuart, and an afternoon coat of Persian lamb in Bergdorf Goodman. She noticed that the color strictures that had been forgotten during the war were back. Whites had been packed away on Labor Day to return next July Fourth, or for the impatient, Memorial Day. Navy was on hold till the spring. Christmas would be a free-for-all. But now browns were the hue of the day. *Vogue, Harper's Bazaar,* et al. said so. She went for another interview, appropriately dressed in a chestnut tweed suit that Rose had taken in to make her look slender rather than gaunt from the weight she'd lost after Max's death, and got the job. A woman called Miss Scobey hired her to work behind a makeup counter at Saks Fifth Avenue. Miss Scobey would have preferred someone experienced in what she called the beauty business, but with women putting on new fall faces, she needed another saleswoman and was willing to take a chance.

The work had plenty of drawbacks. Fanny was on her feet from before the store opened in the morning until it closed in the evening. She was required to wear more makeup than she ever had, more makeup than she thought any woman should. But the most offensive part of it was the endless lying, or what Miss Scobey called saleswomanship. She had no trouble mastering the orange and coral lip and nail colors appropriate to the season and, supposedly, to the current customer's complexion, but she hated telling women of a certain age that one cream would smooth their wrinkles while another would lift their eyelids. She felt guilty assuring an unhappy girl with acne-ravaged skin that the heavy pancake foundation hid every imperfection and selling powder and rouge to a dewy-cheeked teenager who clearly looked better without it. Then one afternoon, three weeks after she'd started the job, she erupted in a burst of truth. She didn't know why she did it. Perhaps it was anger at the job, at any job. Or perhaps she didn't like women being hoodwinked. She especially didn't like hoodwinking them herself.

The customer looked to be about nineteen or twenty. Her complexion wasn't luminous, but neither was it ravaged. A single pimple on the side of her nose was barely noticeable. Miss Scobey noticed it. She asked the girl what product she used to cleanse her skin. In the beauty business, no one ever washed a face. They cleansed skin. This girl, however, did wash her face. She mentioned a brand of soap. Miss Scobey's eyes widened in horror. The girl said sometimes she used another brand. Miss Scobey was not mollified.

"Don't you know that soap doesn't cleanse the skin?"

"I didn't know," the girl admitted, her voice thick with embarrassment.

"But I have something that does," Miss Scobey went on. "A revolutionary new cream that goes beneath the surface of your skin to penetrate deeply." In the beauty business, deep penetration was the holy grail. Cosmetic pornography, Fanny occasionally thought in her rare moments of grim humor. "Think spring cleaning for your pores." Miss Scobey was already on her way to the other side of the counter where the cleansing creams were kept.

Fanny waited until she was out of sight, took a step toward the girl, and leaned across the counter.

"Soap cleans," she whispered. "Soap cleans like nobody's business."

She never knew whether Miss Scobey heard her or simply put two and two together when the girl paid for her lipstick and left. And she had to admit Miss Scobey was nice about it, nicer than she'd been while Fanny was working for her.

"You're just not cut out for the beauty business," she said sadly.

Fanny agreed that she wasn't.

❦

Rose was furious. "Is that what you thought they were paying you for, consumer enlightenment? Truth in advertising?"

"I just got so tired of standing there talking about spring cleaning for your pores with a straight face."

"Poor Fanny." Rose repeated the family mantra, but in her mouth sarcasm replaced pity. "She can't bear to tell a lie, or even to let someone else's lie pass in order to hold on to her job."

"You're the one who's always railing against hypocrisy."

"Hypocrisy applies to politicians, businessmen, and religious fanatics who mouth platitudes in public and fleece the public in private. Not to permitting foolish women to let themselves be bamboozled into one scheme or another to make themselves look prettier or younger or sexier. Do you want to know the number of times a day I have to bite my tongue? 'Perfect,' I tell a woman who insists on a skirt that's too short for her because she had good legs twenty years ago. 'So becoming,' I lie to a woman who's showing too much cleavage because she had a big bust as a girl. And let's not even talk about Dior's New Look."

"What's wrong with Dior's New Look? I think it's chic."

"Chic? 'Constraining' is the word you're looking for. During the war I was altering trousers, short skirts, and jackets so women could actually do things. Now I'm sewing bodices so tight they can barely breathe and ankle-length full skirts over crinolines that keep them anchored in place like dolls. The style is designed to put women who got uppity during the war back in their place. I see my clients admiring themselves in the mirror in the supposedly *new* look and think women haven't been so hogtied since hoop skirts and bustles, or maybe since chastity belts. But I bite my tongue and tell them how stylish they look. I bite my tongue so many times a day it's a miracle I still have one. And while we're on the subject of dissimulation, it wouldn't hurt you to smile a little more."

She held up her hand before Fanny could say anything.

"I know you don't have a lot to smile about these days, but here's a news bulletin for you. The world doesn't care. You think when someone asks how are you, they really want to know? We all soldier through life behind our own little masks. At least we do if we want to survive. So from now on, stop trying to sabotage the cosmetics industry or wherever you end up working next, and start smiling. For your own sake, and for Chloe's."

"What does Chloe have to do with it?"

Rose shook her head. "You're too smart to have to ask me that."

❦

Rose's diatribe had hit home, especially in relation to Chloe. Literature was full of scenes of adults cherishing memories of maternal visits to the nursery, glimpses of mothers dressed in glowing fabrics and glittering jewels, fragrant with heavenly perfumes, radiating fond if distracted love as they bustled off to a mysterious adult existence. She hated to think that all Chloe would have to remember was a grim-faced, grieving mother in a flannel bathrobe who never went anywhere but the past.

Then it got worse. She had no idea where the epiphany came from. It had nothing to do with losing or needing a job. The moment was existential. She was standing on the median in the middle of Broadway at Eighty-Second Street waiting for the light to change. Behind her on one of the benches, a woman with a babushka tied over unruly gray hair was feeding pigeons, crooning encouragement as they pecked. Suddenly it hit her. Max was gone. He had ceased existing. Until then, she'd been obsessed with her loss. Her loneliness. How to live without him. How to go on putting one foot in front of the other in his absence. Everything had been about her. The self-absorption had been a way not to look the fact in the face. Now a different reality crashed into her consciousness. Max was not and never would be again. It seemed impossible, but it was true. There was a hole in the world where he had been.

She sat down hard on the bench beside the woman, who went on feeding the birds as if the earth hadn't lurched off its axis. A pigeon flapped wildly in front of Fanny's face. She let out a scream and flailed her arms.

"There's nothing to be afraid of, dear," the woman said.

Chapter Seven

Rose did not have to bite her tongue with Alice Anderson, the woman who'd told her about the volunteer job handing out tickets to servicemen on leave. Alice, a tall taut woman with a white streak in her dark hair which she refused to dye, had no illusions about short skirts or décolletage tops. She knew her age, even if she wasn't likely to admit it to others. She was partial to severe, beautifully cut suits and understated evening dresses in sumptuous fabrics. She was also, if not exactly a friend of Rose's, then a kindred spirit. She, too, had worked her way up in her profession, though it was not only more lucrative than Rose's, but had the cachet of being mental rather than manual. Not that Alice had any misconceptions about that either. "Nobody ever accused me of writing serious drama," she liked to say about her work in daytime radio serials. "But what I turn out isn't entirely without socially redeeming value. According to the head of the advertising agency that represents the sponsors of all three of my serials, women find worry entertaining." She shook her head. "The male view of the female psyche. But I never argue with sponsors, advertising agencies, or networks. I just try to keep the stories moving along and my listeners happy."

Alice Anderson had another trait that set her apart from her colleagues. She was unflappable. Inebriated actors, incensed sponsors, and late scripts didn't send her into a tailspin. Nonetheless, she was upset that day as she stood in front of the three-way mirror in Rose's fitting room and told Rose that her secretary was leaving to get married.

"I'm happy for her, I guess, but she's going to be hard to replace. I hired her fresh out of high school and trained her in the job. She knows almost as much about radio serials as I do." Despite Alice's lack of pretension, she refused to call them soap operas.

Rose took the pins she was using to fit a seam from her mouth. "I have a replacement for you."

"You have other clients in the business?"

"Remember my niece who volunteered at the network during the war?"

"Not one of those girls who were slaphappy for a uniform?"

"The only uniform she was slaphappy for was her husband's. She was married with a baby."

"Was?" Alice's eyes met Rose's in the mirror. "Divorced or widowed in the war?"

"Widowed after the war."

Alice shook her head. "Poor kid. The short end of the stick without the patriotic sheen."

"You got it."

"Can she type?"

"Like a wiz." It was only a minor exaggeration. Rose had encouraged Fanny to take a typing course in high school. She was determined to make her niece self-sufficient.

"Shorthand?"

Rose stood behind Alice, tugged the shoulders of the suit

into place, and checked the reflection in the mirror. "Do you dictate your work?"

"I make notes longhand and write on a typewriter."

"So who would you rather have, a girl who can take shorthand, which you say you don't need, or a girl with a degree in the liberal arts? A cum laude degree in the liberal arts from Barnard College. In other words, someone who can run the show while you write." Rose stepped back and examined the fit of the suit. "Perfect."

Alice began unbuttoning the jacket. "Tell her to call and set up an appointment for an interview."

Fanny called and scheduled an appointment. As she made her way through Rockefeller Center, blooming once again with mums and marguerite daisies rather than tomatoes and cabbages, she was nervous, but when she reached Miss Anderson's office, she wasn't tongue-tied. They discussed Fanny's credentials and lack of them. Miss Anderson described the duties of the job. She asked if Fanny ever listened to any of the three daytime serials she wrote.

Fanny debated lying, then decided against it. "Only since I learned about the job." She held her breath, waiting for Miss Anderson to be offended. She merely said she appreciated Fanny's honesty and asked when she could start.

❧

The work wasn't difficult. She retyped Miss Anderson's heavily marked-up long storylines, typed fresh copies with carbons for the actors and director after Miss Anderson had edited the other writers' scripts, and learned to recognize on the phone the voices of the sponsors and advertising and network executives who were to be put through immediately and others who were to be put off indefinitely. She remembered how Miss Anderson liked her morning coffee—black—her afternoon tea—one slice of lemon—and whom to call to get tickets for *Kiss Me, Kate* and the Ballet Russe and for tables at El Morocco and the Stork Club.

"I get the tickets, or rather you do," Miss Anderson told Fanny, "because my name and the network command second- or third-row center seats and tables on the dance floor and away from the kitchen, but the men pick up the check. I haven't reached the gigolo stage yet, and I'm never going to. The day I have to pay for companionship, I'll buy a cat."

The sheer bravado of the statement shocked Fanny. Then, the more she thought about it, the more intrigued she became. She couldn't imagine Mimi or her mother or her aunts saying anything like it. She couldn't imagine them living Alice's life or enjoying it as Alice clearly did. Only Rose gave her grounds for comparison, but if Rose had the spirit, her life didn't have the style.

She also made runs to Miss Anderson's Park Avenue apartment to pick up and deliver scripts. Miss Anderson had an office at the network, a handsome corner space with a view of the Chrysler Building that made the opening bars of Gershwin's "Rhapsody in Blue" sing in Fanny's head, but she wrote at her apartment in town or at her house on the East End of Long Island. Alice Anderson was one of the most successful writers in the business. The three serials she currently had running added up, she told Fanny, to a million and a half words a year, give or take a hundred thousand, spoken by more than a hundred and fifty characters, not one of whom, she added, had ever succumbed to amnesia. "That's got to be a record in this racket."

If Fanny didn't find the work difficult, she did find the world, like Alice, different from anything she'd ever experienced. That was all right. That was better. The peculiarity of her new life kept the memories of her past life, her real life, at bay, though sometimes she found herself storing up anecdotes from the office to tell Max. Then she'd remember.

One of the actors, a man named Larry Cunningham, was so vocally versatile that he played four different characters on Miss Anderson's three shows. Only once when he'd been suffering from a cold had an avid listener recognized that one voice was coming out of the mouths of two husbands on two different serials and written to say he might be able to pull the wool over his wives' eyes, but she knew he was a bigamist. Some of the actors, like Cunningham, were happy with their radio careers. Thanks to the American Federation of Radio Artists, he got paid for all four roles, a practice that hadn't been followed in the early days of soaps. But others, who had loftier ambitions, were constantly auditioning for plays and movies. When they didn't get the parts, and they usually didn't, they consoled themselves with tales of famous stars who'd languished in radio until they got their big breaks. Remember Orson Welles, they'd tell one another, and launch into an imitation of Welles delivering the show's opening lines. "Who knows what evil lurks in the hearts of men? The Shadow knows."

"That's actors, for you," Rose said. She, Fanny, and Chloe were having dinner in her apartment. "They're always on stage."

"I didn't realize you were so knowledgeable about the breed," Fanny said.

"Before the war I had friends in the Federal Theatre Project."

"I didn't know that."

Rose shrugged. "My checkered past."

Fanny was also intrigued by the casting choices. Victoria Gibson, the woman of a certain age who played the long-suffering saint on Miss Anderson's most popular serial, *The Three Lives of Ivy Brent,* would, Fanny had heard the director remark, trade her firstborn, if she'd had a firstborn, for a few more lines in a script. Ava Sommers, the villainous home-wrecker on the same show, was a girl in her twenties who cried at tales of lost dogs and cats, cooed over babies, and was indignant about starving children abroad and injustice closer to home. She'd grown up in a devout family and had been tithing into the collection plate since she'd earned her first pennies doing chores for neighbors in a small town in Minnesota. No longer a believer, these days she tithed for a host of charities fighting to save the world.

Fanny knew the phrase "casting against type" from her undergraduate days in the drama club, but Ava was the first professional example she'd encountered. On *The Romance of Helen Trent,* Ava had played someone's naïve kid sister, but Miss Anderson had heard the sultry throatiness beneath the girlish sweetness in her voice and stolen her away to play a vamp. In life, Ava was perhaps not innocent, but guileless. On the radio, she was a Circe who couldn't stop luring men onto the rocks of self-destruction and almost, but not quite, foiling the virtuous heroine. She loved the masquerade. It was always more fun to play a bad girl than a good one, she told Fanny.

The writers were a different breed. Fanny got the impression that unlike the actors, few of them still cherished professional hopes, though according to office gossip, more than one had an unproduced play or unpublished novel stashed away in a bottom desk drawer. The writers came in to pick up what were called breakdowns, outlines of the segment of the ongoing story for the specific scripts they were assigned; deliver the scripts; occasionally sit in on rehearsals and broadcasts; and attend meetings; but, like Miss Anderson, they wrote at home, or, it was rumored in some cases, in diners, cafés, and bars.

One afternoon, she was at her desk outside Miss Anderson's office typing an edited script when she sensed someone watching her. She looked up from her machine to find a man leaning against the wall of Miss Anderson's office. He had a face that was at war with itself. The dark, heavily lashed eyes and sleek black hair put him in the actor category; the long narrow nose and thin mouth belonged to a Talmudic scholar. Something about the way he leaned against the wall with his hands in his pockets made her think he was going to break into a soft-shoe at any moment. She decided he was an actor, and probably one of the more successful ones. His tweed jacket and silk tie, she knew from Rose's tutoring, cost more than she made in a week, despite the fact that her pay these days was respectable, or at least more respectable than it had been behind the makeup counter.

"Can I help you?" she asked.

He took a step toward her desk and lifted the small wooden plaque with her name on it.

"And now *The Romance of Florence Fabricant*, 'the real-life drama of a woman, who, when life mocks her, shatters her hopes, dashes her against the rocks of despair, fights back bravely, successfully, to prove what so many women long to prove, that romance can begin at thirty-five.' Though in your case," he went on in a less dramatic voice, "my money is on a number closer to twenty-five."

She swiveled her chair away from the typewriter and crossed, then recrossed her legs. She wasn't accustomed to sitting at a desk all day. "I take it you're one of the actors."

"You take it wrong. I write this drivel. Though I didn't write the particular drivel I just quoted. I still have a stray scruple or two. Didn't you recognize it?"

"Should I?"

"It's the lead-in to *The Romance of Helen Trent*."

"I never listened to s—" She caught herself. "Radio serials before I got this job."

"Watch your mouth, Florence Fabricant, or we'll have to wash it out with the word that is not spoken in these hallowed halls."

"Isn't *Helen Trent* the competition?"

"Sometimes the competition, sometimes the inspiration. In this business we steal anything that's not nailed down. But I have a special fondness for Helen. She was my last gig. Some cold winter night, I'll tell you the story of my ignominious departure."

She turned back to her typewriter. He was a little too cheeky for her taste. "Be still my heart. I can hardly wait."

"You're a hard woman, Fanny Fabricant."

Her glance snapped from her machine back to him, and when he saw the surprise on her face, he grinned. "I have my sources, Fanny, née Florence." Then he actually did it. He executed a quick buck-and-wing and started down the hall. "Welcome to the wonderful world of daytime serials, Miss Fabricant," he said over his shoulder.

"Mrs. Fabricant," she called after him, and held up her

left hand with the gold band she still wore, the gold band she would never take off. He didn't turn back to see the gesture.

❦

She found out who he was a few days later. His name was Charlie Berlin, and unlike his colleagues who had unproduced and unpublished works moldering in desk drawers, he'd had a drama staged by the WPA Federal Theatre Project before the government closed down the program.

"The way Charlie tells it," Ava Sommers said, "his play was the cause of the federal project's demise."

"Watch out for Charlie," Miss Anderson warned her when she found him at Fanny's desk a few days later and chased him away.

"What should I watch out for?"

"How much time do I have to run the list? He's a good writer. Did he tell you about his play that the Federal Theatre Project produced?"

"He didn't, Ava did."

"I bet Charlie put her up to it. But he really is good. Not to mention the fact that he's the only writer I know who can write when he's drunk as well as sober. A lot of writers think they can. He really can. Unfortunately, drunk or sober, instead of turning in scripts, which he's paid to do, he prefers playing poker with the engineers. He's also the only writer who understands the mechanics of radio transmission. That's what got him in trouble at *Helen Trent.* Did he tell you about that?"

"He mentioned it."

"Almost brought the FCC down on them. Fortunately, the avalanche of complaining letters they were expecting never arrived, so the incident died a natural death. But someone had to take the fall, and Charlie did. With good grace. I'll give him that. Of course, he's a skirt chaser."

"If he's so impossible, why do you keep him on?"

"You've seen his scripts. He's the best writer I have. Better than me, but don't let that get around. Also, and don't let this get around either, I have a weakness for the company of troublesome men. My father was one."

As the weeks went by, Charlie Berlin graduated from hovering over her desk to sitting on the edge of it, bracing himself with one leg on the floor, swinging the other in time to an inner beat. He could be funny. He could also be annoying. Or maybe these days she found any man who wasn't Max an irritant.

But Charlie Berlin was the least of her worries. Her daughter's welfare preyed on her mind. According to newspapers, magazines, and a variety of experts, Chloe was a latchkey child, as they'd begun calling kids who'd been left too much to their own devices during the war. Chloe wasn't left to her own devices. Rose and Charity saw to that. But with no father and an absent mother, Fanny still feared the term applied. And everyone, or at least the experts, knew a latchkey child was on the road to juvenile delinquency.

Fanny did her best to compensate, though she knew her best wasn't nearly good enough. On weekends she took Chloe to the park, museums, and the various shows and movies geared to children that she could afford. The outings weren't always a success. One Saturday at the Museum of Natural History, spotting a father kneeling beside a girl about her own age explaining how the hole in the hip pocket had allowed the dinosaur to walk upright, Chloe inched closer and closer to them. Perhaps she was curious about reptilian evolution, but

Fanny had the feeling she was more fascinated by the father-daughter bond. Chloe stood transfixed, staring at them with wide, unblinking eyes. Fanny had to drag her away. In the park, she stopped to watch fathers tossing balls with children. The sight of men carrying small girls or boys on their shoulders made her face crumple with suppressed tears.

Weekdays were easier. She and Chloe walked home from Rose's, where Chloe went after school unless she was invited to play with a friend, swinging clasped hands. Sometimes they sang. Occasionally they played don't-step-on-a-crack. Over dinner, Fanny asked Chloe about her friends, her teachers, and what she'd done in school that day, and reciprocated with stories about the middle-aged actor who cried like a baby and spoke in the voice of a three-year-old, and the sound effects men who spun the wheels of an upside-down bicycle against rayon fabric to create wind and, though this wasn't necessary on any of Miss Anderson's serials, pounded coconut halves on a board to simulate galloping horses.

One night she brought home the cellophane wrapper from a pack of cigarettes someone had left on her desk. Chloe was perched on the stool in the corner of the kitchen; Fanny was leaning against the counter, keeping an eye on the lamb chops in the broiler.

"Okay, this is a test," she said. "Close your eyes." Chloe closed her eyes. "Now imagine wind."

"Like the upside-down bicycle?" Chloe was proud of her arcane knowledge and occasionally showed it off at school.

"The very same. Now what's this?" She scrunched the cellophane.

Chloe leaned closer, listening intently. Fanny went on crumpling.

"A fire!" Chloe shouted.

"Right! A fire crackling in a fireplace. First prize goes to Miss Chloe Fabricant."

Chloe might not be thriving, but she did seem to be surviving. At least she wasn't as far on the road to juvenile delinquency as her friend Linda, who had a mother who saw her off to school each morning and was there when she got home in the afternoon, and a father who was on the premises every night. When Linda filched a Baby Ruth from the local candy store, that same mother dragged her back to return the candy and apologize to the owner. Chloe, as far as Fanny knew, had never lifted anything in her life. Nonetheless, she worried.

Chapter Eight

SHE'D JUST FINISHED TYPING THE EDIT OF CHARLIE BERlin's script when he turned up at her desk. Miss Anderson didn't edit his scripts as heavily as those of the other writers. "He writes them the way I hear them in my head," she liked to say.

"That's what worries me," he'd told Fanny when she'd repeated the comment. "I'd say I love Alice like a sister, except my sister is what is commonly known as a royal pain, but the day I begin writing the way she thinks characters talk is the day I hock my typewriter and find an honest job."

"Is that my deathless prose?" he asked now.

"She deleted a couple of lines. I guess you wrote too long." Fanny had been surprised. He seemed to have not only the form but the length down pat.

He picked up the script, perched on the edge of her desk, and began flipping through the pages. "Not too long, too dangerous. She caught me in the act."

"Of what?"

"Trying to slip in a forbidden message."

"If you know it's forbidden, why do you do it?"

"That's like asking me why I play the ponies."

"Why do you play the ponies?"

"To see if I can beat the odds."

"What was the message? As far as I could see, the scene was just Louella being evasive or at least changing her tune when her husband asked about the turnout at the garden club meeting. First she tells him thirteen women showed up, then she changes the number to twenty-three, then she admits there were only fourteen besides her."

He looked from the script to her. "Jesus, Fanny, do you even read the papers?"

"Of course I read the papers." She heard the defensiveness in her voice. Rose had said the same thing to her more than once. But let them hold down a job, take care of an eight-year-old who lost her father, cook, clean, and make sure she and Chloe had fresh underwear every morning and a hot dinner every night, and see how au courant with the news they'd be.

"Ever hear of Joe McCarthy?"

"Of course I've heard of Senator McCarthy. Tail Gunner Joe," she added to prove that she did look at the paper, when she had time.

"Then you ought to be able to figure out why Alice didn't let changing the number of women at the meeting get through. It sounded too much like McCarthy, who can't make up his mind whether there are two hundred and five Communists in the State Department or fifty-seven or some number between."

"Why would you want to slip that into a script?"

"Because McCarthy and his fluctuating numbers are worse than a joke. They're a threat."

"True, but people get fired for less."

"So you do follow the news."

A librarian friend of Rose's had lost her job for refusing to sign a loyalty oath, but Fanny saw no reason to cite her sources for him.

"It might not be only you. What about Alice?" She still called her Miss Anderson to her face, but the form of address made her feel infantile when Charlie referred to her as Alice.

"For that matter, what about you?" he said. "When you spotted those subversive numbers in the draft of the script I gave you, why didn't you pick up the phone and call HUAC immediately? That's the House Un-American Activities Committee, in case the acronym got past you in the newspapers."

"I know what HUAC is."

"Then why didn't you call them? You must be a little pink around the edges yourself for letting a spoof of Tail Gunner Joe get through." He slid off her desk, put his hands on the blotter, and leaned toward her as if he was going to impart a confidence. "But don't worry, sweetheart, your secret is safe with me. It's one more thing we have in common."

She sat watching as he soft-shoed away from her desk and down the hall. He really was impossible. He enjoyed driving Alice to distraction by getting his scripts in just under the line. Once, he'd been so tardy that she'd barely had time to edit it, and he'd had to stand over Fanny's desk, pulling each page out as she finished typing it, then race it down the hall to the actors in the recording studio, who'd stood huddled together for the reading because there hadn't been time to make more than one copy. He spent half his time in the office, as Alice had said, playing poker with the engineers, and the other half spouting irrelevant information on arcane subjects like the importance of centering on rare stamps and how the Dewey Decimal System revolutionized library shelving. Fanny was far from his only audience. Charlie Berlin was out to entertain the entire office, the entire world. Secretaries for other shows, file clerks, even elevator operators and messengers were fair game. If an actress came in to audition for a part, she was manna from heaven. Anyone who walked through the door was a potential peanut gallery of admiration for Charlie Berlin. Chained to her desk from nine to five, Fanny was a captive audience.

She came awake with a start. The sudden wrenching into consciousness wasn't unusual. She rarely had trouble falling asleep. If anything, she was exhausted by the time she went to Chloe's room to tuck her in for the night and would have gone to bed herself if she didn't think there was something pathetic about a grown woman turning in at eight or nine o'clock. Staying asleep was another matter. At four or three or even two, the hours of the morning when even the most innocuous concern takes on the hellfire glow of imminent disaster, her mind snapped into action, and she knew trying to fall back to sleep would only make her more anxious.

Sometimes, she turned on the light and picked up a book, but John O'Hara's *A Rage to Live* was on her night table at the moment, and she was in no mood for the sexual longings of others. She got up, pulled on her robe, slid into her slippers, and made her way down the short hall past Chloe's room to the living room. Aside from the creak of the wide oak floorboards, the apartment was silent. A car cruised down West End Avenue, then the world beyond the windows went quiet too. Though she hadn't turned on a light, the illumination from the streetlamps and a full moon hanging over the skyline in the distance spilled into the room through the tall windows. It was bright enough to see that the door of one of the carved walnut cabinets beneath the long, curved window seat was open. The hardware on cupboards, like the building itself, went back to the turn of the century and didn't always catch. The one that had sprung open held games and toys Chloe had outgrown but wasn't quite ready to discard.

Fanny bent to close the cabinet. That was when she saw it. Even in the dim light, even in this room where it shouldn't be, she recognized it. She reached in and took out the small wooden bowl. The familiar fragrance filled the room. Max was there with her. She reached out to steady herself against the wall, then, still feeling dizzy, sat on the window seat.

She didn't know how long she remained there, cradling the bowl in her lap, inhaling the memory of Max, but somewhere toward morning her grief began to give way to guilt. She worried about her daughter. She was on the lookout for filched candy bars and other childish transgressions. But she'd missed this, the fragrant tangible sign of her daughter's pain. She'd been too consumed by her own loss to recognize that Chloe's was at least as vast and deep.

She was still sitting there, chastising herself, when Chloe came out of her room the next morning. Her hair, more strawberry blond than copper, hung tangled around her face, still soft from sleep. She raised a fist to one eye and rubbed it. Then she saw what her mother was holding and stopped. She'd been prepared to be scolded for not wearing her slippers. Her mother was always carrying on about how she would catch cold. But not wearing slippers was nothing compared to stealing.

"I wasn't stealing, Mommy. Honest. Not like Linda and the Baby Ruth."

"Of course you weren't. How could you steal from Daddy? You're part of him. He's part of you. Of us."

Chloe didn't move from where she was standing. Sometimes her mother pretended everything was all right, but the next minute she'd get angry about something else. Chloe still remembered the slap.

"And I don't blame you for wanting to keep it. It was a good idea. I wish I had thought of it."

Chloe was still wary. But as she stood eyeing her mother, her mother lifted one arm in invitation. Chloe scooted across the room and onto the window seat, though just to be safe she tucked her bare feet under her. Then she leaned against her mother.

"You're not mad?"

"Of course I'm not mad. You didn't do anything wrong. It's another way to hang on to Daddy. Like talking about him and remembering things he did and said."

"I remember when I was a flower girl and he pretended to be shot because I looked so nice."

Her mother's face crumpled, like a tissue when you scrunch it up. Sometimes when she talked about Daddy, her mother looked, not happy exactly, but not too sad either, but sometimes, like now, she looked as if she was going to start to cry again. Chloe wished she could tell which it was going to be before she said anything.

Oh god, why did Chloe have to bring up that night? Fanny was on her knees in the big walk-in closet again, pleading with Max not to leave her.

"Like the time you looked so nice," Fanny repeated.

"Everybody looked nice. You and Daddy and me."

Fanny took a breath. The aroma of the shaving cream undid her. People had insisted the pain would ease with time. People had lied. The sob she'd been holding in escaped.

"Mommy." The word was an answering sob in Chloe's throat.

"It's all right, baby. It's all right," she said, and held Chloe tighter.

But they both knew it wasn't.

Chapter Nine

Fanny usually saw Mimi on weekends with the girls in tow, but every two or three weeks Mimi came to Midtown to meet for lunch. Though Mimi never said as much, Fanny always had the feeling that her cousin found the outings disappointing. For Fanny, their lunches were nutritional sustenance and a break from work. For Mimi, they were occasions. No wonder she was disappointed. Sometimes Fanny tried to enliven the event, but unlike Chloe, Mimi had no interest in the sound effects or casting ironies of radio serials.

They usually met at Schrafft's, but when Fanny was feeling financially strapped, they went to the Automat. Mimi hated the Automat. Lunching there was an occasion only if you were young enough to find excitement in slipping nickels into slots, opening small glass doors, and taking out soup, a sandwich, or shrilly colored Jell-O. Mimi always offered to treat Fanny to lunch on the days when she was economizing, but Fanny always refused. It was awkward enough feeling like a poor relation when she and Chloe paid a visit to Mimi's apartment. Fanny's love for her daughter didn't blind her to her faults. She recognized that like most children, and many adults for that matter, Chloe had an unsavory materialistic streak. She envied Belle's toys and games and clothes. She coveted the television in front of which she and Belle sat on the floor, legs crossed, eyes wide with wonder, as Howdy Doody, Clarabell, and the rest of the troop cavorted. The fact that Mimi was generous compounded the awkwardness of the situation. When she bought something for Belle, which she was always doing, she often got an identical or similar item for Chloe, just as Mimi's mother used to for Fanny after her own mother died. Fanny appreciated the instinct to solace, even if it took a strangely concrete form, and she didn't have the heart to make Chloe refuse the gifts, but she had no intention of becoming a charity case herself.

Today they were meeting at Schrafft's. Fanny made her way past the long counter, or cocktail bar, depending on your taste and point of view, where women, only women, sat eating baked cheese soufflé and creamed shrimp on toast or tippling a small Manhattan or whiskey sour, to the dining room where more women in groups of two or three or four gathered at tables covered with ladylike white tablecloths. As soon as she spotted Mimi sitting straight-backed and expectant, she knew something was up. It was more than the fact that she was shedding the weight she'd put on trying to fill the void left by Norman's death. Fanny had been witnessing that change for weeks. This was something different. When she saw Fanny coming toward her, her smile beamed out like the shaft from a lighthouse and her dimples flashed.

"You're looking as if you just won a daily double," Fanny said as she slid into the chair across from her.

"Since when did you begin using racetrack expressions?"

"Sorry. The bad influence of someone in the office."

"The sooner you get out of that place, the better. Especially if that's the kind of thing you're picking up."

"I just meant you were looking especially good today."

"Then you like my hair this way? You don't think it's too short?"

"I don't think it's too short, but it's not the hair. It's the canary you just swallowed. Something's up."

Mimi picked up her menu. "Let's order first."

So that was the way it was going to be. Whatever Mimi's news, and Fanny had a good idea of what it was, she was going to put off the pleasure of springing it.

After the waitress in her starched uniform came, took their order for tuna and vegetable salads, and retreated, Fanny turned back to Mimi.

"Now do you want to tell me what's up?"

Mimi went on smiling across the table. "Guess."

"You met someone."

The smile faded only slightly, then returned. She'd been deprived of the element of surprise but not the delight of the news. "How did you know?"

Fanny smiled back, though she knew the expression was forced. She wasn't envious. Fear was closer to what she was feeling. She saw herself being introduced to a man. He had no face, only a shadowy presence. She sensed him sizing her up. She saw herself trying to make conversation. She imagined . . . only she couldn't imagine it—or rather she could, and that was the problem. Sex had been a mystery when she was a girl. Now that she knew the intimacy of it, now that she'd experienced the emotional as well as physical nakedness, she couldn't imagine committing it with a stranger. She knew as soon as she shook a man's hand or sat across a table from him, she would be thinking about the act. She might as well wear a sandwich board saying *hungry* on one side, *hands off* on the other.

"Call it an educated guess," she said. "Not to mention that piece you clipped for me from *McCall's* a while ago. '129 Ways to Get a Husband.' My favorites were 'Learn to paint and set up your easel outside an engineering school' and 'Have your car break down in strategic places.' I assume by 'strategic' they mean the engineering school and not some dark back road in the boondocks."

"You can laugh, but it had some good suggestions."

"Name one. No, on second thought, tell me about the man you met."

"His name is Howard. He's a widower."

"Did he find you at your easel outside an engineering school? Sorry. That was unkind. Where did you meet him?"

"In his store. I was taking in my dry cleaning. He owns two dry cleaning places, one on Broadway and one on Columbus. He doesn't actually work in them, just owns and runs them, but he was there that day, and we started talking. It came out that I was a widow and he was a widower, and lo and behold a few nights later, he called and asked me out. He got my phone number off the cleaning slip."

"A resourceful man."

"A kind man," Mimi corrected her. "He's the kindest man I've ever known."

"There's a lot to be said for that."

"There's everything to be said for that."

"How long ago did this happen?"

"Two and a half months."

"Why didn't you tell me before?"

"I didn't want to tempt fate."

The phrasing had changed from their grandparents' or even parents' generation. The evil eye had become fate. But the fear was the same. News this good had to be hidden from the vengeful gods, not that Mimi would put Fanny in that category. Nonetheless, she wasn't taking any chances.

❧

When Fanny got back to the office, she found two edited scripts in her inbox. One, from a woman named Tess Whitely who'd been writing for the serials for almost as long as Alice, had a handful of edits; the other, from Charlie Berlin, had one. She'd just rolled a piece of paper into her typewriter when Charlie showed up at her desk. He picked up Tess Whitely's script.

"That's not yours."

"Just checking the competition." He put down Tess's script and picked up his own. "Curses, foiled again."

"What were you trying to sneak through this time? As far as I could see there was nothing subversive or even political. All you did was mention that the stranger who just came to town had lost a son in the war."

"You didn't pick up on the problem because you don't listen, or at least you didn't listen in the past, to the bilge we're churning out. Reality has to be kept at bay at all costs. Characters can be felled by mysterious illnesses and infirmities as long as they're not specifically diagnosed as something the listeners might be worried about. They can come down with blindness, amnesia, inexplicable paralysis at the drop of a hat, but never infantile paralysis and especially never cancer. It was even more extreme during the war. In the wonderful world of daytime radio serials, between Pearl Harbor and V-J Day, nobody ever died in action. No, I take that back. Ma Perkins's poor son bit the dust. I can't remember now whether he was so admirable that he had to go out in a flash of patriotic glory or so venal that he had to be punished. But he was the only one."

She thought of Norman, and all the men who'd died in the war, and of course Max. He hadn't died in the war, but she couldn't get over the feeling that the things he'd seen and endured in the war had somehow contributed to his death. She wondered what Charlie Berlin had been doing while all those other men were risking their lives.

"And I bet you tried to slip in at least a missing-in-action every chance you got."

He looked down at her from his perch on the side of her desk. "Come on, Fanny, spit it out. Ask me directly. Like those cunning little tykes in the propaganda ads for the last war. 'What did you do in the war, Daddy?' You'll be relieved to know I did not spend the years from '41 to '45 turning out radio scripts. I served my country with valor and distinction."

"Only you could make the words 'valor and distinction' sound like bad jokes. What did you do?"

"I commanded an LGD."

She was surprised. She had no idea what an LGD was—she could never keep the acronyms straight—but the last thing she could imagine Charlie Berlin doing was commanding something with initials that landed on beaches or plowed over enemy forces or committed heaven only knew what form of devastation. Her reaction must have shown on her face.

"Do you know what an LGD is?"

"No."

"Large government desk. I wrote films for the army."

"Don't you take anything seriously?"

"I took those movies very seriously. Didn't want to get shipped overseas. I turned out gems. *What We're Fighting For* was full of

Mom and apple pie. Then there was the one with indiscretions that sank ships and got our boys killed. But my favorite was a sexy little flick that warned all those good clean American boys that those sweet young English, French, German, and, heaven forfend, American girls eager to give them a night of bliss might also give them a case of the clap, to put it eloquently."

"Are you trying to shock me?"

"Shock an old married lady like you? Surely it ain't possible."

She felt the color rising in her cheeks and swiveled back to her typewriter.

"I have shocked you." He laughed. "The mention of venereal disease shocks the blissfully married Mrs. Fabricant."

She whirled from her typewriter back to him. "Goddamn you, Charlie. I'm not blissfully married. I'm not married at all. I'm a widow." She shrieked the last hated word.

He looked as if he'd been slapped. "Jesus."

She turned back to her typewriter. She was not going to let him see her cry.

"Why didn't you tell me?"

"Because it's none of your damn business."

He slid off her desk and came around until he was standing over her typewriter. "I'm sorry, Fanny. I really am."

"Just go. Please."

This time he didn't do a soft-shoe on his way out, but he did go quickly. He couldn't wait to get away. And she couldn't wait to be rid of him.

❧

The illuminated hands of the clock on her night table carved a narrow slice out of the night. Two twenty. It was even earlier than usual. She turned on her other side, though she knew it was no good. She wasn't going to fall back to sleep. And the much-touted charm of the book on her night table, *Cheaper by the Dozen,* escaped her. Before Max's death she'd always finished books, even if she didn't like them, but she no longer saw the point in squandering time.

She got out of bed, and without bothering with a robe because the nights were getting milder, made her way to the living room. The wooden bowl of shaving cream had come as a surprise, but she knew exactly where the letters were even though she hadn't read them for some time. She hadn't had to after he'd come home. She hadn't dared to since the awful night of the blizzard. But she needed to now. She'd shouted at Charlie Berlin this afternoon, and the word "widow" had seemed to bounce off the walls of the office and echo down the halls. She needed to drown it out. She needed to remember what it had been like to be connected. She needed to remember Max.

Though the moon was shrouded tonight, the light from the streetlamps trickled through the tall windows. She crossed the living room to the row of cabinets beneath the window seat, bent to the last cupboard on the right, and took out the shoebox. She'd remembered where they were, but she'd forgotten the shoebox. Tomorrow she'd buy something better to keep them in. A handsome wooden box or maybe a leather folder.

She sat on the window seat with the box, her hands cradling it, her mind putting off the moment of opening it and taking out the letters. She was impatient, but strangely fearful—not of the letters but of herself. She was afraid of the dam breaking again.

Finally, she lifted the lid. The letters were stored in the order they'd been written rather than the order they'd arrived. The latter had little to do with the former. Sometimes she hadn't gotten a letter for weeks, then she'd find the small locked mailbox in the building vestibule overflowing with three or five or six envelopes, usually the most recent, though occasionally one from several weeks or even months earlier would be among them. But the strangest aspect of the letters had been their anodyne nature. Even at the time she'd known they were dishonest. Not the paragraphs telling her how much he loved and missed her. She'd trusted those and read them over and over. But she'd been suspicious of the rest of what he'd written, or rather what he'd left out. No one was ever seriously wounded. No one in his care ever died. And, of course, he, the doctor, was never in danger. She wondered if all men at the front or close to it wrote such guarded, protective letters home.

She took one from the box, reached up to turn on the standing lamp, took the letter out of its envelope, and began to read. The words were there, mundane reports of the weather, the food, the wounded GIs who were getting better, but his voice was missing. It wasn't even in the questions about Chloe or the expressions of love and longing. Just as she hadn't been able to recall it during the months he'd been overseas, she couldn't hear it now. She put aside the letter and took out another. His voice wasn't in that one either. She went on that way, pulling out letters, opening the envelopes, reading snatches, and tossing them aside. Max wasn't there. He was missing from the letters just as he was from the apartment and her life and Chloe's. He'd gone AWOL. He'd abandoned them.

Then she did hear a voice, but it wasn't Max's. It was hers. "How could you?" she was shouting. "How could you do this to me? How could you be so cruel? I'll never forgive you. Never."

The last words stunned her into silence. She sat listening.

The refrigerator motor whirred quietly. The old building groaned on its haunches. A car went by, then another, their tires sizzling on the wet pavement like frying bacon. And her own words still beat in the room, or perhaps only in her head. She didn't know if she'd spoken aloud or only screamed in her mind. But it didn't matter. She'd thought the rage. She'd placed the blame.

She began picking up the letters, smoothing them out, and putting them back in the envelopes, careful not to mix them up. Each letter had to go back in the proper envelope. Each envelope had to be restored to the box in the order it had been written. And all the time she worked she kept talking, not in her head now but whispering into the room that was beginning to grow light.

"I'm sorry," she murmured. "I didn't mean it. You know I didn't mean it. I could never mean it. I'm so sorry. Forgive me. Please forgive me." She stopped. "I'm just so lost," she said, and began to cry.

Chapter Ten

Though Fanny and Mimi lunched regularly, Rose usually had a solitary sandwich at her kitchen table between clients or bouts of sewing. Old habits die hard. For years she'd carried her lunch to various factories in paper bags. All the girls had. She remembered one spring day when she was sixteen or seventeen. She could pinpoint her age because she knew when she'd lost her faith, such as it had been. She hadn't told her parents. She hadn't wanted to hurt them. But neither was she a hypocrite. She would not carry a matzos sandwich to the factory. Instead, she'd taken a hard-boiled egg to placate her mother and bought a hunk of Passover-forbidden bread from a vendor on the street. The devout girl at the sewing machine next to hers had been scandalized.

"It's *pesach*!" the girl had hissed.

"A *zissen pesach,*" Rose had answered, and gone on eating.

After that, she'd lunched alone, until she'd made friends with one of the Italian girls in the factory who was an anarchist and ostracized by her coreligionists too. She and Rose got along. In those days, there was nothing Rose wouldn't rebel against.

Over the years, she'd reverted to having a quick lunch alone on working days, so Fanny was surprised when she telephoned that morning and said she had to come to Midtown to find fabric for an evening gown she was copying for one of her clients. If Fanny was free, she'd stop by her office and take her to lunch.

Fanny was free. Unfortunately, Charlie Berlin was at loose ends as well. He turned up at her desk a few minutes before Rose was due. He'd been giving her a wide berth, but now he sauntered up to her desk as if nothing had happened.

"Is this my drivel?" he asked as he took a script from her outbox, perched on her desk, and began paging through it.

This time she didn't mention how many changes there were, and he didn't comment on them. His silence was more awkward than his sarcasm. She went on typing and made three mistakes, but refused to fix them until he left. She wouldn't give him the satisfaction.

He stood, finally, and put the script back in her outbox. That was when she saw Rose coming toward them. She'd never get rid of him now. Rose was a new audience.

"Charlie Berlin," Rose repeated his name when Fanny introduced them. "Weren't you the wunderkind who had a play produced by the Federal Theatre Project?"

"I admit I was pretty wet behind the ears in those days, but wunderkind is hyperbole."

"It was good."

"Is that hearsay or can I assume you were one of the three people who saw it?"

"I not only saw it, I was at the party after the opening."

He looked at her more closely, clearly trying to place her. "Hugo Hayes," he said finally.

"Hugo Hayes," she agreed, and the color flared in her cheeks. It wasn't a blush, it was a flush of pride.

He turned to Fanny. "Why didn't you tell me who your aunt was?"

Fanny looked at Rose. "Because I didn't know who my aunt was."

Rose smiled back at her. "You would have if you'd been paying attention. Don't you remember that Eugene Debs rally I took you to, among other events that would have scandalized your parents?"

"Did you ever take me to hear this Hugo Hayes speak?"

"Hugo wasn't one to give speeches, but you met him briefly at the Eugene Debs rally."

"I was sorry to hear about him," Charlie said.

"Thank you," Rose answered, and this time she didn't look at Fanny.

❧

"Who is this Hugo Hayes?" Fanny asked after Charlie had walked with them to the elevator, told Rose he hoped to see her again, and moved on.

"I wish you'd stop calling him *this* Hugo Hayes, as if there were a bunch of them. And I'll tell you when we get out of here," Rose said quietly.

They took the elevator to the ground floor, crossed the lobby, and went through the revolving door. "Okay," Fanny said as they came out onto Sixth Avenue and began walking. "Who is this—"

Rose shot her a look.

". . . one-of-a-kind Hugo Hayes? And why shouldn't I

mention his name in the hallowed halls—" She stopped again. She didn't like picking up Charlie Berlin's phrases. "In the office?"

"Because these days guilt by association, even distant association with someone who's been dead for more than ten years, is enough to get you hauled before HUAC for questioning. But you're right about one thing. He was one of a kind."

"In that case, why didn't I ever meet him? A brief encounter at a political rally doesn't count. I don't remember even hearing of him. But a complete stranger takes one look at you and connects you to him. You and Hugo Hayes must have been quite an item."

Rose stopped in the middle of the sidewalk and turned to Fanny. A man bumped into her and apologized. The lunchtime crowd flowed around them like a river around an island. But Rose went on standing there with an expression Fanny had never seen on her before. Her mouth had gone soft with memory, and her eyes were tender.

"We were an item. We definitely were."

"So why didn't I ever hear of him?"

"Because an aunt does not tell even a favorite niece about her lover. Not when the niece is five or seven or even fifteen. The affair went on for a while. I was trying to open your eyes to the world, but not that wide. Besides, your parents were suspicious enough of me as it was. If they'd known I was enjoying sex without benefit of clergy, they wouldn't have let me see you."

"I haven't been fifteen or under the parental thumb for some time now."

Rose took Fanny's arm and began walking. "True, but the occasion never arose."

Fanny turned to look at her as they walked. "You mean I never asked. Never showed any curiosity about your life. I was too consumed by my own."

"It's a generational flaw. Young people tend to be self-involved. They certainly don't think old people were ever young."

"Why didn't you marry him?"

Rose's glance slid to Fanny briefly. "I think you're smart enough to figure that out. He was already married. To a devout Catholic. He rebelled against the church and everything else. One of the many things I loved about him. She clung to it."

"Oh, Rose, how sad. For both of you. Tell me more about him. I feel as if I've missed a whole chunk of your life, maybe the most important chunk."

"He was a labor organizer—that's how I met him—with a literary bent. Or to put it another way, he was a Stanford Phi Beta Kappa with a social conscience. By the time your friend Charlie Berlin came along, Hugo was working for the WPA's Federal Theatre Project. Unfortunately, he was too restless for the bureaucracy. He just had to get to the war in Spain. I loved him for that too, though I didn't want him to go. He signed on with the Lincoln Brigade. And was killed five days after he got there. At Jarama. One of the first battles."

Fanny stopped again and stood staring at her. "I'm sorry, Rose. So sorry."

Rose smiled. The tenderness was gone. She was the armored Rose again. "For what? His death? For thinking you were the only widow in the world? Or for assuming that your old spinster aunt could never have loved or been loved? For being as blind and stupid as the rest of the family, the rest of the world?"

"All of the above."

Rose went on looking at her. "You're forgiven. And I'm glad

you finally know. Now there's someone I can talk to about him. Besides your friend Charlie Berlin. But I promised you lunch, and we're going to have lunch. I'll regale you with stories of my star-crossed love affair. Where do you want to go?"

"Someplace where we can get a drink."

Rose looked at her in surprise.

"I just discovered the woman I thought I knew best in the world is someone else entirely."

"Not entirely. I'm still the tough cookie who has spent a good part of her life trying to keep you up to the mark. That was one of the things Hugo loved about me."

"Trying to keep me up to the mark?"

Rose shook her head. "Talk about solipsistic. Being a tough cookie."

❦

"I trust I made clear the answer to the second part of your question about why you shouldn't bandy Hugo's name around your office," Rose told her as they stood saying goodbye in front of Fanny's building. "He missed being dragged through the mud in the hearings about the Theatre Project. The rest of us might not get off so easily. As I said, these days it's guilt by association. And in my case, it's not merely association. I used to be pretty active. It's just lucky I'm only a seamstress."

"I'm only a secretary."

"True, but you work in radio. I can affect the way women look. You, or at least the people you work for—people in radio, television, movies—influence the way people think. And that scares a lot of other people. So be careful." She turned to go, then pivoted back. "Be careful of Charlie Berlin especially."

"I thought you liked him."

"I do. At least I used to. And I remember his play. A little too agitprop maybe, but original. It was good enough for the army to acquire the rights to produce it in Germany under the occupation. They were going to stage it and Arthur Miller's *All My Sons*. Until that rightwing rag *Counterattack* got wind of it and raised holy hell. Can't have our good clean American boys and those innocent Germans who brought you the war corrupted by plays about man's venality and inhumanity to his fellow man. Needless to say, neither play reached Germany. But I'm willing to bet HUAC and other like-minded organizations have folders a foot thick on Charlie Berlin. And there's one more thing that makes him dangerous."

"I know. Alice told me he's a skirt chaser."

"I don't know about that. I was thinking of something more serious. These days most of us old lefties are trying to keep our heads down. Not Charlie."

"He's always trying to sneak subversive messages into scripts."

"Exactly. If ever a man was dying to be hauled before a committee of bombastic pseudo-patriots so he can thumb his nose at them, it's Charlie Berlin."

Chapter Eleven

FANNY DIDN'T TELL MIMI ABOUT ROSE'S PAST, THOUGH Rose was Mimi's aunt too. Fanny had been happy for Rose. Mimi would be scandalized. Besides, Mimi didn't give her a chance to. She had news of her own, though it was scarcely a surprise.

They were sitting on a bench in a playground in Central Park on a mild April Saturday. The rows of daffodils around the perimeter of the paved area stood like bright promissory notes for the coming season. Chloe and Belle had tied one end of their rope to a park bench and were switching places turning the rope and skipping.

Mommy and Daddy
Sitting in a tree
K-I-S-S-I-N-G
First comes love
Then comes marriage
Then comes Mommy with a baby carriage.

"Howard and I are going to be married," Mimi said. "He asked me a few nights ago."

"That's wonderful, Mimi. Though not exactly a surprise. Good luck."

"Good luck? In other words, you think I'm making a mistake."

Fanny turned on the bench to look at her. "I wasn't being sarcastic. It was a benevolent wish, not a taunt. 'Good luck' is what you say when people get engaged and married."

"Most people say 'congratulations.'"

"That's because most people weren't raised by our mothers. Don't you remember the etiquette books they bought us when we were, what, fifteen or sixteen? You're not supposed to congratulate the bride because that implies she snared the groom. You congratulate him, because he snared her, and wish her good luck. So my congratulations to Howard and good luck to you. I'm happy for both of you."

Mimi didn't say anything to that, but went on watching the girls.

A, my name is Alice
And my husband's name is Albert
We come from Alabama
And we sell apples.

"I know you don't approve of him." Mimi couldn't seem to let it go.

"Approve? I'm delighted. Why wouldn't I be? From what I've seen, you were right. Kindness is his middle name." She hesitated for a moment. "If anything, I'm envious. It must be wonderful to be in love again."

Mimi shook her head. "You're one for the books, Fan, you really are."

She tried not to stiffen. "Why am I one for the books?"

"Everyone says you're the smart one, the competent one. A tough cookie, like Rose."

"I can't hold a candle to Rose."

"You have a job. You take care of yourself and Chloe. You know how to balance a checkbook. But sometimes you sound as if you're still sweet sixteen. 'It must be wonderful to be in love again.' I'm not in love again. At least not the way I was with Norman. I was a kid then. And he was going off to war. But I'm comfortable with Howard. And I'm tired of not going out to dinner."

"What are you talking about? You go out to dinner all the time."

"Oh, sure, my parents take me out to dinner, and that makes me feel worse, as if I'm a little girl and they're giving me a treat. Or I go out to dinner with you or a friend whose husband is working late or away on business. Even that's only once in a blue moon. And you of all people know what happens when we do. We get treated like second-class citizens. We are second-class citizens. Women without men. Remember the time the girls were sleeping over at Rose's and we went for something to eat before the movies? You asked if we could have the booth. It wasn't even a fancy restaurant, just a diner. The man said the booth was only for parties of four. Then two men came in, and he ushered them straight to the booth."

"Okay, you have a point, but I'm not sure it's a reason for marriage. It may be an advantage of marriage, but not a reason."

Chloe and Belle were still skipping rope.

T, my name is Theresa
And my husband's name is Thomas

"I was just giving you an example of what life is like being alone. Besides, Belle needs a father."

Fanny wasn't going to argue with that.

"What I'm trying to say is love has nothing to do with it, and the sooner you realize that and find someone yourself, the better off you're going to be."

"Right, I'll set up an easel in front of an engineering school this weekend."

"I mean it. The better off you and Chloe will both be. Marriage is what we're supposed to do. Anything else is unnatural."

"Unnatural?"

"Unnatural. Women are meant to be wives and mothers. All the books and magazines say so. Remember your college graduation? The speaker, somebody in government or the head of a foundation or something. I forget who he was, but I remember he went on and on about how much all of you had learned in your four years there. If you ask me, he could have cut the speech in half. The sun was really hot. But he finally got to the point. He asked what all that education was for. Maybe you don't remember his answer, but I do. To make you better wives and mothers. So you could further your husbands' careers and raise healthy, moral kids who would grow into responsible members of society. In other words, the only job that matters for a girl is taking care of a man and his kids. And if she doesn't have a man to take care of, she's a failure."

Fanny glanced over at the two girls. "You have Belle to take care of."

"It's not the same. More important maybe, but not the same. Belle will grow up. Both of them will be gone before we know it. You can't fight it, Fanny. A girl is supposed to be married. And I'm going to be married to Howard."

"Congratulations."

"Thank you."

❦

Fanny and Chloe walked home through the May evening on the park side of Central Park West. That way they didn't have to stop every block for crosstown traffic but could make their way down the long unbroken expanse of wide sidewalk, interrupted only by the major crosstown thoroughfares. And on that side of the street they could smell the park greening. They swung hands as they walked. Fanny had had two glasses of champagne at the reception in Howard's apartment, which Mimi and Belle were moving into. Mimi had made sure Chloe got one of the roses from the wedding cake.

"Did you have a good time?" Fanny asked.

"It was okay."

"Just okay?"

"Did you?"

"Of course I did. I'm happy for Mimi."

"Are you going to get married?"

Fanny forced herself to keep walking, though she couldn't help glancing at her daughter to gauge whether she was hoping for an affirmative or negative answer. Chloe's face gave away nothing.

"Not in the immediate future."

They walked on in silence for a few moments, still swinging hands.

"Do you want me to?"

"I don't know. I guess it would be nice to have a daddy. But only if he could be like Daddy."

"I'm with you there."

"Not like Uncle Howard."

"What's wrong with Uncle Howard? I think he's nice."

"He's old. And he smells funny."

"He's not that old. And the smell is from his cigars. Anyway, the important thing is that Mimi doesn't seem to mind either." She hesitated. She didn't want to encourage her daughter to betray confidences, but she was curious. "What does Belle think of him?"

"She likes him. She says since Uncle Howard, Aunt Mimi doesn't cry all the time."

"That's something to celebrate."

Chloe looked up at her. "Do you cry all the time?"

"Have you seen me crying all the time?"

"I mean all the time when I don't see you."

"If it's only when you don't see me, it couldn't be all the time, could it?"

Chloe stopped. "Mommy! I mean it."

"I cry occasionally. Don't you?"

Chloe didn't answer, but she started walking again.

"It's all right to cry sometimes. It's just not a good idea to make a habit of it."

"Like Aunt Mimi before Uncle Howard?"

"Aunt Mimi couldn't help herself."

"Why not? If you can help yourself."

"Aunt Mimi didn't have my advantages."

"What do you mean?"

"The things you're lucky enough to get in life. For one thing, I had Aunt Rose."

"Is she an advantage?"

"Is she ever. She taught me all kinds of things. She made me pull up my socks."

"You don't wear socks most of the time. You wear stockings."

"It's an expression. It means stop whining and get on with your life."

"Isn't Aunt Rose Aunt Mimi's aunt too?"

"Let's just say I was more receptive to her coaching."

Chloe thought about that for half a block. She liked Aunt Rose, but when it came to advantages, she'd rather have a bigger apartment and lots of toys and clothes and a television, most of all a television, like Belle did. And there was one more thing, but she wasn't sure she should mention it. She debated for another half a block, then came out with it.

"Aunt Mimi doesn't have to work. Isn't that an advantage? Belle says everyone feels sorry for you because you have to work."

"They shouldn't. I don't feel sorry for myself. Aunt Rose doesn't feel sorry for me."

"You mean you like going to work?"

"It's fun. Sometimes."

"What's fun about it?"

Fanny thought about that for a moment, searching for specific aspects of the job that would appeal to a child.

"The rehearsals, for one thing. There are usually three rehearsals or run-throughs before each show. The first time they let me sit in, I couldn't believe it. During the initial read-through the actors were cutting up and making fun of their lines and pulling off wild stunts. One actress—I told you about Ava—was doing cartwheels between reading her lines. I thought the director was going to get angry, but he just laughed. I couldn't understand it. Then when I watched them do the real broadcast, I figured it out. Some of the lines they have to read are pretty silly. If you've been trained as a serious actress and studied Shakespeare and plays like that, and Ava has, it's kind of embarrassing to deliver those lines. Acting silly in rehearsals is one way to get over the embarrassment so they can be serious in the broadcast. Does that make sense?"

"Kind of," Chloe said.

"And then there's the other stuff that's going on. While the actors are reading their lines, the man who plays the god box—"

"The what?"

"That's what they call the organ."

"Why?"

She could see her mother thinking about it. She liked that. A lot of grown-ups made up answers when they didn't know something, but her mother always admitted not knowing. Aunt Rose did too.

"I'm not sure. Maybe because they play organs in church so hearing it on the radio makes listening to the program almost a religious experience. Anyway, the organist comes in and begins practicing for the show. At the same time the sound man is going through the script figuring out where he has to slam doors and put in footsteps and make it rain or thunder."

"I like the sound effects best."

"I think they're fun too, and if I didn't go out to work, I wouldn't know about them or any of the rest of it. And neither would you. I admit most of what I've learned isn't what anyone would call important. Not like Daddy knowing how to save lives. But it's interesting, and I'm glad I learned about it. I'm really glad I can tell you about it."

"What else do you like?"

"The people. At least some of them, like Ava. It's the rehearsals all over again. There are all kinds of people I never would have met if I hadn't gone to work. And maybe, just maybe, knowing more kinds of people and more about the world makes me more interesting to you and everybody else and even me."

Chloe thought about that. None of it sounded like a reason to feel sorry for her mother.

"Penny for your thoughts," her mother said. "In fact, I'm curious enough to pay a nickel."

"Will I go out to work when I'm a grown-up?"

Her mother stopped walking and stood looking down at her, and now Chloe was sorry she'd asked. She never knew when something she said was going to make her mother sad again, or even angry.

"I never thought about it," her mother said. Then she was quiet for another minute. "I don't see why not, if you want to."

She took her mother's hand and they started walking again. "Only if it's fun like your job."

❧

"That lady you work with," Chloe said a few days later, "the one who does cartwheels?"

"Ava."

"Could she teach me?"

"I bet she could. I'll ask her to brunch next Sunday."

Ava arrived with coffee cake from a local bakery and a book for Chloe. As soon as Chloe tore the paper off, Fanny saw that it was a picture book and too young for Chloe. She waited to see how Chloe would react, but Ava didn't give her a chance to.

"I know it looks too young for you," Ava said, "but I assure you it's not. Lots of grown-ups like it too. It's about a bear who goes into hibernation the way bears do in winter, and when he wakes up in the spring, he finds they've built a factory over him. The problem is none of the people in the factory believe he's a bear. One after another they keep repeating the same line." Ava straightened her shoulders and slipped into the persona of a factory manager. "'You're not a bear. You're just a silly man who needs a shave and wears a fur coat.'"

By the time Ava left, Chloe could do cartwheels and kept dissolving in giggles over the line. "You're not a bear," the three of them kept repeating. "You're just a silly man who needs a shave and wears a fur coat."

"You're really good with kids," Fanny observed when she and Ava were saying goodbye at the door.

"It's the ham in me. Playing to an appreciative audience."

Chapter Twelve

The door to Alice's office was closed, but Fanny could hear them arguing. Alice didn't argue with Charlie Berlin any more than she ran roughshod over his scripts. Sometimes she pretended to be annoyed with him, but whatever he'd done now had really riled her.

"Goddamnit, Charlie," her voice carried through the closed door, "if you want to go down in flames, that's your business, but you're not taking me and my shows with you. This isn't *The Romance of Helen Trent,* and this time it won't be the FCC hauling us up on obscenity charges. These people mean business."

"It was only a joke." Charlie wasn't shouting, and Fanny had to lean toward the closed door and listen carefully to hear. "And more for you than anyone else. I knew you'd catch it."

"What if I didn't? What if I was too busy with the other scripts that need more work than yours? What if it had slipped by?"

"You let something slip by, sweetheart? Don't make me laugh."

Fanny couldn't make out Alice's reply, but she interpreted

the tone. Alice didn't have a weakness for troublesome men. She was a pushover for them.

A moment later, the door opened. Charlie shuffled out grinning and dropped a script in Fanny's inbox.

"Only three changes."

"From the sound of things, they must have been whoppers." She took the script from the inbox and paged through it for the red markings. It was the scene where the two neighborhood boys who have just had a fistfight decide to make peace and prick their fingers to exchange blood so they'll be brothers for life. In Charlie's script one of the boys mentions "blood brothers" once and the two of them swear an oath of loyalty three times. Alice had deleted all three iterations of "oath of loyalty."

He was sitting on the edge of her desk, watching her. "I take it I don't have to explain the reference to you."

Fanny remembered Rose's librarian friend who'd been fired for refusing to sign a loyalty oath. She'd also heard rumors that the network was thinking of distributing a questionnaire to employees that would amount to the same kind of pledge. Some of the sponsors already had them for their own personnel.

"I understand the reference," she said. "What I don't understand is why you keep trying to get yourself and everyone else in trouble."

"I already told you. I'm trying to beat the odds."

"It's not funny."

"You're right, it's not funny, it's ludicrous. Reds in the government. Reds in the movie business. Reds in radio and television. Reds in the closet, reds behind the shower curtain, reds under the beds. Uncle Joe Stalin is lonely as hell because all the Commies have left Russia and set up shop here."

"People are losing their jobs right and left."

"That ought to keep them on the straight and narrow."

"You're such a cynic. Don't you believe in anything?"

He sat looking down at her from his perch on the edge of her desk. "You've got it wrong, sweetheart. The thing about cynics is we believe in so much so fervently that we can't help being disappointed."

"What has ever disappointed you? A horse that didn't come in? A girl who showed up for an audition and resisted your charms?"

"Well, well, well."

"Well, well, well what?"

"Mrs. Fabricant has a bitchy streak."

"Only toward certain people."

He leaned over and put his mouth next to her ear. "That's the nicest thing you ever said to me."

❦

This isn't *The Romance of Helen Trent,* Alice had shouted behind the closed door of her office. The more they referred to the other program, the more curious Fanny became about what had happened there, but she didn't want to ask Charlie. She refused to give him the satisfaction. She couldn't ask Alice. Alice might be clear-eyed about the literary value of her serials, but she didn't take the business side of them lightly. The person to ask was Ava. She'd worked with Charlie on *Helen Trent.*

She and Ava were having lunch at the Automat. Like Mimi, Ava could afford better restaurants, but unlike Mimi, she loved the ambiance of the Automat. According to Ava, the penniless patrons making a meal of ketchup and hot water and the lonely trying to look as if they were enjoying their solitary meals, the greedy loading their trays with too many dishes and the indecisive pacing back and forth between the ham and cheese on rye in one window and the pot roast in another were a gold mine for an actress. It also gave her a chance to flex her charity muscle. She'd been known to buy a second lunch after she'd had one, approach one of those penniless patrons dining on ketchup and water, and explain that she'd just realized she was late for an appointment or had morning sickness or some other excuse, add that with all the children starving in Europe she hated to waste food, and beg the person to take it off her hands. She was studying an older woman in a sad cloche hat and an air of having seen better days when Fanny asked about Charlie Berlin's departure from *Helen Trent.*

"I thought everyone knew the story. It's legendary in the business."

"I wasn't in the business until eight months ago."

"Have you ever listened to *Helen Trent*?"

Fanny shook her head.

"You know the premise, though?"

"That a woman can find romance after the age of thirty-five."

"Helen finds romance all right. The show's been on for what, fifteen or sixteen years, this is the third actress to play Helen, but Helen's still thirty-five, and men still keep falling for her. Helen, however, never succumbs. She frequently begins to—have to keep the plot creeping along—but something always goes wrong. The love interest falls off a cliff while mountain climbing, or turns out to be a bounder, or some monkey wrench gets thrown into the romance. Helen is a professional virgin. If she gave in, the show would be off the air in a month. The incident that got Charlie fired had to do with the professional virginity. Helen has a longtime beau, Gil Whitney, who returns at regular intervals to beg her to marry him. One day when Gil was proposing yet again, a voice came over the airwaves. 'For Christ's sake, lay the dame and get it over with,' the voice growled. Then, as the engineers were running around the building trying to find where the voice was coming from, it went on to tell Gil in graphic detail exactly what he should do to Helen. It was pretty racy."

"And the voice was Charlie's?"

Ava shook her head. "No one ever found out for sure who it was or where it came from, but Charlie, being Charlie, got the blame. He was in the studio that day and had disappeared right before the broadcast. He knows almost as much as the engineers about the mysteries of how we stand in a studio reading our lines and our voices go wafting out to all those listeners. And it's just the kind of stunt Charlie would pull. So Charlie took the fall. That way the network, the sponsors, and everyone else connected to the show could say the culprit had been punished, and the FCC backed off. But the most surprising part of the story had nothing to do with Charlie. Everyone thought there'd be an avalanche of letters from listeners swearing they'd never heard such filth in their lives and would never listen to the show again. Maybe five letters came in." She smiled and pushed her dark pageboy, which kept falling forward, behind her ear. "Which means, according to Charlie, all those women supposedly listening while they're mopping, ironing, and cooking either aren't paying attention or are starved for sex."

"That sounds like Charlie, all right."

"Charlie's okay." Ava put down her coffee cup. "Don't look at me that way, Fanny. I never had a fling with him, if that's what you're thinking. Though to tell the truth, I might have if he'd been interested. But Charlie has a sixth sense."

"For what?"

"Girls who might try to entangle."

❦

When Fanny got back to the office, she found two edited scripts in her inbox. One was by a new writer Alice was trying out. It had so many red pencil marks it looked as if it were bleeding. The other was Charlie Berlin's.

She rolled a clean sheet of paper into her typewriter and started on the heavily edited script. She'd get the harder job out of the way first. She was halfway through it when Charlie showed up at her desk. He picked up the discarded pages she'd already retyped.

"That's not yours."

"I knew that from the red pencil. This from the new guy?"

"If this is any indication, it's not only his first script for Alice, it's his last. Even I could have told him where he went wrong, and that was before I saw Alice's edits."

He perched on the side of her desk. "Where did he go wrong?"

"I know it's only a so . . ." She stopped. "Serial."

"Watch your mouth, Fanny."

"But in the first scene, Gladys shouldn't lose her temper. She shouldn't even get angry. It's too trite. It's what the listener expects."

"What should Gladys do to get the characters where Alice wants them by the end of the scene?"

"Try to understand why Quentin did what he did."

He sat looking down at her. "You mean write the scene backward?"

"I wasn't talking about the chronology."

"Neither was I. Opposite was what I meant. When you sit down to write a script or a play or any kind of fiction, the first instinct, at least for most writers, is to go for the obvious emotion. A woman is abandoned, she's bereft. A man is outmaneuvered, he's angry. But sometimes the emotion or response that isn't the first instinct, that's the opposite of what we assume the character will feel, is more interesting."

"Thank you for the master class," she said, but her voice lacked its usual bite. For a moment she'd been back in her creative writing seminar. Before that, even. She'd started writing short stories in her teens. One day her mother had found one while cleaning out her drawers and been scandalized, not by the evidence of sex, which would be a plot twist in Philip Roth's *Goodbye, Columbus,* that Fanny would read years later, but by the disaffection and restlessness of the protagonist, who was, of course, a badly disguised Fanny.

"You're the one who spotted it," Charlie said now. He went on studying her. "Did you ever think of trying your hand at one of these?"

"No," she lied.

"You ought to."

"Because you sense some hidden gift in me or because you'd have such a good time watching me fall on my face?"

He grinned. "Maybe a little of both."

"Sorry to disappoint you, but I don't think I'll take the bait. I've seen too many would-be writers sail in here on their high hopes and leave with their tails between their legs."

"You have a point."

"Anyway, I thought you thought your work had no redeeming value beyond a paycheck."

"True. But I bet my paycheck is bigger than yours. And I know writing is more interesting than typing."

Chapter Thirteen

The day was too hot for early June. If this was a preview of the summer, Fanny was glad Chloe was going to sleep-away camp. Not that they had much choice in the matter. Max's parents had been eager to have her stay with them on weekdays when Fanny was working, but the city was no place for a child during the summer months. The Health Department was already issuing warnings about swimming pools and other public places. Fanny couldn't get two photographs she'd seen in a magazine out of her head. In one, lines of iron lungs stretched the length of a hospital ward, small heads sticking out of one end of each cylinder. A ghoulish fear had made her lean over the picture to study the individual children. Blondes and brunettes and probably redheads, though she couldn't tell from the black-and-white photograph; boys and girls, preteens and two infants stared back at her. In the foreground of the picture, a curly-haired girl about Chloe's age had twisted her head to look up at a white-uniformed nurse standing beside the contraption. The article said the iron lung was a triumph of innovation. It prevented asphyxiation and death. Unfortunately, it had no effect on other consequences of the disease. In another photograph in the same article, a girl about five in a frilly party dress was leaning on two crutches. A heavy metal brace on one leg weighed her down. Polio was most deadly for children between the ages of five and nine, the caption beneath the picture said.

Thanks to Rose, who'd offered to pay for sleep-away camp, Chloe would spend the worst months of the epidemic in fresh air on a lake in the woods in the Poconos. The only drawback was that Fanny wouldn't be able to visit her. The camp would be in quarantine for the season. But that was still three weeks away, so Fanny was relieved when Mimi called on that first stifling Saturday in June and invited them to Howard's beach club in Long Beach.

"You've saved the day," Fanny said. "We were supposed to go to the Met with Rose, but Chloe would much rather go to the beach than a museum. Thank you." She hesitated. "You're not going to let them in the pool, though, are you?"

"I'm not an idiot, Fanny, even if I didn't go to college. Of course I'm not going to let them go in the pool. But Howard says the ocean is okay."

The consensus of opinion did seem to be that the ocean was safe, or as safe as anything could be during an epidemic. Fanny thanked her for the invitation again, and an hour later, Chloe—bathing suit, towel, and bottle of Coppertone in her beach bag and sunglasses perched on her nose—waved an excited goodbye to her mother from the back seat of Howard's cream-colored Cadillac convertible.

Rose and Fanny came down the wide steps of the museum, crossed the plaza, and turned back to the park. The afternoon was cooling into evening, but still warm for early June.

"If today is a harbinger of things to come," Fanny said, "thank you again for sending Chloe to camp. It really is generous of you."

"What else do I have to do with my ill-gotten gains?"

They sat on one of the benches along the path.

"All the same, I can't help feeling we're exploiting you. I'm sorry I'm not making more money."

"You're doing all right. You've been at it for less than a year. And you weren't exactly brought up to be self-supporting."

"Don't remind me. Chloe and I had a discussion about it on the way home from Mimi's wedding. She said according to Belle the entire family feels sorry for me because I have to work."

"Welcome to the club. What did you tell her?"

"That there was no reason to feel sorry for me. I liked working. In fact, I was so busy painting a rosy picture because I didn't want her to start feeling sorry for me or, worse still, guilty herself, I made life in the wonderful world of radio serials sound like more fun than a barrel of monkeys."

"Good for you." Rose was silent for a moment. "And is it?"

She shrugged. "It's fine."

"How's Charlie Berlin? Still trying to make trouble?"

She told her about the *Helen Trent* episode.

"I remember that."

"You heard it?"

"Don't look at me that way, Fanny. Sometimes I keep the radio on while I'm working, usually to WQXR, though you haven't lived until you've jitterbugged to Benny Goodman or Artie Shaw with the foot pedal of one of those old treadle sewing machines. But Klara—remember the Hungarian refugee who used to help out with some of the sewing?—was there that day, and she liked to listen to soaps to improve her English."

"Was she shocked? The girl who told me the story said they expected to be deluged with angry letters. They got about five."

"Once she understood the gist of what he was saying, she was laughing so hard she had to stop sewing. We both were. If they had more installments like that, I might start tuning in."

"You want to listen to a disembodied male voice on the radio talking dirty?"

"Not particularly, but I might listen occasionally if they weren't so vapid."

"Charlie Berlin thinks I ought to try my hand at a script."

"I knew I liked that man."

"You agree with him?"

"I've been waiting for you to think of it."

"What if I were no good at it?"

"Wouldn't that be heartbreaking? Fanny tries her hand at something and fails. I don't know how you got so timid. Not my example, I'm sure."

They were on their way out of the park when Rose brought up the *Helen Trent* episode again.

"In answer to your question, no, I do not want to listen to a disembodied male voice talking dirty to me on the radio. But you know what I miss, and I bet you do too. Physical touch. Sometimes my skin gets so lonely."

Fanny, who had a good four inches on Rose, stopped and reached an arm around her shoulders.

"Thank you," Rose said.

"Thank *you.*"

❧

"How about a shower to get off the sand and salt water?" Fanny asked Chloe as she hung the wet bathing suit and towel over the shower curtain rod.

"I showered in Uncle Howard's cabana. It's like a little house with a table and chairs, and a patio outside with more chairs, and a little refrigerator full of Cokes and tonic for Uncle Howard's and Aunt Mimi's drinks. Aunt Mimi says she doesn't leave anything else there because it would go bad between visits, but I bet people could live there if they wanted to."

"I bet they could, if they didn't mind living cheek by jowl."

"What's that?"

"Crowded. Too close together. On top of one another."

"You can walk right out of it and jump in the pool."

Fanny whirled around from taking the rest of the things out of Chloe's beach bag. "You didn't go in the pool?"

"Aunt Mimi wouldn't let us. Just the ocean."

"What else did you do besides swim in the ocean?" Fanny asked when they were eating dinner. Or rather, Fanny was eating dinner. Chloe was pushing food around on her plate. Fanny chalked that up to too much sun, salt water, and god knows what junk Howard had plied them with that afternoon. She was willing to bet he'd bought them hot dogs, ice cream, and anything else they'd asked for. Mimi was right. He was a kind man. In this case that was the problem.

"Uncle Howard taught Belle to swim." Chloe pushed peas from one side of her plate to the other. "She kept going under, even though he had his hands under her tummy."

"It's hard to learn to swim in the ocean. All those waves. Daddy taught you in a lake."

Chloe lifted a forkful of rice, then put it down again.

"You're not eating. Do you feel all right?"

"I'm not hungry."

"I fear to ask what you ate all day."

Chloe shrugged. "I was five when Daddy taught me, right?"

"Do you remember?"

"Vividly."

"Vividly?"

"That's what you say when you talk about remembering things about Daddy. Belle is almost seven. She should know by now."

"Maybe she was waiting for Uncle Howard to come along to teach her."

"How come mommies don't teach how to swim?"

Fanny thought about that for a moment. "The phrasing is 'why don't mommies teach how to swim,' but it's an excellent question."

"If it's so good, what's the answer?"

"It's not that mommies can't. It's that daddies usually get there first. Mommies are too busy spreading suntan lotion on everyone and unwrapping picnics and all that."

"I'd rather swim."

"You're in good company."

"Do mommies teach anything?"

"Who taught you to bake chocolate-chip cookies, kiddo?"

"That's different."

"Different, but not less important. If you had to go through life without one of them—swimming or chocolate chips—which would you choose? You don't have to answer that. I also taught you to jump rope and helped you perfect your jigsaw puzzle skills."

"Thank you."

"You're welcome. And I taught you your excellent manners, as you just demonstrated. Daddy was a bad influence in that department."

Chloe's eyes widened. She'd never heard her mother say anything bad about her father. "He was?"

"When we had hot chocolate with whipped cream, he'd compete with you to see who could get the biggest mustache. Of course, he had a head start, because he had a real mustache to begin with."

"I remember that." She didn't, but she wished she did, and now she would. She tried to remember things about her father, but it was hard. She was so little then. But one thing she'd always remember. She'd always see him putting his hands over his heart and staggering backward that night when she came down the stairs to be a flower girl. She bet Belle didn't have anything like that to remember.

"My daddy is going to teach me to swim," Belle had said when they were in Uncle Howard's cabana changing into their bathing suits. Belle didn't have to bring one in a beach bag the way Chloe did because she kept all hers there. Uncle Howard and Aunt Mimi did too, and towels, and shovels and pails, and a big black rubber tube, and all those bottles of Coke in the little refrigerator.

At first, she hadn't understood what Belle was talking about. Belle's daddy had died, just like hers, only before hers. Then she realized when Belle said her daddy, she meant Uncle Howard. Uncle Howard wasn't Chloe's real uncle any more than he was Belle's real daddy. Mimi wasn't her real aunt either.

She didn't have any real aunts and uncles, because her mother was an only child, and her daddy had been too. Like her. She had Aunt Rose, but Aunt Rose was her mother's aunt so it was different.

Chloe told Belle she already knew how to swim. "My daddy taught me."

"Well, my daddy's going to teach me today."

Uncle Howard had taught her. At least he'd tried to. But Belle didn't want to learn to swim. She wanted to show off. Every time a wave came, even if it wasn't big, she screamed and hung around Uncle Howard's neck and yelled, "Daddy, Daddy, Daddy!" She was showing off for Chloe, getting back for all the times Chloe was a year older. Chloe was still a year older—Belle could never do anything about that—but she'd tried to even the score today.

"You're still not eating," her mother said.

"My stomach hurts." It wasn't a lie. Before she just wasn't hungry, but now her stomach really did hurt. She hated Belle.

"Where does it hurt?" her mother asked.

"All over."

"You're sure this isn't just an attack of 'I don't want to eat chicken and peas because I'm full of hot dogs and ice cream'?"

"It really hurts."

"A lot?"

Chloe nodded. The more she talked about it, the worse she felt.

"Okay, forget dinner. Do you want to lie down?"

Chloe nodded again.

After her mother helped her get out of her clothes and into her pajamas and tucked her in, she asked her mother to leave the nightlight on.

"I'm not even sure where I put it. You haven't wanted it for a while."

"Please."

By the time her mother came back with the nightlight, her stomach had almost stopped hurting. But she still wanted the nightlight. She knew what would happen in the dark. Belle would come back screaming "Daddy, Daddy, Daddy!"

❦

After she plugged in the nightlight and kissed Chloe, Fanny went back to the living room and began clearing the plates. Chloe's was still full.

It was only a stomachache. Children had stomachaches all the time. It was the junk food she'd eaten, and the sun, and too many hours in the ocean. She hadn't gone near the pool. Mimi hadn't let her, Mimi had promised and Chloe had reported.

She hadn't gone in the pool, but she'd had lunch around the pool. Were other children splashing in the infected water? And what about the bathrooms? Children never bothered to wash their hands when no adults were around. She never should have let Chloe go. The ocean might be safe, and she wasn't even certain about that, but the beach club was a cesspool of contagion. If Max were alive, he wouldn't have let her go.

She crossed the living room to the window seat. The sky over the Hudson was a riot of pink mauving into purple. As she sat watching the colors deepen, she tried to regulate her breathing. She had to calm down. Chloe didn't have a fever or chills or a sore throat. She had a stomachache. A stomachache wasn't a symptom. At least, she didn't think it was.

She stood, went down the short hall to her bedroom, and knelt in front of the bookcase. She'd had to get rid of so many books when they'd moved. The sunporch in the house had been fitted out with two walls of built-in shelves. But she'd brought a couple of Max's medical dictionaries, partly because they'd been a part of him, partly because they might come in handy.

The novels and short stories were arranged alphabetically by author, the nonfiction by subject, but she'd stuck the medical books on the bottom shelf with the other thick reference volumes. She took out the one on contagious disease, and sitting on the floor, began paging through it until she came to poliomyelitis. Her eyes raced down the symptoms. "Fever. Headache. Sore throat." The list was reassuring. She kept going. "Pain or stiffness of the back, neck, or limbs." Just as she'd thought. Her eye caught on the next entry. She sat staring at the words. "Gastrointestinal disturbances. Nausea. Vomiting. Abdominal pain." The last two words seemed to throb on the page.

Her eyes moved from the list of symptoms to her watch. It said a little after seven. There wasn't much hope the doctor would be in his office at this hour, but it was worth a try. She went back to the living room, found the number on her emergency list, dialed it, and stood counting the rings. A voice answered on the tenth. She knew even before she asked that this was not the doctor's office, but his answering service. He was away for the weekend, the voice reported, but called in for messages. In fact, he had telephoned a short while ago and would again in the morning. If Fanny needed help before then, the voice suggested, she should go to the emergency room. The image of the ward full of iron lungs flashed through her mind. The idea of taking Chloe to a hospital emergency room seemed as dangerous as tossing her into a swimming pool.

She made her way back to Chloe's room. She was sleeping

curled on her side facing the door with her hand to her mouth. Her skin was flushed but that was probably from the sun. Fanny took the few steps to the bed and put her fingers against Chloe's forehead. It was warm but not feverish.

Chloe opened her eyes.

"How's your tummy?"

"What?" she asked sleepily.

"I said how's your tummy? Does it still hurt?"

Chloe shook her head and closed her eyes again.

Fanny tiptoed out, went down the hall to her own room, and picked the communicable diseases dictionary up off the floor. As she closed it, she noticed Max's name written inside the front cover. The familiar lines and curves of his signature looped around her heart. Disaster couldn't strike again. Life was not that cruel. Except that it was. Only a child or a fool would believe that one loss gave her immunity against a lifetime of them.

By the time the doctor returned her call the next morning, Chloe was fine. "Stomachaches happen," he said, not unkindly. He was good with children and patient with mothers.

Three nights later, sometime close to one, Chloe woke with another stomachache.

"Where does it hurt?" Fanny hadn't forgotten the photograph of the iron lung ward, but surely if Chloe had contracted something at the beach club, other symptoms would have shown up in the intervening time. Now she was more worried about appendicitis.

"All over."

"Not just down here?" She pressed gently on her daughter's lower right side.

"All over," Chloe repeated.

"Do you have to go to the bathroom?"

Chloe shook her head.

"Do you feel as if you're going to throw up?"

She shook her head again.

This time she didn't have to consult a book. She remembered the advice from the various manuals she'd relied on when Max had been overseas. Try to distract the child.

"Would you like me to read to you?" She waited to see how Chloe would take it. She'd been reading to herself before bed for some time now and might resent being babied.

She nodded.

"What would you like?"

"*Betsy-Tacy.*"

"The whole series? This is to fall asleep, not set out on a marathon."

"I mean the first book. *Betsy-Tacy.*"

Fanny was surprised. In the first book, both Betsy and Tacy are five. Chloe was working her way through the series and preferred the books where the protagonists were older.

She took the volume from the bookcase, sat beside Chloe with her back against the chintz headboard Rose had sewn, reached her arm around Chloe's shoulders, and began to read. She hadn't gotten far when she heard the change in Chloe's breathing. She was asleep.

❦

Two days later, the school nurse called Fanny at her office and told her to come get Chloe, who was complaining of a stomachache.

"I couldn't find anything specific," the nurse said. "It's not in the area of her appendix. At least, not specifically there. She's not nauseated. She said she doesn't have diarrhea."

"This is the third one in the past week," Fanny told her, and said she'd be on her way as soon as she called the doctor for an appointment.

She got the answering service again. The doctor hadn't been away only for the weekend; he was on vacation.

"Somebody must be covering for him," Fanny said.

The service gave her a name, address, and phone number.

Dr. Ezra Rapaport's office was in the basement of a brownstone on Seventy-Fourth Street between Central Park West and Columbus Avenue. Fanny was relieved. She'd never scrimp on Chloe's health, and if need be, she could turn to Rose or her father, but she didn't think a well-appointed office at an expensive address was an indication of medical expertise. That was Max's influence, again. She remembered a conversation he'd had with one of his colleagues when they'd come back from the war. The friend had been determined to get on the staff of New York Presbyterian. Max was headed for Bellevue.

"Bellevue," the friend had repeated incredulously. "You can do better than that."

"Not if I want to do serious surgery instead of worrying whether there's enough ice in the maternity ward kitchen for the fathers' martinis."

What both of them were too politic to mention was that the point was moot. The friend's last name was Osborn. Max's was the less shiny and more problematic Fabricant. Max had told her about an interview he'd had when he'd applied to Johns Hopkins medical school.

"Fabricant," the interviewer had said. "That's an unusual name."

"I'm a Jew, sir," Max had answered.

It was the only med school he'd applied to that hadn't accepted him. The staff of New York Presbyterian, he knew, wasn't likely to be any more broad-minded.

From the look of Dr. Rapaport's office, he subscribed to Max's view of practicing medicine. The waiting room was small and crowded with a lumpy leather sofa, several straight-backed chairs, and a table littered with outdated magazines and dogeared children's books. There were no other patients. Fanny hoped that was the result of the hour—it was almost six—rather than his diagnostic skills or medical expertise. The secretary or nurse she'd made the appointment with was gone.

A man in a white coat over a white shirt and a blue tie printed with teddy bears—bedside manner for kids—stepped into the waiting room before they had time to sit. He had a shock of unruly brown hair crowned by a cowlick and watchful eyes behind large horn-rimmed glasses. She had a feeling he'd begun taking medical notes the minute he laid eyes on them. She remembered another incident when Max was just finishing medical school. They'd been on a bus.

"Did you notice that woman across from us?" he'd asked when the woman had gotten off.

"She was wearing a nice hat."

"You didn't notice her eyes?"

"I was too busy looking at the hat."

"She has exophthalmos."

"Okay, I give up. What's exophthalmos? More to the point, how do you know?"

"Her bulging eyes. And the visible whites above the irises. It's a symptom of a thyroid disorder."

But perhaps she was only projecting Max onto this new doctor because she was desperate to trust someone with medical expertise.

He introduced himself to Fanny, then to Chloe. He didn't bend down to her level, but he did shake her hand as he had Fanny's. Chloe was shy, but Fanny could tell she was pleased.

He ushered them into an even smaller room with a desk, one chair behind it, and two in front of it; gestured them to the chairs; then sat behind the desk and began to ask questions, some of Fanny, others of Chloe. He kept eye contact as he listened and only after each of them had finished talking did he make notes. Finally, he led them into the largest of the three rooms, though that wasn't saying much, and positioned a small step so Chloe could climb up on the examining table.

Fanny stood looking over his shoulder as he lifted Chloe's dress and palpated her stomach, moved a stethoscope over her chest and back, looked in her ears and nose and mouth, and finally told her to sit up.

"You look healthy as a horse, or in this case a filly," he said when they were back in the consulting room.

"Then you don't think there's anything wrong?" Fanny asked.

He leaned back in his swivel chair. "I can't find anything, but just to be safe let's try a bland diet for a while." He turned to Chloe. "Chicken and mashed potatoes, no hot dogs or pizza or soda. Just for a few weeks. Do you think you can handle that?"

Chloe nodded.

"And now don't get upset. I know you're not a baby. Third grade is practically on your way to college. But I'm going to put you on baby food just for a week or so."

Fanny waited for Chloe to protest. She nodded, as if she and the doctor were in medical cahoots.

He looked from Chloe to the notes he'd made before he'd examined her, and hesitated. Fanny waited. Was there something he wasn't telling them?

"Fabricant," he said, and now he looked up at Fanny. "There was a Max Fabricant in my med school class. Any relation?"

Fanny felt a flash of pride. Max lived, if only in people's memories. She felt irrationally grateful.

"He was my husband."

"Was?" He hesitated, gauging the proper response. Divorce had been almost as rampant after the war as marriage before it. She could tell from the uncertainty on his face that he didn't want to imply a tragedy if it was merely a mistake. On the other hand, he didn't want to seem callous in the face of a war casualty.

"He died."

"I'm sorry. Last I heard he was in France."

"It happened after the war."

The mask of professional kindness fell, and emotions raced across his face. Sympathy gave way to shock, then fear. The war had changed the natural order of the universe and sent the young to their graves before the old. But the war was over. Young men, his contemporaries, weren't supposed to die before they'd had a chance to live. It took him a moment to recover and slip back into his professional mien. "I'm sorry," he repeated.

"Thank you," she said, her words as rote and meaningless as his.

She opened her handbag and began to take out her wallet.

He held up his hand, palm toward her. "Professional courtesy for Max's family," he said.

❦

Though Chloe hadn't balked at the idea of baby food in the doctor's office, Fanny was prepared for a fit of embarrassment or at least a sulk when they stopped at the market to buy several jars on the way home. But Chloe seemed to enjoy debating between the pureed chicken and beef, peas and carrots, bananas and apples. The real wonder, however, came a few days later when Fanny picked her up from a play date at a friend's apartment. The friend's mother had a Lord & Taylor shopping bag hanging on the doorknob.

"I left it here to remind me to give it to you," she said, and held the bag out to Fanny.

Fanny couldn't imagine why the woman was giving her a gift. She looked inside. There were several jars of baby food.

"I swear Billy can read a calendar. The day he hit six months, he began pushing baby food away and reaching for the solids on the table. These are still good, and I hate to see them go to waste."

Fanny thanked her and asked how she knew about Chloe's new diet.

"I heard her telling Karen. She's a real trouper. Karen would keep it a deep dark secret, if I could get the stuff down her at all, but Chloe seems to think it's a joke."

It occurred to Fanny on the way home. For Chloe the baby food diet wasn't a joke, it was a kind of solace. The first stomachache had occurred the night she'd been to the beach club with Mimi and Howard. A few days later she'd brought up the incident again and confided that every time a wave had come, Belle had hung on to Uncle Howard and screamed "Daddy, Daddy, Daddy!" The stomachache hadn't been caused by the food Chloe had eaten. It had been triggered by the incipient love affair she'd witnessed. The malady and its treatment not only made Chloe, who'd been only a spectator that day at the beach club, the center of attention. It also took her back to an earlier time when the world had been intact.

Chapter Fourteen

The stomachaches disappeared. When Fanny reported the improvement to Dr. Rapaport, he said Chloe could go back to normal food but to keep it fairly bland for a while. Fanny followed his advice, but now she had another concern. It wasn't exactly medical, but she couldn't think of anyone else to consult. After all, it had to do with Chloe's psychological well-being.

She called the doctor's office. The nurse said he was with another patient and asked if it was an emergency. Fanny said it wasn't. "It's just a question about my daughter. He saw her in the office ten days ago, and we spoke last week." The nurse said he'd return the call at the end of the day. Fanny wasn't sure what the end of the day meant, so she gave the nurse both her office and apartment numbers and explained that she'd be at the office until five and home by six.

"The doctor starts returning calls at five. Except on Wednesday evenings when he has late office hours. Then he returns calls after seven," she added briskly. Clearly Dr. Rapaport was the one in the office with the bedside manner.

Fanny was pulling on her white cotton gloves when the phone rang a little after five.

"I hope it isn't the return of the stomachaches," the doctor said.

"None since you put her on, then took her off, the baby food. It's something else. Or rather it's related to the stomachaches, but more psychological than physical. At least I think it is. I'm sorry to bother you with it, but I don't know whom else to ask."

"You're not bothering me. It's my job."

She told him about the summer arrangements. "She'll be out of the city for July and August. The camp will be quarantined all summer. Not even parental visits. That's the only drawback. That's what I'm worried about."

"That you won't be able to see her?"

"That it's not a good time to send her off. It didn't occur to me until after the stomachaches stopped." She told him about the day at the beach club, the swimming lesson, and the "Daddy" chants. "If she's still so fragile about losing her father, and how could she not be, is it wise to send her away on her own? It'll be like losing her one remaining parent."

He was silent for a moment, and she pictured him sitting behind his desk in the slightly shabby office, pondering the problem.

"First of all," he began finally, "she didn't strike me as fragile. She struck me as pretty strong in view of the trauma. The stomachaches may have been a symptom, or a protest, but she was functioning. Second, I still think getting her out of the city for the summer is a good idea. She can't go to a pool. I don't think a playground is a great idea either. A quarantined camp in the country sounds like the safest bet."

"Even without me."

When he answered, she could hear the smile in his voice. "Who are you worried about, Mrs. Fabricant, you or Chloe?"

"Both of us, I suppose."

"My diagnosis is that you're both going to be fine. Though that doesn't mean she won't have a few days or nights of homesickness. Or that you won't have bouts of Chloelessness."

It occurred to her as soon as she hung up the phone. He hadn't charged her for the office visit and he hadn't rushed her off the phone now. A thank-you gift was in order, but what did you give someone whose tastes and interests you didn't know? She could get him something for his desk, though he didn't seem particularly office proud. A picture frame was a possibility. She hadn't noticed a photograph of a wife, or a wife and children, on his desk. But that would have to be good leather and pricey. She could send him a plant for his office. A plant was about as anodyne as a gift could be. But that dark basement would be a death sentence for any form of vegetation. A gift certificate was too crass. The only solution was a book, even if she didn't know his predilections in reading or anything else. If he didn't like what she chose, he could exchange it.

She thought of stopping on the way home, but she was already late. And there was no rush. Chloe was leaving for camp next week. She'd have plenty of time, too much, on her hands after that. Instead of grabbing something on the run in a local bookstore, she'd stop at Scribner's during her lunch hour or after work and find the perfect book to say thank you to Dr. Rapaport.

❦

The yellow school bus idling at the curb on Central Park West was frying like an egg in the hot sun. A little distance away, girls and mothers milled about in the shade thrown by a canopy of trees. Some of the girls held their mothers' hands; others who knew one another shouted and squealed and giggled. Dressed in identical shorts and T-shirts with the words "Camp Winding Wood" across their narrow or chubby chests, each wore a name tag and, suspended from it, a doctor's certificate verifying that she was free of any symptoms of illness. Chloe wasn't holding Fanny's hand, though she was staying close to her, despite the fact that her friends Karen and Linda would be boarding the same bus to the same camp and would even be in the same bunk. Belle was not among the campers. She would be staying in the city for the summer with access to the ocean if not a pool, and a mother who would be home all day. Fanny felt a flash of guilt, then remembered the conversation with Dr. Rapaport. Camp was the safest place for Chloe. The best mother in the world was no match for a city that was likely to be a breeding ground of poliomyelitis.

Several older girls, counselors and junior counselors, wearing the same uniform of shorts and camp-emblazoned T-shirts, moved among the children and their mothers, introducing, greeting, encouraging, consoling.

Fanny bent to embrace Chloe. Chloe clung to her.

"I'll miss you, sweet pea," Fanny said as she tried to let go.

Chloe went on clinging for a moment, then released her.

"I'll write," Fanny said. "I'll write every night. You write too. I'd hate to see all those stamped, addressed postcards moldering in your duffel all summer. And don't forget the ones addressed to Grandma and Pop Pop. Remember to thank them for the tennis racquet."

Chloe nodded. Fanny could tell she was trying to hold back her tears. They hugged again, then Chloe broke away and ran to join the line beside the bus. As she reached the door and climbed the first step, she turned back to wave.

On the bus, Karen was saving a seat for her. Chloe slid into it and leaned past Karen to look out the window. The mothers stood in groups of twos and threes, waving. Not a single father had come to see anyone off. She waved back at her mother and stopped being sad. Camp was going to be okay.

❦

"How are you holding up?" Rose asked that evening. She was standing at her kitchen counter tossing a salad while Fanny set the table. She'd had no intention of letting her niece have dinner alone tonight.

"I haven't fallen apart yet."

"And you're not going to." Rose carried the bowl to the table, then stood with her hands on the back of a chair, looking at Fanny. "Funny thing about mothers and children."

"I can tell a cosmic observation is on the way."

"Don't be disrespectful to your elders, but you're right. It's the only love affair that has to end in a breakup to be successful."

"You have a point," Fanny said. "A depressing point, but a point nonetheless."

❦

She realized as she came out of the office the next evening that there was no reason to procrastinate. She'd go to Scribner's now. The longer she put off letting herself into the empty apartment, the better.

Her shadow cast by the lowering sun behind her led her east on Fiftieth Street. A truck passed, blotting out the light, erasing the silhouette, deleting her. She was back in the Pennsylvania Station, watching Max disappear into the crowd of men pounding down the steps to the track, hollow, insubstantial, with only Chloe clutching her as an anchor. But Chloe was no longer here. How had so much of her life become being left? The truck passed. The shadow reappeared. It straightened its shoulders and quickened its pace.

When she reached the bookstore, she stood for a moment in front of the large plate-glass window, studying the book jackets gleaming in the evening radiance. Behind them, more volumes were heaped on display tables and shelves. Surely somewhere in that vast array lurked the perfect gift. She pulled open the door, stepped into the aroma of fresh print, and began to browse. A bestseller would be the safest bet, but so many of them were war stories. *The Naked and the Dead. The Young Lions. Crusade in Europe.* Those books were for the home front. When Max had come back from the war, he hadn't wanted to read about it. Dr. Rapaport probably wouldn't want to either.

She climbed the wide staircase to the wrought-iron balcony and made her way to the history section. There were books by Churchill and about Roosevelt. Those were safe bets too. Then she remembered a volume she'd given Max for his birthday when he was at Bellevue. *The Age of Jackson* by Arthur Schlesinger, Jr. "You know me like a book. I've been wanting to read this since it came out," he'd said, and put it on the night table on his side of the bed. Each night he'd gotten through three or four pages before, exhausted from the hospital, he'd fallen asleep with it on his chest. She could see him lying there, his hair mussed from the pillow, his reading glasses askew over his closed eyes, his face unguarded. The image made her reach out to steady herself against a wooden library ladder.

She retraced her steps to the ground floor. Piles of *Shake Well Before Using* by Bennett Cerf took up one table. That was it. Something light and entertaining after a day of seeing patients. He wouldn't fall asleep over that, and if he did, it wouldn't matter. She picked up a copy and started toward the register, then stopped. Perhaps it was too light and entertaining. Perhaps he'd think she was frivolous. She returned the book to the stack. Now she was angry at herself. What did she care what he thought of her? She was giving him a thank-you gift, not asking for his stamp of approval. She took a copy of *Behind the Curtain* by John Gunther from another table. Max had read one of Gunther's books on the ship coming home and been enthusiastic about it. And the reviews of this one had been good. Then, as a reward for her labors, she picked up a copy of Mary McCarthy's new collection of stories, *Cast a Cold Eye*. She needed something astringent to ward off the melancholy of her daughter's departure.

When she reached the register, she realized she didn't have the doctor's office address with her. That was all right. That was better. The office wasn't far from her apartment. She could leave it with his unfriendly nurse on her way to or from work tomorrow or the next day.

Another idea came to her on the walk home. The nurse had said he had office hours till seven on Wednesdays, then returned calls. Today was Wednesday. By the time she got uptown, it would be a little after seven. She could give him the book and thank him in person.

The waiting room was as empty as it had been the evening she'd taken Chloe for her appointment. Now that she knew him, she found the shabbiness even more forgivable, almost admirable. He was interested in practicing medicine, not impressing patients. He was like Max. While she was debating leaving the book on the table with a note, the door to his consulting room opened and he came out. When he saw her, he looked surprised.

"I thought I heard someone come in. Not Chloe's stomach again, I hope."

"She's fine. At least I assume she is. She left for camp yesterday. I just wanted to drop this off." She held out the gift-wrapped book. "To say thank you."

"That's kind of you," he said as he took the book from her. "There was really no need, but I'm grateful. Should I open it now?" he asked as he began tearing off the paper. "How did you know? I've been wanting to read this since it came out."

The words had an echo. "I hope you enjoy it."

"I'm sure I will," he said as the door to the street opened again and another patient came in. Only this girl couldn't be a patient. She looked to be in her early twenties, too old to be seen by a pediatrician, and she didn't have a child with her. Neither did she have the hesitant or worried air of a patient. Her glance around the room was proprietary. Something about it made Fanny think she was going to run one white-gloved finger over a surface to check for dust. Something about the firm set of her pretty mouth made Fanny think she'd find it. She wasn't dressed for a doctor's visit either. When she crossed the small room to where Fanny and the doctor were standing, the skirt of her dotted swiss dress was so voluminous that it swept over the furniture. If it was a copy of a Dior New Look—and it probably was because you didn't see too many girls on the Upper West Side in the real thing—it was a good copy. For all Fanny knew, Rose had made it. The girl looked as surprised to see Fanny as Dr. Rapaport had been.

"Am I early?" she asked the doctor. "You said you'd be finished by seven."

"Mrs. Fabricant is an old friend," the doctor said. "Or rather, she was married to an old friend from medical school."

The girl turned to Fanny. There was a moment of sizing up before she held out her hand. "I'm Joy Geller. Ezra's fiancée. I'm so glad to meet you." Fanny sensed another moment of being sized up. "You're a doctor's wife too? I guess I shouldn't say 'too.' We're not married yet."

"Mrs. Fabricant was just dropping this off." Dr. Rapaport held up the book.

"A thank-you for treating my daughter. Successfully."

The girl slipped her arm through the doctor's. "That's my Ezra."

Fanny smiled, told Joy Geller it had been nice meeting her, and started for the door.

"I hope I'll see you again," Joy called after her. "You and your husband both."

Fanny didn't turn back. Let the doctor explain, or not.

❧

She argued with herself all the way home. She hadn't done anything untoward. She'd given him a book in thanks. It was only good manners. There was absolutely no reason to be embarrassed.

Nonetheless, she must have needed absolution, or at least reassurance, because a few nights later, she brought up the incident with Rose. They were on the way to an air-conditioned movie theater to see *A Letter to Three Wives*.

"The girl, his fiancée, had on a dotted swiss copy of a New Look that was close to the real thing. You haven't by any chance run off any dotted swiss knockoffs lately?"

Fanny admitted it to herself if not to Rose. She was curious to know more about Dr. Rapaport's fiancée.

"Not lately or even before that," Rose said as they reached the ticket booth.

"Let me," Fanny said, and took out her wallet to pay for the tickets.

Rose let her. She knew what it felt like to be the poor relation, even if you were poor because you'd spent too many years supporting too many other family members.

"I didn't make the dress, but I'm glad you gave him the book," Rose said when they'd found two seats close to the screen. They were both myopic.

"It was the least I could do. He was awfully good with Chloe."

"That's not what I meant."

Fanny turned to her. "What did you mean?"

"It's nice to see you coming back to life," she whispered as the lights began to dim.

"I just wanted to say thank you," Fanny murmured.

"If that's your story, you stick to it," Rose whispered.

"Shush," a voice behind them said as the newsreel began.

❦

The next day Alice left town to work at her house on the eastern end of Long Island for a week, and Fanny arrived back from lunch to hear Charlie's voice coming through the open door to Alice's office. That didn't surprise her. He had a habit of occupying her office when she wasn't in town. Whether Alice didn't know or didn't mind was none of Fanny's business. The fact that he'd left the door open and that his voice carried indicated that his presence was no secret. What did surprise her was his conversation. Somehow, she'd never thought of Charlie Berlin as having a family. Then again, she hadn't expected Dr. Rapaport to have a fiancée. She wasn't sure why. There was nothing surprising about either fact.

"I don't know what you did to be cursed with a son like me either, Ma. You'll have to consult your conscience on that one."

He was silent while Fanny took off her gloves and put them and her handbag in her bottom desk drawer.

"I know I'm a smart aleck, but just cash the check, will you? I may be worthless, but it's not. Now would you put Dottie on?"

She took the cover off her typewriter, put it in another drawer, and sat behind her desk.

"Because she's my niece and I'd like to talk to her. That's why. To give her some of that bad advice you're always warning her against."

She took Alice's expense account from her inbox.

"That was a joke, Ma. Just put her on. Please."

This silence went on for a bit longer. Fanny's hands hovered over the keys, but she didn't begin typing.

"Reading books is not going to ruin her eyes, Ma. Marrying her off at eighteen to one of those guys you and Estelle keep setting her up with will ruin her life. Look what it did to Estelle."

She heard the squeak of Alice's chair and imagined him swiveling to look out the window at the view of the Chrysler Building.

"He may be a good provider, and boy do I love that term, but if he's such a prince among men, what's he doing taking a pop at his wife? And if you believe Estelle that it was only that once, I have a bridge to sell you. Now, will you please put Dottie on?"

This pause was shorter. His niece must have been hovering.

"Hi, sport, what'd you think of the books I sent?"

In the silence that followed, Fanny started typing. When she heard his voice again, she stopped.

"It's called an hourglass effect. And I'm not talking about your shape, which your mother and grandmother seem to think is your ticket to happiness. It's good, I'm happy to say, but nobody can go through life on that. I'm talking about the structure of the novel. When it begins, Dick Diver is strong and whole, and Nicole is a fragile flower, to say the least. By the end, Dick's a mess and Nicole is all set up."

He fell silent again, and she began typing. This time she didn't stop when she heard his voice, though now and then she caught the title of a book or the name of a character above the sound of the keys striking the roller. He must have sent his niece half of Scribner's.

She pulled a sheet of paper out of her typewriter and began to roll in another.

"Okay, I hear Grandma in the background yelling at you to get off," Charlie said finally. "But don't forget. We have a date. Saturday after next. I have two tickets to *South Pacific*. If Grandma or your mother tries to stop you from coming into town, tell them the tickets cost a bundle. That'll give them pause. In the meantime, take care of yourself, sweetheart." He pronounced the endearment without a whiff of irony.

"Didn't know I was a family man, did you?" he said when he came out of Alice's office and saw Fanny at her desk.

"What do you mean?"

"Don't pretend you weren't listening."

"I won't pretend I wasn't listening if you don't pretend you weren't playing to the crowd. For all I know there wasn't even anyone at the other end of that telephone line, and it was all a ruse to make you look like a devoted uncle and show off your literary expertise. And while we're on the subject. What is it with all those learned lectures on arcane subjects you're always delivering?"

He perched on the end of her desk. "The autodidact's revenge."

"Autodidact?"

"I didn't have your advantages. No fancy private school. Not even City College. I'm a proud graduate of the New York Public Library. Forty-Second Street campus. Want to come to my next reunion?"

"Thanks, but I think I'll pass," she said, though her tone was less cutting than usual. Charlie Berlin being embarrassed about his lack of credentials was even more surprising than his having a family. No, that wasn't entirely true. At the risk of sounding like her freshman psych course, anyone who was on stage that much had to be compensating for something.

Chapter Fifteen

THE TWO MEN DIDN'T LOOK ALIKE. ONE WAS DARK, THE other fair. The dark one must have been more than six feet; the fair one was not much taller than Fanny would be if she were standing rather than sitting behind her desk. The short one carried his belligerence before him as if he were leading with a pair of boxing gloves; the tall one gave off an aura of calm that was even more menacing. But despite the differences, she sensed a similarity between them, and it went deeper than the identical inexpensive blue suits and the gray fedoras they held beside their thighs. Both bore little resemblance to the writers, directors, and actors who frequented the office or even to the sponsors and ad men who occasionally descended on it. They were more conventional than those denizens of Madison Avenue. Alice had entered their names in the appointment book Fanny kept for her, but without any indication of who they were or why she was seeing them. The appointment was for nine thirty. They appeared in front of Fanny's desk at nine twenty-eight.

Fanny pushed the switch on the intercom and told Alice that Mr. Garrison and Mr. Hagerty were here, Alice said to show them in, Fanny led them to the door of Alice's office, stood aside for them to go in, and closed it after them. She sensed that the meeting would be quiet. No voices would be raised in artistic protest or commercial reprimand.

An hour later, Garrison and Hagerty came out of Alice's office, filed past Fanny's desk, and made their way toward the bank of elevators, still holding their gray fedoras against their thighs. A moment after that, Alice buzzed and told her to call Charlie Berlin and tell him to get over here as soon as possible. "And that means now," Alice added.

"Nice that you're so eager to see me," he said when Fanny relayed the message on the phone.

"Alice's impatience, not mine."

"You really know how to break a guy's heart."

He sauntered in fifteen minutes later. She had a feeling the saunter was a ruse. She'd called him at his apartment on Sixty-Eighth Street. At this time of day there would be traffic. He must have told the cabdriver to step on it.

"Did you have a siren on top of the taxi or run all the way?" she asked.

"You do know you're beginning to sound like me, don't you, sweetheart?" he said as he went to knock on Alice's door.

"You can't say you weren't warned," Fanny heard her say before she closed the door.

Charlie was closeted with Alice for almost as long as the two men had been. By the time he came out, the rumors had begun to fly. They were only rumors, though later in the day one of the actors saw Charlie going into a meeting on the eighteenth floor, and a few minutes after that Ava shared an elevator with two unsmiling men in shiny blue suits coming down from the same level. Later still, an executive showed up in Alice's office. Fanny never would have known about the visit or overheard the conversation if she hadn't been working late—

she had no one to rush home to these days—and gone to the ladies' room before she left. When she returned to her desk to get her hat, gloves, and handbag, she heard one of the voices she'd been trained to put through immediately coming out of Alice's office. The door was open a crack, an oversight that never would have occurred during working hours.

"I don't care if he's your best writer, Alice. He could be Shakespeare, Dickens, and Dostoevsky rolled into one. We're not in the business of nurturing good writers. We're in the business of business. And that business is selling time to advertisers."

"We ought to at least look into the charges before we do anything."

"It's not up to us to disprove allegations. That's his job. It's up to us to keep the sponsors and the agency happy."

"The Guild will protest," Alice said.

"You know my door is always open." There was a finality to the statement, then a moment's pause, long enough for someone to cross an office to the door.

Fanny grabbed her handbag and gloves and started down the hall to the bank of elevators, but the conversation followed her home. The first thing she did when she got there was call Rose.

"Alice tried to stand up for Charlie. When I got back to my desk, the network man was ranting—no, those men never rant—he was saying he didn't care how good a writer Charlie was, and it was up to Charlie to clear himself, not for them to fight the charges."

"I wouldn't count on Alice to save Charlie."

"She's crazy about him."

"She's more crazy about her little fiefdom of soaps. A few years ago she wrote a Jewish character into one of her programs.

I know because she was so proud she couldn't stop talking about her courage. I swear she was on the verge of telling me some of her best friends were Jews. The sponsor told her to take the character out. He might offend the antisemites. She took the character out."

"What about *The Goldbergs*?"

"What about them?"

"That's a soap full of Jewish characters."

"Exactly, a Jewish soap. For Jewish listeners. Antisemites don't tune in, so they can't be offended enough to stop buying the sponsor's products. Besides, the Goldbergs are having their own problems these days. Rumor has it that Philip Loeb, who plays Jake Goldberg, is about to be blacklisted. It won't be pretty. He's the sole support of a really troubled grown son."

"How do you know these things?"

"Old lefty friends—not that I have any other kind of friends, old or new—keep me informed. The point is Alice isn't going to risk her career to save Charlie's. He's the only one who can do that. And I wouldn't count on him any more than I would on her."

❦

"What are you going to do around here without me?" Charlie asked as he dropped a script on her desk a few days later.

"Aren't you being a little dire?"

"'Optimistic' is the word you're looking for. Now that I'm unemployed I'll have more time to spend at the track."

She swiveled her chair to face him. "Are you serious?"

"About spending more time at the track or being unemployed?"

"Charlie!"

"I am no longer writing scripts for these or any other soaps. I'm allowed to use the word now that I've been canned."

"What happened? You write the best scripts on all three of Alice's shows."

"Things are already looking up. Those are the first kind words you've ever spared me."

"The blacklist?" she asked in a whisper.

"Nice to know you're becoming informed. I ascribe that to your aunt."

"It is that, isn't it?"

"I don't think we should discuss this here, unless you want to begin spending your days at the track with me. Meet me for a drink after work, and all will be revealed."

She hesitated.

"Come on, Fanny. You don't have to rush home to your daughter. She's away at camp. And you know you're curious."

She still didn't answer.

"Just a drink, sweetheart. Surely you wouldn't deny a farewell drink to an unemployed man who's walking out of your life forever."

"Since you put it that way."

"Are you this gracious with everyone, or do I get special treatment?"

"You're sui generis." She asked where she should meet him.

"Smart girl, not wanting to be seen leaving the premises with me."

"It's not that," she said, though it was, but not for political reasons.

"Gino's. I assume you know where it is. Not so far from the

office to be inconvenient, but sufficiently distant to make it unlikely that we'll run into people from here."

❦

She came out of the glare of the July evening into the shadowy gloom of the bar and lounge of an Italian restaurant several blocks from the office. It took a moment for her eyes to adjust, then another for her to find him in the after-work gathering of people in search of drink or food, conviviality or solace, and air-conditioning. He was sitting at a corner table with a drink in front of him. She threaded her way through the tables. When she reached his, he made one of those half-hearted feints at standing. Her first thought was that it was more than she'd expected. Her second was that she didn't mind, or to put it another way, she was often of two minds about the gesture. She believed in manners when they put others at ease, but having men jump up, bumping tables and sloshing liquid over the tops of glasses, rarely put her at ease.

She sat across from him, took off her white cotton gloves, put them in her handbag, and put the handbag at her feet. The table was so small she had to shift her legs to keep their knees from touching. He asked what she wanted to drink, she said a gin and tonic, and he ordered one for her and another for himself.

"This place used to be a speakeasy," he said. "Bet you didn't know there were more than a hundred thousand in the city during Prohibition."

"I'll make a note of it."

"You wouldn't have been allowed in this one, though. Women weren't until after repeal."

"They still aren't."

"You're sitting here, aren't you?"

She pointed to a sign over the mirror behind the bar.

LADIES ARE NOT PERMITTED AT THE BAR UNLESS ACCOMPANIED BY GENTLEMEN

"That's one rule I don't understand."

He raised his eyebrows. "You don't?"

"Why would the management care who's drinking as long as they're paying customers?"

"The assumption, Fanny, is that any woman alone at a bar is a working girl."

"I'm a working girl."

"That's not the kind of work they have in mind. The sign is to discourage ladies of the night. Women of easy virtue. Prostitutes. Hookers."

"You're kidding."

"It's been known to happen."

"Well, it's not fair to the rest of us. What if a woman is dying for a drink and doesn't have a man around?"

"Anytime you're dying for a drink, sweetheart, just give me a call."

The waiter came with the drinks and a small bowl of peanuts, and after he retreated, Charlie raised his glass to her. "Here's to my new life of leisure."

She raised her own glass. "Are you going to tell me what happened?"

"First tell me what they're saying at the office."

"That the two men who came to see Alice were either from the FBI or detectives hired by the network, the sponsor, or the advertising agency."

"The stories aren't mutually exclusive. The two men used

to be with the FBI, but they decided there's more money, and fun, out on their own. They started a consulting firm for radio and television, advertising, that kind of thing. The Anti-Communist Enterprise. ACE for short. As in in-the-hole. They charge a fee, anywhere between fifty and fifteen thousand dollars, to investigate people in the business. I tried to find out how much they charged for me. I'd hate to think I was at the low end of the scale. I have my pride. But the word 'investigate' is a euphemism. Fishing for gossip and innuendo is more like it. Then they turn what they've dug up, or made up, over to the client, and the client acts accordingly, though sometimes it's a dicey business deciding which way to go. A bunch of rabid so-called patriots threatened to boycott General Foods unless they fired Jean Muir, who played Henry Aldrich's mother on the program. Then a group of liberals threatened to boycott if they did fire her."

"What did General Foods do?"

"Apparently the American Legion, Catholic Vets, and various like-minded groups eat more breakfast cereal than liberals. Muir went quietly, and the brouhaha died. My case will attract even less attention. Jean's an actress. Her face was on television and she got billing. I'm just an anonymous typewriter in Alice's stable."

"You had that play."

"Part of the problem. I'm finished, Fanny. As those two goons informed me, unless I clear myself, no one in the business will touch me with a ten-foot pole. I have to admit I had trouble keeping a straight face when they used the phrase. No cliché is too tired for those guardians of the public virtue."

"They said unless you clear yourself. What would you have to do?"

"Write a letter. They're all heart about that. It doesn't even have to be public in a magazine or newspaper. That shows how low I am on the entertainment totem pole. Bogey had to publish a piece in *Photoplay*. 'I'm No Communist.' Boy, was that a stomach-turner. All I'd have to do is send a private billet-doux to ACE, expressing profound regret for my past transgressions, saying I was duped, and promising to be a good red-baiting boy in the future. They'll pass the exculpation on to the sponsor, the advertising agency, the network, and anyone else who's interested."

"So you're not fired. All you have to do is write a letter denying the charges."

"You're not listening, Fanny. To call them charges is to praise with faint damnation. I belonged to a bookshop association in the Village that held literary and musical evenings. That was in my misspent youth before I discovered less lofty pastimes. I subscribed to the *New Republic*. I was once overheard by a friend, now a former friend, making a joke about the absurdity of separating the blood of Negroes and whites in blood banks. And don't forget that play you mentioned. Of course, I was in good company there. ACE also questioned the loyalty of Christopher Marlowe, whose plays were being staged by the WPA Theatre at the same time. They didn't seem to realize it was a little late to go after him. Fortunately for their purposes, I'm still around. They quoted chapter and verse from the play, including a line about the immaculate misconception. They claimed it undermined not only religion but female chastity. You know what the real crime was there? I thought the phrase was clever at the time. But as your aunt pointed out, I was a mere slip of a boy in those days."

"That's ridiculous."

"Unfortunately, the men from ACE don't share our sense of the absurd."

"Can't you say you outgrew the ideas?"

"Tell a lie? Fanny Fabricant, you shock me. Besides, there's another reason I can't write the letter."

"Which is?"

"To try to clear myself when I haven't done anything wrong is un-American." He grinned across the table at her. "Don't look so surprised, Fanny. I warned you about cynics becoming cynics because they believe too fervently."

She picked up her glass again to hide her embarrassment. When had Charlie Berlin become a moral arbiter?

Chapter Sixteen

Just as she'd still felt Max's presence on the premises after he'd shipped out, she couldn't get used to Chloe's absence from the apartment. Standing at the kitchen counter, she'd sense her daughter in the doorway and look up only to find uninhabited space. In the middle of the night, she'd be halfway down the hall to check on her before realizing Chloe was asleep in a camp cot a hundred miles away.

It wasn't all pain and longing. There were moments of disorienting freedom. She didn't have to rush home to make dinner. She didn't have to make dinner at all if she didn't feel like it. She could have a salad or some fruit or nothing if she wasn't hungry, though she felt guilty for enjoying the abandon. Sometimes on nights when she stretched out on the long window seat with a pillow propped against the northern wall so she could look up from her book by one of the Elizabeths—Janeway, Taylor, or Gaskell—to see the sun sliding toward New Jersey and color seeping into the sky, she found comfort, almost, in Rose's observation about the necessary breakup of the mother-child love affair.

"Now you have no excuse," Rose said. "Except fear."

They were sitting on a bench in the shade of a stand of trees a little distance from the model boat basin in Central Park. The heat had drawn half the population of the city out of their apartments on this Saturday afternoon. Families strolled, couples held sweaty hands, people wolfed down hot dogs slathered with mustard and sauerkraut and licked melting ice-cream cones. Small boys—they were all boys—and their fathers sailed miniature skiffs in the pond.

"No excuse for what?"

"Not trying your hand at one of Alice's scripts. You have plenty of time now that Chloe's away at camp. And you could certainly use the money."

"I'm sorry I'm such a freeloader."

"That's not what I meant, and you know it." She signaled to a man pushing an ice-cream cart around the plaza. "And if it'll make you feel any better, you can pay for the ice cream."

They sat working on their cones in silence for a while.

"I don't know anything about writing a radio script."

"You've been typing them for almost a year. You must pay some attention while you work. You majored in English lit in college. And I seem to remember a minor brouhaha the time your mother found one of your stories when she was cleaning out your drawers. I told her that was what she got for invasion of privacy." She shook her head. "If I had your gumption, Fanny, I'd still be doing piecework back on the Lower East Side." She held the cone out in front of her to let it drip on the ground rather than her skirt and leaned forward to lick the sides. "It's not just the money," she went on as she took the last bite of the cone, "though god knows it's nicer to have some than not. I'm an old union maid, as the song goes. I believe in the dignity of work well done, even if the work is knocking off expensive clothes for women whose husbands can't afford or won't let them buy the real thing, or writing silly scripts to keep other women company while they feed, clothe, and clean up after men and children." She wiped her mouth, took Fanny's napkin, crumpled it with hers, and tossed them into the wire trash basket a few feet away.

"Nice shot."

"Try it, Fanny. Just try it."

❦

Alice was putting scripts into her briefcase when Fanny appeared in the open door to her office. It was a Mark Cross case embossed with Alice's initials in discreet gold letters. She looked up.

"If it's anyone but Ned Griffin from the sponsor or someone from the eighteenth floor, I've left for the day."

"It's me. I."

"Pardon me?"

"Do you have a minute?"

Alice looked at her watch. "Exactly three. I have an appointment at the hairdresser."

Fanny stepped into the office, then stood there.

Alice went back to putting papers in the briefcase. "The three minutes are flying, Fanny."

"It's about the scripts."

Alice looked up from the case again. "You want to have a try at one."

"I wouldn't ask to get paid."

Alice laughed. "You wouldn't get paid, unless we used it, which is highly unlikely. Still, I was waiting for this. One of the things I liked about your predecessor was her total lack of ambition. If she hadn't gone off to get married, she wouldn't have left here until they carried her out feetfirst. As they'll carry me. But you're a different breed. I figured it was only a matter of time. Unless you, too, went off to get married. Okay, I'll look over the breakdowns tonight and find one for you to try your hand at." She snapped the clasp on the briefcase closed. "But a few words of warning. Don't try for witty. Wit is death to radio serials. No sexual innuendo. Though I have a feeling I don't have to worry about that with you. I'm not commenting on your personal life, only your discretion. And one more caveat. Your aunt recommended you on the basis of your education. Literary doesn't fly. Emotion flies. You have to grab listeners by their guts and hearts. You have to get them to love and hate these characters they spend time with every afternoon. You have to make them tune in tomorrow because they're worried sick about what's going to happen, not because they're analyzing character and plot. Hell, the last thing we want them to do is analyze anything. Including, or maybe especially, the promises of how this cake of soap or that face cream will change their lives."

Fanny said she'd keep it in mind.

Rose had said she must know how to write a script because she'd been typing them for almost a year. Rose had it wrong. A complete novice would think it was easy. She or he would look at Alice's breakdown, which was an outline of the scenes from the ongoing story that would be in that day's installment, and think all that had to be done was supply the dialogue. But a novice wouldn't realize how many ways that dialogue could go.

She thought of Charlie's line about writing a scene backward. Alice made it clear you had to get from point A to point B, but didn't say how you had to get there. Someone who hadn't been typing scripts for the better part of a year might not see all the possible paths. Fanny did. Or if not all, enough of them to give her pause. By ten o'clock her wastebasket was overflowing like a prop in a bad movie about a struggling writer. Only she wasn't a struggling writer who was going to find acclaim at the end of the film. She was a reasonably intelligent college graduate trying to grab listeners by the gut and the heart so they'd tune in tomorrow to find out if a girl from a small Midwestern farm could find happiness on the stage and still retain the good clean American values she'd been raised to revere. And that was only the main protagonist. There were eleven others in the installment Alice had given her.

At ten thirty, she gave up, rolled a piece of stationery into the typewriter, and began a letter to Chloe. For once she had news. Ava had progressed to handstands at rehearsals. *"She's promised to teach you those too when you get home. And we both want to know about the flora and fauna (that's flowers and animals) at Camp Winding Wood. Have you run into any silly men who need shaves and wear fur coats?"* Then she told her how much she loved and missed her and signed off.

❦

With the exception of Sunday brunch with Ava, who'd just broken up with her current boyfriend and turned up looking sensational in a yellow sundress and straw hat with a matching grosgrain ribbon she'd splurged on at Bergdorf's as balm, Fanny spent the weekend holed up in her apartment struggling with the script. By Sunday evening she was changing words, paragraphs, and entire scenes in the most recent version back to the way they'd been in earlier drafts. It was clearly time to give up. She typed a clean copy and told herself if nothing else she could tell Rose and Charlie that she'd given it a try. Not that she was in touch with Charlie these days, but she could justify herself to him in her mind.

Monday morning she arrived in the office before Alice, as she always did, slipped the script into Alice's inbox, and waited. Monday went by without a word. Of course it did, Fanny told herself. Alice wasn't going to drop everything to read a script written by her secretary. She didn't bring up Fanny's attempt on Tuesday. By the end of the day on Wednesday, she still hadn't mentioned it. Fanny couldn't decide whether Alice was a busy woman or a sadist.

"Sadist," her former roommate Susannah pronounced when they met for dinner that night. Her husband Jeffrey often stayed late at the law library, and since she'd thrown her typewriter at the magazine editor, she had too much time on her hands. She was trying to get pregnant, she confided, but how much time did that take? Fanny admired her nonchalance about the matter. She was sure in Susannah's place, she would be more impatient, even desperate, one of those girls who peer into baby carriages on the street and wonder aloud what's wrong with them. Susannah was cavalier. "If it happens, it happens. If it doesn't . . ." She shrugged. "Who knows. Maybe I'll go to law school."

"Are you serious?"

"Kind of. The way I figure it, living with Jeff has given me a running start. He's studying for the bar, and the law is all he can talk about. Last winter when he was laid low by the flu, I even went to classes to take notes for him."

"That must have been strange."

"It was interesting, in more ways than the law, though I liked that aspect of it."

"What do you mean?"

"The other students couldn't have been nicer. Some of them offered to let me copy their notes, in case mine weren't up to scratch. How could I have a legal mind if I had breasts, not to mention the other paraphernalia. And anything for good old Jeff, as long as he was out of commission and not competing with them for a job. But the strangest part of it was the one girl in the class."

"I'm assuming she had breasts and the other paraphernalia too."

"Actually, she was a knockout, but it didn't help. If anything, it probably made things harder for her. As helpful as the men were to me, that was how awful they were to her. They barely talked to her. They sure didn't offer to lend her their notes. And, of course, they didn't invite her to join any of their study groups. The professors were even worse. They either ignored her or fired questions at her, then made fun of her answers."

"And you're telling me you want to go to law school?"

"I figure I'd have Jeff behind me. And it would only be three years. Then, who knows, maybe I'd end up winning a case against one of them in court. But at the moment I'm more worried about your sadistic boss. If she doesn't say something by the end of the week, ask her."

Late the next afternoon she said something. Fanny was slipping the cover on her typewriter when Alice came out of her office and put the script on her desk. It was marked up, but not embarrassingly so.

"Some of the scenes are good," she said, and Fanny could

tell from her voice that a caveat was on the way. "But the woods are full of one-or-two-good-scene scriptwriters."

Fanny didn't know what to say to that.

"Are you serious about this or just marking time till some man comes along to sweep you off your feet?"

"I'm serious," Fanny said, though until that moment she hadn't been sure she was. Maybe it was Susannah's influence.

"In that case I'll give you a few more breakdowns to try your hand at. You won't be paid until we can use one. But I'm willing to edit them, which is worth its weight in gold, if you swear you'll try to learn from the edits, and I won't be wasting my time."

Alice was no sadist.

❧

When she opened the metal door in the line of mailboxes in the vestibule of the building that evening, she found, among the flyers and bills, one of the stamped, addressed postcards she'd put in Chloe's duffel.

Dear Mommy,

Tell Ava I taught cartwheels to all the girls in my bunk. I can't wait for handstands. There are no bears here, just silly men who need shaves and wear fur coats.

Love,

Chloe

Chapter Seventeen

She spotted him standing under the marquee of the building from half a block away, only she wasn't sure it was Charlie. Then it occurred to her that this was Charlie when he wasn't onstage. He was standing with his hands in the trouser pockets of a surprisingly somber dark blue suit, staring down Amsterdam Avenue at the oncoming traffic. At first she thought he was looking so morose because he was having trouble finding a cab in the drizzle, but two taxis went by without his trying to hail them. When he caught sight of her, his face rearranged itself into the familiar Charlie expression.

"I figured if I stood here long enough, someone would turn up with an umbrella."

"Seems like a pretty futile way to spend time."

"You forget how much of it I have on my hands these days."

"How are you?" she asked, though she didn't expect a straight answer.

"Not bad, in view of the day."

She closed her umbrella since they were standing under a marquee. "It's not raining that hard."

"I wasn't talking about the weather."

"Then what?"

"Look around you, Fanny."

She did. Her umbrella had been open so she hadn't noticed the words on the marquee, but now she saw them on the front of the building. Riverside Memorial Chapel. The odd thing was not that she hadn't noticed where she was, but that she was here at all. She usually went out of her way to avoid the place, but she'd stopped at the shoe repair shop to pick up the navy spectator pumps she'd had reheeled and taken the most direct route home because of the rain.

"You've been to a funeral?" She heard the faint incredulity in her voice. Somehow the idea of Charlie and funerals didn't go together.

He nodded.

"I'm sorry."

He didn't say anything to that. For once she didn't blame him. She knew there was no answer to those words.

"Someone close?"

"Not particularly."

She was surprised again. He didn't strike her as the kind of man who went out of his way to pay respects if he could help it.

"It was a matter of showing the flag," he went on. "The deceased was a writer. Not a particularly accomplished one, if you'll excuse me for speaking less than glowingly of the dead. Done in by good old ACE, Inc. I suppose there's a certain irony to that. You don't have to have a lot of talent, only a handful of beliefs they don't agree with for them to go after you."

"You think the blacklist had something to do with his death?"

"Do I think the blacklist had something to do with his death? The guy had been all over town, the West Coast, and points between, and couldn't sell a script if his life depended on it, which

apparently it did. His wife took the kids, cleaned out what was left of the bank account, and exited. So he went into the garage of the house in Westchester that was mortgaged to the hilt, closed the door, and turned on the engine. No, Fanny, I don't think the blacklist had something to do with it. I think the blacklist had everything to do with it. That's why I'm here. I wanted his wife and kids, who came back for the funeral, to know he still had some friends. God knows few enough of them showed up. Besides, I wouldn't give those bastards at ACE the satisfaction of not showing up. You can bet they had someone taking down the names of everyone who went in and out this afternoon. In fact, you're taking a chance now standing here talking to me."

"I'll risk it."

His eyebrows lifted. "What do you know? Maybe there's a streak of your aunt in you after all. Did she tell you we had dinner?"

"You and Rose had dinner?"

"Don't sound so surprised. We were both planning to eat that evening and decided it would be more pleasant to do it together."

She started to ask him how they'd even been in a position to arrange it, then changed her mind and said she had to be getting home, though if he'd seen Rose, he knew Chloe was still away at camp and she had nothing to get home to. That was assuming they'd discussed her. She started to turn away, then turned back.

"Are you okay? I mean really okay."

His grin grew wider, and now he was the familiar Charli "You're all heart to ask, sweetheart, but don't worry. I do have a car or a garage, and I've got a bundle riding on tom row's fifth at Belmont, so I certainly won't do anything r

before then. Though if the horse doesn't come in, who knows what'll happen after?"

❦

She called Rose as soon as she got home.

"You never told me you had dinner with Charlie Berlin."

"I didn't tell you I had dinner with my librarian buddy, the one who was fired for refusing to sign a loyalty oath, a few nights ago either. Oh, and did I mention I went to the movies last night with Faith Kaminsky, a friend from the old days? *My Foolish Heart*. I thought it would be good because it's based on a short story by J. D. Salinger. 'Uncle Wiggly in Connecticut.' Based on? Everything has been changed *except* the names. It's one of those Hollywood weepies where the heroine has sex out of wedlock once and spends the rest of her life paying for it."

"Very funny. I mean I didn't know you were in touch with him."

"He called and said he wanted to talk to me about something."

"Am I allowed to ask what or is it on a need-to-know basis?"

"Mainly old times, when he was the boy wonder of the Federal Theatre Project and I was a little shorter in the tooth and living in delicious sin with Hugo. Why are you so surprised?"

"Why am I so surprised? You run into a man in my office, a man you haven't seen in more than a decade, the two of you don't even recognize each other at first, and suddenly you're having dinner with him."

Rose laughed. "I swear, Fanny, if I weren't of such advanced years, I'd think you were jealous."

"It's just that I never thought you shared Alice's taste for troublesome men."

"Charlie Berlin isn't so troublesome."

"He could have fooled me."

"Apparently he has. I wouldn't say he's a sheep in wolf's clothing, but when it comes to dyed-in-the-wool louses, he isn't near qualifying. And trust me, I've known enough of them over the years to recognize the breed."

"I thought you were living in what you just called delicious sin with Hugo."

"That's how I met the louses. There's a certain breed of man, for all I know it's most of the sex, who believe if you're easy, to use their expression, for one man, you will be for all."

"That's a nuanced view of the world."

"Mine or the men's?"

"Both."

"Maybe, but mine is accurate. For a plain-looking girl, I attracted more than my share of men."

❧

She was surprised when Charlie turned up in the office a week or so later. He hadn't been there since the day he'd dropped his final script on her desk.

"I thought you'd been banned from the premises."

"Nice of you to notice my absence. But you know Alice can't resist my charms. Not to mention the fact that the Radio Writers' Guild is pretending to make some sort of sham protest about my getting sacked. I'm on my way upstairs now, but I knew you'd never forgive me if I didn't stop by to say hello."

He picked a script up off her desk.

She reached for it. "You don't have snooping privileges anymore."

He took a step back so the script was out of her reach and stood reading it.

"So you finally took my advice."

"It was Rose's suggestion."

"Great minds and all that." He went on reading. "First scene's not bad, though you could tighten the exchange at the end."

"Thanks for the editorial advice."

"What does Alice say?"

"That the woods are full of one-and-two-scene wonders."

"She's right." He dropped the script on her desk. "Good luck with it, sweetheart. I'll stop by on my way out to tell you how the meeting went, as if we didn't know now."

"Good luck to you," she said.

"Good luck? Against ACE, the sponsor, and the network? Surely you jest." He didn't do a buck-and-wing, but he did manage a jaunty step as he made his way down the hall.

She was surprised when he hadn't returned by five. Perhaps the outcome of the meeting wasn't a foregone conclusion after all. Perhaps the Guild really was defending him. Or perhaps he'd decided not to stop by on his way out. Even Charlie Berlin could feign insouciance for only so long.

She was considering the possibilities when the phone on her desk rang. Alice was gone, but the sponsor, the advertising agency, and the network bosses kept longer hours. It was as if they were afraid that the minute they left their offices their competitors and enemies would establish beachheads. She picked up the phone.

"Mrs. Fabricant?"

The voice was vaguely familiar but she couldn't place it.

"This is Mrs. Fabricant."

"It's Ezra Rapaport."

It took her a moment to recognize him. The first name threw her. She wondered why he was calling. It couldn't be bad news. He'd filled out the medical forms for Chloe to go to camp, but he wasn't affiliated with the camp.

"How's Chloe?" he asked.

"Fine, last I heard."

"Enjoying camp?"

"She's the junior diving champion."

"So I was right." She could hear the smile in his voice. "Camp was the best thing for her. How are you getting along without her?"

"Fine." She couldn't imagine where this phone call was going.

"I enjoyed the book."

"I'm glad."

There was a moment of silence. She racked her brain to fill it. The awkward evening in his office when she'd delivered the book still rankled. She decided to ask after his fiancéc. That would prove that she really had been dropping off a thank-you gift and hadn't had ulterior motives.

"She's not my fiancée."

"What? I'm sorry," she added quickly. "But I suppose it's better that it happened now. These things generally work out for the best."

"Dr. Pangloss, I presume," a voice behind her said.

She swiveled her chair around. Of course it was Charlie. She motioned for him to leave. He went on standing there.

"In fact, that's why I'm calling," the voice on the line went on. "I've been debating the ethics."

"The ethics?"

"Ethics?" Charlie repeated. "Did I hear the word 'ethics' spoken in the hallowed halls of soap land?"

"I couldn't ask you to dinner if you were my patient," the doctor went on, "but I think it's allowed if Chloe is my patient. I haven't consulted the AMA, but it sounds aboveboard to me."

"What?"

"I'm asking you out to dinner, Florence."

"Florence was for the medical records. My friends call me Fanny."

"Of whom she has many," Charlie said.

She motioned for him to go away again. He merely grinned.

"Would you like to have dinner, Fanny?"

The invitation threw her off balance. Or maybe it was Charlie. Of course she wanted to have dinner. Why else had she shown up at his office with a thank-you gift? But now that it was a possibility, she had second thoughts. Did she really want to venture into that dangerous no-man's-land where men and women met, mingled, and had their hearts broken or at least their feelings mauled in a hundred different ways? Wasn't she better off as she was?

"Are you still there, Fanny?"

"I'm still here, Doctor."

Charlie perched on the edge of her desk and folded his arms.

"The name is Ezra."

"I'm still here, Ezra."

"Ezra," Charlie repeated quietly. "Guy in the Bible who reintroduced the Torah to the Jews. I bet you didn't know that."

She put her hand over the mouthpiece. "Would you get out of here."

"What did you say?" the doctor asked.

She took her hand off the mouthpiece. "I'm sorry. Someone turned up at my desk."

"Look, I don't seem to be handling this very well. I'm a free man. Not engaged. Never was. If that's what's worrying you. I'll explain over dinner. Thursday? I'll pick you up at eight. Okay?"

"Fine."

"Thursday at eight," he said.

"Thursday at eight," she repeated.

"Thursday at eight," Charlie echoed as she hung up the phone. "Tune in tomorrow for the next episode of *The Romance of Fanny Fabricant*."

"Did it ever occur to you that a call might be personal?"

"On a company phone? I'm shocked. Of course it occurred to me. Why do you think I was eavesdropping?"

"You really are impossible."

"Some people say that's my charm."

She leaned back in her chair and looked up at him. "You really believe that, don't you?"

He shrugged. "Just waiting for a good woman to come along and save me. Want to apply for the job?"

She stood and began taking her gloves and handbag from the bottom desk drawer.

"You've been reading too many of your own scripts. Good women don't save wayward men. They just get dragged down by them."

❦

Ezra arrived promptly at eight. Somehow she'd known he would. They came out of her building into a soft summer evening. The air was warm, but the heat wave of the past few days had broken, and a mild breeze made the pleated skirt of her white linen dress flirt around her legs. He lifted an arm to hail a cab, then dropped it and turned to her. "Unless you'd rather walk. It's such a beautiful night. And the restaurant isn't far."

She said she'd rather walk.

"Do you like French food?" he asked as they started up West End Avenue.

"Does anyone not like French food?"

"You must move in rarified circles. Plenty of people don't like French food. Too rich. Too full of garlic. Too exotic."

"I like French food."

"Excellent, but don't expect anything fancy. This is just a neighborhood bistro. Though the food's pretty good. And it has one more thing to recommend it. A garden. Which would be perfect on a night like this. With any luck we can get a table outside."

It wasn't luck. The owner's wife, a stern-looking woman with gray hair pulled back in a severe French knot, broke into a broad smile when she saw him. As she was kissing him on both cheeks, the owner came out from behind the small zinc bar to shake his hand.

"This man saved my husband's life," the wife told Fanny as she showed them to a table in the garden.

"'With any luck we can get a table outside,'" Fanny repeated after the wife had seated them and gone back to her station inside. "I have a feeling I've been snookered. How did you save his life?"

The wife returned before he could answer. "The usual?" she asked him.

"What's the usual?" Fanny asked.

"Dry martini."

She hadn't had a martini since Max. Somehow it seemed too festive, or maybe only too strong for a single woman. She caught herself. When had she begun to think like Mimi? She said she'd have a dry martini as well.

"How did you save his life?" she asked again after the wife had retreated with their drink orders.

"One night I stopped for a drink on my way home from work. He was behind the bar, and I noticed when he put the glass down, the left side of his face suddenly drooped. It was very quick and pretty dramatic. He was having a stroke. I told her to call an ambulance and got him to the hospital."

The wife returned with the drinks in time to hear the last few words. "This man is a hero." She put the stemmed glasses, full to the brim, on the table without spilling a drop, leaned over, and planted another kiss on his cheek.

"Don't let it get around," he said when she was gone, "but it wasn't exactly a difficult diagnosis. And while we're on the subject, a confession. That's why I brought you here. I was trying to impress you."

It was the kind of ploy Max had been prone to. He'd say something self-aggrandizing or self-effacing, then own up to both the act and the motive. She lifted her glass to him. "You've succeeded."

The wife brought the menus, and while they studied them, another piece of etiquette advice came back to her. Going out to dinner with Ezra Rapaport—with any man, she supposed—was taking her back. The girl never gives her order directly to the waiter. She tells the man, and he relays it to the waiter. What she didn't understand, what she'd never thought of until this moment, was why she was capable of ordering for herself when she went out with Rose or Ava or Susannah—even Mimi had known how to tell the waiter what she wanted before she'd remarried—but wasn't permitted to when a man was at the table. Perhaps the idea was that the man knew best what was good for her, as he knew so many things. *Steak is a man's meal, dear. You'll be happier with the chicken.* She told the wife she'd have *ris de veau,* and as she did, she was back in the small apartment with Max recently returned from the war teaching her to roll her *R*s as he'd learned to do in Rouen. He made the name of the city sound like a growl. Clearly the evening was exerting a centrifugal force, spinning her out into too many memories.

"You've been admirably discreet," he said when the wife had retreated again.

"I have?"

"You haven't asked about the fiancée who never was. After that incident in my office, aren't you curious? Maybe even suspicious?"

"I'll settle for curious." It was true. Something about him encouraged trust. Perhaps it was his treatment of Chloe. Or maybe it had something to do with his connection to Max, at least in her mind.

"When I was overseas, Joy wrote to me just about every day. I was grateful. Not to mention lonely. She began to talk about marriage. I didn't think I should tell her in a letter that wasn't part of the plan."

"More honorable to do it face-to-face?"

"Exactly." He smiled. "Also, easier to procrastinate. I guess that's what I was still doing that night in my office."

"What finally gave you the courage, if you don't mind my asking?"

She watched him mulling the question. The garden, surrounded by brownstones, was darkening, and the only light came from the flickering candle in the hurricane glass on the table between them and the strings of colored lights looped through the trees overhead. The sounds of urban life came to her muted: a passing car, a horn, a woman's voice calling from above to someone in the street. The sensuous promise of a summer night in the city seemed to tremble in the air.

"That night in my office."

"You mean her announcing that she was your fiancée?"

"Her announcing that she was my fiancée to *you*."

Coming from some men, the words would have sounded like a line. To her surprise, she believed them.

The wife brought their dinner, and they were silent while she placed the plates and poured the wine. After she retreated, they moved on from his broken engagement to the stories of their lives, replete with what each hoped were amusing anecdotes. She told him about her past before Max, about not being cut out for the beauty business, and about her job now. They discussed Chloe. She didn't say anything about Max, and he didn't ask. She was glad. She liked catching the occasional glimpse of Max in him, but didn't want him leaving his fingerprints on Max.

Then it was his turn. He'd grown up in Brooklyn, the youngest of three boys. Fortunately, they'd all managed to come home from the war. One brother had been in the ETO, the other stateside, and he'd ended up in the South Pacific.

"Did you always want to be a doctor?"

He smiled at her and took a sip of his wine. "You're probably not going to believe this. With good reason. It sounds apocryphal to me. My father owns a store. What they call an army-navy store, or a close relative of it. Men's work clothes. Women's underwear, and I mean underwear, not lingerie. My mother went to work there as soon as my brothers and I were in school. When my brothers graduated from high school, there was no discussion of what they were going to do. There had never been any question. My father had made it clear from the beginning that they'd go into the store with him, and they did. Finally, my mother could stay home, and he could stop being ashamed."

"Ashamed?"

"If a man's business is doing well enough that he can take in his sons, it's a source of pride. If things are so tenuous that he needs his wife to work with him rather than stay home and take care of the household, it's a reason for shame."

"How did you manage to escape?"

"That's the part that sounds so perfect it has to be apocryphal. My father may be dictatorial, but my mother is no shrinking violet. As the story goes, when my father came to the hospital after I was born, my mother greeted him with an announcement. 'This one is mine,' she told him. 'This one is the doctor.'"

She laughed. "It's a wonderful story, even if it is apocryphal."

The ease continued through dinner and on the walk home. He took her arm when they crossed streets, but didn't try to hold her hand or put his arm around her. When they reached her building, he followed her into the vestibule. She turned and held out her hand.

"Thank you. I had a good time. Really."

"You didn't need the 'really.' I believed you." He leaned over, kissed her on the mouth, but lightly, said good night, and made his way out into the clement summer night.

She went on standing in the vestibule, feeling strangely

girlish. The evening had taken her back. Again she remembered the do's and don'ts in the book her mother had given her years ago. Never let a boy kiss you on the first date. He'll think you're easy—the word Rose had used recently. Funny how you could get past those silly strictures but not forget them.

She climbed the stairs to the apartment. The evening had been pleasant. Being with a strange man, a man who wasn't Max, hadn't been as awkward as she'd feared. So why did she feel an amorphous sadness welling up? It came to her as she was brushing her teeth. That often happened. Something about confronting herself in the mirror, face scrubbed, hair clipped back, clarified matters. She'd kept catching glimpses of Max in Ezra. But he wasn't Max, and looking for traces of Max was only a greater disloyalty to Max. If she was going to take up with another man, she ought to find someone as dissimilar to Max as possible. But Max had been so right for her. Why would she want his opposite? No matter which path she chose, it was still betrayal.

They had dinner again the following week. This time when he came to pick her up, she asked if he'd like a drink. He said he would. She went into the kitchen to fill the ice bucket. When she returned, he was standing with his back to the room, looking at the framed photograph of Max on the mantel above the fireplace. At first, she'd kept the picture of him in his uniform there, but after a while she and Chloe had decided they preferred the more informal photograph of him taken before he went into the service. In the military picture, the brim of his hat shadowed his eyes so you couldn't really see them, and as a newly minted officer he was trying too hard to look serious. He ended up looking unhappy. In the civilian shot, his wide mouth hovered on the cusp of a smile that made you want to know what he found so amusing. She stood holding the ice bucket, watching Ezra take in the picture. Then he must have sensed her behind him, because he turned. So far none of this was odd. What she did find peculiar was that he didn't say anything about the photograph or Max. Then it came to her. She'd been a widow—she still hated the word—long enough to understand his reaction, or lack of it. Death embarrassed people. They didn't want to talk about it. They didn't want even to think about it. Doctors were no exception, despite their intimate, if secondhand, knowledge of the experience. Max used to joke that they became doctors to keep their own illness and death at arm's length. The ploy obviously didn't work. The picture of Max must have reminded Ezra of the fact.

They graduated from one dinner a week to two. Facing off in front of the bathroom mirror after the most recent evening out, she realized another subject made him uncomfortable, though this one wasn't a matter of life and death. She'd mentioned over dinner that she was trying her hand at scripts.

"Alice—the head writer I work for—said she's willing to edit them if I'm serious about scriptwriting, but if I'm not, she doesn't want to waste her time."

"Sounds pretty high-handed to me."

"She's a busy woman."

"You're a busy mother," he added, and changed the subject.

Thinking about it now, standing in front of the unforgiving mirror with a mouth full of toothpaste again, she realized why he'd changed the subject. She couldn't imagine how she hadn't seen it before. The fact that she worked troubled him. He never said "poor Fanny" as her family did, but she had a feeling he thought it. And, she realized as she went on brushing, the pity he felt put pressure on him. You didn't get mixed up with a girl like that unless you were prepared to save her.

Chapter Eighteen

THE BUS CAME TO A STOP, THE COUNSELOR GAVE THE word, and the girls jumped up and began pushing into the aisle.

"In order, Winding Wood campers, in order," the counselor shouted. "Front seats first, then row by row to the back of the bus."

Chloe didn't push into the aisle, but she couldn't help stamping her sneakers in impatience. Next to her, Karen's feet kept a similar beat. Through the windows on the other side of the bus, she could see groups of mothers milling around, but she couldn't find her mother among them. The idea came to her out of nowhere. What if her mother wasn't there? What if she'd forgotten when Chloe was coming home? No, that couldn't be. Her last few letters had listed the days till her return. Six days and counting, her mother had written. Four days and counting. Two days, fifteen hours, and forty minutes—assuming the bus is on time. But what if something else had happened to her? That night her father had carried her from the car into the house—she didn't remember, but her mother had told her—and when she got up in the morning, he was gone. What if her mother had had an accident on the way to the bus? A taxi could run her over. Anything could happen. Then Chloe would be a whole orphan instead of a half. Where would she go? Who would she live with? She never should have left her mother.

The line had stopped. She pushed forward to get it moving. Linda told her to stop shoving. She bent to look out the windows again. There she was. Chloe waved through the window, but her mother didn't see her. She was too busy watching the door of the bus.

The line started moving again. Chloe reached the door and jumped from the top step to the sidewalk. The counselor yelled at her to be careful, but she was too late and anyway, the counselor no longer had any power over her. She was running toward her mother, and her mother was running toward her. She felt the familiar hair against her cheek, and something else. She'd always known about Daddy's smell. That was why she'd taken the wooden bowl of shaving soap. But she hadn't realized until she went away and came home again that her mother had an aroma too. It wasn't perfume. It wasn't even soap or shampoo, though they were part of it. It was Mommy.

The three of them were walking up West End Avenue. When they'd set out, Chloe had been in the middle between her mother and the doctor, but when they crossed the street, she managed to switch places so she was walking on the inside of the sidewalk with her mother between her and the doctor. It wasn't that she didn't like him. He was going out of his way to be especially nice to her. That was the problem. She didn't want all that attention.

She remembered a night right after her father died. She was lying in bed, almost asleep, when she heard a man's voice in the hall outside her room. It could have been Grandpa or Pop Pop—her grandfathers had different names to tell them apart—or someone else. Uncles and aunts, cousins and people she'd never heard of kept coming and going in the house. It wasn't a party. Nobody laughed or even smiled, and they all talked really quietly. Sometimes, when she was outside, because Aunt Rose and Aunt Mimi kept sending her out to play, she watched the people come out of the house and walk to their cars. By the time they got there, they still looked sad, but they were talking in normal voices. But what she really remembered from that time, besides the slap, was the man's voice outside her room. It wasn't a dream. It was real. It was Daddy. She was sure of it. She kicked off the covers and sat up. The voice was still going on, but it wasn't Daddy. Now that she was really awake she knew that. It couldn't be. Daddy had died. He'd never be back. The doctor was nice, but he'd never be her daddy. No one would ever again.

❦

The following Sunday, the three of them went to the zoo. The week after that, the doctor took her to a baseball game. Just the two of them. At first she didn't want to go without her mother, but she hated to be a baby and she'd never been to a baseball game. She liked it, and she liked the way the doctor explained everything. He bought her a hat too, with "*Dodgers*" written on it. She was going to wear it to school on Monday.

❦

She and her mother and the doctor were coming out of the park, and Aunt Mimi, Uncle Howard, and Belle were going in. Everyone was in the park that day because the leaves were beginning to turn. As the grown-ups stood talking, Chloe maneuvered her way around her mother until she was next to the doctor and took his hand.

❦

Fanny noticed her daughter take Ezra's hand. She knew the gesture had to do with Belle's presence, but she was happy that Chloe was warming to Ezra. It wasn't only that she was warming to him too. It was that she would have hated her daughter to become a one-man woman at the age of eight. Still, it hurt.

❦

The slip of the tongue was perfectly normal. The only surprise was that she hadn't made it before. She was standing at the kitchen counter dicing mushrooms. Ezra and Chloe were sitting side by side on the living room sofa, leaning over the coffee table where they were putting together a jigsaw puzzle of American presidents that he'd brought her. Fanny was about to call into the living room to ask if he wanted a drink. She opened her mouth. The name Max came out. She tried to swallow the sound, but it was too late. The syllable flitted around the apartment like a bird suddenly free of its cage. She stood waiting. The only sound was the murmur of Chloe looking for Abraham Lincoln's stovepipe hat. She dried her hands, went into the living room, and asked Ezra if he wanted a drink. He looked up from the puzzle and said thanks, he did. She'd never know whether her voice hadn't carried or he was being tactful.

❦

They were having lunch in Schrafft's again when Mimi broke the news.

"Have you told Belle?"

"It's too soon. I'm going to wait till I show."

"How's Howard taking it?"

"He's in seventh heaven. He said he never knew whether it was his fault or his late wife's that they didn't have children."

Fanny thought of Susannah. "I wouldn't say 'fault.'"

"That's what he calls it. But now he knows. And he's thrilled."

Fanny sat studying her across the table. "You know something? Your dimples are back. They've been back for some time, but now they're back in spades."

Mimi put down her menu. "That's because I lied to you. Last spring. That day in the park when I told you I was going to marry Howard. Only I didn't know it was a lie then. Or rather it wasn't a lie then, but it is now. What our mothers and all that generation said is true. You can learn to love someone."

"I'm happy for you, Mimi. You deserve it."

"We all deserve it. But I'm lucky enough to have found it. And if you're smart, you can be lucky too. You're a fool if you let Ezra get away."

"As soon as we finish lunch, I'm going to the nearest hardware store to buy leg irons."

"You're such a smart aleck, but you know what I mean. He's a catch. Grab him before someone else does."

A catch. The expression took her back. There had been a tea for the wives and fiancées of the graduating doctors. A woman who was married to one of the deans had hushed the group of fifteen or twenty girls and delivered an informal talk. Informal, but not unprepared. She said she gave it every year to the wives and fiancées, and she wasn't going to stop because of the war. Peace would break out someday, soon they all hoped, and when the men came home, the advice would be as relevant as ever.

"Your husbands will be establishing practices," she told them. "When you see them off to their offices and hospitals each morning, make sure you're nicely dressed and fully made up. No flannel bathrobes and naked faces. And absolutely no curlers. Do you know why?"

"To keep up their morale?" one of the braver wives ventured.

"To save your marriages," the woman corrected her. "They'll be spending their days in contact with other women. Nurses, patients, secretaries, even salesgirls when they go into shops to buy you birthday and anniversary presents. Many of those women are going to be looking for husbands. Your men are catches, girls. Remember that when you send them off in the morning and when you welcome them home at night. Don't risk losing the catch you've reeled in."

"Why are we never the catches?" Fanny asked Mimi now.

"Because girls aren't. That's the way the world works. And it's even more so for you and me. Widows with children. Most men aren't eager to take on someone else's child."

"Ezra loves kids. They're his specialty."

"Then he's even more of a catch than I thought. And I hate to say it, Fanny, but you and I have one more strike against us. We're damaged goods."

"You make us sound like something at a clearance sale."

"You may not like it, but it's true. Men prefer virgins."

"I thought it was blondes."

"I'm serious. They may fool around with girls who are easy, but when it comes to marriage, they want virgins."

"Even if they've spent the war hopping in and out of beds?"

She'd never asked Max. She'd been more worried about his survival than his sexual fidelity. But Ezra had been single. He could have cut a swath through the hospital nurses and local girls, both professional and amateur, with a clear conscience.

"That's different. They're men. They can do anything they want. But girls are supposed to be virgins."

"If the issue ever came up, I'd say I did a lot of horseback riding in my youth, but Chloe's the giveaway."

"It's not a joke," Mimi insisted. "Some men can forgive you for having been married. Howard did. Of course, he was a widower. But Ezra has never been married. He could have any virgin he wanted."

"Surely not any."

"What I'm trying to say, Fanny, is maybe he can forgive you a husband, but not fooling around with anyone else. And that includes him. He won't buy the cow if he gets the milk for free."

"One of the more egregiously offensive warnings of our misguided youth."

"Our youth wasn't misguided, and our mothers were right." She was silent for a moment, then went on. "But I have a feeling it isn't a problem with Ezra. I have a feeling he's not pressuring you."

Fanny was surprised. Mimi wasn't usually so perceptive. "What makes you say that?"

"It's obvious. He respects you."

Fanny would have thought Rose and Mimi were in cahoots, if they hadn't been in complete disagreement on the subject.

A few days after that lunch at Schrafft's, Rose brought up the matter in a fitting room at Jay Thorpe.

Rose made most of her own clothes and many of Fanny's and Chloe's, but occasionally, for birthdays and other gift occasions, she liked to buy them something. Her motive was moral as well as generous. She had no compunctions about knocking off a Balmain or Balenciaga, but she refused to steal from less pricey designers, half of whom, she insisted, were perpetually on the verge of bankruptcy. She also accompanied Fanny on shopping trips because though she trusted her niece's sense of style and what suited her, she had less faith in her knowledge of seams, buttonholes, and other details that signified a garment was well made and worth the price rather than designed to catch the eye and last for only a season.

Fanny was facing the three-way mirror in a gray wool suit, with Rose standing behind her pinching the seams of the long narrow skirt where she said it needed taking in, when she spoke.

"Incidentally, or not so incidentally, anytime you want me to take Chloe for a sleepover rather than just dinner so Ezra can spend the night, let me know."

"Thank you."

Rose raised her eyes to meet Fanny's in the mirror. "You don't seem particularly enthusiastic about the prospect."

Fanny dropped her gaze. "Let's just say I'm of two minds."

"You mean Max steps into the picture at inconvenient moments?"

"I guess I'm just not ready. And please don't tell me three years is a long time."

"I wasn't going to. People mend at different rates in different ways. I had a friend who was devastated after her husband died. He was killed in the same battle as Hugo. She swore the only thing that got her through the first few months was an affair with his brother."

"What about you?"

"I went back to being the spinster you see before you. But I was older than you are now. And it's not a condition I recommend."

"There's also Chloe."

"That's why I'm offering to take her for the night."

Fanny stepped away and sat in one of the spindly velvet-upholstered chairs indigenous to fitting rooms in better stores. "I'm still her mother. Even if she's not under the same roof. I have to protect her."

"From what, a mother who's human?"

"You don't understand."

Rose took the chair facing her. "Because I don't have children?"

"I'm sorry, but yes."

"Don't be sorry. It's true. I come at this from a different angle. But if I were a mother, I'd hope I wouldn't stop being a woman."

"I haven't stopped being a woman."

Rose's eyebrows went up a fraction of an inch. "Look, it's okay if you're not ready. As I said, people mend at different rates in different ways. But don't use Chloe as an excuse." She stood. "Okay, I'll mind my own business."

"It isn't as if there's no physical affection," Fanny said. "That touch your skin was lonely for."

"If there weren't, I'd be really worried." She started to take another suit off the hanger, then changed her mind and turned back to Fanny. "Okay, so I can't mind my own business. The physical affection raises one more question. What about the other character in this drama? Isn't he getting a bit, shall we say, impatient?"

"He respects me."

"I can always tell when you've been talking to Mimi. Either that or regressing to your childhood."

"I think in this case she may have a point. In his mind I'm a *nice* girl, as the expression goes."

"You are a nice girl. That didn't stop Max. I was a nice girl once. That didn't stop Hugo."

"Let's just say Ezra is old-fashioned."

"That's what worries me."

"He's a decent man, Rose. Would you prefer I take up with a skirt chaser like Charlie Berlin?"

"There's a wide spectrum of men between skirt chasers and the saving-it-for-marriage types. Besides, what makes you think Charlie's a skirt chaser?"

"Alice."

"Alice has a rich fantasy life."

"She knows him better than you do."

"Possibly, but as I said, she has a rich fantasy life. I have a gimlet eye."

Chapter Nineteen

Fanny was surprised when she picked up the phone that afternoon and heard Charlie Berlin's voice. In the three months since he'd been fired, the two since she'd run into him on that drizzly afternoon in front of the memorial chapel, she hadn't heard from him or even about him.

"Alice isn't back from lunch yet," she told him.

"And what if I'm calling you rather than Alice?"

"I can't imagine about what."

"Have a drink with me tonight, and I'll explain. And don't tell me you have to rush home to your daughter. I happen to know she's having dinner at Rose's."

"How do you know that?" she asked before she realized there was only one way he could know.

"Your aunt and I have no secrets from each other. Come on, Fanny, a drink won't kill you. And I have a proposition."

"I bet you do."

There was a moment's silence. "This is going to come as a shock to you, sweetheart. You're a good-looking girl. In the gams department, you could give Grable a run for her money. And for all I know you've got that Ezra guy tied up in knots."

"How do you know about Ezra?"

"The Joe who reintroduced the Torah to the Jews? Don't you remember? I was there when it all started. But as Fats Waller puts it, 'You're not the only oyster in the stew,'" he sang, in imitation of Fats. "This proposition is strictly business."

"Such as?"

"Have you ever heard of switchboards and the operators who listen in on them? Have a drink, Fanny, and I'll tell you about it."

The picture of him standing in the rain in front of the memorial chapel flashed through her mind.

"Where?"

"Our place."

"I didn't know we had a place."

"That's the way I think of Gino's."

He was sitting at the same table in the corner when she arrived.

"I was going to wait at the bar," he said as she took the chair across from him, "but it didn't seem fair. If you're not allowed to drink there alone, why should I be?"

The waiter came and took their order.

"I bet you campaigned for us to get the vote too."

"That was a little before my time, but I've done my part. When I was in the service writing those films, I helped a woman named Margaret Sanger in her campaign to persuade the army to distribute contraceptives to WACs. Like the business of who can sit at the bar, it seemed only fair, since they were spending millions passing them out to GIs."

"I bet you were going to hand them out yourself."

"Only to certain WACs under certain conditions. But I did write a nifty little script for a film to further the cause. Not a word about women and sex. I knew how the brass would feel about that. If the gals weren't afraid of getting pregnant, they'd behave as badly as we do. And those men had wives and daughters as well as girls on the side. The message of the movie was that if they wanted to beat Hitler and Hirohito, they couldn't afford to have half the WACs in uniform mustering out to be mothers."

"Did the film persuade them?"

"It never got made. But I have the screenplay somewhere if you're interested."

He asked how Alice was.

"You haven't spoken to her?"

"Alice may have a soft spot for troublesome men—"

"You know about that?"

"She mentioned it once or twice over drinks."

She wondered just how close he and Alice had been.

"But," he went on, "her instinct for self-preservation is stronger. Remember the ten-foot pole with which no one in the business will touch me. Being the woman she is, Alice can't afford to know me. And believe it or not, troublesome as I am, I like her enough not to want to embarrass her."

He asked her how her script attempts were coming along.

"Alice says I'm getting close."

"That's good news."

"The only problem is now that Chloe's home and I still have to spend the hours from nine to five supporting us, I don't have much time for extracurricular script writing."

"What I have in mind won't take much time. Have you ever heard the term 'front'?"

"As in communist-front organization?"

"What I have in mind is a variation on the theme. Think

of it as a writer front. Someone who passes off another writer's work as his own. Or in this case, her own."

"I believe that's known as plagiarism."

"Oh, Fanny, I love it when you get on your moral high horse. But you're not far off. This is like plagiarism in that the real writer doesn't get credit. The front gets that. But the writer gets paid. Minus the split with the front. Which is only fair. The front is the one taking chances. The writer hiding behind him has nothing left to lose." He stopped, as if he'd suddenly heard his own words. "Not that there's much risk involved. Even if the people who are buying the scripts twig to who's really writing them, they tend to look the other way. They're too desperate for good material. And some of them know they've behaved like bastards in the first place."

He sat waiting for her to say something.

"Do I have to spell it out for you, Fanny? I write the script. You submit it to Alice as your own. We split the money. I don't know what Alice is paying you, but I'm willing to bet this arrangement will boost you into another tax bracket."

She stared at him. "Isn't what you're suggesting illegal?"

"Misleading, perhaps. Maybe even dishonest. But do you know a law against it?"

"There must be."

"There isn't, though I'm sure ACE is trying to figure out how to pass one."

"All right, it's not illegal, but it's unethical."

"There's that moral high horse you're determined to climb on again. What's unethical about it?"

"I'd be passing off your work as mine."

"Exactly. It can't be unethical if I'm asking you to do it."

"It's unethical to Alice and the sponsor and the network."

"Alice maybe, but you're using the word 'ethics' in the same sentence with 'sponsor' and 'network'? Who do you think makes the blacklist possible?"

"All right, forget them. I'd be lying to Alice."

"If I remember correctly, you sat right here a few months ago and urged me to lie to clear myself."

"That was different. You were trying to save yourself."

"Now I'm asking you to help save me. And don't give me that line about good women not saving wayward men, just being pulled down by them. It was a quick comeback, I'll give you that, but in this case it doesn't apply."

She thought about that. "Only it does in one way."

"How?"

"Chloe. I can't afford to be pulled down, or more to the point, hauled up before some committee. It's not only that I'd lose my job and wouldn't be able to get another. It's one thing for you or me to be labeled red or commie or bolshie. It's something else for a child. She has a hard enough time being the only one in her class who doesn't have a father and whose mother works. I can't have her being taunted on the playground for having a pinko mother."

He had no argument for that.

❦

Fanny was on her way to the kitchen with the dinner dishes when the phone rang. She put them down on the counter and made a dash for it.

"Guess what," Susannah said.

Fanny carried the phone to the window seat, which was as far as the cord would reach, kicked off her shoes, and sat.

"When's the momentous date?"

"I start next week."

Fanny began to say that she'd meant when was the baby due, then caught herself. "Start what?"

"I have a job. Now that Jeffrey passed the bar and can practice, I talked the civil rights lawyer he was doing research for into letting me step into his shoes. It wasn't easy. The lawyer insisted on Jeffrey's permission."

"I assume he gave it."

"He didn't have much choice. It was either a working wife or a divorce."

"Don't you need grounds for the second? Jeffrey never struck me as the philandering type."

"I'd hire a divorce Jezebel."

"A what?"

"Girls you hire to be caught in compromising positions with the husbands in trumped-up divorce cases. You can get one for eight or ten dollars."

"How do you know something like that?"

"I'm becoming well versed in the niceties of the law."

"Apparently. What kind of research?"

"Do you know what a Mississippi appendectomy is?"

"An appendectomy performed in Mississippi? Unless it's another legal nicety like a divorce Jezebel."

"It's a lot worse than that. A Mississippi appendectomy is a slang term for forced sterilization. That's how common they are in the South. Mostly of Negro women there, though in other parts of the country like California and the Southwest the victims are usually Mexican. The lawyer I'm going to work for is part of a group who are bringing a suit on behalf of women who were sterilized against their will. More than against their will. Without their knowledge half the time. Can you imagine? I've read some of the interviews. Middle-aged women still trying to conceive, who think there's something wrong with them because they can't, and don't know they lost any chance at fourteen or fifteen or younger when some county hospital or social service do-gooder decided to play god and determine who could bring children into the world and who couldn't. I joke that I'm missing the maternal gene, but even I can understand how that must feel. So I'm going to help sue the hypocritical bastards who did it, or at least the organizations behind them. Forget divine retribution. Give me human every time."

"I know you sat in on those classes to take notes for Jeffrey when he was sick, but do you know enough law?"

"The lawyers do the law. I'll be collating the interviews, whipping the data into shape, finding the best cases. Though there's nothing to stop me from picking up a little law along the way."

"I'm in awe. I never knew I was rooming with Portia. Shakespeare's character, not the soap opera version."

"To tell you the truth, I never knew it either."

"When did you find out?"

"When I started listening to your boss's programs."

"*Portia Faces Life* isn't one of hers."

"I didn't mean listening to a soap about a lawyer, I meant listening to her soaps."

"You never told me that."

"It's not the kind of thing you want even your dearest friends to know. I pretended I was doing it out of loyalty to you, keeping up with Fanny's life and all that, but when I found myself looking forward to tuning in tomorrow, I knew it was time to take action. And you know something else?"

"I suddenly feel there's a lot I don't know."

"I'm going to open my own checking account."

"Why? You always said Jeffrey never stopped you from buying anything you wanted, providing you didn't have to go into hock for it. And you were never one to splurge on yourself."

"I just like the idea of it. A kind of declaration of independence. 'In the course of human events' and all that. Now when I buy a birthday present or something for him, he won't be the one paying for it. It came to me on his last birthday. He was dying for the binoculars I bought him, then he felt guilty that I'd spent so much on them. If I had my own account, he never would have known."

Fanny congratulated her and told her again that she was in awe.

"You had something to do with it."

"Me?"

"I envied your having someplace you had to go every morning. Like when we were at school. We'd complain about dragging ourselves out of bed for class, but we had a purpose. I know it wasn't easy with Chloe and all. And I knew you weren't exactly saving the world in that job. But I was still a little jealous. And lest I sound too high-minded, I also kept thinking of your getting dressed every morning, looking spiffy in your working-girl suit and heels and sometimes even a hat—I was green with envy of that gray cloche your aunt gave you last spring—while I was lounging around the apartment in a ratty bathrobe."

"Now I'm the one who's going to be envious. You really will be saving the world."

"Let's just say making a minuscule contribution, but thank you."

After Fanny hung up the phone, she sat thinking about the call. Something nagged at her, and it had to do not with Susannah or that army of unfortunate women, but with Chloe and her, with the least important part of Susannah's announcement. She was going to open a checking account. Fanny had a checking account, but there was never much in it. Charlie had said his scheme would put her in a different tax bracket. She thought of all the small luxuries she'd be able to afford. Piano lessons for Chloe. Rose had offered to pay for them, but they already took too much from her. Besides, they'd need a piano for that. Okay, forget piano. Violin lessons. Theater tickets. Weekend jaunts to Philadelphia to see the Liberty Bell and Independence Hall, Boston to walk the Freedom Trail, Washington to see the monuments, so Chloe would have something to talk about when her class did show-and-tell. And it wasn't only the small indulgences. It was the peace of mind. She was so tired of worrying about money. But she couldn't do it. What good would a star turn on the show-and-tell circuit do Chloe if she was walking around the playground with her mother's scarlet *C* on her chest?

❦

"So you turned Charlie Berlin down," Rose said.

They were in the living room of Mimi's apartment. She had refused their offer of help and gone off to the kitchen to check on the pot roast. Chloe and Belle were in Belle's room playing with the fully equipped toy kitchen Howard had brought home from FAO Schwarz. The gift was supposed to prepare the ground for the news that Belle had a half sibling on the way. To paraphrase Charlie Berlin singing Fats Waller, she would no longer be the only oyster in the stew. Howard and Ezra, whom Mimi had invited to the family dinner in an effort to move things along, were in the study watching the Gillette Friday Night Fights. Every now and then Howard's voice, shouting tactical advice to one of the fighters, filtered down the hall. Ezra was more restrained.

"I couldn't take the chance. It's one thing if I'm disgraced, but something else if Chloe is."

Rose's eyebrows shot up. "Disgraced?"

"A pinko mother."

"Or perhaps a mother who's fighting injustice."

Fanny leaned forward to center her drink on the crewel coaster on the coffee table. "Oh, please, Rose, fighting injustice? By signing my name to soap opera scripts I didn't write to make more money."

"And helping someone who's been blacklisted."

"As you and Alice and several other people pointed out, he was practically begging for it. Besides, according to him, he can always make a living off the horses."

"Sometimes I worry about you, Fanny. I'm not saying he never places a bet, but anyone can see the racetrack business is an act."

"I'm sure there are other jobs he could get."

"After he's been blacklisted?"

"I heard of someone who used to work at the network who's making industrial films."

"I'll match that with his friend who went into the garage, closed the door, and turned on the engine."

"Charlie's not the type for that."

"You think there's a type?" She stood, went into the hall where she'd left her handbag, came back carrying a newspaper clipping, and handed it to Fanny.

"This is a letter from the wife of a Stanford research scientist who committed suicide after he was raked over the coals by HUAC. The committee wouldn't let her read it at a hearing, but she managed to get it printed in a newspaper."

Fanny took the clipping and began to read.

> **You have helped to kill my husband and make my four children fatherless. You have committed a greater crime against the children of America and of the world. My husband thought he had found a clue to the understanding of schizophrenia. Perhaps he was mistaken. Only time and the opportunity to pursue his research would have told. You took away both.**

"You carry around clippings like this?"

"Not all of us want to avert our eyes from the scene of the crime."

❦

Fanny was surprised when Ava turned up at her desk that morning. She'd picked up her latest scripts two days earlier and wasn't in the segment they were broadcasting today.

"Is Alice here?" she asked.

"I gather from your whispering that you do not want to see her. That, more to the point, you don't want her to see you. You're in luck. She's writing at home today."

"I have news that I definitely do not want her to know. At least not yet. I don't want anyone around here to get wind of it until it's final. That's why I didn't call. The switchboard operators would have it all over the building in minutes, and I'd end up with egg on my face if it doesn't come through. But I have to tell someone. I'm even afraid to tell you. Not because I don't trust you," she added quickly, "only because I don't want to jinx it."

"If the news is top secret, it can't be that you're in love again."

"I resent the 'again.' It's not love, it's my so-called career."

"Not so-called. You get lots of fan mail."

"Beatrice gets lots of fan mail. Most of it telling her what a terrible homewrecker she is. But this is a real part. In a real play. On Broadway. I've been called back twice, and my agent says they've just about made up their minds."

"This is fabulous. What part? What play?"

Ava leaned closer. "A George S. Kaufman play. Can you believe it? It's called *Fancy Meeting You Again,* and the part isn't just a walk-on or the maid who gets to say 'Dinner is served, madam.' I play the handmaiden to the leading lady, Leueen MacGrath, Mrs. George S. Kaufman to you."

"The handmaiden?"

"The play takes place over five thousand years with the same characters reappearing in different guises. I keep coming back scene after scene. In contemporary times, I'm her secretary. You know, the smart sardonic working gal with all the good quips. I can't wait to get my teeth into the part. We open in January."

"I love the *we*."

"No more than I do. Oh, Fanny, I can see my name on the marquee now."

"Is the part that big?"

"Okay, on the poster, somewhere in the small print below the title, Kaufman, MacGrath, and the actor who's playing the male lead. Walter Matthau. But still. Ava Sommers." She made a space between her forefinger and thumb as if to encase the letters. "And everyone back home laughed when I changed it."

"I never knew you changed your name."

"It's not something people go around announcing."

"What was it before?"

"Astrid Spongberg."

"You're right, Ava Sommers is better on a poster and in a playbill. It's only a matter of time until it's on the marquee as well. We should celebrate."

"Not till the contract is signed. I'm superstitious. Hell, I'm in the real theater now, the legitimate theater, I have to be superstitious. It comes with the territory."

"Okay, no celebrations, and my lips are sealed, but when you do sign the contract, I'll buy the champagne."

"I'll buy the champagne. I'm going to be a legit actress. A legit actress makes grandiose gestures. But you'll help me drink it. We'll even give Chloe a sip. Then the three of us will come up here, and she and I will do cartwheels around the office."

Chapter Twenty

ROSE STEPPED OUT OF THE BUILDING INTO THE GATHERing autumn dusk and smoothed her newly done hair. She'd learned years ago that nothing much tamed her frizz, but a good cut helped. Until she'd met Hugo, she'd hated her hair, but he'd come from a long line of straight-haired women who were continually perming, and he had loved to tousle her curls. Sometimes he'd called her Curly, other times Red. He'd also quoted Thomas Wolfe about "melon-breasted Jewesses from New York." She didn't fit that bill as closely as she did Curly and Red, but he'd said the women in his family ran to flat chests as well as straight hair, and she came near enough to Wolfe's description for him. And he'd marveled at her complexion. God, she missed him.

Warmed by the lights in the shop windows and the memories of Hugo, she started west on Fifty-Seventh Street. That was when she spotted Charlie Berlin coming toward her. She wasn't surprised at how glad she was to see him, but she was at how pleased he seemed to see her. She wondered if old friends had begun cutting him. A lot of that was going on. He didn't so much shake her hand as take it and hold on to it.

"You've done something to your hair. Very soigné."

That was the thing about Charlie Berlin, he looked at women, even older women.

"Thank you. Blame it on Mr. Jonathan."

"Mr. Jonathan knows his way around a haircut. It seems a shame to take it home and hide it from the rest of the world. It deserves a drink in a swanky setting. Unless you have something planned to show it off."

She started to say he was the one who must have better things to do, then caught herself. She suspected these days he was a man with plenty of time on his hands. She told him she'd love a drink.

"How about the Plaza?" He took her arm, turned her around, and they started east.

When they reached the hotel, they made their way through the revolving door and across the thickly carpeted lobby to the Oak Bar. She waited until they'd settled in one of the deep leather banquettes and ordered drinks before she brought up the subject.

"I'm sorry Fanny didn't go for the front arrangement."

He shrugged. "I always knew it was a long shot. And I can't blame her for not wanting to get the kid involved."

"Getting the kid involved is one of the reasons I thought she might do it. She could use the money. I do what I can to help, but I'm not exactly Daddy Warbucks."

"I bet you come close. Anyway, I'm working on some other possibilities who might be willing to sign their blameless names to my deathless prose."

She knew from the way he said it that he was lying, and dropped the subject.

The incident occurred on their way out of the hotel. It had

nothing to do with the drinks. She'd had one whiskey sour. If she was going to blame it on anything, it would be the snag in the red carpet runner on the steps. Her heel caught, and she began to pitch forward. Charlie grabbed her before she went down, and held on for moment. She was an old woman, and he was a young man, and their winter coats were bulky between them, but somehow the human touch came through, and for a minute she thought she was going to weep at the relief of it.

❧

This time Ava used the telephone. "I want the whole building to know. I want the whole world to know. I got it! I got the part!"

"Congratulations!" Fanny shouted as loud as she dared in the office.

"I can't believe it. I've been pinching myself ever since my agent called."

"This is terrific. Fantastic. When do you start rehearsals?"

"In two weeks."

"Are you going to ask Alice to send your character on vacation, throw her off a cliff, or hire another actress?"

"I'll let my agent negotiate that."

"Aren't you the cavalier one?"

"Euphoric. Euphoric is the accurate term. I figure I can always get another part on a soap—there, I said the word—but I'm hoping I won't have to. Not after a juicy part in a George S. Kaufman play."

"You're right. As soon as we get off the phone, I'm going out to buy that champagne."

"I told you. I'm buying. I'm a legitimate theater actress now."

❧

Fanny wasn't surprised when the two men in the identical shiny blue suits and gray homburgs turned up at her desk again. They'd been back once since Charlie Berlin had been fired. A few weeks after their second visit, one of Larry Cunningham's characters had been written out of the show and three new actors with dramatically different voices had been hired for his other parts. There would be no more listeners writing in accusing characters of bigamy. He'd left joking that he was a man of a thousand voices and not one of them was employable. Apparently, the way to go out was laughing.

This time the two men were closeted in Alice's office for only a few minutes before she came out and told Fanny they wanted to talk to her.

"Me?" Fanny's voice was more surprised than frightened.

"Don't worry, it's not about you. They just want to ask you a few questions."

"About Charlie?"

"Charlie's ancient history."

"Then about whom?"

"They're in my office, Fanny. Don't keep them waiting," Alice said, and started off down the hall.

The door to the office was open. Fanny stepped through it, then stopped. The two men were sitting in the chairs in front of Alice's desk. Alice's chair was empty. Fanny went on standing. For some reason an incident from her childhood flashed through her consciousness. She had wandered off to a far corner of the park playground, where two bigger boys cornered her. One held her while the other dropped worms down the back of her middy blouse. "Jew girl," they'd called her. "Kike. Christ-killer."

"Close the door, Mrs. Fabricant," the taller, dark-haired one said. Again, she heard the menace behind the soft voice.

She closed the door, but didn't step farther into the office.

He told her to sit and indicated the sofa. She hesitated, then perched on the edge of it. They swiveled their chairs to face her.

"Relax, Mrs. Fabricant," he said with a smile that conjured up the worms again. "You have nothing to worry about. We know enough about you to know you'll want to help us."

"Help you?"

"By answering questions," the shorter, fair one said sharply. He'd be the one to hold her while his colleague dropped the worms.

The other man shot him a look, then turned back to her.

"We understand you and Ava Sommers are friends."

She waited.

"What can you tell us about her?"

"She's a good friend. She's a good person. She doesn't have a mean bone in her body."

The short one snorted a harsh laugh. Fanny turned to him. She wanted to slap him. She turned away.

"What else can you tell us about her?" the tall one asked. "What do you know about her life outside of her work here?"

"She collects for all kinds of charities. She performs for free at benefits. And she and a friend put on puppet shows for kids in a home for newly arrived war orphans."

"So she likes children."

"She cares about humanity." Fanny regretted the words as

soon as they were out. Caring about humanity sounded like part of a communist manifesto. "Especially children."

"Does she spend much time with your daughter?" the dark one asked. "Chloe, isn't it?"

Fanny shuddered. Chloe's name in his mouth was worse than the worms down her back.

"The three of us spend time together. She babysat for me once."

"What did they do when she babysat? Did she tell Chloe stories or read to her?"

"As far as I know, they practiced handstands and cartwheels."

Even the unruffled one looked a little surprised by that.

"What else?"

"I don't know if they read that night, but sometimes she brings my daughter books. I told you, she's generous."

"What books does she bring her?"

"The latest installment in a series she likes."

"Which series?"

"Betsy-Tacy."

The two men looked at each other blankly. The Betsy-Tacy series must not be on the list of suspect books.

"What else?"

"A children's biography of Eleanor Roosevelt."

Now the glance they exchanged was dour.

"I think Mrs. Roosevelt is a great woman," she said, and could hear Charlie Berlin laughing. Fearless Fanny has the temerity to tell ACE she's a fan of the former first lady. What will she risk next?

"Can you recall any other books?" the dark one asked.

"Yes, but it was only a picture book." Surely they couldn't

find anything subversive in a picture book. "Too young for my daughter, but she loved it. I did too."

"What picture book?"

"*The Bear Who Wasn't.*"

This time their glances glinted off each other like knives.

"Why do you think she gave your daughter a book that was too young for her?"

"Sometimes people who don't have children of their own can't gauge reading levels. Although I don't think that was the case here. The book appeals to all ages. The story is witty and the illustrations are wonderful."

"Your book that appeals to all ages is communist propaganda," the short one said.

"It's about a bear."

"Who makes fun of capitalism," the calm one said. "That's the way propaganda works, Mrs. Fabricant. Obliquely. The enemy doesn't come out and say capitalism and God and America are bad. They undermine subtly. Did you know that Ava Sommers collected for the American Negro College Fund?"

"She might have mentioned it. I don't remember."

"Did she try to get you to contribute?"

"She knows I don't have much money."

They went on that way for some time, asking her about what Ava said and read, the organizations she belonged to and the people she knew, the charities she collected for and the causes she espoused. Finally, the short one brought out an old newspaper clipping and handed it to her. She sat staring at his outstretched arm. He jabbed it toward her. She took the clipping from him, but didn't look at it.

"Look at it," he said.

She glanced down. The date on the top was October 20,

1947. Max was still alive. Barbara's wedding and that awful night were still in the future. She'd known nothing of jobs or paychecks or anti-communist interrogations. She didn't know Ava. She hadn't known people like Ava existed.

"Do you recognize Ava Sommers in the picture?"

Her eye moved from the date to the headline above the photograph.

NAACP PROTESTS SCREENING OF
BIRTH OF A NATION

She looked at the picture. Men and women holding signs circled beneath a movie marquee. She made out the lettering on some of the signs. BIRTH OF A NATION REVIVES KKK. BAN HATE FILMS. BIRTH OF A NATION SLANDERS NEGRO AMERICANS.

"What do you know about this?" the tall one asked her.

"I never saw it, but some people think it's the greatest movie ever made."

"I'm not talking about the movie, Mrs. Fabricant. I'm talking about the demonstration against it."

She read the lettering on the signs the protesters were carrying again. Something Rose had told her years ago came back.

"When the movie was shown originally, lynchings in some southern states shot up."

"We're not asking about lynchings," the fair one growled. "We're asking about that picture you're holding. Do you or do you not recognize Ava Sommers in it?"

Fanny looked again. Most of the protesters were Negroes, but there were a handful of white faces. One might have been Ava. She couldn't be sure. The photograph was grainy, and it looked as if it had been fingered a lot.

"The date says October 20, 1947. That was before I knew her."

"She couldn't have changed that much in a few years. Do you recognize her?"

She looked again. "I'm not sure."

"Several other people are sure."

"Then you don't need me to identify her."

"But we do," the dark one said quietly. "We're thorough, Mrs. Fabricant. We accumulate as many corroborations as possible. And," he went on in a voice so soft she had to lean toward him to hear, "we need to believe that like any upstanding American citizen, you want to help us. Look at the picture again."

She gazed down. It did look a lot like Ava. She lifted her eyes. "I'm not sure. It might be Ava."

"Right!" the shorter one said.

"Or it might not be."

❦

Fanny and Chloe sat side by side on the bench, looking down at Ezra on his knees on the rubber matting surrounding the rink in the sunken plaza at Rockefeller Center. He was lacing Chloe's skates.

"Shouldn't they be tighter?" Fanny asked.

"They will be," he said without looking up. "The trick is to lace it all the way to the top, then start at the bottom again, tightening as you go." He finished one skate, and Chloe stuck out her other foot.

Fanny bent and went to work on her own skates, following Ezra's method. When he'd suggested they go skating, she'd told him she hadn't skated in so long she'd probably forgotten how, and hadn't been very good to begin with. He'd replied that it was like riding a bicycle. It would come back to her.

"Tight enough?" he asked Chloe.

"I think so."

He stood and held one hand out to each of them. "Here we go."

The bicycle analogy turned out to be only partially accurate. Fanny remembered what she was supposed to do, but she did it even less well than she had when she was still in practice. Forty-five minutes into the two-and-a-half-hour afternoon session, she clumped off the ice just as a couple were getting up from a ringside table at the English Grill, took one of the chairs, and when the waiter came, ordered a pot of hot chocolate. The sun was almost directly overhead, and the surrounding skyscrapers cast no shadows on the ice that glinted in the hard light. She took a pair of dark glasses from the pocket of a boiled wool jacket that went back to her undergraduate days, slipped them on, turned her chair for a better view of the ice, and sat sipping the chocolate and watching Ezra teach Chloe to fall and get up. They both seemed to be having the time of their lives. A little while later he came off the ice and clumped the few steps to her table.

"She's a natural and I'm rusty so I hired one of the instructors for the last half hour."

"You're too generous. Thank you."

"Selfish is more like it." He pulled the chair out, sat across from her, and turned so they were both facing the rink. "I get a kick out of watching her."

The first time Chloe skated by, she waved. After that she was too busy concentrating on the instructor and her feet. Ezra ordered another pot of chocolate, and they sat side by side tracking Chloe among the skaters. The piped-in music went from a tango to a waltz.

"This is peaceful," he said after a while.

"Thank heavens."

"Too much ice?"

"Too much office this week."

He poured more hot chocolate into her cup, then his. She waited to see if he'd ask what had happened in the office. He never had in the past.

Chloe glided by again. Fanny waved, but her daughter didn't notice. She knew from the expression on Chloe's face that she was practicing for the Ice Follies.

Another few minutes went by.

"I was grilled about a friend," she said.

"What?" he asked distractedly, his eyes still on the rink.

"At the office. Two men from something called the Anti-Communist Enterprise came to the office and questioned me about one of the actresses on one of the serials. Ava Sommers. You've heard me mention her."

He was no longer watching the skaters but had turned to her. "Why did they question you?"

"Because we're friends."

"Does that mean you're your friend's keeper?"

"Apparently it does. But they didn't ask anything about me. They only wanted to know about her."

"What about her?"

"If I recognized her in a picture of an NAACP demonstration. They were picketing a theater screening of *Birth of a Nation*."

"Is this Ava Sommers a Negro?"

"No, but would it bother you if she were?"

"Of course not. I was just curious because you said she was picketing with the NAACP."

"She also collected money for Israel."

"Then she's Jewish." He didn't try to hide the relief in his voice.

"She was raised Lutheran, but she has an ecumenical conscience."

He shifted in his seat. "Collecting for a good cause is one thing; picketing is another."

"Don't tell that to my aunt Rose."

"What do you mean?"

"Back in her sweatshop days, Rose was a union organizer. She got roughed up by policemen more than once."

"All I meant was that your friend could have been hurt. Especially if she was picketing with a bunch of Negroes. Don't get me wrong, I'm not prejudiced, and I hate people who are, but a white girl getting mixed up in a situation like that, who knows what could happen?"

"Apparently nothing did at the demonstration, though I guess it's come back to haunt her."

"What else did they ask you?"

"What magazines she subscribed to, books she read, that kind of thing." She had to smile when she remembered it, though she hadn't been amused at the time. "They even asked about a book she'd given Chloe. It's called *The Bear Who Wasn't*. Chloe loves it. I do too, for that matter. They insisted it was propaganda."

He shook his head. "We live in dangerous times."

She agreed that they did, but she was still thinking about the book. "I think I'll get a copy for your waiting room. What are you smiling at? My buying so-called propaganda for your waiting room?"

"You giving me books. Remember the John Gunther *Behind the Curtain*?"

"If I hadn't given you that book, we wouldn't be here."

"Don't you believe it. I sat up and took notice the first time you walked into my office."

"You did a good job of hiding it."

"Professional demeanor. All the same," he went on as Chloe stepped off the ice onto the rubber matting, "I wish I'd been there when those two men grilled you."

"I managed to handle it."

"I'm sure you did, but you shouldn't have to. Now that I'm around."

Chapter Twenty-one

At first Fanny thought it was Ava's agent's doing. She must have found a way to get Ava out of her contract, because the character she played was written out of the story and a new vamp written in.

"It was time," Alice said. "The character was getting stale." Though the explanation sounded reasonable, the fact that she didn't meet Fanny's eyes when she spoke should have been the giveaway. But Fanny was too busy typing up revised scripts for the following week to notice. Changes weren't usually made so quickly.

"At least this will give Ava a week or two off before she starts rehearsals for the Kaufman play," Fanny said.

Alice looked at her for a moment, then headed back to her office. Later, Fanny would blush at her naïveté.

Fanny was at the small desk she and Rose had found in a secondhand furniture shop and placed so it had a view through the bay of tall windows, studying the scripts she'd written and Alice had edited. She'd barely looked at them since Chloe had come home from camp, but Charlie's request that she act as a front had made her start thinking about writing again.

When the telephone rang, she looked at her watch. It was almost midnight. No one would call to chat at this hour. But someone would call in a crisis. Someone would call with dire news. As she started for the phone, she thought that Ezra was right when he teased her about her tendency to expect the worst. She didn't tell him that until the night she and Max had driven home through the blizzard, she hadn't expected the worst. She'd hadn't told him about that night either. She wasn't sure why. Perhaps it was miserliness on her part. She was hoarding every bit of Max, even the awful moments. No one was entitled to any of him except Chloe. Or perhaps it wasn't her stinginess with Max, but Ezra's reluctance to admit he existed. Had existed. It was like her job, a part of Fanny he didn't want to think about.

As she reached for the phone, she had a premonition of what the bad news would be. Mimi had called that afternoon. She'd begun to spot, and of course once she saw the blood, she felt cramps. She hadn't let on to Howard. She didn't want to frighten him. He had his heart set on this baby. But she had to talk to someone.

She picked up the phone. At first she couldn't recognize the voice that came intermittently through the sobs.

"I lost it."

Poor Mimi. Poor Howard. Before Fanny could say anything, the voice went on.

"I lost the part." A sob exploded on the other end of the line. "They changed their minds. They want someone else for it."

"Oh, Ava, I'm so sorry."

This time Ava sounded as if she was being strangled by the sob. In the moment of silence that followed, Fanny heard other voices and an automobile horn.

"Where are you?"

"On the street. In a phone booth. I've been walking for hours." Another sob came over the wire. "Ever since my agent called. That was around six, I think."

"Where on the street?"

"I don't know. I can't see the sign."

"Listen to me, Ava, get yourself in a taxi and get over here right now. You shouldn't be wandering the streets at this hour. You especially shouldn't be wandering the streets at this hour in your condition."

"I haven't had anything to drink."

"We'll take care of that as soon as you get here. Do you remember the address?"

"Of course."

"Then hail a cab and give it to the driver."

The downstairs buzzer rang only a few minutes later. She must have been around the corner. Fanny went out on the landing and stood at the top of the stairs watching Ava climb. She kept her eyes on the worn carpet runner, but as she turned the last landing, she lifted her face. Under other circumstances, Fanny would have laughed. They both would have. She was a circus clown with two black streaks running down her cheeks.

When she reached the landing where Fanny was standing, Fanny put her arms around her. The gesture was more compassionate than wise. It opened the floodgates again. Fanny led her into the apartment, settled her on the window seat, and said she was going into the kitchen to find out what kind of alcohol she had on hand.

"Rubbing will do."

Fanny stood looking down at her. "You're going to be okay. Anyone who can fire off a comeback like that isn't going to be done in by losing a part."

Ava started to cry again. "You don't understand. It's not just this part. It's any part. I've been blacklisted."

"Are you sure?"

"My agent said the backers are afraid of people picketing the theater. In North Carolina an audience actually stoned the screen of a Katharine Hepburn movie because of a speech she gave in Hollywood, in a flaming red dress no less, about liberty of conscience."

"Don't take this the wrong way, but I didn't think you were that well known."

"My agent said ACE would make me well known. The way they did the actress who played Henry Aldrich's mother. No one will ever hire me. Or by the time they do, by the time the blacklist is lifted, if it ever is, I'll be too old. I won't even be cast as a grandmother or a dowager, because I won't have any credits. I'm finished, Fanny. I'm a twenty-four-year-old has-been."

Fanny started to say it couldn't be that bad, but she knew it was. Instead, she went into the kitchen to find them both something to drink.

There was scotch in the cupboard. As she poured it, she thought that she should have lied. She should have said the girl protesting the screening of *Birth of a Nation* was definitely not Ava. But she knew it wouldn't have made any difference. As they'd said, they already had other corroborations. They just liked throwing their weight around, humiliating people, turning them into quislings.

She carried the drinks back to the living room, and they sat on the recessed window seat facing each other with their legs stretched out and their backs against the opposite walls. Fanny started to ask what she was going to do, then caught herself. It was too soon for that. But Ava was ahead of her.

"I can't go home," she said. "I won't go home."

"'Home is the place where when you have to go there, they have to take you in.'"

"Robert Frost doesn't know my family. The worst of it is—" She stopped. "No, the worst of it is losing that part and not being able to get another. But it doesn't help much that I didn't save a penny."

"You always were too generous. Those lunches at the Automat for total strangers, and every charity that appealed to you."

"That was penny-ante stuff. Plain old extravagance did me in. I used to joke that they should send my paycheck directly to Bergdorf's. Some joke. Like these trousers." She lifted expensive-looking flannel fabric between her thumb and forefinger. "I bought them last week because I thought they'd be perfect for rehearsals." Now she was on the verge of tears again.

"Look on the bright side. You've still got the wardrobe. You didn't blow all the money on the horses."

"Charlie's all right." She blew her nose. "Better than all right. If there were more people like Charlie, maybe the world wouldn't be in such lousy shape."

"Let's not get carried away."

"Didn't I ever tell you about him and the girl on *Helen Trent*?"

"From what Alice says there was more than one girl on more than one serial."

"It's not that kind of story. One of the actresses on the

program needed a, you know, an abortion. Charlie not only found a doctor. A refugee from Germany or Czechoslovakia or someplace like that who couldn't practice here legally until he passed his New York State Boards. Anyway, Charlie not only found him and checked out his credentials, he paid for the operation."

"Isn't that the least he could do under the circumstances?"

"You don't understand. He'd never done any more than flirt with the girl, the way he can't help doing. I don't think he ever got more intimate than shaking her hand. But he gave her the money, told her not to worry about paying it back, and here's the part of the story where I don't come off too well. I was supposed to go with her, but I got a callback from an audition that day. So Charlie went with her." She stopped and thought about it for a moment. "And now he's blacklisted too. What a rotten world." She took a wadded-up handkerchief from her pocket and blew her nose. "All the decent people in the world are blacklisted. Except you."

Perhaps Ava planted the seeds of the idea in Fanny's mind with those last two words. Or maybe Rose had when she'd given her the clipping about the Stanford scientist who'd committed suicide. Or perhaps it hadn't been a matter of seeds at all, but of an epiphany the Friday night she came home to find Ava sitting on the floor of the vestibule of her building.

She hadn't been thinking about Ava at the time. Her mind had been on Max. Even now, three years later, he stalked her life, sometimes as unobtrusive as her shadow on a bright day or moonlit night, others an intense presence watching her, walking beside her, judging her actions, in regard to Chloe, in regard to the world. Tonight it had been an echo from that night shortly after he'd come home from the war when a friend had said he could do better than Bellevue and Max had made a joke about cocktail hours in the maternity wards of swanky hospitals. The same stories churned through her mind again and again.

There had been no cocktail hour in Mimi's room at Mount Sinai this evening, but Howard and Mimi had clearly been giddy with happiness. That morning she'd delivered a seven-pound, nine-ounce boy. The spotting had turned out to be nothing. Everything had gone smoothly. She'd been in labor for fewer than three hours; six hours less than her delivery of Belle. Fanny had taken flowers, oohed and aahed over the wizened little face indistinguishable from the other wizened little faces behind the glass wall of the nursery, and promised to give the cigar Howard handed her with a flourish to Ezra later that night.

She took the crosstown bus home from the hospital and walked the rest of the way to her building. She was happy for Mimi and Howard. Who could be so churlish not to rejoice in the birth of a baby, especially one so desperately wanted? But the joy made her uneasy. It made her guilty. Though she knew she ought to want to be in Mimi's shoes, she didn't. She loved Chloe, but that was different. Chloe was her child. She'd never been an indiscriminate fan of babies simply because they were babies. She'd never thought motherhood was unmitigated bliss. She wasn't talking about the practical frustrations of sleepless nights and toilet training and tantrums. She meant something at once deeper and more amorphous. Her former roommate Susannah maintained she lacked the maternal gene. Fanny was pretty sure she didn't share the deficiency. Her pleasure in

Chloe was proof. But she felt no urge to have another child. More than that, she couldn't imagine having another child. She couldn't imagine having a child with anyone except Max. Again, it came back to Max. It wasn't the act of conception, though she still hadn't quite come to terms with that. It was the actual child. She wasn't a fool. She knew people divorced, families shattered, parents turned children against former spouses, children took sides. But none of that could undo the bond of having made a human being together. At least it couldn't in her mind.

She pulled open the outer door to her building. Ava was hunched on the floor. At least she thought it was Ava. Her knees were pulled up, her head was resting on them, and her hair cascading over them hid her like a curtain. She looked up at the sound of the door groaning on its hinges. Black streaks ran down her cheeks again, but this time her eyes were still heavily made up with shadow and mascara. The look was out of character. Ava never wore much makeup. She must have had an audition. That was good news. Though from the look of things, she hadn't landed the part. Nonetheless, someone must have been willing to consider casting her. Perhaps there were still pockets of the theater or movies, television or radio the blacklist hadn't penetrated.

Ava stood. "I'm sorry to turn up like this again."

"Delete the 'again.' Last time you called, and I ordered you over here." Fanny unlocked the inner door and pushed it open. "I take it from the makeup that you've been to an audition."

"I'll tell you about it when we get upstairs." She stopped halfway up the first flight. "Is Chloe there?"

"She's at Rose's."

"Thank heavens." She started climbing again.

"She's seen women cry. For a while her mother was perfecting the art."

"I'm finished crying. I've moved on to anger. Rage."

Fanny unlocked the door to the apartment, stood aside for Ava to go in, and followed her.

"At the director? The producer? Whoever wrote whatever you were auditioning for?"

"At myself."

"You can't blame yourself for not getting a part."

Ava threw herself down on the window seat. "I got the part."

"Then why are you crying?"

"Because I should have known. I did know. But I refused to believe it."

"I think I missed something here."

Ava looked up at Fanny and, childlike, rubbed her cheeks with her fists. Now the black streaks were smudges. "The audition was for a girlie movie. A stag film. Whatever you want to call it. I should have known when I got the call."

"Your agent didn't tell?"

"I don't have an agent. She hasn't exactly fired me, but you can bet she's not out hustling parts for me. Oh, she tried for a while. Once a casting director told her he wanted someone like Ava Sommers. She said she could get him Ava Sommers. He said someone like Ava Sommers who wasn't blacklisted. This audition was through a friend of a friend. As I said, I should have known. I did know. But I went anyway. That's how desperate I am."

"Okay, you're desperate. You went to the audition. They said you could have the part. You realized what it was. You told them you weren't interested. And you left."

Ava dropped her gaze to the floor. "I didn't leave. I auditioned."

Fanny took a moment to interpret her words. "What exactly does that mean? How do you audition for a movie like that? My guess is it doesn't entail reading lines. I'm not being facetious. I'm just trying to figure out why you're so upset."

"Because I went along with it."

"Went along with what?"

"First they asked me to take off my blouse. I figured no big deal. Then my bra. I wasn't comfortable with that, but I told myself that was my problem. In acting classes the instructors and the other actors were always telling me I was too prim, too bottled up. If I wanted to be a real actress, I had to let myself go. So I took off my bra. Then one thing led to another. It seemed silly to suddenly say 'I can't do this' when I'd already begun to do it."

"So you took off your clothes. That doesn't sound so terrible," Fanny said, though it did to her. "I knew a girl in school whose idea of a good time was playing strip poker with a couple of boys from Columbia."

"I wasn't playing strip poker. I wasn't doing anything but standing there, like a piece of meat hanging on a hook. There were five of them, and believe me they weren't Ivy League undergraduates. You should have seen their faces. You should have seen their eyes." She shuddered. "They kept telling me to turn this way, do that, assume this pose. One of them got so close, he burned my shoulder. I can still feel it."

"He burned your shoulder?"

"He had a cigar chomped in his mouth."

Fanny thought of the cigar in her handbag that Howard had given her for Ezra.

"Okay, but the important part is that you got out in time." She hesitated. "You did get out in time."

"I wasn't raped, if that's what you mean. Though god knows they were thinking of it. That's what I meant about their eyes."

"Okay, you got out in one piece. And you said no to the part. That's what counts."

"But I didn't say no."

"You told them you'd take it?"

"I told them I had to think about it."

"Fine. You've thought about it. And you've made up your mind. You're not going to do it. The incident is closed. No one will ever know about it."

"Except the five men in that room."

"And if you do it, try five hundred or five thousand or however many men watch those things. For all we know, the upstanding city fathers of that town in Minnesota screen them at chamber of commerce meetings."

"I suppose you're right."

"You suppose?"

"I know you're right. Maybe that's why I turned up here. I knew you'd tell me what I already knew."

"Anyone would tell you the same thing."

"You don't know some of my actress friends."

"In that case, I'm glad to be of service. Now do me a favor, go into the bathroom and wash your face. You came in looking like Clarabell. Now you're a walking Rorschach test."

Ava went into the bathroom, and when she returned, her face was scrubbed clean, and she was smiling; not a happy smile but an expression somewhere between rueful and relieved.

"I'm glad to see you've cheered up," Fanny said.

"I was just thinking of what I'd escaped. I never saw a script, if there was a script. All I know was there was a dog in it."

"Please tell me you're making this up."

Ava raised her right hand. "Swear on a stack of Bibles. An inappropriate oath under the circumstances." She started to laugh. At least Fanny thought she was laughing. The sound was a little too hysterical for her to be certain of the emotion it was expressing.

❦

She decided not to procrastinate. If she gave herself time to think, she might lose her nerve. As soon as Ava left, she picked up the phone and dialed Charlie Berlin's number.

"A call from Fanny Fabricant. How did I get so lucky? Wait, let me guess. You're dying for a drink at the bar in Gino's, and they won't let you sit there without me. I'll be right over."

"Don't bother. I have a dinner date in"—she looked at her watch—"twenty minutes."

"The Joe who reintroduced the Jews to the Torah?"

"It's none of your business with whom."

"Okay, my apologies. What's up?"

"You remember your suggestion?"

"About fronting?"

"I thought we weren't allowed to talk about it on the phone."

"We're not allowed to talk about it when network switchboard operators are listening. I doubt Ma Bell's minions are eavesdropping or would care if they were."

"I'll do it."

There was a moment's silence. "Are you sure?"

"No, but I'm willing to risk it."

"What made you change your mind?"

"Ava."

"You mean the fact that she was blacklisted too?"

"Let's just say I don't want you reduced to writing stag movies. If they're even written."

"Jesus, don't tell me she's doing that."

"She's not, but it was a close call."

"How do you know?"

"She just left here."

"And you talked her out of it?"

"She'd talked herself out of it. She just needed someone to say out loud what she was thinking."

"You know, Fanny Fabricant, I'm beginning to think maybe you're more than a pretty face and a good pair of pins after all."

"Is that supposed to be a compliment?"

"Yes. The question is can you accept it."

"I'll take it under consideration. Now what's the plan?"

"Tell Alice you want to try your hand at another breakdown. Then we'll do the drop. Don't worry. If you're afraid of letting me up to your apartment or coming here, you can leave an envelope on a park bench. Spy craft stuff."

"I don't think we have to go that far. I'll let you know when I have it."

"Wait. Aren't you forgetting something?"

"I said I'll call you when I have the breakdown."

"Money. Filthy lucre. The financial arrangement. Unless you're doing this out of the goodness of your heart."

"I'm not," she said, more harshly than she'd meant to.

"Fine. How about we split it fifty-fifty."

"That doesn't seem fair."

"Okay, you take sixty, I'll take forty."

"No, I meant fifty-fifty doesn't sound fair to you. You're the one writing the script."

A faint laugh came over the wire. "It's clear you don't have your aunt's business acumen."

"Okay, fifty-fifty," she said.

She was just hanging up the phone when the downstairs bell rang. Either Ezra was early or she'd been on the phone with Charlie for longer than she'd realized. That was all right. It wouldn't take her long to wash her face and put on powder and lipstick, and he knew his way around the apartment well enough to make drinks for them.

She went into the hall and leaned over the banister to watch him climb the stairs. From this angle, his cowlick was even more noticeable. It was funny how the physical traits and personality quirks that seemed strange or even off-putting at first could become endearing with time. A stray thought streaked through her mind, quick and surreptitious as a cat darting through the apartment. Perhaps it was part of her new recklessness. If she was taking practical chances, and she was in this arrangement with Charlie, she might as well risk an emotional gamble.

He must have sensed her leaning over the banister, because as he turned the last landing, he looked up. Surprise, then pleasure crossed his face. She didn't usually come out to the hall to greet him.

When he reached the top of the stairs, she took a step toward him and put her arms around his neck.

"Where's Chloe?" he asked.

"At Rose's. She and Belle are having a sleepover." She lifted her face to his. He didn't taste risky; he tasted safe.

They let go of each other, finally.

"If this is what a visit to the maternity ward does to you, I'm all for it."

She'd forgotten her visit to the hospital. That was before she'd found Ava despondent on her vestibule floor and set out on a life of crime or at least deceit with Charlie Berlin.

"How are they?"

It took her a moment to realize he was asking about Mimi and the baby, not Ava and Charlie, and as she did, the moment passed and she turned away from him.

Chapter Twenty-two

“I THOUGHT YOU’D GIVEN UP,” ALICE SAID WHEN FANNY told her she wanted to try her hand at another script.

“I was busy getting Chloe back to school, but I’ve been studying your edits. I think I’ve finally gotten the hang of how it’s done, so if it’s all right with you, I’d like to give it another try.”

On her way out of the office that evening, Alice handed Fanny a breakdown.

She called Charlie as soon as she got home. He said he’d stop by the next evening to pick it up.

She hesitated.

“For Pete’s sake, Fanny, I’ll wait in the lobby, and you can come down and hand it over there if I make you that nervous.”

“I don’t have a lobby. I have a vestibule and a hall. I’m not in your tax bracket, as you pointed out.”

“Yet.”

“And you don’t make me that nervous. But no smart aleck repartee, please. My daughter is of a tender age.”

“How tender?”

“Eight.”

“I’ll keep it in mind.”

The next night the downstairs doorbell rang as she was washing and Chloe was drying the last of the dinner dishes. She buzzed him up, and when she opened the door, found him standing in the hall with a book. At least it looked like a book. She couldn't be sure, because it was wrapped in gift paper.

"Don't worry," he said. "This isn't for you. I know we're on a strictly business basis. It's for the daughter of a tender age."

She called Chloe from the kitchen and introduced them.

"Pretty name," he said. "Do you know where it comes from?"

"My mommy and daddy gave it to me."

"I mean the origins of it. When people first started calling people Chloe. It's from Greek mythology. An alternative name for Demeter. She was the goddess of agriculture and fertility."

"Charlie," Fanny said.

"What's fertility?" Chloe asked at the same time.

"If you can grow lots of flowers and fruits and vegetables and stuff in the soil, it's said to be fertile soil. The name Chloe's also associated with spring. It means 'young green shoot.' And come to think of it, you look like one."

Chloe didn't know how to deal with that.

"I meant it as a compliment," he said, and held the book out to her. "This is for you."

She took it and thanked him. "Should I open it now?"

"Can't think of a better time. And in case you think I'm insulting your intelligence, don't let the pictures fool you. It's not a baby book. It's a book for all ages. One of my favorites, and I'm pretty ancient."

She unwrapped the book and, clearly perplexed, looked from the cover with the familiar title and drawing of the bear to her mother. Was she supposed to pretend she didn't already have it?

Fanny started to laugh. "Ava gave her *The Bear That Wasn't* some time ago. And just for the record, the book was one of the things that got her in trouble with ACE."

"It figures," he said to Fanny, then turned back to Chloe and pretended to study her. "You're not a bear . . ." he began.

"You're just a silly man who needs a shave and wears a fur coat," Chloe chimed in.

"Your daughter and I have a lot in common," he said after Chloe went off to her room with the book, which he'd told her to feel free to exchange for something she didn't have.

"Only she doesn't play the horses."

"Give me time." He saw the look on her face. "That was a joke, Fanny."

"Sorry, I don't have much of a sense of humor when it comes to her." Then, because the book had been a nice gesture and she really had been humorless about his joke, she offered him a drink.

When she came out of the kitchen carrying the ice bucket, he was standing in front of the fireplace, studying the picture of Max on the mantel.

"I take it this is your late husband."

She felt herself tense. Of all the people she didn't want to touch Max, Charlie Berlin was high on the list. She murmured an assent.

"He looks so young. Just a kid."

"That was taken before he went into the army." She hadn't meant to say that. Max was none of his business.

"How old was he when he died?"

At least he used the word and not some euphemism. She

hated it when people did that. Passed away, passed on, passed. They thought they were being kind, or at least polite. What they were doing was cheapening the horror, the finality of his death. Maybe that was why she answered again. "Twenty-eight."

"ETO or the Pacific?"

"It wasn't the war. It was after."

She saw him swallow the question.

"An aneurysm to the brain." Her words shocked her. The doctor had pronounced them, but she'd never repeated them to anyone. Where was all this coming from?

"Jesus!" he said, then quickly added, "I'm sorry." He turned away from the photograph, finally.

After she poured drinks for both of them, she went to her desk, took out the breakdown, and handed it to him.

He took it from her, but instead of glancing at it put it down on the coffee table in front of the sofa and sat. "There's one more thing we ought to discuss."

"Further financial arrangements?"

"More serious than that."

She sat in the chair across from him and waited.

"If you're going to get into this—"

"I already said I was."

". . . you ought to know more about me."

"Do I have to?"

"Now who can't be serious? They're blacklisting a lot of people like Ava who never did anything but subscribe to a magazine they don't approve of or collect contributions for a cause they don't like. They're also blacklisting current and former party members."

"You're about to tell me if you are now or ever were a member of the Communist Party," she repeated the familiar mantra.

"I'm not now, but I was."

"Am I supposed to be surprised?"

"I just wanted to make sure you knew."

"Did you ever spy for the Soviets or turn over top secret information?"

"Only tips on various horses."

"Okay, now I know. But I'm curious about one thing. When did you lose faith? Or more to the point, when did you join and why did you leave?"

"I signed up in '36. I was seventeen, and my social conscience was working overtime. Like my glands. The world was still a mess. Men had pretty much stopped defenestrating, but the country wasn't exactly on easy street. Millions were out of jobs. People who'd worked hard all their lives were eating out of garbage cans. Clearly the old system wasn't working. So I signed on for a new one. I warned you about cynics being lapsed true believers. Then came the war, and the Soviet Union was our ally. Hell, if FDR could be taken in by Uncle Joe Stalin, who was I to be suspicious? After the war, I got mixed up with a small theater group. They were going to produce one of my plays."

"I didn't know there was more than one."

"I had a lot of time on my hands commanding that Large Government Desk. This one was about a professional heel who does everything in the book to get ahead. Please, no digs about its being autobiographical. The director and a couple of other people in the group kept suggesting changes. I figured okay, I'm open to constructive criticism. No prima donna, Charlie Berlin. It turned out they didn't want a play about an individual heel. They wanted an indictment of a whole class of capitalist heels. They wanted a proletarian play. I objected. They told me I had to discuss the matter with someone higher up. I refused. They washed out the play. I left the theater group, and the party. I like to think the experience opened my eyes to the moral and social bankruptcy of the cause, but maybe it just hurt my feelings."

"What happened to the play?"

"It's in my bottom desk drawer where all failed plays, scripts, and novels go to die. Anyway, I just thought you ought to know whom and what you're getting mixed up with." He picked up the breakdown. "Have you read this thing?"

"I'm not an idiot. I've not only read it, I've made a copy of it. And I'll commit the script to memory once you write it. I'm not about to give Alice something I've supposedly written and know nothing about."

"That's a relief."

"What's a relief? That I'm not an idiot?"

"That we're back to bickering. Makes me feel like an old married couple."

"I hate to disillusion you, but the bickering part is an old wives', or in this case a confirmed bachelors' tale. The real thing isn't like that."

"The real thing?"

"The real thing," she repeated with certainty. "Bickering is too petty for that." She remembered the night she'd lain awake on a quilt in the guest room because the house was still only half furnished, swearing that when dawn came she'd take Chloe and leave. She hadn't known until then the rage love could engender. She wasn't going to try to explain that to Charlie Berlin, but when he spoke again, she realized he must have understood.

"You mean it's the cynic business all over again. Extremes one way or the other."

"Exactly."

His eyes cut to the picture on the mantel, then back to her. "He must have been quite a guy."

"He was."

She'd just closed the door behind him when a thought occurred to her. She opened it again.

"Wait," she said.

He stopped at the top of the stairs and turned back to her. "Second thoughts so soon?"

"Only a caveat. No funny business like slipping in veiled references to Joe McCarthy, the Hollywood Ten, or loyalty oaths."

He shook his head. "To quote my new collaborator, I'm not an idiot."

He wrote the script the next day, but they decided not to give it to Alice until the following week. Fanny's turning in a polished script in twenty-four hours wouldn't look suspicious; it would be a dead giveaway.

Alice pronounced it pretty good. "There are still some rough spots, but I can take care of those."

The script with Fanny's name on it was pretty good. If Charlie's name had been on it, Fanny knew, it would have been excellent. At first she ascribed the difference to Alice's weakness for troublesome men. Then she realized it had to do with her, Fanny, rather than Charlie. Alice couldn't accept the fact that the secretary who'd managed a decent scene or two but never a full script in the past could suddenly turn in one that needed almost no edits. And, of course, she hadn't.

Charlie laughed at the heavier edit now that he was writing under the name of Florence Fabricant, but he found the pay differential less amusing. Alice had told Fanny she'd be getting fifty dollars a script.

"I used to get a hundred," he said.

"I didn't think it would be wise to make the comparison."

Two days later Alice gave her another breakdown. "I probably wouldn't be giving you so many so quickly, but with Charlie gone, I'm shorthanded."

"I appreciate it," Fanny said.

"All the same, I have a feeling I'm going to rue the day I turned you into a scriptwriter. I give it two months, maybe three, before I have to find a new secretary."

Fanny assured her that she had no plans to quit in the foreseeable future.

"Maybe not, but I don't see how you'll be able to manage working here from nine to five, taking care of your daughter, and writing scripts."

Fanny looked up from the new breakdown she was studying. Surely the words were a warning. Alice knew what she and Charlie were up to. But Alice had already picked up the phone on her desk and swiveled her chair to look out at the Manhattan skyline as she talked.

❧

Alice began giving her two breakdowns a week. Charlie began turning up twice a week to pick up the new breakdowns and deliver the scripts he'd written for the previous ones. Sometimes he brought Chloe a book or a puzzle or something for her dollhouse. Fanny told him not to.

"I may be living in reduced circumstances, as the women in

that position politely put it," Charlie said, "but I'm not broke yet."

"If you keep this up, you will be," she warned, but she was more concerned about Ezra than Charlie. One evening Ezra noticed a duplicate copy of *Carney's House Party* by the author of the Betsy-Tacy series.

"Why didn't you tell me you'd already bought Chloe this?" he asked.

"I hadn't. Rose gave it to her, and I didn't have the heart to tell her you'd beaten her to the punch."

"I guess Rose and I are going to have to compare notes from now on."

"Incidentally," Fanny said to Rose the next time they spoke, "if you run into Ezra at one of Mimi's matchmaking family dinners, you gave Chloe the second copy of *Carney's House Party*."

"Who am I fronting for?"

"The same man we're all fronting for. Charlie Berlin. He brought it for her when he came to deliver a script."

Rose was the only one Fanny had told about the arrangement with Charlie. The secrecy bothered her. She felt as if she were back behind the makeup counter, but now she was lying to people she cared about rather than strangers.

Once or twice she'd almost slipped with Ava, except she knew that it wouldn't have been a slip. She wanted to show off that she was doing something to fight or at least undermine the blacklist. Ava had recovered from her brush with pornography, partly thanks to Rose, who'd heard through an old friend in the alterations department at Saks of an opening for a model in their Salon Moderne.

"Apparently, the blacklist hasn't infiltrated the world of

fashion," Ava reported when she landed the job. "How much propaganda can I spread when I spend my days walking around the salon dressed to the nines repeating 'crepe de chine evening dress in lagoon blue' or 'afternoon sport frock in Harris tweed'?"

She'd almost slipped with Susannah too, and again she knew it wouldn't have been a slip, but a message. You're fighting to redress injustices against women in the past. I'm doing my best to help right the wrongs people are suffering now.

She hadn't come close to slipping with Mimi. She wanted admiration for the chance she was taking, not disapproval.

But the one she should have told, the individual it touched more closely than any of her friends, was Ezra. She tried to justify herself with the excuse that she wasn't really keeping anything from him since he never asked about her work, but she knew he'd be interested in this aspect of it. He'd be horrified by this aspect of it. Didn't she understand the chance she was taking? She could be hauled before a committee and blacklisted herself. And what about Chloe? She knew every argument he'd make because she'd made them to herself. And even if he could understand the moral justification for what she was doing, he'd object to whom she was doing it with.

She kept resolving to tell him. Surely she could make him understand. If he didn't care about someone like Charlie being blacklisted, especially since Charlie had been asking for it, he'd have to recognize the injustice of Ava's predicament. And what about the Stanford scientist who'd left four fatherless children? As for the effect on Chloe, she'd come to agree with Rose. Better that she learn to deal with peer disapproval now than grow up morally unmoored. But every time she started to broach the subject, she lost her nerve. Then one Sunday afternoon when they were handing sections of the paper back and forth between the big easy chair where he was sitting and the sofa where she was stretched out, she decided the time had come. She had to tell him. She sat up and faced him.

"Listen to this," he said, and began to read from an article about the first nuclear test the Soviets had carried out the previous summer. "Makes you wonder what these people they're hauling before committees were thinking."

"I imagine they were thinking about the mess the country was in during the Depression. Most of them joined in the thirties."

"If you ask me, they were just plain naïve, no matter when they joined."

"Or idealistic."

He smiled and shook his head. "My soft-hearted Fanny."

She didn't like having her moral stance dismissed as sentimental claptrap, but before she could justify herself, he put aside the article on the Soviet nuclear tests and turned to her. She could tell from his expression that this was more serious than a nuclear apocalypse. This was personal.

"Did Howard adopt Belle legally?"

"Not to my knowledge."

"You'd think he would now that there's another child."

She sat waiting. This wasn't about Howard and Mimi.

"I just want you to know that I'll adopt Chloe. If you'll let me."

She knew she should be grateful. As Mimi had said, most men weren't eager to take on someone else's child. Heaven knew the arrangement would make their life easier. No more sitting at her desk jockeying bills to figure which could wait for a few more days or weeks, no more borrowing from Peter to pay

Paul, as her father called it. But she hated to think of herself as the kind of woman who would marry for money. She and Chloe were fine as they were.

"I hadn't planned to say that," he went on when she didn't answer. "I've been thinking it, but I hadn't planned to come out with it. At least not yet. I'm not trying to rush you. Three years is a long time for some people, but apparently not for you. I know you're not ready. You're still married to . . ." He hesitated and glanced at the framed picture on the mantel. ". . . him."

"I'll always be married to him."

"Part of you will always be married to him," he corrected her, "but you need someone to take care of you, you and Chloe both do. He'd say the same thing if he were here."

She wondered if he would. Would he say my old medical school pal is a good guy, walk into his open arms and take Chloe with you, or would he tell her to get that bastard out of the apartment and let me go on living on the mantel and in your heart and mind? He'd been an altruist in his work, but he'd had a jealous streak. Doesn't everyone?

"Just think about it," Ezra said.

She promised to.

Chapter Twenty-three

THE FRONTING ARRANGEMENT WAS WORKING OUT BETTER than she'd dared hope. Alice had no suspicions. The network and the sponsor were pleased. They'd gotten rid of the commie troublemaker, whom Alice had told them in a half-hearted defense was the best writer she had on all three shows, and the scripts hadn't suffered. More to the point, the network was still selling time and the sponsor was still selling soap flakes. Though Fanny hadn't gone into it for the money, or not only for the money, she had to admit the extra—and unearned, she kept reminding herself—cash made life easier. Strange the headiness of no longer watching pennies at the butcher's, greengrocer's, or Zabar's. Sometimes she thought the small luxuries made her feel richer than a real windfall. Chloe's piano and violin lessons hadn't materialized, and ice skating was impractical as anything but a special treat from Ezra, but her new passion was ballet. Every Saturday, Chloe and her friend Karen went off to Miss Vasiliev's studio with their shoes in cloth bags slung over their narrow shoulders. Fanny loved standing in the window watching them glide up West End Avenue in that exaggerated toe-pointed, plié-push ballet walk.

Nonetheless, something was still bothering her about the

arrangement, something more than keeping what she was up to a secret from Ezra and almost everyone else. It took her a while to realize what it was. She felt guilty. Charlie was doing all the work while she was getting half the money. He told her it wasn't work. He could churn out soap scripts in his sleep. But, he pointed out, he couldn't sell them without her. Still, the agreement struck her as lopsided. Then one night when she was curled up in a corner of the window seat reading the script Charlie had delivered earlier that evening, she realized what she felt was more than guilt. It was envy. She remembered how pleased she'd been when Alice had praised a scene or a line in the scripts she'd really written, not merely put her name on. Now when Alice admired something she turned in, she averted her eyes and mumbled a half-hearted thank-you. She took less pleasure in getting undeserved credit than in pocketing unearned money.

She looked down at the script again. There was nothing wrong with it. The dialogue stayed true to the characters. That was one of Charlie's strengths. He could do voice. If anything, the problem lay with the breakdown. Alice prided herself not only on never having given a character amnesia, but on at least a modicum of psychological veracity. In this scene, however, the actions were completely out of character. Fanny didn't believe this woman, or any woman for that matter, would confide such intimate thoughts to her closest friend, let alone a neighbor who'd dropped in for coffee, as so many of Alice's characters spent so much of their time doing.

She looked up from the script. The lights of the apartment buildings across the street burned holes in the darkness. In one square, a couple was dancing cheek to cheek. That hurt. In another, a woman bounced a crying infant in her arms as she paced back and forth. At least Fanny assumed the infant was crying. The windows were closed, but the woman looked frazzled. In a third illuminated rectangle in a different line in the building, another woman stared out into the darkness as she washed dishes. If life were a comic book, there would be a bubble of print over her head. The question was what would be in the bubble. That was it.

She knew she was breaking the rules. "Literary doesn't fly," Alice had told her the first time she'd given her a breakdown to try her hand at. But it wasn't literary if you didn't call it stream of consciousness. It was what women did as they went about their daily lives. Show me a woman, Fanny challenged the rules she was arguing with in her head, who doesn't gnaw on her worries and hopes while she washes dishes or vacuums or pursues any of the mindless chores of keeping house. Alice didn't know that, because with all her money and swanky restaurants she probably hadn't washed a dish in years. Charlie probably didn't own a dish. But most women who spent too many hours performing monotonous repetitive tasks did know. Unless, of course, they were listening to a soap. That was another problem with the idea. Characters on soaps never washed dishes or ironed clothes or mopped floors. The sponsor was selling escape along with laundry detergent or floor wax. But if the character's mind was far away from the mundane task at hand, the listener would forget what she was doing and follow the drama of her musings.

She stood, went to her desk, and pushed aside the typewriter. She didn't want the noise to wake Chloe. She'd write the scene longhand and type it up when she got to the office in the morning, before Alice got in.

❦

Charlie liked to compare the changes Alice made to the scripts with Fanny's name on them to the edits she used to make when she knew he was the writer. He saw the heavier revisions as a moral victory over his firing, or at least retaliation for it. When Fanny gave him the most recently edited script, he was almost exultant.

It was a Saturday afternoon. Since Chloe had begun ballet lessons, he'd taken to coming by on Saturdays to deliver scripts and pick up breakdowns.

"We really put one over on her this time." He was leaning against the counter in the kitchen, reading the pages while she made coffee. "She rewrote the entire scene. She never would have done that if my name had been on it."

Fanny kept her eyes on the coffee she was scooping into the percolator basket. "She didn't rewrite the scene, I did."

He looked up from the pages and stood staring at her.

"You rewrote the scene?"

She put the coffeepot on the stove, switched on the flame, and turned to him. "Don't sound so surprised. You adhered to the breakdown, but the breakdown didn't make sense."

"Soaps don't make sense, Fanny. That's the point."

"Not necessarily. Look at *Against the Storm*. It won a Peabody Award."

"Since when did you start researching soap history?"

"I like to be informed."

"So you've decided to single-handedly improve the quality of what we're writing."

She reached up and took down two cups and saucers. "Not single-handedly. I didn't change anything else in your script."

"You realize you could have thrown a monkey wrench into the whole arrangement?"

"But I didn't. Alice loved the scene. Though I admit she didn't mention that it veered from the breakdown. You're just envious that you didn't think of writing it as stream of consciousness."

"Stream of consciousness. Let's not get carried away. This isn't exactly Molly Bloom's soliloquy."

"I didn't say it was. Merely better than Alice's breakdown and your scene from it."

"I still think you had chutzpah."

"That's the first time I ever heard you use a Yiddish word."

"It's not a Yiddish word, it's a New York word, and I still think you had it."

She turned from the cups and saucers she was arranging on a tray to face him. "Whose name is on these scripts, Charlie?"

He went on looking at her for a moment. She couldn't read his expression. He pretended he took no pride in the work, but even a cynic couldn't put in as much time and effort, no matter what he said about turning out scripts in his sleep, without having at least a little ego implicated. The moment went on. Then he started to laugh. "Your name. And I have to hand it to you. Unlike Alice, I remember what I wrote. You made it better."

"Thank you." She turned to take the percolator off the stove. "So I guess from now on we really collaborate." She hadn't known she was going to say that. She'd been thinking it, but she wasn't sure she was ready to propose it. She started for the living room with the tray.

He followed her. "There's only one problem with that."

She sat and began pouring coffee. "You're going to tell me again that the woods are full of one-scene writers."

"I'm going to tell you the fifty-fifty split of the filthy lucre doesn't fly anymore. Not if you're writing half the script as well as fronting for my half."

"You can take me out to dinner," she said, and surprised herself more. "That was a joke," she added quickly.

❦

He didn't take her out to dinner. He tried to, but she always found an excuse.

"Is it because Ezra wouldn't like it?"

"He wouldn't."

"So he dictates your life?"

"He doesn't dictate my life."

"That's what it looks like from where I stand."

"If he dictated my life, I wouldn't be fronting for you or collaborating on the scripts."

"Does he know you're fronting for me and collaborating on the scripts?"

"That's not the point."

He grinned. "So he doesn't know. Are you going to marry him?"

"That's none of your business."

He held up both hands. "Don't get touchy. I'm only asking in the interest of my future job security. Though far be it from me to let my livelihood interfere with the course of true love."

❦

"I've been thinking it over," Alice said one afternoon shortly before Christmas. "Good scriptwriters are harder to come by than competent secretaries. Do you think you're up to five scripts a week?"

Fanny called Charlie as soon as she got home that evening. "We're up to five scripts a week." She practically sang the news.

"It's about time," he said. "At how much?"

"I didn't ask."

"For Christ's sake, Fanny. I don't know why I put up with you."

"Because, as you point out, you can't sell the scripts without me. These days you probably can't even write them without me."

"Talk about swelled heads. Ask her for a hundred a script. Don't settle for a penny less than seventy-five."

"That's between five hundred and three seventy-five a week!"

"And they said you weren't good with numbers."

"I can't ask her for that."

"Why not?"

"I'm making fifty-five a week now."

"As a secretary."

"What do I do if she says no?"

"Tell her you're going to another show."

"We are?"

"You are." He was silent for a moment. "Look, maybe you should let Rose negotiate for you."

"I can negotiate for myself, thank you."

"I love it when you get huffy, sweetheart."

❧

She'd told him she could negotiate for herself, but every time she screwed up her courage to go into Alice's office, she found something else to do. At lunchtime she went down to the lobby and called Rose from a phone booth.

"There's a trick I used when I was starting out on my own,"

Rose said. "When I began setting prices for my work, I pretended to myself that the money wasn't for me or the work I was doing, but for the girls in the sweatshops or their unions or some good cause."

"What difference did that make?"

"We're raised to selflessness. You weren't sent into the sweatshops to send your nonexistent brothers through school, but there are more subtle forms of telling you you're worthless. Pretend the money isn't going to you. In a way, it isn't. Charlie will get half, and you'll spend the rest on Chloe."

"Look who's talking."

"How do you think I got so smart about it?"

As soon as Alice returned from lunch, Fanny went into her office.

"About the five scripts a week," she began.

"We'll start as soon as you train your replacement."

"I think I should get a hundred dollars a script."

Alice leaned back in her swivel chair and stared at Fanny.

Fanny opened her mouth to explain, then closed it and went on standing in silence.

"A hundred a script," Alice agreed. "I think I've created a Frankenstein monster," she added as Fanny started out of her office.

"Or trained a good scriptwriter," Fanny said over her shoulder.

❦

The three of them stood staring at the television. Actually, Fanny and Rose stood staring at it. Chloe was dancing around the coffee table where the delivery man had placed it. She was no longer the only kid who didn't have one.

"It's a Philco," she sang. "Linda has a Philco. But her screen isn't as big. This is sixteen inches!"

Fanny wondered when her daughter had become so knowledgeable about electronics.

"Of course, we can't keep it," Fanny said.

"Mom-my," Chloe wailed.

"Why not?" Rose asked.

"I'm not taking a television set from Charlie Berlin."

"It's only a table model," Chloe insisted.

How had she raised this child?

Rose picked up the card that had arrived with the set.

> A Christmas or Chanukah (I'm ecumenical) gift for Chloe, the only one of her friends who doesn't have one, and a token of gratitude to my meal ticket.
> Charlie

"It's a thank-you gift," Rose said.

"A thank-you gift is flowers or a book or a bottle of champagne. That's acceptable. Expensive gifts from strange men are another story."

"Now you sound like Mimi. First of all, he's scarcely strange. He's your collaborator. And the prohibition against expensive gifts has to do with the laws of barter. What he might hope to get in return for a television. I don't think you have to worry about that with Charlie."

"Why not?"

Rose laughed. "Don't sound so affronted, Fanny. I wasn't suggesting he's not interested, only that he doesn't have to buy affection, or even sex."

Fanny glanced at Chloe. "Come into the kitchen," she said to Rose. "You can help me make tea."

"Sorry," Rose said as Fanny began filling the kettle. "From now on there will be no mention of any connection between you and sex in front of your daughter."

"Even if I could square taking it from Charlie, how could I explain it to Ezra?"

"Why do you have to explain it to Ezra?"

"Be realistic, Rose. He walks into the apartment, sees an expensive new television set—"

"It probably isn't so expensive. As Chloe pointed out, it's a table model."

"I don't believe this. My two experts on television sets. Whatever it costs, it's more than I can afford on my salary. My salary as a secretary rather than a professional front and collaborator."

"All right, say I gave it to you. Or your father did."

"That means asking Chloe to lie."

"Then tell him the truth. If not about fronting for Charlie, then at least about collaborating on the scripts. You're going to have to eventually."

"Eventually isn't now."

"What's wrong with now?"

"I'm not ready."

"First you're not ready to sleep with him. Now you're not ready to lose him. Do you really care that much?"

"I don't know. I'm trying to find out."

"Fair enough. Then don't lie. Just don't tell him the whole truth. You work in show business. It's a flamboyant world. People in it are given to grand gestures. Sterling silver cigarette cases. Gold lighters. Horses."

"Horses?"

"I read in a column about some movie mogul, I forget which one, who gave an actress a horse when they finished shooting the movie."

"I guess I should be glad it's only a television."

"Just tell Ezra one of the writers on the show was grateful for some favor or other and wanted to say thank you."

"Some favor or other? If ever I heard a compromising term."

"Only to someone with a suspicious mind. I was thinking extra typing. Covering for him when he was late with a script. You come up with something. You're the one who works in the business."

"I guess, but I can't get over the feeling it's an inauspicious start."

"It's either that or a precipitous finish. Take your choice."

Chapter Twenty-four

Chloe met Ezra at the door with the news. "We have a television. Sixteen inches."

She took him by the hand and led him across the living room to the set, not that he could have missed it. Fanny hadn't found a place for it yet, and it was still sitting on the coffee table.

"Congratulations. Now you're not the only kid on the block without one."

"Not just the block. Practically all my friends have one."

"It's just an expression, but congratulations all the same."

"I'll show you how it works." She turned the knob, and they stood waiting for the set to warm up. When it did, there was snow in the picture, and she adjusted the antennas until it cleared.

"You're quite an expert."

"I had to teach Mommy how to get rid of the snow."

"I take it from whatever smells so good that she's in the kitchen."

On Fridays and Sundays, Fanny cooked for the three of them. On Saturday nights, she got a babysitter or Chloe had a sleepover, and she and Ezra went out to dinner.

"Don't you want to watch it?"

"Later. For now, I'll let you and Kukla hold down the fort while I see what's up in the kitchen."

Fanny was at the counter trimming string beans. He came up behind her, put his arms around her waist, and kissed her neck. Max used to do the same thing, only he used to put his hands on her breasts. Ezra would have if Chloe hadn't been in the next room. She supposed the gesture was universal, even prehistoric. Man returning to the cave from the hunt found woman preparing whatever she'd gathered that day, sidled up behind her, and slid his hands inside the animal skins that covered her nakedness.

"I can't decide which smells better, dinner or you."

"A man of the people, torn between sautéing onions and Chanel 22."

"Let's just say a man of varied appetites." He let go of her and took a step back. She turned to smile at him. He looked perfectly at home in her kitchen, jacketless with loosened tie, leaning against the counter with his hands in his pockets fiddling with keys or a lighter or change. "Chloe just showed me the new addition to the apartment and demonstrated her expertise with it."

She continued trimming the beans.

"I knew it was only a matter of time until Rose gave in," he went on.

She forced herself not to look at him and told herself to let it slide. There was no need to contradict him. If Chloe hadn't mentioned the provenance of the television yet, she wasn't likely to. Rose could have given them the set. She probably would have in the near future if Charlie hadn't beaten her to it. Besides, she didn't owe Ezra an explanation. At least not yet.

"It was generous of her, but I admit I'm embarrassed," he said.

She turned her head to look at him again. "Why should you be embarrassed? You're not the one who keeps taking things from her."

"I knew how much Chloe wanted one, and I thought of buying one for the two of you. For the three of us, really. I spend a lot of time here."

"You shouldn't be buying us televisions." She tossed the ends of the beans in the trash. "We're not exactly one of the *Times*'s Hundred Neediest Cases."

"I didn't mean to suggest you were. But I decided there was no point in buying a second set. I already have one, and we're not going to need two, much as it would delight Chloe. We probably won't have room for two in the beginning. Besides, I had a more important gift on my mind."

She bent to the bottom cabinet to take out a pot for the beans. When she straightened, she saw it on the counter. A small velvet box.

He came around to face her, picked up the box, and opened it. The small diamond winked at her. She'd never liked men who winked, but you couldn't muster animus against an inanimate gem. Nonetheless, the thumb of her left hand rubbed the underside of the gold band on her finger.

"It's beautiful," she said, though she knew that was neither the point nor what he wanted to hear. "I don't know what to say."

"Try yes."

She heard the clock ticking in her head. She felt him standing beside her, waiting. She'd told Rose she needed more time. She'd said the same thing to him and made it clear in countless ways. But how long could she go on needing more time? They weren't kids.

"Yes," she said finally, and turned to him. She put her arms around his neck and lifted her face to his. "Of course, yes."

Now you do sound like Molly Bloom, Charlie Berlin whispered in her head.

❦

The subject of the television didn't come up again that night or for the rest of the weekend. Chloe was glued to it. Though Fanny knew she'd have to set limits to her viewing time, she didn't have the heart to that first weekend. Besides, she had other matters on her mind.

She'd explained to Ezra that she had to tell Chloe about the marriage in her own time and her own way. They had to be alone. It had to be a discussion, not a proclamation. It couldn't look as if the grown-ups were ganging up on her. Chloe had to be reassured that she still came first in her mother's life. Rose said that was no way to raise a daughter, but then Rose had never brought up children, unless you counted Fanny.

There was also the issue of Fanny's job, but since he didn't bring it up, she saw no reason to. The ring was a more immediate problem. Standing in the kitchen, he'd started to slip it on her left hand, but the gold band was already there. She thought of saying that she didn't want to wear it until she told Chloe, but she didn't like the idea of exploiting her daughter in her stratagems. Besides, he'd probably say that Chloe was too excited about the television to notice a new piece of jewelry on her mother's hand, and even if she did, she wouldn't necessarily grasp its significance. That was the drawback of getting mixed up with a man whose specialty was children. Instead, she gave him her right hand and explained that the wedding band had become tight with the years and she'd need soap to get it off.

She'd take care of it later, she promised. She was too excited now. But as she set the table and served dinner, she was acutely aware of her hands. They felt heavy, stiff, strangely clumsy, as if she were a puppet on one of Chloe's television shows whose movements were being manipulated by others. But at least she and Ezra weren't talking about the television.

❦

Chloe could tell something was up. Her mother was pretending it wasn't, but Chloe knew. She recognized the difference between her mother when she was really happy and when she was only acting that way. She hoped it didn't have to do with the television. Nobody was saying anything about it while they ate, but every once in a while, her mother glanced over at it. It was sitting right there on the coffee table, the screen black now because her mother had made her turn it off when they sat down. Chloe hadn't forgotten her mother's reaction when it came. She said they couldn't keep it because it was from Mr. Berlin. Aunt Rose had talked her into not sending it back. But maybe her mother had changed her mind again. She wondered if her mother would have wanted to return it if Uncle Ezra had given it to them. Come to think of it, she wondered why he hadn't. He was around a lot more than Mr. Berlin. She couldn't decide which of them she liked better. Until now, she'd been pretty sure it was Uncle Ezra. It wasn't just the skating at Rockefeller Center and the baseball game and stuff like that, though that helped. He was really nice to her. But Mr. Berlin was nice to her too. And now there was the television. Sometimes she thought about which one she wanted her mother to marry. She didn't mean which of them would give her more presents. She meant who she'd rather have around. But the more she thought about it, the more she decided it didn't matter. She just wished her mother would get married. It wasn't only that then they'd be more like normal families. It was that she wouldn't feel so responsible for her mother. "Responsible" was Aunt Rose's word. She never said anything to Aunt Rose about the times she felt bad leaving her mother alone, but somehow Aunt Rose knew. She'd told Chloe it wasn't her job to take care of her mother. But if it wasn't her job, whose was it?

The following Saturday, Charlie was still there, sitting on the sofa going through breakdowns, when Chloe returned from her ballet lesson.

"How are you and the telly getting along?" he asked. "That's what they call it in England."

She crossed the room to him. "It's wonderful."

"I'm glad. Your thank-you note was nice, but I like a little in-person enthusiasm as well."

She stood for a moment, debating. "I could hug you."

"Not only could you, I think you should."

She bent to the sofa and put her arms around him. The gesture was quick and shy, but it was unmistakably a hug.

"Thank you," he said when she let go. "Which are your favorite programs?"

She thought for a moment. "I like *The Lone Ranger* and *The Magic Cottage*." She thought some more. "But my favorite is *Kukla, Fran, and Ollie*."

"That's one of my favorites too."

"You're teasing me."

"Scout's honor." He held up his right hand. "It's supposed

to be for kids, but lots of grown-ups like it. Like *The Bear Who Wasn't*. It's for all ages. Anyone who has a funny bone."

"A funny bone?"

"Anyone who can laugh at funny things."

"I hate to break up this discussion of the nature of comedy . . ." Fanny began.

He stood and picked up the breakdowns. "I was just leaving."

She turned to Chloe. "And you better get ready if you're going to Karen's for a sleepover."

Fanny was still putting away the scripts and breakdowns she and Charlie had been going over when Ezra arrived.

"That woman doesn't pay you enough for the amount of work you do for her."

She looked at her watch. "The afternoon got away from me."

"It frequently does."

Chloe came out of her room carrying her overnight bag, and Fanny said they'd drop her off at Karen's on their way to the restaurant.

"I have a better idea," he said. "I'll take her now, while you get ready. That way she won't be late, and you won't have to rush."

"How did you become such a sterling human being?"

"Hard work and good genes."

She stood in the doorway watching her daughter and the man she was going to marry chatting volubly as they went down the stairs. She still hadn't told Chloe about the engagement—she was waiting for the right moment—but she didn't have to worry about her daughter's reaction.

Twenty minutes later, he came back into the apartment saying it was a frigid night out there, and when he bent to kiss her, his mouth was icy against hers.

"You need a drink," she said.

He agreed, and she went into the kitchen. When she came back carrying two glasses, he was sitting on the sofa. She handed him one of the glasses and sat across from him with her own.

"Feels like snow," he said.

"It's not in the forecast."

"If we get a couple of inches, we can take Chloe to the park, sledding."

"That would be wonderful," she said, and didn't add she'd never been able to do it herself. Even a flurry still reminded her of that brutal night.

They went from the weather to his practice, the patients he'd seen that week, a pediatric convention he was debating attending, new equipment he was considering buying. When they finished their drinks, she stood and carried the glasses into the kitchen. She was surprised when he followed. He often kept her company in the kitchen while she was cooking or cleaning up and even took a towel and dried dishes on occasion. When Fanny had mentioned that to Mimi, she'd been appalled. "A man's place is not in the kitchen," she'd insisted. "Don't tell that to Escoffier," Fanny had answered. But there was no reason for him to follow her now.

He leaned against the counter with his hands in his pockets again, a man at ease in her kitchen.

"Who's Charlie Berlin? Or Mr. Berlin, as Chloe says you make her call him, though he told her Charlie was fine with him."

She'd been careful never to mention Charlie when she talked about the office. And he hadn't been important in Chloe's life until recently. She began to run the water. She'd wash the glasses now.

"I take it you and Chloe had a talk on the way to Karen's apartment." She put one clean glass on the drainboard.

"We were discussing the new television. I remarked that her aunt Rose was a very generous woman, and one thing led to another until it came out that Rose didn't give you the television, someone called Charlie Berlin did. So naturally, I'm curious to know who Charlie Berlin is. And why you told me Rose had given you the set."

"I didn't tell you Rose had given us the set. You assumed."

"You're right, I assumed, but you didn't set me straight, so naturally I'm curious who Charlie Berlin is."

She turned off the faucet and swiveled to him. His expression was perfectly controlled. Clearly this was a man who was going to be reasonable.

"Maybe we should go into the living room and sit down to discuss this," she said.

"I'm fine here."

They were face-to-face without much space between them. The proximity made her lean her upper body back, but he was still feigning ease.

"He's a scriptwriter on the programs," she said finally.

"Who gave you a television set for Christmas."

"It's show business, even if it's the lowest rung. He's really a playwright." She wished she hadn't said that. Keep Charlie out of it. Keep it generic. "You know show business."

"I don't, but you seem to."

"People are extravagant. They make grand gestures."

"How grand? Did this Charlie Berlin give all the secretaries televisions?"

"I'm the only secretary on Alice's shows."

"So you're the only secretary he gave a television?"

"I told you, there aren't any others, and he wanted to show his appreciation."

"For what?"

"Helping him."

"Helping him do what?"

She'd been cantilevered back, but now she pulled herself up and away from the counter. "Not anything close to what you're implying."

"I'm not implying anything. I'm just asking you how you helped him."

The answer was spooling through her mind. Charlie's blacklisting, his friend's suicide, Ava's stag movie. A man who branded idealism as naïveté would never understand.

"Typing scripts after hours when he's late, which he is all the time. Covering for him then."

"Does he pay you for that?"

"That's why he gave us the television. It was for Chloe too."

"So he's grateful to the entire family."

"He's met Chloe when he's come here to drop off scripts. I've taken her to the office on occasion." Her mind was racing through the unlikely possibilities. "And once I saved a script for him."

"You mean he threw it out by mistake, you found it in a wastebasket, and he gave you a television in thanks? That's an extravagant gesture, all right."

"There was a really bad scene, and I spotted it." She remembered something Alice had told her when she first met Charlie. He's the only writer I know who can write when he's drunk as well as sober. "He must have been drunk when he wrote it."

"Is he a drunk?"

"I don't know if he's a drunk. I keep telling you, I don't know him that well."

He was silent for a moment, and she could see again that he was determined to be reasonable. "Look, Fanny, I'm not suggesting you did anything wrong."

"Thank you for the vote of confidence."

"But you don't know men."

"Possibly."

"This Charlie Berlin is working up to something."

"Which evidently I'm incapable of handling."

"I'm not saying that. I'm just warning you to nip it in the bud."

Maybe it was the cliché that did it. She turned away from him and walked out of the kitchen. He followed her into the living room. Now they were standing a few feet apart.

"All right. Maybe he is just grateful. I don't believe it, but I'll give you the benefit of the doubt."

"Give him the benefit of the doubt."

He ignored that. "And maybe it is a flamboyant business. But you have to admit it looks pretty compromising to the rest of the world that isn't in the business."

"What does it matter what the rest of the world thinks? Unless you want to think those things along with them."

"We don't live in a vacuum. It matters what my colleagues and friends and patients think."

"Your patients are children. They'd like nothing better than being given a television set out of the blue."

"Be serious, Fanny. How does it look that my wife is taking television sets from another man?"

"Television set, singular. And I'm not your wife yet. If this is how little you trust me—"

"I said I didn't think you'd done anything wrong."

". . . maybe I shouldn't be."

He stood staring at her for a moment. "I had a feeling we'd get to this point."

"I didn't do it alone."

She asked him if he wanted the ring back, and he told her not to be silly. They went on that way for a while, swinging and jabbing, feinting and pummeling, coming close and backing off, like a couple of punch-drunk prizefighters who want to call off the match but have no referee to step in and do it for them. Finally, one of them—she couldn't remember who—said perhaps dinner wasn't a good idea, and the other agreed.

He went to the closet, and she followed him and stood waiting while he put on his hat and coat. Neither of them looked at the other. He opened the front door and hesitated for a moment with his hand on the knob.

"I'll call you tomorrow," he said, but he still wasn't looking at her. Then he was gone.

This time she didn't watch him go down the stairs.

❦

She woke with a start, anger coalescing as she gained consciousness. It took her longer to figure out what she was angry about. He should have stood up for her. What kind of a husband lets his friend insult his wife? Then it came to her. She had the wrong argument. She was fuming at the wrong man. Her troubled sleep had taken her back in time.

She sat up in bed and turned on the night-table lamp. The

small room fell into place. The mirror over the dresser threw back an image of a woman with a sleep-smudged face and tangled hair alone in a narrow bed. She was in the apartment where she and Chloe lived alone, where no Max existed. But for a moment, as she'd struggled up to consciousness, she'd been back in that other life. Odd how even the unhappy moments could make you ache with longing.

She and Max had argued rarely. When they did, it tended to be about something minor. She had a feeling that was true of most couples. They threatened immediate divorce and undying enmity over wet towels thrown on a bed, too many after-work drinks with the boys, or impulsive bank-breaking purchases. But the punier the cause, the greater the passion. Shame at your own pettiness can have that effect. Her worst argument with Max, however, hadn't been about something either of them had done. It had been triggered by something he hadn't done.

They'd had one of Max's doctor buddies from the war and his wife for dinner, and the conversation had turned to the Truman Doctrine or the Marshall Plan or something to do with foreign policy. She couldn't even remember the topic now. She'd said something—she couldn't remember what, either—and the friend had told her she didn't know what she was talking about and shouldn't try to discuss things she was incapable of understanding. Max had sat at the table concentrating on his wineglass as if it were tea and he was trying to read the leaves.

"How could you let him get away with that?" she demanded as soon as he closed the door behind them.

"Get away with what?"

"Calling me stupid."

"He didn't call you stupid."

"He said I didn't know what I was talking about and shouldn't try to discuss things I was incapable of understanding. That's a longwinded definition of stupid."

"You're right, I should have taken a poke at him." He began carrying the cake-and-icing-smudged plates into the kitchen.

"It's not funny." She followed him, but her hands were empty. She was too angry for domestic chores.

"Of course it's funny. You know more about the subject than he does."

"All the more reason to stand up for me." She followed him back to the dining room. This time she began clearing the table.

"Standing up to fools is a fool's errand."

"Oh, good, let's have some aphorisms."

He let that one go.

"Besides, I thought the fool was your friend," she insisted.

"Let's just say there's a bond. Sixteen-hour bouts of surgery side by side in a field hospital tend to forge that sort of thing."

"So your allegiance to him is greater than your allegiance to me."

He stopped with several glasses in his hands and turned to face her. "Don't be s—"

"Stupid?" she cut him off.

"I was going to say 'silly.' You're my wife. He's just someone I served with. And didn't want to fight with. Any more than I want to fight with you now. It wouldn't have been worth it."

"I'm not worth it?"

"If he took a swing at you, I would have stepped in. Hell, if he made a pass at you, I would have stepped in."

"That's because a pass at me is an encroachment on you, or at least your prerogatives."

"But I didn't think a difference of opinion about foreign policy," he went on as if she hadn't spoken, "warranted calling out an old buddy."

"It's not the difference of opinion that bothers me. It's your sitting there staring into your wineglass, pretending to be somewhere else, while he insulted me."

"You're right. I did want to be somewhere else. Just as I do now."

"Don't let me keep you."

"Fine." He started out of the kitchen. "I'll see you upstairs."

He wouldn't see her upstairs. She was too angry. She spread a quilt on the floor of the unfurnished bedroom and had a tortured night plotting life without him. He'd had one too, she was delighted to discover in the morning.

They'd made up, of course, but she was still wounded enough a few days later to mention the incident to Rose.

"You do see the irony, don't you?" Rose asked.

"What irony?"

"You were angry the friend belittled you. Then you turned on Max for thinking you could take care of yourself."

"Sometimes you make me so mad."

"Only when I'm right."

Remembering the quarrel now, she knew her argument with Ezra couldn't hold a candle to it. This disagreement had been more substantial, but her reaction to that incident with Max had been more painful. Perhaps the deeper feeling for Max had made for deeper disappointment. She'd expected more from him. But she'd known what Ezra's response would be. That was what gave her pause about him.

❦

He'd said as he'd left the apartment that he'd telephone tomorrow, but the phone was silent except for a call from Mimi and another from Max's parents, who wanted to take Chloe to see *The Nutcracker,* the Christmas show at Radio City Music Hall, and the holiday windows at Lord & Taylor.

"Leave some treats for the rest of us," she managed to joke, then made plans with them for the various outings.

After that she spent the rest of the day vacillating between ambivalence that it was over and anger that his not calling was a ploy to punish her. She couldn't call him. This was one area where the rules of her adolescence still held sway. Or perhaps only her pride did.

Chloe asked where Ezra was. She'd grown accustomed to his being around on Sundays. Fortunately, he hadn't promised her a particular outing for this Sunday. Fanny told her he had to work.

Chloe had already gone to bed when the phone rang.

"How was your day?" he asked.

"Not a lot of fun."

"I know what you mean. I guess we both got a little hot under the collar."

She made a noncommittal sound.

"But you have to admit it looks pretty peculiar."

"Let's not start that again."

"You're right. Let's forget the whole thing. Let bygones be bygones. Couples fight. You ought to know that. You were married."

Funny that after rarely referring to her marriage or Max, he chose to do so now. But she decided to ignore the comment. The last thing she wanted was a repeat performance of the previous evening.

❦

The first week in January, the show Ava had been cast in, then blacklisted from, folded after five performances.

"I suppose there's a kind of justice in that," Fanny said when Ava called to tell her. Fanny had seen the announcement in the paper but hadn't mentioned it to Ava because she didn't want to open old wounds. She should have known they'd never healed.

"Except that the actress who stepped into my part got good reviews. Now she has press clippings, and I spend my days walking around Saks selling the dress off my back."

That same week, Alice hired a new secretary. Fanny trained her to get Alice's black coffee in the morning and tea with lemon in the afternoon, to recognize on the phone the voices of the sponsors and network executives who were to be put through immediately and others who were to be put off indefinitely, and whom to call to get tickets for the theater and ballet and tables at swanky restaurants and nightclubs. She was a better and faster typist than Fanny, especially when she was racing to get to the end of a storyline or script to find out what was going to happen. The girl was a fervent fan of all three of Alice's serials.

Fanny didn't tell Ezra she was no longer working for Alice, because she was. The job was simply different. But one Saturday night in January she mentioned that she was writing a script. They were back in the French restaurant where these days the husband-and-wife owners, who'd broken out a bottle of Dom Perignon when they'd heard about the coming marriage, treated her almost as warmly as they did him.

"Why?"

"Because it pays better. And it's more challenging."

"Well, you won't have to worry about either of those things after this summer." They'd decided on a summer wedding, but hadn't yet set a date. "I'll bring home the bacon, and Chloe and I will provide all the challenge you need. Not to mention other small people running around the apartment, or should I say house, in due time."

"But until then," she went on, though she knew she should let it go—the summer was months away, other children even more distant—"Chloe's in school all day and you're in your office. I'll have plenty of time on my hands. Other wives shop or play mahjong or take French cooking classes. I prefer to write scripts."

"French cooking classes. Now there's an idea. I can already smell the simmering cassoulet and rising soufflé as I walk in the door."

"The aromas you smell are coming from the kitchen here, and I promise you my soufflé would be flat as a pancake."

"I beg to differ. You're an excellent cook."

"I'm not a bad scriptwriter either."

"Maybe, but you seem to forget my part in all this. What would I tell people?"

"That your wife writes good scripts. You could brag about that as easily as a soufflé, if I ever did manage to get one to rise."

"I'd brag if we had friends for dinner and you served a soufflé. I wouldn't be crowing if you were turning out soufflés in a restaurant kitchen. I'd be too ashamed that my wife had to work."

"Not had to, wanted to."

"Fine. I'll send out an announcement. The way I did when I opened my office. Dr. Ezra Rapaport would like to inform you it's not that he can't support his wife, only that she likes to make it look that way."

She started to say she didn't care what people thought and he shouldn't either, but they'd been through that before, and she didn't want a replay.

"Can't you see, Fanny? It's one thing if a woman has to work, the way you did when you were alone with Chloe. People feel sorry for her. But if she's married and has to work, they feel sorry for him. Correction, they laugh at him. Snicker behind his back. What kind of a man can't support his wife?"

She thought of Max's mother, who'd told her a few weeks earlier that she was going to retire next year. She'd gone back to teaching high school math as soon as Max had started school, and he and his father had always been proud of her. According to Max, if she'd been a man, she would have been a first-rate mathematician. Or, to put it another way, which he never had but Fanny realized now, she was a first-rate mathematician who'd never held a job commensurate with her talents. But she didn't think Ezra would find the example of Max's mother persuasive.

There was a moment's silence. Then they each started to speak at the same time.

"You'll change your mind once we're married," he said.

"You'll change your mind once we're married," she told him.

They sat looking at each other. Then they laughed. Neither of them wanted another row, and there wouldn't be one. He was sure she was just suffering from premarital jitters. She knew he was too reasonable a man not to see reason with time.

❧

She hadn't planned to mention the discussion—it wasn't an argument—to Susannah at lunch the following week, but when she heard Susannah's news, she couldn't help herself. She and Jeffrey were moving to Alabama for a year.

"That's exciting for you, but what's Jeffrey going to do in Alabama?"

"That's the best part. He decided he was getting tired of my moral superiority. I was saving the world—my husband is prone to hyperbole—while he was drawing up contracts to enable people to make or keep more money. So he quit the firm and signed on with the group of lawyers who are running the project. We'll be poor as church mice."

"Only you could make that prospect sound like a lark."

"It'll just be for a year. When we come back, we'll have credentials that will be unusual, to say the least."

"I'm green with envy."

"That we're going to be poor as church mice in Alabama?"

Fanny was silent for a moment. It wouldn't be betraying Ezra, merely a discussion of an issue that Susannah had some experience with.

"Ezra doesn't want me to work." She hesitated again. "We had, not an argument exactly, but words about it last Saturday night."

"Tell him not to worry. His shirts will still find their way back and forth to the laundry, and dinner will still be on the table every night. If he doesn't believe you, tell him to call Jeff."

"That's not the problem. I admit he's having fantasies about soufflés, but it's more than that. He says he'd be ashamed."

"I only met him a handful of times, but he didn't strike me as an intellectual snob."

Fanny laughed. "Now who's the intellectual snob? He wouldn't be ashamed I was writing for the soaps. He'd be ashamed I was working at all. He says people will think he can't support me."

"Tell him to call Jeff about that, too. A couple of months of coming home to a stir-crazy wife will change his mind. I was hell on wheels until I went back to work."

Chapter Twenty-five

SHE NO LONGER WENT TO THE OFFICE. SHE WROTE THE scripts at home. The problem was where to collaborate on them. She didn't want Charlie in her apartment all day. She especially didn't want him there when Chloe came home from school, though her daughter got along with him as well as she did with Ezra. Charlie's apartment was out of the question. A widow, the mother of a young girl, didn't spend her days hanging around a man's apartment, even if her scruples about it made her feel like Mimi. Charlie came up with the solution.

"Do you know the New York Society Library?" he asked.

"Society Library? I doubt they'd let me in. I know they wouldn't let you in."

"I'm already a member."

"How did you manage that?"

"Filled out a form and paid my annual dues. It's a subscription library. No pedigree required. Eighteen bucks gets you a year's membership. It's mainly a circulating library, but there are places to write as well. Desks in the open stacks. A couple of small private rooms. Don't worry, they all have judas windows in the doors. Kind of like a psychiatric asylum or prison for writers. The point is, we could hand scenes back and forth as we wrote them. We could even try out ideas—forgive me for using the word in this context—on each other. The scripts would go faster. I'll take you for a tour and introduce you to the librarians. Needless to say they're all crazy about me."

The library was an unlikely place for Charlie Berlin, at least for the Charlie Berlin she knew. Inside the gray-stone Regency building rising five stories above the busy street, he led her up a short flight of marble steps into a lobby with a long dark oak desk. Through a set of carved double doors, a paneled room housed a wall of wooden card catalogs. Even Charlie lowered his voice on the premises. On the second floor, a large drawing room with a fireplace at one end and three tall French windows opening onto East Seventy-Ninth Street invited readers to curl up with a book or magazine. An old-fashioned open-cage lift took them up through twelve levels of book stacks and out through a hall to the private workrooms. They returned to the lobby in another small elevator. This one was wood paneled with a velvet cushioned seat.

"I had one of the more memorable experiences of my adult life in this elevator," he said as they descended.

"I'm afraid to ask what it was."

"You have a salacious mind, Fanny. The experience was literary. I was coming down in it with a woman of a certain age whom I'd seen around the place occasionally. I remembered her because she had the most remarkable blue eyes. The color of a prairie sky, or the color I imagine a prairie sky to be, since I've never been west of the Mississippi. Hell, I've never been *to* the Mississippi. I was carrying a stack of books, and she wanted to know what I was reading. I told her I'd just finished a terrific novel called *Sapphira and the Slave Girl* and asked if she'd heard of it. 'I wrote it,' she said."

Fanny filled out the application and became a member on the spot. They began working there most weekdays. She left her apartment in the morning shortly after Chloe set off for school and usually arrived at the library before Charlie. In her imagination she saw him sleeping off the night before. Sometimes she saw a woman in the rumpled bed beside him.

She was usually early enough to get one of the private rooms with a big desk and a window overlooking the roofs of the neighboring buildings, but when those were taken, she found a smaller writing table in the stacks. She loved the dry, faintly acrid smell of paper and print and the fortress-like safety of nesting among all those volumes. Sometimes a gilt-lettered spine or colorful jacket seduced her, and she took the book down from the shelf and spent half an hour wandering among old master paintings or corresponding with Abigail Adams or hobnobbing fictionally with the mighty or the destitute. Though she felt a twinge of guilt when she did, it didn't stop her, but after she lost the better part of an afternoon to *Phineas Finn,* she was careful not to take a desk near the Trollope shelves.

Charlie usually arrived an hour or two later, but occasionally he didn't get there until lunchtime. Now and then she made a crack about his tardiness, but she didn't really mind. He was a faster and more facile writer than she was.

They worked separately, but exchanged pages and compared notes frequently. She'd carry her sheets of paper from one small room to another; he'd ferry his up or down through the stacks. They spoke in whispers. It was, after all, a library. The murmured exchanges gave them a sense of intimacy. So did the work. They pretended not to take it seriously, but they couldn't help themselves. He was a pro and she was becoming one. If you took on a job, you did the best you could. Occasionally he accused her of being lazy.

"I get here before you do," she said the first time he criticized her.

"I'm not talking about how long you work. I'm talking about settling for the word or phrase or solution that comes easily even if you know you can do better."

When she turned the same accusation on him, he said he rued the day he'd begun encouraging her.

Occasionally one of them turned up where the other was working to find the desk empty.

"This is silly," he said one day when she came back from lunch to find him sitting at the desk she'd taken that morning. She'd left her things when she'd gone out. "Admit it, you time yourself so we don't run into each other at the local greasy spoon or the Longchamps down the block."

She didn't answer, because it was true.

"From now on, we break for lunch together," he went on. "Nothing personal. It's just that we'll get more done before you have to beat it home in time for Chloe. Or Ezra."

"I thought we weren't going to talk about him."

"That was a slip. And Dutch treat. Television sets are one thing, but I refuse to start springing for your daily chicken sandwich, and especially not for shrimp or crab salad at Longchamps."

He didn't mention Ezra again, but the reference made her realize he'd never remarked on the small diamond solitaire on the third finger of her left hand that had replaced the gold band.

They began going out for lunch together, usually to what he called the local greasy spoon, but occasionally, when work was going well or they had more time, to Longchamps at Seventy-Eighth and Madison, where the red, black, and gold art deco spectacle was intended to dazzle the middle-class eye while the prices and no-tipping policy took into consideration the middle-class pocketbook. On those days he had a drink, and as he lingered over it, he plied her with lore.

"This was the original restaurant in the chain," he told her the first time they went there together. "Lustig, the owner who'd started out selling produce, was staked to it by his brother-in-law, Arnold Rothstein. You know, the guy who may or may not have fixed the 1919 World Series and was the inspiration for Meyer Wolfsheim in *The Great Gatsby*. Not that Lustig's hands were particularly clean. He kept two sets of books, siphoned off millions, and ended up in the federal slammer. But I have a soft spot for him. Before the IRS caught up with him, he owned two racehorses. Ergo, Longchamps after the Paris racetrack."

Despite Charlie's foray into local history, the talk was usually about work, though sometimes the conversation strayed to Chloe or Rose, books or politics, the theater or television. He said he could feel the last nipping at his heels. It was a new world, even worse for actors than writers. The situation was the reverse of what had happened when talkies had arrived in the movies. Then the actors who'd looked great but had squeaky voices or thick accents or couldn't get through a sentence without a verbal stumble were out of work. Now actors with the great voices needed faces and bodies to match, and had to be photogenic in the bargain or they were finished. Another reason it was a shame about Ava. "The camera would have loved her," he said.

"Television shouldn't frighten you," she insisted. "You've written real plays. You've even had one produced."

"That was in a theater with actors treading the boards and live humans sitting in the audience, coughing when you don't want them to and not laughing when you do. This is another beast entirely. When you write a television drama, you're not thinking about character and motivation, you're worrying about staging action that the camera can track. You get only a few days of rehearsal, and that's more for the crew so they can work out the shots and angles from the different cameras. Want a costume change? Fit it into a commercial break. And speaking of commercials, how do you write a realistic play, a little slice of life, which is what they say they want, when you're selling a pill or a soap or a tire that's going to improve your life overnight? I'm used to that on the soaps, but I'm talking about a real play. Even if you manage to pull off all that, it still won't come out right, because the picture and the sound are so unreliable. And if you blow it, which you're likely to under those circumstances, you can't reshoot the way they do in the movies or hope you'll get it right the next night in the theater. Live drama on television may be fun for the great unwashed American public, but it's hell on earth for a playwright."

She sat grinning at him. "I take it from that diatribe that you've been thinking about writing a drama for television."

"Hell on earth," he repeated, "but better than soaps."

A few days later she brought up the subject again. They were in their usual booth at the back of the coffee shop where the manager always seated them, because, Charlie insisted, it was the most private table in the place.

"You mean he knows we're working?" she asked.

"He thinks we're having an affair."

She was sliding onto the leatherette seat and stopped half-way in. "How did he get that idea?"

"I told him." He read her expression. "That was a joke, Fanny."

She asked how the television drama was going.

"I'm not writing it."

"Yet," she finished for him.

He shrugged. "A producer I know who works for one of the programs said he'll look at anything I have—providing I submit it through a front. They're desperate for material."

"It's nice to be needed."

"The money's a lot better."

"That's nice too. When do we start work?" Now she was the one who read his expression. "You mean *we* don't. I'm just a front again."

"I've never collaborated on a play."

"There's a first time for everything."

"This isn't a soap, Fanny. It's the real thing, or close to it. Close enough that after some of these things run on television, they go to Broadway or the movies."

"In other words, out of my league."

"It's not that. It's just that, as I said, I've never collaborated on something serious."

They made their way back to the library in silence. She stopped under the awning and turned to him. The wind coming off the park a block away stung her cheeks and burrowed down the collar of her coat. She pulled her scarf tighter.

"Aren't you afraid that if you don't let me collaborate on the script, I won't front for it?"

"No."

"Because I need the money?"

"Because I know you."

"You mean I'm easily exploitable?"

"For Christ's sake, Fanny, I've been at this for years. I've written half a dozen plays."

"And had one produced."

"That was below the belt."

"Kind of like telling me I'm a no-talent soap hack."

That afternoon neither of them carried pages to the other. She didn't know about him, but she didn't even manage to write any. He was as bad as Ezra. Worse. Ezra didn't want her to work because of some misguided principle. Charlie thought she didn't have what it took.

❦

"I know it's a lot to ask," Ezra said, "but I have a full schedule, and I'd hate to have to cancel patients."

"It's not that it's a lot to ask, only that I'd feel awkward. I didn't know the woman. I don't know her family. I'm a stranger. Worse than that, an interloper. I'd be intruding into a private ordeal."

"Private? There'll be dozens of people at the funeral. Maybe hundreds. Her husband is an important man. And I knew her. At least met her. You're my fiancée, soon to be my wife. You'll be representing me. I'd go if I could, but like I said, I'd hate to cancel appointments. On the other hand, the soaps won't go off the air if you take a few hours away from the office."

The mention of the office where he still thought she went every morning did it. She agreed to go to the funeral of the late wife of an older physician who'd taken him under his wing. She'd go as his fiancée, his soon-to-be wife, his representative, his appendage.

She'd agreed to attend the memorial service, but she had no intention of going to the cemetery. She hadn't, however, counted on the funeral director and his minions. One of them ambushed her as she came out of the chapel and began steering her toward the line of limousines waiting on Amsterdam Avenue. She told the man, who wore a black suit and a face of professional mourning, that she'd come only for the service, but he was having none of it. He strong-armed her onto the jump seat in one of the waiting cars and closed the door with the finality of a man accustomed to closing coffins.

She twisted around to see four gray-haired women crushed together on the back seat and another beside her on the other jump seat. Three were wearing mink coats, one was in Persian lamb, and the woman on the other jump seat was in cloth. Perhaps the seating arrangement indicated the pecking order. Their hats were black, and, she knew thanks to Rose, pricey.

The woman in Persian lamb asked how she knew the deceased, but before she could explain that she hadn't known her but was there to represent Dr. Rapaport, whom the deceased's husband had trained, one of the minks said she must be Ethel's niece.

"Ethel talked about you all the time," the woman said. "I'm sure you'll miss her."

"She's not Ethel's niece," another mink said. "I've seen pictures of Ethel's niece. Ethel's niece has dark hair. As close to black as natural hair gets. Unless you're Chinese."

The woman in the cloth coat observed that women were known to change their hair color.

"I know a natural redhead, or at least an auburn, when I see one," the mink said with a look of satisfaction in Fanny's hair and her own acute eye.

"I have to find a new hairdresser," the Persian lamb complained. "Mr. Anthony's been putting too much blue in my rinse."

A discussion of blue rinses in general and the Persian lamb's in particular got them almost to the cemetery. Only when the driver had helped them out of the car and they stood at the entrance to the graveyard did the question of her identity come up again.

"If you're not Ethel's niece," one of the minks asked, "who are you?"

The question was not quite an accusation, but it came close. She said she was a friend of the family.

As she made her way through the gate, she was thinking that the ride out had been ludicrous, but at least she could dine out on it. Rose would enjoy the story. Ezra would see the humor, especially after she told him she had signed his name in the guest book in the chapel. The burial would be over in thirty minutes, she'd be back in town in an hour, and she'd have committed a kindness, to Ezra if not the deceased Ethel.

She started to follow the mourners toward the graveside, then stopped. She hadn't been to a cemetery since that awful afternoon three days after the blizzard. Since they'd buried Max. Since she'd refused to bury him and walked away from the open grave. She stood immobilized now in the cold afternoon. The trees were bare again, but no snow softened the landscape. In the glare of an unforgiving winter sun, marble and stone monuments sprouted from the brown earth like cautionary tales. Her gaze ricocheted from slab to slab. Beloved husband of. Devoted wife of. All those tributes chiseled into stone. All that love and regret and rage, as many sentiments as there were headstones howled silently into the cold afternoon.

Behind her the line of limousines stood empty, their drivers leaning against hoods in groups of two or three, hiding their cigarettes in cupped hands to shroud their disrespect. Ahead of her, the mourners were mustering around the open grave. She tried to walk toward it, but her legs wouldn't move. Her mouth was dry as parchment. Her stomach churned. The nausea mounted. She put her hand over her mouth. To hold in what? The vomit? The venom? The scream? She turned and started back to the line of cars. The driver of the one she'd come in took a last puff of his cigarette, stamped it out in the road, and came around to her.

"Not feeling well?" he asked.

She nodded.

"Funerals have that effect on some people." He held open the door for her.

She climbed into the back seat and sat waiting for it to be over. It wasn't Ezra's fault, not really. He had no experience of the intimacy of such rites. She remembered how she'd hated the intruders who'd come to pay their respects, as Ezra put it, at Max's funeral. Death, like love, like sex, was private. It couldn't be shared.

Chapter Twenty-six

SHE DIDN'T GO TO THE LIBRARY THE NEXT DAY OR THE day after that. She could work perfectly well at home. Though it had been convenient to swap ideas and hand scenes back and forth, the proximity wasn't necessary. She'd have to see Charlie before the week was out and get his scenes to turn the scripts in to Alice, but she wasn't ready quite yet.

The evening of the second day she didn't turn up at the library, he called and asked if she was all right.

"I had to go to a funeral."

"I'm sorry. Someone close?"

"Not close," she said.

"Forgive the indelicacy, but was it a two-day funeral?"

"I've been busy."

"I think angry is the word you're looking for."

She didn't say anything to that.

"I'm glad."

"You're glad I'm angry at you?"

"I take it as a compliment. You once told me that if you really care about somebody, you don't bicker. It's too petty. You go for the jugular, or something to that effect."

"I was talking about love."

"Exactly. Come to the library tomorrow, Fanny. Let's get back to work."

She agreed to go to the library the following day. "How's the television drama coming?" she asked before they hung up.

"Lousy."

"Good."

"You're all heart, sweetheart."

❦

The next morning Fanny was putting on the new camel's hair polo coat she'd indulged in to leave for the library when Ava called to say she'd just gotten a telegram from London.

"Saying?" Fanny asked.

"There's no blacklist in London."

"You get telegrams telling you that?"

"I get telegrams telling me I got a part in a play called *Bet Your Life*."

"That's wonderful. Were they casting over here?"

"They didn't come over here to cast, but the director was someone Charlie knew from the war. When he was in Washington making films for the army. The director was in New York a few weeks ago. Charlie had a drink with him and told him about me. I read for him, he was impressed, and I'm on my way to London."

"I think it's time to break out the champagne that's been cooling in my fridge since last fall."

"I'd love to, but I have too much to do. I leave in two days."

"I'll come down to the ship to see you off."

"Ships are for the hoi polloi. They're flying me over. Pan

Am's Stratocruiser. I'm terrified, but I'll risk it for this part. Hell, at this point I'd risk it for any part. Charlie's an angel, a saint in my own personal pantheon."

"If you say so."

"You never did like him."

"For Pete's sake, Ava, I like Charlie. I like him a lot. And I'm not immune to his attractions. He gives off a lot of heat. But unlike you and my aunt, I can't afford Charlie. I'm a widow trying to raise a daughter in a conventional world that feeds on other people's scandals, which Charlie is always more than ready to provide."

There was a moment's silence. "I should have realized," Ava said. "I'm sorry."

"No more than I am," she answered. "That was a joke," she added quickly.

❧

Several days later, she looked up from a desk in the stacks to see Charlie making his way toward her through the shelves of books.

"Why are you limping?" she whispered when he reached her.

"That's my impression of a man walking with his tail between his legs."

"Because?"

"How'd you like to collaborate on a television drama?"

"I thought you never collaborated on plays."

"There's always a first time, as you pointed out. And it seems I've forgotten how to write alone." He pulled over one of the ladders on rollers scattered throughout the stacks to reach the top shelves and perched on it. "You want to know the truth?"

"It'll be a change."

"Actually, this is more in the line of confession. I've always had a hard time writing female characters. Lots of male writers do, but they won't admit it." He was still whispering, and now he dropped his voice even more. "I need you, Fanny."

"What did you say? I didn't hear you."

He stood. "Don't push your luck," he said, but before he went off to find a place to work, he bent over her desk and put his mouth beside her ear. "And they said it wouldn't last."

❧

He turned up at her desk at lunchtime. "If we're going to work together on this thing, we better start having lunch again."

"Do you want to tell me what it's about?" she asked when they were in their usual booth in the back of the greasy spoon.

"Isolation. Disillusion. Connection."

"That's right. Don't let the cat out of the bag with your collaborator."

"Guy comes home from the war. Was a poor kid before it. Grease monkey. Or drove a hack. You get the idea. In the war he's a flyboy."

"And he's disillusioned when he comes home to discover he's not a flyboy anymore, just the same old working stiff."

"If I'd known you were going to go for the clichés, I wouldn't have asked you to collaborate on this thing. He comes home to a new life. More than he ever dreamed of. Goes to college on the GI Bill. Nobody in his family ever finished high school. Gets a good job where he sits behind a desk in a white shirt and no grease under his fingernails. He's a success. He's also a fish out of water. We see that in a twenty-four-hour slice of his life. In the office his colleagues condescend to him. When he pays a visit to his family that night, his father and brothers think he's too big for his britches. His mother and sister resent the gifts he brings. They think he's showing off. By the time he returns home, his wife is asleep and he's despondent."

"How despondent? Suicidal?"

"I'm not sure. He'll let me know when he's more fleshed out."

"What saves him? My only experience is in soaps, but even I know you can't end one of these television plays with a suicide or even total despondency. Wait, I know, the love of a good woman."

"Bingo! But not in the way you think. She doesn't rescue him from his situation. She just makes him realize he's not isolated. He's connected to another human being."

"I see you've been studying your E. M. Forster."

"I only steal from the best."

"I like it. But don't ever call yourself a cynic again."

"This is a play, sweetheart, not my life."

❦

She and Ezra came out of the movie theater into the February night. Above them, the marquee, still lit up, advertised *People Will Talk*.

"Taxi or walk?" Ezra asked.

"Walk. We need fresh air after all that time in the restaurant and then the theater."

"Even in this weather?"

"I don't mind the cold. As long as it doesn't begin to snow."

"What do you have against snow? Most people think it's the only justification for putting up with the cold."

"Too slippery. And I'm not most people."

"You can say that again." He took her arm and folded it against him as they began to walk. "What I want to know is how Hollywood comes up with these plots. A medical student is about to begin carving up his cadaver, looks down, and realizes the body's still alive."

"Actually, it's based on a German play called *Doctor Praetorius*."

"That explains it. The Krauts."

"I don't know if it was in the original play, but the scene where Cary Grant refuses to name names to clear himself has to be a reference to the HUAC witch hunts."

"If you say so."

"The screenplay was good. One of the reviews called it sharp as a scalpel."

"Scalpels are my specialty, but I leave screenplays to you."

They'd reached a corner and stood waiting for the light to change. She'd made up her mind to tell him half a dozen times. Not about collaborating with Charlie. Certainly not about fronting for him. About the fact that she was no longer a secretary who went to the office every morning but a scriptwriter who went to a library across town to write.

"I'm glad you think I know about screenplays." She waited for him to say something, but the light changed and he started across the street. He was still holding her arm tightly, and there was nothing she could do but keep in step. "Because I'm writing them. Full time. I'm not Alice's secretary anymore. I'm a scriptwriter."

He was still walking. "You never mentioned it."

"Actually, I did mention it. At least I mentioned the part about the scripts. I said they paid better and were more of a challenge. And you said after next summer I won't have to worry about money, and you and Chloe will be all the challenge I need."

They'd stopped for another light, and he turned to her. His face was open and trusting and so damn happy. "And I still say it. The way you are with Chloe is one of the first things about you I fell in love with."

He started walking again, and again she fell in step. At least she'd told him.

❧

Alice had her working on all three shows now, as she'd once had Charlie doing. They were up to eight scripts a week. They could handle it. Charlie wrote fast. She was learning to. The problem was that it didn't leave much time for the television drama.

"We're under the gun, Fanny. The guy wants to see something in a couple of weeks. Half the writers I know and all the blacklisted writers who have fronts are trying to get a foot in the door. I don't want him to lose interest."

They began working in her apartment on Saturday afternoons. The arrangement made more sense than wasting the few hours Chloe was in ballet class going back and forth to the library. She no longer worried about Chloe's coming home to find Charlie there and papers spread all over the living room. Her daughter and her collaborator had forged a bond of their own. Sometimes Charlie asked her what she'd been up to in class that day, and she'd demonstrate steps. Sometimes he asked her what she thought of a sentence or a word. Fanny got a kick out of listening to her daughter discussing the work in progress.

Charlie was scrupulous about not leaving traces of himself. Once or twice he'd even carried the ashtrays full of his Camel butts into the kitchen to dump in the trash. He'd never said anything, but she had a feeling he'd noticed when she'd missed an ashtray of Ezra's Pall Malls from the night before.

The work was paying off. Not only were they getting the soaps in on time, but in another week or two the television script would be ready to show.

At the moment they were struggling with a scene halfway through. She was sitting at her desk at the typewriter, he was stretched out on the sofa. When they'd started working that way, she'd asked how he'd managed to get his scripts typed before.

"Hunt and peck. A paid typist. The occasional girl who was crazy about me."

"Woman's eternal problem."

"Being crazy about me?"

"Competence leading to exploitation."

"The scene doesn't work," she said now. "It telegraphs too much. The viewer will see the ending coming a mile away."

"And if we don't have any foreshadowing, the ending comes out of the blue."

"I'm not saying we don't need any forewarning, but does it have to be so heavy-handed?"

He sat up, ground out his cigarette in the ashtray on the coffee table, crossed the room, and bent over her to look at the page in the typewriter. As he did, she could feel his face against her hair. She told herself to lean away from him. She remained where she was. He went on reading the page. Or did he? He had to be as aware of their closeness as she was.

"Fine," he said finally. "Take out the line about the childhood memory. I never liked it anyway."

"You never liked it? You were the one who wrote it."

She turned her head. Now her cheek brushed against his. That was when she realized. His skin was smooth. That was odd, because he had a heavy beard that often in the old days in the office had shown traces of five-o'clock shadow by this late in the afternoon. She leaned away from him. He took another moment before he turned and went back to the sofa.

❧

Nothing had happened. She had no reason to feel guilty. And she didn't. Something else was gnawing at her. She tried to quiet it, but the craving persisted. Conversation with Ezra over dinner didn't distract her. Food didn't fill the hunger. Wine, and she drank more of it than she usually did, only made it worse. They went to a movie after dinner. Marlon Brando was no help. If anything, he exacerbated the itch.

Later, close to midnight, she and Ezra were tangled on the sofa in her apartment, the same sofa that Charlie had risen from that afternoon to come and stand behind her chair. She wasn't thinking about the afternoon, at least not consciously. She wasn't thinking at all. She was acting on instinct when she did something she'd never done before. She reached down and put her hand on his trousers. She didn't unzip the fly. She just put her hand there.

His moan came from deep within and echoed back through months of longing. And she was glad, finally.

He took her hand from him and held the palm against

his mouth. "My god, Fanny," he murmured into it, "I'm only human."

But after that she wondered if he was.

❦

There was no recurrence of the incident. She was too ashamed. Or maybe anger was the operative emotion. Whichever it was, she was glad he was away the following weekend.

"Are you sure you don't mind?" he'd asked when he told her about the plan. He and a couple of his buddies from the army were going to a ski lodge, as they had every year since the end of the war. It wasn't anything as formal as a reunion, merely a few friends getting together and remembering.

"Why should I mind?"

"Are you kidding? Last year one of the guys had to buy his wife a gold bracelet before she'd let him go."

"The girl's a piker. I'd insist on diamonds or emeralds at the least," she said, and didn't add that the timing was perfect. If she and Charlie wrote through the weekend, they could have the script ready to show the following week.

Chapter Twenty-seven

CHLOE TOOK THE NEWS THAT CHARLIE RATHER THAN Ezra would be there that evening with equanimity. To think Fanny had ever worried that her daughter would be a one-man woman. She had only a single question.

"How come Mr. Berlin and Uncle Ezra are never here together?"

"Why are Mr. Berlin and Uncle Ezra never here together?" she corrected her daughter.

"Okay, why?"

"They don't know each other."

"They both know us."

"Are all your friends in the same place at the same time?"

"I guess not," she said, and headed for her room. The conversation wasn't interesting enough to pursue.

"I thought you were going to bring dinner," she said when she opened the door to find Charlie empty-handed and the hall definitely not redolent of anything mouthwatering or even edible.

"Be patient. All will be revealed in due course. In the meantime, you can offer me a drink."

"I thought we were working."

"You know what Alice says about me. I'm the only writer she knows who can write as well drunk as sober."

"I didn't know *you* knew what Alice said about you."

"Who do you think feeds her her lines? And incidentally, that's a nice sweater. New, right? Glad to see this collaboration has catapulted you from wool to cashmere."

Half an hour later, the downstairs buzzer rang again. She started to go to the intercom. He told her not to bother. "It's Sardi's."

"You're bringing dinner from Sardi's?"

"Actually, a waiter from Sardi's who's in hock to me is bringing dinner from Sardi's."

"You may have some redeeming traits after all."

"I've been waiting for months to hear you say that," he told her as she started toward Chloe's room to get her for dinner.

It was close to eleven when she pulled the last page of a scene out of the typewriter and said she didn't have another word in her.

"That makes two of us," he agreed. "But the least you can do is offer me another drink before you send me out into the cold."

She went into the kitchen, and when she came back, he was leaning over the window seat looking out at the checkerboard of lighted windows across the street.

"There's a couple dancing over there."

"They do that all the time."

"What are you, a voyeur?"

"Look who's talking."

"Doesn't that give you any ideas?"

It did. On the nights she saw them dancing, she ached with memory. The night of the blizzard, she and Max had foxtrotted and waltzed, rumbaed and jitterbugged through the wedding.

But like the negative of a photograph, memory is only a ghostly outline of the real thing.

"Not a single idea," she said, "except sleep."

He turned to the radio on one of the shelves beside the window seat and switched it on.

"You'll wake Chloe."

"She'd have to be a bat to hear it at this volume," he said as he waited for the set to warm up, then turned the volume even lower. He dialed slowly through the stations until he found dance music. The strains of "Isn't It Romantic" seeped into the room.

He turned and held out his arms. "Dance with me, Fanny."

She took a step back.

"I'm suggesting a dance, not a weekend tryst."

He closed the distance between them, put an arm around her waist, and started to move to the music. He was a good dancer. She'd known he would be from those impromptu steps he used to do in the office. She wasn't. She'd never thought much about the inadequacy. Now she felt suddenly awkward.

"I'm no good at this." She started to pull away.

"Do you hear anyone complaining?"

They'd been moving slowly, but now he twirled her out, and when he brought her back, he rested his cheek against hers.

She thought about that for a moment. Then she stopped thinking about it.

"See," he said after a while, "you're fine when you stop worrying."

She started to pull away again. She didn't like his knowing

her that well. He went on holding her. She gave up and fell in step with him again.

The music came to an end. The room went silent, except for the sound of Charlie's breathing, and her own. He didn't let go of her. No, that wasn't the entire story. They didn't let go of each other. Then a voice announced the orchestra was coming to them from the beautiful Crystal Ballroom of the world-famous Empire Hotel in New York City. She started to step back. He held on to her. The orchestra launched into their version of Benny Goodman's rendition of "Body and Soul," and there was nothing she could do but go on dancing, because it had been so long.

The song came to an end. She turned her head to tell him nicely, calmly, that this had been fine, but it was time for him to leave. That was all it took.

The surprise wasn't that he was kissing her. The unholy shock was that she was kissing him. She wanted to kiss him. She was dying to kiss him. She was upending her life and all her plans to kiss him. She tried to hold on to some thread of who she was, but that was another part of the shock. This was who she was now. Not Max's wife. Not Ezra's fiancée. Only herself alone with Charlie Berlin in this room, with a dance band halfway across the city egging her on.

Without letting go of her, he started moving toward the sofa. Her body followed. No, she wasn't following. They were perfectly in step.

Maybe she imagined the sound. Maybe it was the echo of her conscience reverberating from Chloe's room, reminding her what she'd told Ava a few days earlier, what she'd known all along. She couldn't afford Charlie Berlin. She pulled away.

"Chloe," she whispered.

He stood looking at her for a long moment. Then he took a step back. This was a battle he knew he couldn't win.

Chloe had a sleepover on Saturday night. Fanny thought of canceling it, but she refused to penalize her daughter for her own weakness. She thought of telling Charlie she couldn't work that day, something had come up, but he'd promised the producer he'd deliver the script sometime this week. Then she told herself this was ridiculous. She had nothing to fear from Charlie. More to the point, she had nothing to fear from herself. She was in love with Ezra. Last night had been an aberration born of exhaustion and the intimacy of working together. She'd come close to being done in by her loneliness and need, but reason had prevailed. Nonetheless, she was careful to put on a woolen cardigan over an old silk shirt she could no longer wear to the office because of an ink stain on the cuff. The new cashmere had been asking for trouble.

He arrived a little after noon. As soon as she saw Chloe off to her ballet class, she made a pot of coffee and they got down to work. Neither of them mentioned the night before. By midafternoon she'd persuaded herself it hadn't happened. They broke for a makeshift dinner. He had a drink. She abstained. Last night hadn't happened, but she didn't want to take a chance of it happening again.

It was after midnight when he crushed out another cigarette and sat up from the sofa. "That's it. Type those two bittersweet words 'The End.' From now on we'll just be making it worse."

He stood and crossed to the wall of windows. They were dark and threw back a reflection of the room uninterrupted by any lighted squares across the street.

"The dancers must have called it a night," he said.

"Obviously sensible people." She stood and started for the closet to get his coat. Unlike Ezra he never wore a hat. A decade later he'd insist he'd started a trend and take credit for JFK going bareheaded at his frigid inauguration.

He crossed the room to her. She put out her hand to stop him from getting closer.

"Last night was a mistake."

"Only because your heart wasn't in it."

"That's what I'm trying to tell you."

"I mean your heart wasn't in the resistance. You said no, but it sure as hell felt like yes."

He took a step closer and put his arms around her. She didn't move. Then he was kissing her again, and she was kissing him back again.

He began to unbutton her blouse. Good god, his hands were smooth on her skin. His cheek wasn't. His five-o'clock shadow set up an irresistible itch.

She forced herself to take a step back and closed her eyes to escape his gaze. She opened them. He was there. He was real, more real than anything in her world at this moment.

He put his arms around her again, brushed his mouth back and forth against hers, not passion but tenderness, not sex but the promise of it. They went on that way for a moment, then the framed photograph swam into view over his shoulder. Max smiled at her from the mantel. His expression was still enigmatic.

She pulled away and started buttoning her blouse. "It's no good, Charlie. I'm going to marry Max."

He stood staring at her. "Max? I thought it was Ezra."

She shook her head. She really was unhinged. He'd unhinged her. "That's what I meant. I'm going to marry Ezra."

"Let me know when you make up your mind."

"I've made up my mind. You're just confusing it."

"It didn't take much."

She took another step back. Now she was angry. "What's not much to you may be a lot to me."

"I said what happened wasn't much. I didn't say it didn't mean much to me."

Now she turned away, put the room between them, and sat on the window seat. "Oh, please, what happened last night and tonight mean something to Charlie Berlin, the champion skirt chaser according to Alice, the man with a sixth sense that sets off an alarm when girls likely to entangle get within ten feet according to Ava."

"Did it ever occur to you that the alarms went off with them because I wasn't interested?"

"What occurred to me is that I'm engaged to marry someone else, and you always want what you can't have. You said it yourself when I first knew you."

He stood in the middle of the room, suddenly serious.

"All right, let's talk about those early days. Do you remember the first time we talked?"

"No," she lied.

"I do. It was the day after you came to work for Alice. I said welcome to the wonderful world of daytime serials, Miss Fabricant. And you flashed that gold band and told me it was *Mrs.* Fabricant."

"I would have thought someone as observant as you would have noticed the ring."

"This is going to come as a shock to you, Fanny, but most men don't look at women's hands when they meet. They notice faces, bodies, the way they move. They may even listen to their voices and what they say. With me it's the legs and what comes out of the mouth. That's what got me in trouble with you from that first day when you swiveled away from your typewriter and crossed those gams. Then you started to spar with me. I was hooked. But when you flashed the ring, I figured okay, off-limits. You see, I'm not the heel you think."

"I never thought you were a heel."

"You put on a helluva good act. Then I found out you weren't married."

"At least you had the good grace to be embarrassed at your joke about the blissfully married Mrs. Fabricant."

"I was more than embarrassed. I was ashamed."

"That's a bit much. It was a normal assumption."

"I was ashamed because I was so damn happy that it was indecent. Someone, your husband, had died, and I was over the moon. Suddenly you weren't off-limits. So don't tell me last night didn't mean much to me. And don't for god's sake tell me I want you only because you're unavailable."

She suddenly believed him. That made it worse.

He went to the closet as she'd started to before and put on his coat.

She followed him to the door. "I'm sorry," she said.

"For what? Last night? Now?"

She thought about that for a moment. "Yes, though not in the way you think. I'm still going to marry Ezra, but for what it's worth part of me will always regret letting you walk out now."

He shook his head and she saw him slipping back into his public persona. "Regret? I'll see you and raise you, sweetheart. I'm going to be in mourning for it for the rest of my life."

Chapter Twenty-eight

Ezra had said he'd be back Sunday evening, though he wasn't sure when. It depended on the driving conditions in Vermont and the traffic going into the city. He called from a gas station and said with any luck he'd be home in an hour. Forty-five minutes later, the downstairs bell rang. She buzzed him in and went out to the hall to meet him. He took the stairs two at a time.

"This is crazy," he said halfway up the last flight.

"What's crazy?"

He reached the top, kissed her, and went on holding her. His ski jacket still held the cold, but he gave off a lot of heat. She was glad.

"Waiting till the summer is crazy," he went on. "Sheer lunacy. There isn't a reason in the world we can't be married right away."

"Let's go inside and talk about it."

He began following her inside. "It came to me in a blinding flash. I was going up in the chairlift when the realization hit. What are we waiting for? I don't care about a big wedding. And it isn't as if it's your first."

She'd been walking ahead of him, and now she turned to face him.

"I'm sorry. It never occurred to me. You didn't have a big wedding the first time, did you?"

"The war."

"Do you want one now?"

She thought about that. If she hadn't had a big wedding with Max, she certainly didn't want one with Ezra. A crowd of people watching her say vows struck her as embarrassing; a big party obscene. "Not particularly."

"Then let's not wait."

"I thought we were going to time it to the end of the school year. We'd get married, Chloe would go off to camp, and we could have a honeymoon."

"We can have a honeymoon a couple of months after the wedding. Chloe will still be going off to camp. The city is already talking about closing pools and playgrounds. They're even thinking of encouraging people not to sit too close together in movie theaters. She'll go off to camp, and we'll take a couple of weeks in the country. It'll be safer than traveling." He went on looking at her. "You don't think it's a good idea?"

"Of course I think it's a good idea. You just hit me with it so suddenly."

"Okay, you have ten minutes to get used to it. Then we start making plans. How about over Chloe's Easter vacation? She can stay with Rose, and we can get away for a couple of nights. A pre-honeymoon honeymoon."

"That's less than two months away."

"Exactly. What do you say?"

She said yes.

❦

Four days later, on Thursday afternoon, Charlie turned up late at the library. She made a show of looking at her watch. "I know we finished the television script, but we still have four of Alice's to write. Or now that you're a real playwright again are you too important for that?"

"Soon, sweetheart, soon. What are you doing tonight? No, let me put it another way. Whatever you're doing tonight, cancel it."

"I'm going home to make dinner for Chloe. It's a weeknight."

"You're having drinks at Ned Kagan's apartment."

"Who's Ned Kagan?"

"The television producer. He's hot on the script, but he says he can't go to the network with it until he's met you. Your name is on the title page and will be on the contract. Don't worry, he knows you're more than a front. That's another reason he wants to meet you. If we pull this off, he wants more from both of us under your name. Though of course he can't put it that way. According to him, I have nothing to do with this script or any other he's likely to consider. I'm merely a friend of yours who still knows some people in the business."

"Why his apartment? I thought television people met somewhere swanky like Sardi's or 21."

"Give a girl a Sardi's dinner one night and it goes to her head. Television people do; blacklisted writers don't. He's spotted having a drink with me, then turns up with a terrific, if I do say so myself, script by an unknown who's never sold anything before? Why not just shout 'front' from the rooftops?"

"I'll call Rose and see if she can stay with Chloe."

Fanny went out to the phone booth on the corner and called Rose.

"I'll take her for the night," Rose said. "I don't want you turning into a pumpkin just when the producer begins to talk about other scripts you have up your sleeve or how to stage this one. You're in the big time now."

"As Alice warned me, the woods are full of single-scene or in this case single-play successes."

"Keep thinking that way, and it will be a self-fulfilling prophecy."

"You're right. Thank you for that, and for taking Chloe tonight." She started to get off the phone, but Rose stopped her.

"Fanny . . ."

Fanny waited.

"I'm proud of you. No, I take that back. Proud implies I had something to do with it. I'm impressed by your achievement."

"Stick with 'proud,'" Fanny said. "You had everything to do with it."

❦

By the time she left the library, it had started to snow. As if she wasn't nervous enough. Not to mention the sartorial challenge. She didn't want to show up at Ned Kagan's apartment in galoshes. As she changed, she decided she wasn't likely to ruin her shoes merely going from building to taxi to building. By the time she left her apartment, the snow had diminished to flurries. By the time she reached the lobby of Ned Kagan's building where Charlie was waiting, it had started again. At least if she ruined her shoes, she'd do it after the meeting.

The elevator opened directly into the apartment. Ned Kagan was waiting for them, a short man with a ready smile she didn't believe for a minute and strands of dark hair combed across a shiny bald pate. He ushered them through the foyer into a sunken living room and asked what they wanted to drink. A moment later a man appeared with their orders on a tray. She wondered if he'd been eavesdropping at the door.

Ned Kagan gestured her and Charlie to a long, deep sofa facing the windows overlooking the park. That was no accident. The view was impressive, though it was beginning to be obscured by the snow that was coming down faster. She turned from the view to Ned Kagan.

He was telling her how much he liked the script. He asked how she'd come up with the idea. He said he was grateful to Charlie for introducing them. He inquired about other scripts she had in the works. From the way he talked, she could have sworn the apartment was bugged or perhaps the manservant eavesdropped for ACE and the FBI. No one could accuse Kagan of buying a script from a front. His hands were clean.

After an hour or so of the charade, he stood and began ushering them toward the door. When they reached it, he turned to her and held out his hand.

"I'll have the legal department draw up the contract tomorrow morning. Florence Fabricant or Fanny Fabricant?"

She thought about that for a moment. "Florence Fabricant in the contract. Fanny Fabricant in the credits."

"Fanny in credits, Florence on the contract it is." He shook her hand again, then turned to Charlie.

"Thanks, Charlie," he said. "You always did have an eye for talent," he added with a perfectly straight face. Maybe there were hidden cameras in the apartment as well as bugging devices.

They stood in silence, staring at the gray uniformed back of the operator as the elevator descended. Ned Kagan wasn't the only discreet actor in this farce. They crossed the lobby. The doorman held open the door for them. They burst out of it into the night. The snow was coming down fast. She barely noticed.

Charlie turned, threw his arms around her, and practically lifted her off the pavement. "Florence on the contract," he shouted. "Fanny in the credits. I love you, Fanny Fabricant, I really do."

"Be careful," she said, "you'll slip in the snow and we'll both end up with something broken." But her laughter bubbled up to meet the falling flakes. "We did it."

"You did it." His arm was still around her, and he started to cross the street to the park. "We wrote the script, but you pulled off the charade. Maybe you ought to act as well as write," he said as they reached the park side of the street.

"Where are you going?"

"*We're* going for a walk in the park."

"It's snowing."

"That makes it even better."

"It's dangerous."

"Says who? The murderers and robbers are all home in front of their respective fires." He grabbed her hand and started to run.

"I can't," she said, but she was managing to keep up with him. She'd forgotten about ruining her shoes.

They reached a bench and he sat and pulled her down on his lap.

"You can," he said. "You are. We both are. I'm back in business as a writer. And not just of soaps. And I've got my girl sitting on my lap."

"Since when did I become your girl."

"Since we started collaborating. In certain circles, like the one we're moving in as of tonight, writing together is like being married. Only more so. You each know what's going on in the other's mind. Tell me what's more intimate than that."

Clouds shrouded the moon, but the light from the park lanterns pierced the darkness and sparked off the carpet of snow that softened the harsh lines of the landscape. The world had gone quiet. Even the sounds of cars beyond the park were muffled.

He brought her head down to his. As his face drew closer, she saw the snowflakes caught in his long black lashes. His cheeks were cold, but his mouth was warm. She felt her hat fall off. Now the snow was falling on her lashes and face and hair. She went on kissing him. The other night he'd told her she'd said no, but felt like yes. She wasn't saying no now.

Then she remembered. She was going to marry Ezra. She hadn't thought of him in hours. She pulled back.

"I can't do this," she said.

"You could have fooled me."

"I mean it. I like working with you. You're a good friend."

She'd expected him to balk at the word. He just shook his head and brushed the snow from her mouth with his thumb. "Haven't you heard, friends make the best lovers. Everyone else is a flash in the pan. Friends have staying power."

He began kissing her again, and she couldn't do anything but go on kissing him back. She felt her stomach lurch. That was when she knew she had no more arguments. He must have known it too, because he let go of her and they stood and began making their way out of the park. She didn't ask where they were going, and he didn't say. They both knew. It would have to be her apartment. She didn't have a doorman or elevator operator. An apartment building wasn't like a hotel. No one would stop them. But she was still a nice girl. A nice girl, she told herself, hell-bent on what nice girls were warned never to do.

She felt him behind her as they climbed to the third floor. He didn't touch her, but she knew he was there. Her hands were surprisingly steady with the key. He pushed open the door, followed her in, and switched on a lamp.

"Don't," she said, but she was too late. The picture of Max flared into view. She'd known it would. That was why she hadn't wanted him to turn on the light. But there it was, and suddenly the smile wasn't enigmatic at all. The smile was permission. She wasn't free of him. She'd never be free of him. She didn't want to be free of him. But the smile said she didn't have to be free of him. The smile was complicit, approving, encouraging. Grab life and wring the living daylights out of it, the smile said. For you. For Chloe. For all the years I didn't have.

They never made it to the bedroom. At least they didn't make it to the bedroom the first time. They were too impatient. Her hunger frightened her. It aroused him. They tumbled onto the window seat. Somehow that seemed appropriate as they wrestled each other out of their clothing. Then they were only skin, and she was falling, and he was rising, and then she was on top, and he was arched beneath her. She didn't want to stop. It would be agony to stop. But she knew she had to.

"I don't have . . . ," she began.

He reached up and put his hand over her mouth. It tasted of her. "I do."

He fumbled in the tangle of clothing on the floor until he came up with it, and everything started again, and went on and on until her cry cracked open the night and stars fell out of it, and his shattered the sky a moment later.

They made love twice more. Her bed was narrow but that was all right. They had to stop only because he had no more condoms.

"I could go out to an all-night drugstore."

She sat up with her back against the headboard. They'd knocked the pillows to the floor. "It's too cold out there. And if you left, it would be too cold here. But do you mind if I ask you something personal?"

"As if this weren't."

"Do you always carry three? I'm not prying, merely curious."

He reached up and pulled her down again. "The hell you're not prying. But for your information, only since last Friday night."

"Pretty sure of yourself."

"Pretty sure of you."

Somewhere around two they realized they hadn't eaten in they couldn't remember how long. She got up, went into the living room, and came back wearing his shirt. She could have put on a robe, but she liked the idea of being inside his shirt. She was pretty sure he'd like the idea too.

She handed him his boxer shorts and they went into the kitchen. She opened the refrigerator and bent to peer in.

"Cold chicken?"

"Cold chicken is the ticket."

They sat across from each other at the small table, devouring the food, but keeping their eyes on each other. They couldn't stop smiling. Afterward they went back to bed and lay holding each other, carefully, chastely, sensibly, because he hadn't gone out into the snow to find an all-night drugstore.

The windows were still dark and threw back a reflection of themselves when they got out of bed and went into the living room to retrieve the clothes they'd left on the floor. When she picked up her slip, the ring fell out. He caught it and handed it to her. She took it but didn't say anything.

"When are you going to tell him?"

"I have to find the right time."

"There's no right time for something like this."

She didn't say anything to that, and he stood watching her.

"You're not going to tell him. You're going to go through with it."

"How can I? After this?"

"I don't know," he said finally, "but I have a feeling you'll find a way. He's safe, Fanny, and that's what you're looking for. Maybe that's what you were raised to. Maybe that's what losing Max has driven you to. Whatever it is, that's what you want. That's what you need. And I'm not safe. I'm not nearly as dangerous as you think, but I'm not safe. You know why? Not because I play the horses or provoke the authorities or don't have a steady job. Because I make you care. And that means you have a hostage to fortune. And we all know how fickle fortune is. It broke you once. It can do it again."

He walked to the door. She followed him. He bent to kiss her. "I'll call you later."

"After that indictment."

"A guy can hope."

❦

She waited until almost eight to call Rose and ask if she could come over.

"There's no need," Rose said. "Chloe's about to leave for school. She can manage not seeing her mother one morning."

"To see you."

"I take it from the urgency in your voice that the meeting didn't go well."

"The meeting went extremely well. They're drawing up the contract for Florence Fabricant as we speak. Fanny Fabricant gets billing."

"Congratulations."

"Thank you. Can I come over?"

"I'm putting the coffee on now."

❦

They sat at the white enamel table in Rose's kitchen with two cups of coffee. Rose asked if she wanted toast or coffee cake or anything.

"I had cold chicken somewhere around two or three this morning."

Rose's eyebrows made twin arches in her forehead.

"We were hungry."

"We? Ezra finally overcame his Victorian scruples?"

"I spent the night with Charlie."

"Lucky girl." Rose hadn't missed a beat. Fanny was surprised.

"That's all you have to say?"

"In your place it wouldn't have taken me so long."

"I thought there wasn't anyone after Hugo."

"There wasn't anyone after Hugo because there wasn't anybody worth it after Hugo. No Charlie Berlins walked into my life."

"You and Ava." She shook her head. "What is so wonderful about Charlie?"

"You tell me. You're the one who spent the night with him."

"All right, I'm attracted. But I can't afford him."

"Why not? Because he's not reliable? Steady? Husband material, as Mimi would say?"

"Exactly."

"And Ezra is?"

"Yes. He's all those words you make sound like character flaws."

"I never said they were character flaws. They're admirable traits. If you happen to love him."

"I do."

Rose sat staring at her in the hard winter light that beat off the snow on the roofs across the street and slanted into the kitchen.

"It occurs to me there's another choice going on here, and it's not between two men. It's between two versions of yourself. One Fanny goes as someone's appendage to the funeral of a complete stranger and comes away feeling like an interloper and hating herself. That Fanny bakes soufflés and ends up listening to the soaps she used to write. The other Fanny heeds her own instincts rather than bowing to society's or her husband's dictates and does work that gives her satisfaction, or from what I remember about writers from my time with Hugo, delivers frustration and heartbreak, but at least she's doing something she cares about."

"You make it sound so black-and-white."

"That's because it is. Maybe it wouldn't be if you were marrying someone else, but you're marrying a man who doesn't want you to work because it would embarrass him. I'm not against marriage. Far from it. I would have married Hugo in a minute if he'd been free. I'm just against marriage to someone who wants to clip your wings."

"Ezra doesn't want to clip my wings."

"Right, only take away your typewriter."

Chapter Twenty-nine

SHE DIDN'T GO TO THE LIBRARY THAT DAY. SHE WAS afraid Charlie would be there. She was afraid he wouldn't. Instead she walked. Up West End Avenue, down Broadway, through the park to Fifth. The streets were slushy, but the sidewalks had been shoveled, and the park was still a pristine Currier & Ives print. She stood, her mittened hands in her pockets and her hat pulled down over her ears, staring at the Great Lawn dozing under a blanket of white. Here and there paw prints frolicked, accompanied only occasionally by human treads. And as she stood there, she realized the only chill she felt was from the weather. The snow held no menace.

But the lighthearted mood didn't last. Last night dogged her steps. Tonight, Friday night, when Ezra would reappear, loomed ahead of her. She went into a Chock full o'Nuts and ordered a cup of coffee and a nutted cheese sandwich. She couldn't eat the sandwich. She drank the coffee, left, and decided she'd go to Fairway to get some vegetables and greens for a salad. Did the fact that she was buying things for dinner mean Charlie was right, she wasn't going to tell Ezra?

As soon as she stepped into the store, she was sorry. Mimi

was standing in front of a mountain of apples. She started back to the door, but Mimi had already seen her.

They embraced, then began making their way through the fruits and on to the vegetables, squeezing, examining, selecting. Fanny asked about the baby. Mimi said he'd rolled over.

"Can baseball be far behind?"

"According to your soon-to-be husband, we can start trying solid foods next month."

"Congratulations." Fanny reached for a head of iceberg lettuce.

"Where's your ring?" Mimi asked.

Fanny looked down at her hand. Charlie had handed it to her, and she'd taken it from him, but she hadn't put it on.

"Home on the kitchen counter, bathing in a saucer of ammonia," she lied. "I want it to sparkle."

Outside the market, free of Mimi, she started to walk again. When she found herself a block from Chloe's school at a little before three, she decided she'd pick up her daughter.

As she stood outside the door waiting, she remembered the day in Penn Station when Max had shipped out. Chloe's weight in her arms had kept her from floating off. That was what she needed. Rose had mixed her up. Chloe, the responsibility of Chloe, would ground her.

The doors burst open and kids came rushing out, an explosion of pent-up energy and earsplitting anticipation. It wasn't just the end of the day; it was the end of the week.

Chloe didn't see her. She was too busy chattering and laughing with a gaggle of girls. Fanny recognized most of them and started toward the group. Chloe caught sight of her. Fanny was sure she would never forget the expression on her daughter's face. She looked suddenly trapped.

"Mom," she said. The word underlined the expression. Somehow Fanny hadn't noticed when she'd gone from being Mommy to being Mom. Or maybe the change in name wasn't a function of time but of place. At home, in the primal setting, she was still Mommy. Out in the world, in front of Chloe's peers, she was Mom.

"I thought we could walk home together," Fanny said.

"Mom!" Now the syllable held exasperation rather than surprise. "I told you we were going to Judy's after school."

Fanny said she couldn't imagine how she'd forgotten, told her daughter to have a good time, and escaped from the crush of noisy, jostling kids. She walked home quickly. There was no need to slow her steps for a child to keep pace. Chloe had let go of her some time ago.

She pulled open the outer door to her building, unlocked the inner one, and stepped into the small hall. Charlie was sitting on the bottom stair.

"How did you get in?"

He stood. "Now there's a welcome. I'd like to tell you I picked the lock. It would reinforce your view of me. But one of your neighbors let me in. She seemed to think I had an honest face. Where have you been? You weren't at the library."

"Were you?"

"Only to look for you. You weren't home either. I've been calling all day."

"I was walking."

"I thought you hated snow."

"I seem to have been cured of that particular phobia."

"You must be freezing." He pulled off her gloves and began rubbing her hands.

"Are you checking for the ring?"

"In addition to not wanting you to get chilblains."

"It's not there."

"So I see. Are you going to invite me up?"

She looked at her watch.

"Don't worry," he said. "I'll get out in time. I won't even ask if you're going to tell him. There's something I have to tell you before you do—if you do."

"That sounds ominous."

He didn't say anything to that. She started up the stairs. He followed her.

"Can I at least take off my coat?" he asked when they were in her apartment. "You make me feel like a door-to-door salesman with a foot wedging it open."

"Go ahead," she said, but didn't take it from him to hang up or take off her own. Now that she'd stopped moving, she suddenly felt the cold.

"You're shivering." He dropped his coat on the window seat, took a step toward her, and began rubbing her arms and shoulders.

"I thought you had something to tell me."

He stopped trying to warm her, but didn't let go of her. "I love you, Fanny. I've never said that to anyone."

"At least not when you were sober and both fully dressed."

Now he took a step back. "Jesus, I'm trying to tell you something. I can't marry you."

"In other words, you have a less binding arrangement in mind."

"I, we, don't have a choice. How long do you think it would take ACE to add your name to the blacklist if we were married? Then neither of us could sell anything or get a job. I may not be the most reliable Joe in the world, but I do understand the need for food and shelter. So until this thing is over—"

"In perhaps a decade or three or four."

"There was a red scare after the First War too. That passed. But until then we'll have to be living in what Rose calls delicious sin." He tried a smile.

She didn't meet it. "I never heard her use the term," she lied.

"You never knew about Hugo Hayes either, until I came along."

Now he was the one who looked at his watch. He picked up his coat.

"I find it interesting," she said as she watched him put it on, "that you didn't mention any of this last night."

He'd reached the door and now he turned back to her. "For one thing, it would have been presumptuous. Why would I mention marriage or lack of it to a girl who could barely bring herself to carry on a civil conversation with me? For another, you're a smart cookie. I assumed you'd already figured it out. Why else would you agree to front for me?"

She followed him to the door. "You're right. I'm sorry."

He stopped with his hand on the doorknob and turned to her again. "That's the first time you've ever apologized to me."

"Don't worry, I won't make a habit of it."

He smiled. "That's the Fanny Fabricant I know and love." He pulled open the door, did a quickstep into the hall, and started down the stairs fast. No one was going to pity Charlie Berlin.

❦

After he left, she went into the bathroom, stood under a pounding hot shower, and rehearsed conversations. None of them sounded right. When she was dressed, she went back to the living room. The ring was still on the coffee table where she'd put it when Charlie had handed it back to her that morning. She slipped it on.

She didn't bring up the subject during dinner. She couldn't very well with Chloe there. Besides, no sensible woman would determine her life on the basis of a single night, no matter what Rose said.

After she and Chloe had cleared the table and Chloe had drifted off to her room, Ezra wandered into the kitchen while she was doing the dishes. She wished he hadn't. The first conversation, the only conversation, they'd had about Charlie had taken place in the kitchen. He'd also asked her to marry him in the kitchen. Perhaps this was a cosmic message. He was a domesticated man.

He leaned against the counter with his hands in his pockets as he had that night, but now the ring was on her finger.

"I've been thinking," he said. "Lots of wives teach school for a year or two after they get married. Until the babies start coming. I wouldn't like us to wait too long. We're not exactly kids. But I suppose there wouldn't be much harm in your writing for the soaps for a while."

She went on scouring a pan. "Are you sure you wouldn't find it too embarrassing?"

He laughed. "Come on, Fanny. You know what I mean. I'm trying to be reasonable. You said you wanted to go on working for a while. I'm saying that's okay with me. For a while."

She put the pan in the drying rack, shut off the water, and turned to face him. They were only inches apart. Why did they always have these conversations in such close quarters? Hand-to-hand combat.

"I'm not writing soap scripts anymore. Or rather I won't be in a few weeks."

"I always knew you'd see the light." He leaned forward to kiss her.

She cantilevered her upper body back over the counter. "I sold a play to television. A real play."

He took his hands out of his pockets. "Without telling me?"

"You've never asked what I was writing."

"That's because I trusted you. You said you were writing soap scripts."

"It had nothing to do with trust. It had to do with lack of interest."

She could see him counting to three or ten or whatever the magic number was. "Okay, I'm interested. What's this play about?"

"A disaffected vet and his wife. A postwar marriage."

"It's not autobiographical, I hope."

"Not in the least."

"But it's going to be broadcast?"

"That's the general idea."

"And your name will be in the credits?"

She remembered the night he'd come back from walking Chloe to her sleepover and sat having a drink for almost an hour before he brought up Charlie and the television he'd given them. It hadn't occurred to her until now that he'd known all along what she was up to, what she and Charlie were up to, and that was why he didn't want her to work.

"Who else's name would be in the credits?" she asked.

"So I'll be known as Mr. Florence Fabricant."

She didn't know whether she was relieved or disappointed.

"Actually, it'll be Fanny in the credits. But I doubt it's going to attract that much attention."

"But this is only the first, right? There'll be others."

"I certainly hope so."

"I thought you wanted children. Who's going to take care of them while you're writing these scripts?"

"Television pays better than radio. I'll be able to hire help. Part time at least."

"Wonderful. Now you're the one supporting us."

"I didn't say I'd be supporting us. I said I'd be able to hire someone to take care of the children. Who don't even exist at the moment."

"I don't understand you, Fanny. What's the point of having children, if you don't want to raise them?"

"I'm going to raise them. I'm just not going to spend every waking minute with them. You certainly won't."

"That's different."

"Why? You're always telling me Chloe needs a father."

"It just is, Fanny, and you know it. Read the books. Look at the studies."

"The books. The studies. A few weeks ago I caught Dr. Spock on television with a bunch of fathers. They were all chuckling about how rough it was on them to come home from a hard day's work and be expected to discipline the children who'd been misbehaving all day."

"That's beside the point. No hired help is going to bring up any child of mine."

They were too close physically for this conversation. She turned, went into the living room, and sat on the sofa. He followed and sat across from her in the club chair.

"I don't know how we got here," he said. "I came in to tell

you I understood about your wanting to work. I thought you'd be happy."

"I am," she lied.

"Then everything's fine." He stood. "But I've had a long week. And you probably have too." He hesitated. "It isn't every day a girl sells a play to television. In fact, I think we ought to go out and celebrate tomorrow night. Not the usual neighborhood bistros. A nightclub or better yet a hotel rooftop with dancing. We've never done that, and I think it's about time."

She walked him to the door. "I almost forgot," he said. "My mother's going to call you tomorrow."

"About what?" She heard the churlishness in her voice. Why shouldn't her future mother-in-law call her? "I'm sorry. I mean, about anything in particular?"

"She has a lace veil that she wore and her mother wore before her. I told her it wasn't going to be that kind of wedding, but she said it doesn't have to be a big fancy wedding to wear a piece of lace her mother brought from Hungary. She seems to think it's a good-luck keepsake. But don't let her browbeat you. If you don't want it, tell her so. I'll back you up, I promise." He leaned down, kissed her goodnight, and started for the stairs. He wasn't as fast going down them as Charlie had been, but then, as he'd pointed out, he'd had a hard week.

After he left, she stood in the living room staring at the picture of Max on the mantel. The night before, she'd been sure he was giving her permission, but that had been a fantasy, or maybe only an excuse. She'd been the one giving herself permission. Standing there now, fresh off another disagreement with Ezra, she couldn't help wondering how Max would have reacted to her working. But that was ridiculous. He'd been proud of his mother.

She turned away from the photograph. Suddenly there was nothing she could count on. Not her memory of Max. Not even herself. Especially not herself.

❦

The phone rang a little before ten the next morning. Ezra's mother asked if she could stop by Fanny's apartment in an hour or so.

"I have to come into Manhattan anyway, and I'd like to bring the lace to show you. Ezra says it's not going to be that kind of wedding, but I know once you see it, you'll want to wear it."

There was nothing Fanny could do but tell her to come by. She went into the kitchen to make a fresh pot of coffee.

Fanny didn't know much about lace, but Rose had taught her enough to recognize a well-made piece.

"This is so generous of you, but—" Fanny began.

"Generous? What are you talking, generous? It's not like I'm giving it away. I'm keeping it in the family. You and Ezra have a son, the girl he marries can wear it. God willing. Or a daughter. She can walk down the aisle in it."

Fanny noticed Chloe wasn't included in the line of succession, but she took the lace, wrapped it in the tissue paper his mother had brought it in, and put it carefully on her desk. She could give it back later.

"I knew once you saw it, you'd understand," Ezra's mother said, added she had a lot to do, and started for the door, but when she got there, she stopped and turned to Fanny. "Do you mind if I say something?"

"Please," Fanny answered, and wondered what was coming.

"When Ezra told me about you, I wasn't happy. A widow, I

said. With a child. What do you need that for? A young man starting out, weighed down with responsibility that isn't even his. But then I met you. More important, I saw my Ezra. And I said to myself, if this is what he wants, if this makes him happy, who am I to stand in his way?" She went up on her toes to hug Fanny. "Be happy," she said. "Be happy with my Ezra."

When she let go, Fanny had to wipe her eyes, though she wasn't sure if she was moved by his mother's emotion or ashamed of her own inconstancy.

She stood in the window, watching Ezra's mother make her way down West End Avenue, an old woman in an unstylish coat clutching a large handbag under her arm because who knew what thieves and bad actors were in the streets. It would have been easy to laugh at the woman; not at her appearance, but at her sentimental selflessness. She was the cliché of a Jewish mother. Of mothers in general, for all Fanny knew. If you're what my Ezra wants. Be happy. Be happy with my Ezra. She thought of Chloe. If you had a child, the wish didn't sound like a sentimental cliché. It sounded hopeful.

She went to the phone and dialed Charlie's number, though she had no idea what she was going to say when he answered.

Chapter Thirty

1955

FANNY WAS WORKING IN THE APARTMENT WHEN THE call came, not the apartment with the three bay windows overlooking West End Avenue but a larger place with a sliver view of Central Park. She no longer went to the library to write, though she was still a member. So was Charlie. They ran into each other there occasionally.

When she picked up the phone, she heard Harris Yost's voice on the other end of the line. Harris was her agent. Whether he knew he was also Charlie's agent was anyone's guess. The political situation wasn't as dicey as it had been. The previous March, Edward R. Murrow had broadcast an indictment of the red scare. "We must not confuse dissent with disloyalty." Three months later, the attorney Joseph Welch demanded of Joe McCarthy in a nationally televised senate hearing, "Have you no sense of decency, sir?" But networks and sponsors still weren't taking chances. Harris sold the scripts Fanny delivered to him, took his 10 percent, and asked no questions.

"Ready for some good news?" he asked now.

"You sold *Circles of the Moon*."

"Better than that. *Talking to Strangers* was just nominated for Best Original Teleplay of the year."

Talking to Strangers was the third script she and Charlie had written for the Theater of the Air.

She didn't bother to hang up. As soon as Harris got off, she pressed down the lever to get the tone and dialed Charlie's number.

"Do you remember telling me some time ago that writing a script together is more intimate than marriage?" she asked when he answered.

"I'm not likely to forget it."

"In that case what's a nomination for Best Original Teleplay? Benefit of clergy?"

"'Until the real thing comes along,'" he sang in his Fats Waller imitation.

"I still don't think it's fair."

"That you get all the credit?"

"That I have to go to the awards ceremony alone."

"You could always take Ezra."

"That's unkind. Besides, I don't think his wife would like it."

Joy Geller, Ezra's self-proclaimed fiancée, had gotten her way in the end, or rather six months after Fanny had told Ezra she couldn't marry him and given him back his ring, which, she noticed when she ran into the happy couple on Broadway, he hadn't passed on to Joy. She was wearing a larger diamond on her left hand. For some reason, the size of the stone assuaged Fanny's guilt. She took it as a sign that, as she'd said to Ezra when he'd called to ask her to dinner the first time, everything was working out for the best. He'd behaved well during the encounter, as Fanny had known he would. He asked after Chloe. He even said he'd seen the broadcast of the teleplay she'd written. "It was good," he added, and managed not to sound surprised. She'd always known he was a decent man.

Mimi was less forgiving. No matter how many times Fanny told her she was the one who'd broken off the engagement, Mimi persisted in believing Ezra had treated her badly. It wasn't that she thought Fanny was trying to save face, only that Mimi had a fierce tribal instinct and a wide protective streak. Ezra, the former catch, was now a devious Don Juan.

Poor Fanny clearly wasn't any good with or about men. Charlie Berlin was another example of her ineptitude. Mimi knew nothing about the fronting arrangement, and if she suspected an affair, she pushed the discomfiting thought from her mind, but she did know Charlie figured somehow in Fanny's life. She couldn't imagine what Fanny, and for that matter Rose, saw in him. Mimi didn't like men who weren't susceptible to her iron femininity.

Fanny was touched by Mimi's outrage, and if her attempts to introduce her to eligible men were annoying, Fanny knew they were well intentioned. What she couldn't abide was the pity. Sometimes she wanted to scream at Mimi, at the world, that she was not a lonely widow who warranted the word "poor" before her name, but a woman who loved and was loved.

There were other times, however, when Fanny took a secret pleasure in hoodwinking the world. It was like the fronting arrangement, only more visceral. But the aspect of the masquerade that she couldn't forgive herself for was lying to Chloe. Though Chloe liked Charlie, she wouldn't be as enthusiastic about a mother who was the subject of gossip and scandal.

Like most children, she was sufficiently innocent to be judgmental.

What Fanny didn't realize was that she needn't have worried. The idea of an affair didn't occur to her daughter, at least not yet. Chloe was perfectly willing, or almost, to accept the idea that her mother and late father had engaged in the mechanics of sex once. After all, here she was. But surely no one as old as her mother would dream of doing it again. Sex didn't worry her, but marriage intrigued her. Mothers were supposed to be married. They got married when they were girls. If they were widowed like her mother and Aunt Mimi, they remarried. Her mother was much nicer than Mimi, and prettier too, so why wasn't she married? Was it Charlie's fault? Maybe he was what Aunt Mimi called a confirmed bachelor. You could tell from the way she said it what she thought of the breed. Or maybe her father was to blame. Her mother just couldn't get over him. She took the question to Rose rather than her mother. She knew she stood a better chance of getting a straight answer from her aunt.

"Charlie's around a lot," she began.

"He's a friend of the family," Rose said. "I knew him before your mother did."

"And they like each other a lot."

Rose waited.

"So why don't they get married?"

It was the opportunity Rose had been waiting for. She delivered a crash course in red scares going back to the aftermath of World War I and bringing it up to date with the current blacklist. She'd sowed the seeds. She only hoped she'd live to see them flower.

❦

The summer after *Talking to Strangers* was nominated for Best Teleplay was the first summer Chloe didn't have to flee the city. A doctor named Jonas Salk had developed a vaccine against polio. But camp had become a tradition, and Chloe loved it. Moreover, that summer she'd be in the senior bunk. That wasn't a position she was likely to relinquish after working up to it for so many years.

Fanny and Charlie flirted with the idea of traveling while Chloe was away, but hotels still insisted on seeing the titles Mr. and Mrs. in the register. If the couple checking in seemed bogus or nervous, some even asked for a marriage license. Real estate people were less intrusive. Once the check for the rent cleared, agents minded their own business. They took a cottage on a lake in Connecticut.

In the morning, they awakened to mist rising off the water. In the afternoon they worked, then went for a swim while small white sails ghosted beneath a Wedgwood sky and canoes cut silently through the shimmering surface. When the voices of mothers shouting at children to get out of the water this instant drifted across the lake, one of them went inside and brought out gin and tonics, and they sat side by side in Adirondack chairs watching a gaudy sun slip into the stand of pines on the far shore. And they made love. After their first week in the house Fanny wrote Rose a postcard. *"Sin really is delicious."*

"You're more right than you know," Charlie said when he saw the postcard. They were sitting side by side in bed. He was reading. She'd just finished a letter to Chloe.

"I was joking. I don't regard what's going on here as sin."

"I do."

She pulled back to look at him. She knew a joke was coming, but she couldn't figure out what it would be.

"The original sin wasn't sex. It was knowledge. And that's what love is. Knowing the other person."

He put his book on the night table, took off his reading glasses, and turned to her. "Knowing the other person almost as well as yourself. Maybe better. Knowing and forgiving. Knowing and not blaming in the first place. Knowing, knowing, knowing."

❦

At the end of August, they returned to town, and Chloe came home from camp. She'd grown at least an inch and was wearing a bra beneath her Camp Winding Wood T-shirt. Bras had been only one bone of contention between her and her mother for the past several months. Chloe didn't need one—she was a leggy coltish kid with a flat chest—but some of her friends did, and she'd begged Fanny to buy her a double A or at least what was called a training bra. All in good time, Fanny had insisted. There was also the problem of pierced ears. Fanny put her foot down about those too.

"What's wrong with pierced ears?" Chloe demanded.

"You're too young. And I don't believe in self-immolation."

"Only my mother could call piercing your ears self-immolation. Karen's mother took her to have hers pierced."

"Next time around have the sense to be born to a mother like Karen's."

Though Rose didn't interfere openly, she did point out to Fanny that she was trying to keep Chloe an innocent child because she saw herself as a louche mother, or would be thought so in the eyes of the world. But that summer at camp Chloe had outsmarted her. She'd persuaded a girl in her bunk to trade one of her bras for a snazzy beaded belt. Fanny told Chloe the other girl had gotten the better deal and let it go. She even gave her daughter points for resourcefulness.

❦

Four and a half years later, in January of 1960, Otto Preminger announced that he had hired the blacklisted Dalton Trumbo to write the screenplay for his forthcoming film *Exodus*. Network executives and television producers breathed sighs of relief and tossed their copies of *Red Channels* into wastebaskets or put them through shredders. Rose said wasn't it a shame that lost years and lives cut short by suicide weren't so easily undone, but she was pleased.

A week later, Chloe, who'd come home from her freshman year at Smith for the weekend, stood leaning against the doorjamb of Fanny's room, watching her mother fasten her pearl necklace. It occurred to her that it was the same pearl necklace her mother had worn that night so long ago when Chloe had stood with her hand in her father's, watching her mother descend the stairs. She barely remembered the house, but she could recall that night, or at least that moment. She'd been a flower girl in Aunt Barbara's big splashy wedding. Now she was going to be a witness, she and Rose both, to her mother's marriage in a judge's chambers.

"So you're finally going to make an honest man of Charlie."

Fanny met her daughter's eyes in the mirror. "Did he put you up to that?"

"He didn't have to. I've been hanging around him, or rather

he's been hanging around us, long enough for me to make the crack on my own."

She went on watching her mother close the clasp on the necklace and smooth the twin strand of pearls on her navy-blue suit. Rose had forbidden beige. She said it screamed second wedding. Chloe was glad her mother and Charlie were marrying. As a child, she'd wished desperately for her mother to remarry. She'd wanted to be like other families. And as she got a little older, she'd wanted her mother to release her grip. No, that wasn't fair. Her mother had never clung. She'd had her work. She'd even had Charlie, though it had taken Chloe a while to realize that. She didn't know when the truth of their relationship dawned on her. It seemed to her now that she'd always known, though that couldn't have been. At ten or twelve or fourteen, she would have been scandalized. She was grateful to her mother for keeping the information from her. But somehow she'd figured it out, not suddenly but gradually. And now that she was old enough not to be scandalized, she was glad. She would hate for her mother to have been alone all those years.

She was glad, too, that her mother had ended up with Charlie rather than Ezra. Though she hadn't been sure of her preference in those days, she knew now that life with Ezra would have been explosive for her if not for her mother. Over the years, she'd run into him a few times. He and his family had moved to New Rochelle, but his office was still in the neighborhood, though according to her mother in a swankier building. He was always unfailingly friendly, but as she grew older, she could sense his growing disapproval. The last time she'd seen him, only a year or so ago, he hadn't been able to hide it. "You're such a pretty girl, Chloe, but you'd be even prettier if you didn't wear all that black. And put on a little lipstick." Okay, she admitted it. That day she was looking especially Beat. She and Charlie were a better fit. Charlie had given her a copy of *On the Road*. On the other hand, with Ezra as a stepfather, she might have become a different person, though she doubted it. Not only did Rose and her mother set an example, their blood ran in her veins.

The funny thing was that as happy as she was that Charlie was in her mother's life, as well as she and Charlie got along, well enough to sometimes gang up on her mother, she'd never seen him as a replacement for her father. The wound she'd suffered that night when she was almost six was like the lingering injuries of the returning war veterans that these days acted up only under certain weather conditions. She could go for weeks at a time without thinking about her loss, then some temperamental storm or meteorological depression made it ache all over again.

❦

It took another several years for Charlie to get official credit for the eight plays he and Fanny had written together and the two Best Teleplay awards they'd won.

❦

Fanny and Rose never would have seen the demonstration—neither of them would be caught dead watching the Miss America Pageant of 1968 or any other year—if Fanny hadn't been switching channels. Rose was in bed, and Fanny had gotten up to turn the dial on the television set Charlie had moved to the bedroom from Rose's sewing room when she came home from the hospital after her stroke. Shots of the demonstration outside Convention Hall in Atlantic City flashed on the screen. Fanny stopped switching channels.

Several hundred women, most of them young, and a sprinkling of men were marching and shouting and pumping fists and signs into the air. NO MORE BEAUTY STANDARDS. WELCOME TO THE CATTLE AUCTION. ERA YES. The camera zeroed in on a trash can with a sign on it saying FREEDOM CAN. Women were dancing around it, tossing in high heels, curlers, copies of *Playboy* magazine, bottles of dish detergent, and bras. The reporter said the demonstrators had hoped to burn all the items, but had been unable to obtain a fire permit from the city. "Bra burners," he snickered.

As Fanny and Rose watched, a protester dashed up to the can, whirled a bra around her head like a lasso, and tossed it into the trash can.

"Men burn their draft cards," Chloe shouted into the reporter's microphone as her face filled the screen. "We burn our own forms of injustice and oppression."

The reporter stopped chuckling. "And now, back to the contest for Miss America."

Rose, who'd sat up at the sight of Chloe on the screen, leaned back against the pillows. "Now I can die a happy woman."

"Don't say that. You're not dying. You've had a stroke, but you are not dying. I won't permit it."

"Okay, but when I do, I'll go knowing I left my fingerprints on two generations."

Fanny sat on the side of the bed and took Rose's hand.

"Fingerprints? Don't be modest. You're the Rodin of our existence. Without you we'd still be a couple of lumps of unformed clay."

"You do know it took some time for Rodin's genius to be recognized, don't you?"

Fanny stood and moved to the television. A bevy of young women in bathing suits filled the screen. She switched off the set, returned to the bed, and took Rose's hand again.

"Exactly. He was ahead of his time. A visionary. Like my aunt."

THE TROUBLE WITH YOU

by Ellen Feldman

A Reading Group Gold Selection

About the Author

- A Conversation with Ellen Feldman

Behind the Novel

- A Letter from Ellen Feldman

Keep On Reading

- Reading Group Questions

Also available as an audiobook
from Macmillan Audio

For more reading group suggestions
visit www.readinggroupgold.com.

A Conversation with Ellen Feldman

Many of your earlier novels (*Paris Never Leaves You, The Living and the Lost,* and others) were set against World War II, both on the home front and abroad. What led you to leave the war behind in this book?

The Trouble with You is actually an outgrowth of those books. During the war years, women stepped out of their traditional roles and into the greater world. They went to work in factories and offices, rolled bandages, stood on roofs identifying aircraft, and delivered military planes. Then the men came home, and the women were sent home. Some women were pleased or relieved; many others were furious. Susannah throwing her typewriter at the editor who has come to reclaim his job is based on a real incident. I wanted to explore how, in the postwar years, various women reacted to their new and definitely not-improved place in the world.

The change in women's lives you describe sounds abrupt.

In a way it was. Overnight, magazines that had featured tips for getting dinner on the table in twenty minutes because women didn't get home from work until six or later began featuring recipes for elaborate French cuisine designed to keep a woman in the kitchen all afternoon, if not the entire day. In the novel Rose rants against the new fashions that render women unable to move freely or even breathe. But if the phenomenon occurred suddenly at the end of the war, it grew even more repressive as the years passed. Women were objectified, rated on their appearance,

judged by their sexual behavior. Expectations were upside down. Articles warned girls to remain erotic innocents until their wedding nights, then chastised the wives those girls became for being frigid. Similarly, the girls who had become competent women during the war were expected to become helpless, dependent children after it.

You speak about societal changes, but Fanny's struggle seems deeply personal.

You're absolutely right about that. While I wanted to explore the rules imposed on Fanny by the world, I was even more intrigued by the psychological barriers she erected for herself. Society established job and pay discrimination, rules for where women could go, and guidelines for how they should behave. But what of the strictures and fears Fanny visits on herself, as so many women of that era did? What did it take for a woman to flaunt convention and to thumb her nose at the regulations she was raised with, to risk having her family and friends ostracize her, and the man who proclaimed love for her as a good girl disdain her as a self-realized woman? Societal restrictions are unjust, but we can protest them as Chloe does in the book. Self-imposed limitations are more subtle. You can't demonstrate against yourself.

Did you have to do much research to bring this period to life?

I did less research for this book than any I have written. Strangely enough, I wish that weren't true. I wish the strains of this repressive misogynist world hadn't lingered into my own youth. Girls who wanted to go to graduate school, as I did, were thought to be both marking time until they found a husband and limiting their chances of it because everyone knew too much learning scared off a man. That said, I did delve into books and magazines from the period to flesh out my picture of it. Two of my favorite articles were "The Neurosis of the Working Woman" and "How to Succeed in Business and Fail at Being a Woman." The "experts" Mimi keeps citing in the novel really did pontificate this drivel.

Other areas required more research. I knew about television soaps from a later era because as a young novelist I was hired to be trained to write for one—there were four of us; we called it soap school, and we all flunked out, or at least weren't hired for a permanent position—but I did have to read up on radio soaps. Similarly, for Ava's career I looked at a lot of plays from the period and can say that the one she loses the part in deserved to close after five performances. My experience with the political climate of the day was similar. Though I'd already read a great deal about the plague of McCarthyism, I did probe more deeply into the effects of the blacklist on radio and television.

Can you speak about the inspiration for the various characters in the book?

Building characters is a dicey business for a novelist, at least for this novelist. Sometimes a character springs whole cloth from your imagination. That doesn't mean you don't have to develop and deepen him or her as you struggle through various drafts. Others are inspired by

people you've known over the years. I've written elsewhere about the book being a kind of fantasy attempt to give my mother a do-over for her life. I knew a lot of well-behaved girls in my youth, and Mimi was inspired by one in particular who not only lived by the rules, but was determined to make sure I did as well. Similarly, Ezra resembles many young men I encountered, decent fellows for the most part, but products of their era and upbringing. The father of a male friend once told me that another family in the neighborhood was very strange, because the daughter was smarter than the son. I didn't come across many Roses, but when I did, I was always drawn to them. There was one woman in my mother's circle I remember especially vividly. She was a fundraiser for a large charity organization. Even as a child, I sensed her passion, drive, and the fact that she always seemed to be taking a bigger bite out of life than most of the stay-at-home wives and mothers. As for Charlie, I can't tell you where he came from. He simply danced onto my laptop screen one day and refused to leave. Writers pray for that experience.

Your earlier books, especially *Paris Never Leaves You* and *The Living and the Lost,* were concerned with large moral issues experienced in deeply personal terms. Do you think this novel also wrestles with moral issues on a personal scale?

Much of Fanny's story is concerned with her individual struggle against the sexism, both societal and self-imposed, of the era, but as she grows as a woman, she finds she can no longer stand on the sidelines of the major moral issue of the day.

McCarthyism was a cancer on American society. At first she thinks she can avoid taking a stand against it. It doesn't concern her personally. The attitude is an internalization of a patronizing platitude of the time. "Don't bother your pretty little head about it." But gradually she finds that to ignore injustice is to be complicit with it. At first, she defends her inaction as an effort to protect her daughter. Finally, she comes to realize that protecting Chloe means setting a moral example for her.

Do you think the book, set in the middle of the twentieth century, has relevance for the twenty-first?

Unfortunately, I think it is all too relevant to our times in two areas. It's a truism that the daughters of the women who were sent back to domesticity after the war made the feminist revolution of the seventies. Those women were not going to be relegated to the kitchen and bedroom as their mothers had been. But these days we seem to be backsliding. Reproductive rights have been snatched away. The glass ceiling has been splintered perhaps but not shattered. Men's groups, threatened by the loss of their cherished male prerogatives, rail against women's progress, power, and freedom. Politicians and religious leaders thunder that a woman's place is in the home.

At the same time, books are being banned as they were under McCarthyism. Teachers are being fired for trying to open young minds and teach children to think. People are being punished for how they identify themselves and whom they love. To paraphrase the old adage about not remembering, therefore being doomed to repeat history, forgetting the injustice of our recent past invites its rebirth. That is why we must keep reading and discussing and remembering it.

Can you tell us anything about your next book?

I've moved ahead, but not by all that much. I'm working on a novel, spanning the decades from the sixties to the nineties, about a group of women and men, both real and fictional, who came of age in an era of enormous hope and saw the world darken into war, assassination, broken promises, and dashed dreams.

A Letter from Ellen Feldman

Dear Reader:

While *The Trouble with You* is not autobiographical, the inspiration for the book is deeply personal. Many years ago, on a night my parents, sisters, and I returned from a family celebration, my father, age forty-six, with a clean bill of health he'd received from his doctor after a checkup that afternoon, collapsed and died. I was seven years old.

As a grown woman, I continue to feel the pain much as Chloe experiences her father's death in the novel. "The wound she'd suffered that night was like the lingering injuries of the men returning from the war that these days acted up only under certain weather conditions. She could go for weeks at a time without thinking about her loss, then some temperamental storm or meteorological depression made it ache all over again."

But the story I chose to write, felt compelled to write, was not about my father's death but about my mother's life after it.

Like Fanny in the novel, my mother was raised to be a wife and mother. That was fine with her. She knew little about the greater world but felt secure of her place in the smaller domestic sphere she inhabited. In that confidence she was, like most of the women she knew, like Fanny and Mimi in the book, a creature of her time.

Then, suddenly, while she was still in her thirties, her identity was snatched from her. She was still a mother, but no longer a wife, and in that world,

the only world she knew, a woman without a man was a frozen asset, an object of pity, a failure. There was, however, one compensation.

As family and friends moved somberly through the saddened rooms to pay their respects to my father's memory and to try to comfort my mother, they repeated a mantra. "At least she doesn't have to go to work." The message was clear, even to a child. The only misfortune worse than being a widow, or her equally unlucky but more disreputable sister, a divorcée, was to be a woman who had to work.

Not until I was starting out on a career of my own did I recognize the fallacy of their intended consolation. My mother never recovered from my father's death. I don't suppose one does from the loss of a beloved husband cut down before his time. But a life outside the home she'd built with my father, for my father, and demands beyond those of her three daughters might have forced her to move on in more practical and eventually psychological ways.

The world that shaped my mother lingered through my youth. In college a professor said he'd be happy to write a recommendation for me for graduate school because it would give me something to do until I married. The lecture Fanny receives in the novel about holding on to a husband by being perfectly groomed morning and evening was actually delivered to a friend of mine when her husband was in medical school.

I went to graduate school and forged a career. The friend didn't worry about how she looked when her husband set out for his office in the morning because she'd already left for a job of her own.

The Trouble with You is my attempt to give my mother a do-over, to imagine a happier existence for her in the wake of my father's death—a life lived for herself as well as her husband and children. And while I have no didactic intentions, I wouldn't mind if you saw Fanny, Mimi, and Rose as both cautionary tales and inspiration in this era of dangerous backsliding.

But most of all, I hope you enjoy the novel.

Ellen Feldman

Reading Group Questions

1. Fanny travels a long way from the girl she was brought up to be to the woman she becomes. What do you think were some of the pivotal moments in her transformation?
2. At one point, Rose tells Fanny she wanted to open her eyes to a greater world but knew her parents disapproved. Do you think Rose had the right to go against Fanny's parents' wishes?
3. What kind of woman do you think Fanny would have become if Max had lived?
4. What do you think is meant by Mimi's "iron femininity"?
5. Fanny makes two major choices in the book. The first is to act as a front for Charlie. Do you think she was wrong to expose her daughter to the practical perils and social risks of her decision, or do you agree with Rose that she was setting a moral example?
6. Rose tells Fanny it's all right if she doesn't want to sleep with Ezra, but that she should not use Chloe as an excuse. Discuss the conflicts between motherhood and a woman's self-actualization.
7. Fanny thinks the people who joined the Communist Party during the Depression were idealistic. Ezra thinks they were naïve. Do you agree with Fanny or Ezra?
8. Should Fanny have told Ezra who gave her the television instead of letting him assume it was Rose, thereby lying to him and implicating Chloe in the deception?

9. Fanny's other choice is between two men and, as Rose points out, two ways of life. Were you rooting for one or the other? In view of the world in which she lived and the fact that she had a young daughter, do you think Fanny made the right choice?

10. Years before the novel begins, Rose had a long-standing affair with a married man, behavior which was thought immoral then and is still frowned upon today. Does that color your view of her?

11. Fanny's boss, Alice, fires her best writer and an excellent actor because of the blacklist. Do you think she should have risked her own career to at least try to protect her people?

12. The world in which the book is set is rife with conditions that are offensive, even illegal, today. Jobs listed by sex. Women's colleges educating girls to be good wives and mothers. The government providing men but not women with contraceptives during the war. Signs preventing women from sitting in parts of a restaurant without male companions. Girls who aren't virgins being regarded as damaged goods. Men who forbid their wives to work. Books, magazines, and "authorities" sending the message that if women didn't marry, they were failures. Were you surprised at just how bad things were? Do you feel we're backsliding?

About the Author

Laura Mozes

Ellen Feldman, a 2009 Guggenheim Fellow, is the author of *The Living and the Lost, Paris Never Leaves You* (translated into thirteen languages), *Terrible Virtue* (optioned by Black Bicycle for a feature film), *The Unwitting, Next to Love, Scottsboro* (short-listed for the Orange Prize), *The Boy Who Loved Anne Frank*, and *Lucy*.